A CHOICE IN CHAOS

TOBY SANDERS

Cover design by the author

ISBN: 9798862562873

Published by Amazon

FROM THE AUTHOR

Thanks for looking at my book! I'm a self-published author on a mission to share my stories with readers like you. If you've enjoyed the journey so far, I'd be honoured if you could take a moment to leave a review on Amazon. To connect with my Amazon page, simply follow me on Twitter (X) for a quick and easy link @Toby_Author.

For Tenzi

CHAPTER 1

Kyle Frost tried very hard not to die.

It wasn't easy. Most of the world had died. All but a handful of people struggling for existence in the shattered remnants of the British Isles, sheltering in the ruins of the old world.

Some said it was dumb luck that had saved them.

He didn't feel particularly lucky as the grey skinned Wretch shrieked its awful hunting cry and lunged forward to kill him.

*

It was the smell of the apocalypse that always got to Kyle. Not the lines of rusting cars, not the cracked tarmac, worn by two decades of unrelenting British weather. Not even the sky that seemed perpetually overcast, the encroaching weeds and brambles or the ever present threat of death.

Rather, it was the stink of smoke in every breath, the faint whiff of rot as the bone of a sun bleached corpse crunched under his boot, the nauseating smell of stagnant water blown by a sudden gust of wind.

There were other smells too. The damp fabric that held his combat gear, the plastic stock of his rifle as it rested against his cheek and the sharp, rotten egg stink of smoke as he pulled the trigger.

Bang

The human-shaped figure before him was flung backwards, spilling onto the wet ground. It twitched feebly as a stream of black liquid oozed into the puddles.

"Let's move!"

Kyle acknowledged the voice of his patrol commander with

a flicker of his hand, flipping his safety catch and turning to move. Around him, the other Militia moved into a ragged formation, their eyes roving the ground ahead and to their sides.

"Frost! Up front!" Corporal Sinclair's voice was insistent now. He'd slowed from a jog to turn and shout the order and Kyle hastened to overtake the older man. A crackle sounded from the cracked plastic headset that Sinks wore over his ears and Kyle knew the other patrols would be reporting in. He overhead a faint segment of chatter

"... moving north, numbers exceeding expectations.."

"How many?" he hissed back at Sinks but the soldier just gestured angrily at him to move on. Ahead, the ancient roadway was empty, the vehicles abandoned during The Fall long since shunted to the side to allow the Militia and trade caravans to pass through. Not a spark of life filled the damp air and Kyle instinctively slowed his pace, eyes swivelling from left to right.

"Kyle! Get a bloody move on! There are more than we thought..." Sinks' voice trailed off as Kyle came to a stop, rifle now in his shoulder.

"Enemy front!" he suddenly bawled as a grey skinned figure lurched out from under the rusted remnants of a lorry.

"Stop!" snapped Sinks and Kyle's finger hesitated on the trigger then he was shoved unceremoniously aside as Sinks closed on the Wretch, kicking one leg out from underneath it, dropping a heavy knee onto its chest and driving his knife into the beast's eye socket "Get a move on!" he snapped at the Militia who were gawping.

As if responding to his order, an awful, shrieking cry came from behind them and Kyle found himself driven forward by instinct, a terrible fear making his feet move.

"Stay in formation! Remember the RV point..." Sinks saved his breath for running as the small group sprinted forward. Ahead, a grey concrete bridge spanned the roadway, its sides weathered and worn. Atop it, Kyle could see the distinct figures of another patrol and as they came into sight, one of them raised a hand and a moment later, a hand-woven rope ladder clattered down to the tarmac below.

"Let's go!" Sinks was shouting orders, Kyle knew, to remove any hesitation and to make them hurry. He felt a flash of annoyance at being treated like a child and he slowed to allow another Militiaman to scale the ladder first.

"Frost! Up the bloody ladder!" Sinks snapped but Kyle had turned on his heel and was sighting his rifle down the road.

Where a grey tide of death was sweeping towards them.

A wall of figures, human in shape and movement but otherwise as alien to Kyle and his fellows as anything the animal kingdom had ever birthed. The closest Wretches shrieked a hunting cry as they sighted their prey and bounded forward, their torsos bent close to the ground as though the upright stance of homo sapiens no longer benefited them. A second later, the awful stench of decay, death and disease washed over Kyle and he gagged, dropping the barrel of his rifle.

"For God's sake!" Sinks was snarling at him as another of the Militia began to climb the ladder first, taking Kyle's place "How many times do I have to give you –" Sinks words were cut off as, with a splash that surely saved Kyle's life, another Wretch launched itself towards him. Sinks tried to shove Kyle out the way but he was too slow and Kyle tried to raise the rifle whilst pivoting through forty five degrees but the Wretch was too close and he gave a pathetic cry as the monster knocked him to the ground.

"Shit!" Sinks swore above him. Kyle, his left forearm jammed under the grey skin of the Wretch's throat yelled at his friend.

"Shoot it!" but Sinks could not fire for fear of hitting Kyle and above them on the bridge Kyle could hear the Militia shouting at them to hurry up the ladder, that the Horde was drawing close.

Something clicked in Kyle's head as he saw that Sinks could not help him and the thousands of hours of training his friend had subjected him to took over. He pivoted his hips, his arm still firmly pinned beneath the snapping jaw of the Wretch and, with a cry of disgust he flung the creature away. Grey skin splashed into a water filled pothole as lank strands of black hair oozed liquid.

Bang

Kyle shot the Wretch in the chest, a solid blow which floored the creature, black liquid oozing from the gaping wound.

"Now, up the sodding ladder!" Sinks fury had returned and he shoved Kyle towards the rope ladder.

Behind him, the Horde howled and Kyle could hear bare feet slapping the tarmac, the lying water amplifying the sound. Above, the Militia began to fire their rifles, bringing down the fastest of the Wretches. Kyle let his rifle hang by the sling and gripped the rope sides of the ladder in both hands, placing his boot on the lowest rung

Movement.

A spray of filthy water and black goo erupted from the filthy strands of hair on the Wretch's scalp as it leapt from the ground and into Kyle. He fell backwards off the ladder, keeping his balance as panic gripped him. The droplets of water whipped through the air between them and spattered across his face.

At once, fear and disgust gripped him. His eye had closed instinctively but some liquid had gone in and furiously pawed at it with his tight fitting gloves. Bile rose up in his throat at the thought of that black blood running into his body and he gagged in horror.

"Kyle!"

Sinks' voice had passed fury and was filled with desperate fear and Kyle remembered where he was. He frantically tried to drag the short barrel of his rifle up with his left hand but the Wretch had closed the gap and swatted the rifle down with a vicious blow. Kyle looked into the creature's eyes.

Blank and white, totally devoid of any iris or sense of humanity and shot through with vivid red veins. The skin of the whole face was a terrible mottled grey and stretched too thin as though it were the skin of a corpse.

Bang

Sinks fired his own rifle, the bullet shearing through the strands of black hair and tearing a chunk of the Wretch's head away. Instantly, it collapsed, the virus that had infected it gone. A mass of gooey brain matter splattered the wet surface of the road and then Sinks was grabbing his arm, urging him onwards, under the bridge because there was no time to climb the ladder and the Horde had caught them.

Kyle ran, faster than he had ever run. Beside him, Sinks sprinted hard, his legs moving in a blur as the two men used the only advantage they had over their Infected enemy.

Speed.

The Wretches were close behind them though. Kyle knew most were slow moving like the one Sinks had just killed but there were always a handful of sprinters at the front of a Horde.

Bang-bang-bang-bang

Shots whistled past them and Kyle said a silent prayer of thanks for the marksmanship of his comrades as they shot their pursuers whilst avoiding drilling he or Sinks in the back. He risked a glance behind him to see the grey line of the Horde had reached the bridge where the white eyes of the Wretches glared up at the Militia, well out of reach.

"Here!" Sinks spat the word out and Kyle, ignoring the burning pain in his chest followed the older man left, ducking between two parked cars and vaulting the crash barrier. A dense tangle of brambles shifted in front of them and suddenly the bushes were dragged aside and another patrol of Milita was there. As Sinks and Kyle collapsed through the gap, they shoved the carefully constructed barrier back into place, effectively sealing them off from the road.

"Back – back to the RV!" Sinks snapped at the patrol commander, his status as a legitimate soldier automatically outranking any of the Militia.

"I – I got it in my eye!" Kyle, to his shame, felt tears well up as Sinks' expression turned from one of anger to a look of concern.

"Alright." He signalled to the other Militia to take a knee as he turned to Kyle "Just breathe for a second. What went in your eye?" for a moment, he was just Kyle's friend and not his commander.

"The blood... when it swung its head." Kyle swallowed a sob.

Sinks nodded "It was in the puddle though, wasn't it? It could've just been the water."

"It – it was bleeding in the water though. It was when it swung it's head..." Kyle felt sick. That terrified him. Was that the first symptoms of Infection?

"Alright." Sinks looked Kyle in the eye, the air of command filling his voice once again "What are your drills for a suspected infection?"

"B – booster jab and e – evac." Stuttered Kyle. He rested his rifle against his thigh and patted the velcro pocket on his sleeve. Tearing it open, he withdrew a plastic vial filled with a yellow liquid. Trying to stop his hands shaking, he tore off the plastic cap to reveal a small needle which he stabbed into his forearm. The liquid vanished into his vein and he stood, shock beginning to set in.

"Take a knee, for a minute." Sinks ordered, keying the talk button on his radio and alerting the other patrols to Kyle's status as a casualty.

Kyle knelt on the wet ground trying to control the panic. The Wretch's blood had entered his eye, possibly carrying with it the awful virus that would spell his death. The yellow booster he had just injected himself with was notoriously ineffective and he knew that at the first sign of infection, his fellow Militiamen would put a bullet in him and leave him here in the rain.

Or perhaps, Sinks would make them take him home. After all, Holden's medical facility had a moderate success rate with disease, illness and infections. In Kyle's mind floated the bespectacled face of the doctor, a robotic woman with thin grey hair and heavy wrinkles and he clung to the image desperately.

Rosie was the first to reach them, shoving the bushes aside, heedless of the noise. She knelt next to Kyle, seeing the empty vial, her quick mind taking in the scene.

"Oh, Kyle..." She looked stricken. Kyle had known Rosie since The Fall. In a way, they'd grown up together, both orphans and had joined the Militia together, competing every step of the way. Where Kyle was tall and strong, she was fast and intelligent, where Kyle could wrestle like an anaconda, she could shoot the wings off a fly. They were rivals, usually friends and on one drunken night, almost lovers but now she was staring at him with despair on her face.

"Suspected infection. Not confirmed." Sinks reminded her in the crisp voice he used for giving orders. Quickly, he pushed Rosie into a defensive position, facing outwards so they covered all approaches to their position. Kyle didn't think the Horde would follow them here but he saw the sense and aimed his own rifle obediently away from the group.

The rest of the patrols converged a minute later. Sinks crossed to brief the Mayor, a tough looking woman of indeterminate age who turned a blank expression to Kyle and nodded once before turning away to manage the rest of the fight.

"Alright." Sinks stepped in front of Kyle "C patrol, Rosie, Kyle – you're with me. The rest of you stay with Mayor Friend." Sinks beckoned once and turned, leading them at a hard paced run towards home.

CHAPTER 2

Home was a sturdy collection of rusted shipping containers, looming guard towers and wooden buildings organised into four walls which enclosed the area where Kyle had lived since the age of six. The name was painted in neat letters above the gate.

Holden.

As they approached, Sinks was already keying his radio, reporting Kyle's condition to the town. For his part, Kyle couldn't understand how the older man had the breath to speak. Every one of the Militia were hanging out, panting and sweating although none of them had dropped off the hard pace set by the burly soldier ahead of them.

The gate lifted open just enough for them to scramble underneath before it crashed back down into the concrete trough that sealed the entrance. Almost immediately, the wall guards were on Kyle, taking his weapons and binding his hands gently but firmly with strong cords. A bite proof mask was hooked over his mouth and nose with the loops pulled over his ears. Sinks held Kyle's gaze, his expression carefully blank but even so, Kyle felt the concern of his friend and he tried to remain stoic.

Rosie didn't try to hide her emotions, staring with grief on her face. Kyle held her gaze briefly before he was led away.

*

The quarantine building was cold and damp with concrete walls and no windows. One half of the roof was covered only by thick iron bars which left the room exposed to the gaze of the guard sitting atop the roof above Kyle. He'd been tossed in unceremoniously and the door slammed shut behind him, a couple of thick coats, a blanket, and a bucket his only comfort.

He knew the symptoms of the infection usually showed within a few hours but every man, woman and child in the village had seen the virus rage in as little as a few seconds, to as long as several days. The quarantine period for a suspected infection was one week.

The guards, armed with old but serviceable double barrelled shotguns would watch him the entire time and Kyle sat on the damp straw that acted as a bed and tried not to give in to despair. It was difficult.

The monotony was broken after only an hour as the guard above him stood and spoke to someone outside the building. Kyle heard words exchanged and then the heavy metal door swung inwards and Doctor May strode in.

"What are your symptoms?" she demanded. Not 'how are you feeling' or 'are you okay?'. Not called the 'Maybot' for nothing, the woman was notoriously uncaring although her skills in medicine were second to none in the entire region. Kyle knew that he was lucky to have grown up in a town with someone of her skill.

"None... yet. The blood went into my eye."

"How much?" The Maybot had remained by the door, keeping distance between her and Kyle.

"I don't know.... a drop maybe?"

"It sprayed after you shot the Wretch?"

"No. It's hard to explain. The Wretch was lying in a puddle after I'd shot it. Or I *thought* I'd shot it but maybe I didn't. I don't know. He – it jumped up and its hair flicked with the water and the liquid splashed across my face."

Dr May considered this for a few seconds, her face unmoving. Behind her through the still open door Kyle could see another of the wall guards, his shotgun held ready should Kyle succumb to the first violent urges of the Infection and move to attack the doctor.

"It's highly likely that no infection occurred. Typically, a bite or direct exposure to an open vein is required for the virus to be passed."

Kyle nodded. They all knew how the infection was passed but he felt an overwhelming sense of relief wash over him and a weight lift from his shoulders. He was going to be okay! But Dr May's next words soured his mood almost as quickly as it had lifted.

"Of course, we don't really have any way of telling so there's every chance you'll be Infected and we'll have to shoot you."

"Charming." muttered Kyle.

"Quite. Anyway, take these -" she took another two vials from her pocket, one containing a similar yellow liquid to the emergency vial he'd stuck himself with earlier and the second a dark green concoction "- the yellow in the morning but the green immediately. If you're still alive to take the yellow, you'll probably be fine." She made to turn away but stopped "If you should feel your mental health is under threat, notify the guard and I'll provide a sedative."

Thanks for nothing. Thought Kyle moodily as the heavy iron door slammed shut. He scooped up the vials and jabbed the green liquid into his arm, wincing at the sting of the short needle. He felt no different but stepping towards the door had moved him into the uncovered section of the quarantine room and the first drops of rain immediately made themselves known. He shivered and hurried back to the pile of straw, drawing the thick layers of the coats and blanket around him.

The guard on the roof shifted position to see him better, leaning forward to keep the shotgun out of the worst of the rain. Patrick was a plump man, seven or eight years older than Kyle and had washed out of Militia training into the wall guards. Kyle knew him well enough and caught his eye. Patrick gave him a wry thumbs up.

"Good news, eh? Maybe I won't have to blast you after all!" He joked.

Kyle nodded glumly.

"Cheer up! At least you get a few days off!" He grinned hugely as Kyle screwed his eyes shut and tried his best not to die.

CHAPTER 3

A week later, Kyle emerged from the quarantine cell as the sun began to fade. Rosie and Sinks were waiting for him. She was grinning, Sinks was his usual cool self but he gripped Kyle tightly by the shoulder as Rosie hugged him.

"Glad you're alright."

"Yeah. Me too." Kyle smiled at them both.

"You bloody stink though." Rosie pulled a face as she released Kyle.

"A week of not washing will do that."

"Right. Well, you can go to the bathhouse, then we're getting drunk. It's not optional!" she declared.

Rosie led the way down the crushed concrete that made up the walkways between buildings in their hometown. Holden was a neat square of flat ground, filled with regular rows of buildings, perhaps forty or so in number. Some were larger than others like the long, low hut that served as a cookhouse, village hall and general assembly area. The bath house was adjacent to it, a tall building that reached above the level of the wall that stood close behind it. A steady stream of steam issued from the chimneys that ran along the roof and the scent of the raw soap manufactured in the town filled the air. Sinks had thought to bring Kyle a fresh shirt and trousers and he tossed them to the younger man as they approached the building.

"You coming in with me?" He joked to Rosie who stuck her finger up at him.

"We'll be in the pub. Don't be long!" She warned as she and Sinks threaded their way through the buildings towards the Ridged Back pub.

Half an hour later, Kyle had emerged from the steaming

hot water, his arm weak from working the shower pump but feeling significantly cleaner and more human than he had. He strolled towards the pub, dropping his soiled clothes into the laundry as he went. One of the cleaners would take care of them and they'd find their way back to his narrow bed in the bunkhouse where the single men slept.

The armoury lay in the other direction to the pub but Kyle headed there anyway. He felt naked without weapons, despite the wall guards who were always visible. The walls were uniform on three sides and only broken on the fourth by the heavily armoured gate that allowed entry and egress to the town. Hefty shipping containers, packed with earth and rubble formed the base and atop these, a sturdy line of corrugated iron panels made up the height. A wooden fire step ran the entire length of the walls and it was along this that the guards patrolled.

At each corner of the town, a tall tower rose. These were the only breaks in the uniformity of the defences. Each had its own character and was heavily customised by the section that was responsible for its upkeep.

The towers stood at the four points of the compass and the sections that manned them were known by the same names. Each patrolled the section of wall to the right of the tower and the town itself was divided up into quadrants of north, east, south and west. The bathhouse was in west, the pub in east and the armoury, south.

Everyone had a job in Holden. The children went to school and learned how to raise crops, how to shoot, town politics, history, survival, and the all-important building maintenance skills which were the secret to the longevity of their four walled town. Kyle was a Militiaman, part of the para-military group that was responsible for keeping the Wretches away from their lands and protecting the trade routes that flowed like arteries into the town. Sinks, the towns military liaison, oversaw their training although Kyle could not remember the grizzled northerner ever shirking his own combat duties, getting stuck into any fight.

Kyle turned to his right as he left the bathhouse and passed by townsfolk who were winding down from the day. The weather had remained grey and overcast all week and didn't look like it would improve any time soon. The farmers were worrying, Kyle knew, about the harvest and the labourers would be steeling themselves for the long, gruelling hours in the fields.

A pair of engineers nodded to Kyle as he headed south. One was up a ladder which was propped against a building as he threaded a new cable between family homes. His assistant, a youth who Kyle had known from the schoolhouse was keeping the ladder steady and he called a greeting to Kyle as he past.

"Didn't get turned then?"

"Nah mate. Too much beer in the blood. Keeps me pure." Kyle grinned as the lad turned back to his task.

Electricity was a luxury that attracted traders and drifters to Holden. Not every building had it and use was strictly controlled but the engineers kept the wind turbines spinning and the solar farms reflecting and Holden did not struggle to keep its citizens warm nor its streets illuminated. The building at the north end of the Ridged Back was one that always had the lights on and the heaters glowing in the dark winter months. Holden didn't actually allow new citizens to take up residence, but the council kept the well-furnished guesthouse to attract the traders and wanderers who braved the wastes of the region.

The armoury was another building that the power always ran to. A hefty set of double doors kept the humidity out but Kyle found them unlocked as he slipped inside.

"Militiaman Frost!" Jane McDonald was an enormously fat woman who doubled up as both the armourer and a bar woman in the Ridged Back. Popular all over town, she was obscenely cheerful, come rain or shine and flirted outrageously with the young men of Holden.

"My God am I glad to see your muscly arms back in front of

me! I was saying in the pub just last night if you were Infected, I'd still let you take me to bed but I have to say, my heart wouldn't really be in it!"

Kyle grinned at her. He liked Jane although her innuendos and grabbing hands weren't always welcome. But dry humour was rife in the town and it wasn't done to avoid a joke.

"I missed you too, you know." Kyle joked in return.

"Oh yes? All tucked up in your bed at night I bet you were thinking of me! I know what you boys are like..." Jane threw her head back and roared with laughter as her chins wobbled dangerously.

Kyle rolled his eyes. Jane was separated from him by a thick wire grill and a locked door that kept him from the stacks of weapons the town had scavenged over the two decades since The Fall. Weapons weren't tightly controlled in Holden, indeed, it was considered odd for people *not* to be armed but the Council did enforce regulation of what weapons were owned by who. Everyone had to at least register the fact that they owned weapons, be they knives, bows or guns and many chose to store their rifles and shotguns in the armoury, carrying only scavenged handguns or knives on their person.

"I suppose you're feeling a bit undressed without a piece..." As with everything, Jane couldn't even talk shop to Kyle without making it seem sexual. He rolled his eyes again but she was already waddling to unlock the door to the side of the metal grate. As he stepped through, she intentionally stood in his way, forcing him to sidestep past her and unable to avoid at least partially rubbing against her.

"Oooh. Still smell of the bathhouse. All pink and shiny and clean for me."

He pulled a face and stepped through into the storage room which was lined with racks of rifles, shotguns and the crates of explosives that were only issued in an emergency. Jane elbowed past him and led him towards the handguns, sliding open a drawer labelled 'FROST, K'. She pulled the drawer out of the cabinet it rested in and lowered it carefully onto an empty table in the centre of the room put there for that purpose. She may have been mostly jokes but Kyle knew that Jane always took this part of her job seriously.

"Glock seventeen gen four... one" she laid the black pistol down on the table "Holster, one." She looked up at Kyle "You be careful with that tucked down your waist band! Don't want you shooting off the important bit" her eyes lingered for a second.

"Ammo?" Prompted Kyle, hastily.

"Magazines, three, fighting knife, one, utility knife, one and... That's the lot!"

Kyle pulled the pistol from the holster, checking the chamber was empty before he began loading rounds into the magazines. Jane scooped one up and helped.

"You in the pub tonight?" He asked.

"Not tonight. Got to stay here and work on those SA80's you lot scavenged for me the other week."

"Oh yeah? How are they turning out?"

She snorted, her chins wobbling again "Rubbish. Useless! And that was before they were left to gather dust for twenty years! Dunno why you bothered. Half of them will go for scrap but we should get a few firing. You'd have done better to find some half decent ammunition! Bloody stuff's becoming rarer than gold dust these days!"

Kyle nodded sagely as he finished loading the pistol magazine. He pushed the full mag home, cocking a round into the chamber before removing it again, replacing the loaded round with another and pushing the magazine home once again.

The holster fitted into his trousers, over his appendix and he carefully pushed the pistol home. He pocketed the spare magazines. The fighting knife also went into his belt while the folding knife he used for general tasks clipped into his trouser pocket.

"Better?"

Kyle patted the various weapons breathing a sigh of relief

"Yeah. Much!"

"Well like I said, don't go shooting off bits before I've had a chance to see them!" She leered at his groin again. Kyle snorted, thanked her, and left.

CHAPTER 4

If the air outside was dark and cold, the inside of the Ridged Back in the East Quarter was a vibrant, bustling and brightly lit haven. Kyle stepped through the threshold, the strong smell of stale beer, burning wood and the mouth-watering scent of a roasting joint striking his nostrils.

The pub was built in the style of a Nordic longhouse. Kyle knew the proprietor, Jason Mitchford, had built it this way intentionally because as he put it 'the beer tastes like shit so people need something to look at'. The result was a long, cosy room lit by the glow of the fire and dim electric lamps placed several metres apart so that natural pools of shadow formed between the tables.

The centre was a long bar; two lengths of flat plywood topped by a solid oak counter between which the bar staff drew foaming pints of dark, bitter ale into the fired clay mugs that were the norm in Holden. Next to the bar, a glowing fire pit heated the slowly turning hunk of meat that Kyle had smelled the moment he walked in.

Licking his lips, Kyle peered around, looking for Rosie and Sinks who beckoned him over from the far side. He passed the bar on his way and Jason, the landlord pressed a foaming pint into his hands "Glad to see you back, Frosty!" He grinned before turning to pull another pint from the wooden barrels that sat beneath the counter.

Kyle edged his way through the closely packed tables, nodding in greeting to familiar faces. He ducked once or twice under the lower beams and almost tripped over the tail of one of the many dogs that seemed to be the general property of the entire town. He bent down to pat the bitch who thumped her tail in response and then followed him as he squeezed past a table packed with off-duty wall guards and approached Sinks and Rosie.

"You've been a while, Jane finally got hold of you, did she?" was Sinks' opening remark.

"Not smelling the way he does." Interjected Rosie, pretending to wrinkle her nose in disgust.

Kyle affected a wounded silence as he lowered himself into the chair they'd saved for him and ignored them both, turning instead to pet the dog, running his hand down the prominent ridge along her back that all the dogs shared.

Better cared for than some of the humans in the town, Holden's dogs were mostly a mixture of ridgeback and shepherd, built for their guarding ability and invaluable in their prowess for sniffing out the Wretches that prowled the lands outside their four walls. It was often said that Holden had long since 'gone to the dogs' and it was a compliment. The dogs earned their keep as much as the humans.

"Do you two need a minute?"

Kyle looked up to see Rosie smiling jokingly at him and he gave the bitch one final pat before picking up his tankard and taking a deep swig of the dark brown liquid. He grimaced at the bitter taste.

"This stuff never gets any better, does it?"

"In fact," Sinks observed "this batch seems worse." He sipped and grimaced "Christ, what's he been putting in it, mud?"

Kyle and Rosie nodded sagely. The criticism of Jason's beer was as popular a subject in the town as discussion of the weather or the patterns of the Hordes. The next few minutes were wrapped up in various complaints or reminisces of a favourite batch of the home brewed beer. The dog leaned against Kyle's thigh and he patted her absently with one hand while the other mechanically raised and lowered the clay tankard.

The pub was packed and the temperature beneath the sharp angles of the ceiling began to rise. People nudged into Kyle as they sidled past, muttering apologies or shooting jokes at him. A part of him noticed as always that Sinks was given a respectful berth by the townsfolk, even those who were half a dozen pints deep. The faded camouflage of his military uniform might look out of place but his status as a genuine member of the army earned him a deep rooted respect from the citizens of Holden. Sure, Kyle and Rosie were in the Militia but that was just another job. The army was controlled by Parliament and particularly for those who had been born here or had been children during the Fall, the concept of an army or even a world outside the few thousand acres that Holden laid claim to, was as legendary as an aeroplane or the internet.

Of course, Kyle considered himself almost as important. His friendship with Sinks was one most of the Militia shared. Sinks was responsible for overseeing their training and directing their patrols and discipline. The trade routes were the life blood of Holden and without them, the town would long since have starved. Kyle had spent many weeks of his young life slowly walking along the cracked roads, bored out of his mind or, in contrast, sprinting away from Wretches as they lured a Horde away from their lands. It was one such operation that had lead to the events of a week ago and it was to this that their conversation naturally turned as they drank and Jason brought over a second round of beers.

"Have you seen any more of the Horde?"

Sinks burped gently, shaking his head as he did so "No. Plenty of stragglers, mostly the slower ones but no big groups." He took a sip and the images flashed through Kyle's mind. The slowest of the Infected, barely even mobile were those who had decomposed almost completely. The X2H virus slowed decomposition after its peak and Kyle had seen Wretches that could easily have been Infected around the time of the Fall, twenty years previously. Some, of course were fast like those that had chased he and Sinks but they typically formed the front of a Horde, their slower brethren following their lead and it was rare to find them alone.

They were easier to spot in the thick woodland that surrounded the town, throwing themselves mindlessly through bushes and thickets to attack the patrols. Their strong scent, far more pronounced than the slower varieties gave the dogs little trouble in identifying them.

Bloats were another rare enemy. When corpses fall into water and decompose, they begin to swell as the water is absorbed and the same was true for Wretches. Their skin was stretched taught and the stench of the rot was enough to make you vomit. Kyle had only seen one once, a great swollen monstrosity with its arms stuck out to the sides like a teddy, almost unable to move. One of the wall guards had shot it and the shotgun blast had ripped into the stomach, making it burst open like a dam releasing a flood. Black, rotted organs had spilled out and the creature, unable to support its own weight had flopped onto its back and flailed wildly. The stink had carried across the entire town and for hours the dogs had howled and barked as the residents of Holden choked on the awful miasma.

"Was the Mayor pissed off about me?" Kyle asked.

"I bloody was." Sinks growled and Kyle glanced at him wide eyed "Remember when I told you to get up that ladder?"

"I –"

"And you swore you'd follow orders when I gave them to you?"

"Yes, but–"

"You see, Kyle–" Rosie had taken over the ribbing "when you disobey an order, you disrupt us all. It causes a breakdown in the structure of the patrol and puts other Militia in danger."

Kyle glowered at her in silence.

"And, it makes you look a complete pillock. You –"

"Alright! Alright. I was wrong to ignore you." Kyle held Sinks' gaze "I'm sorry. I won't do that again."

"Bloody right you wont! Anyway, no, the Mayor wasn't pissed off because I didn't tell her you're a stubborn, lanky, ugly, southern tosspot."

"Thanks."

"You're welcome." Sinks rolled his eyes "She didn't bloody listen to me though."

"About what?"

"The Hordes! That's what, the fourth this season?"

"Two of them were small." Argued Rosie.

"Small! It only takes one to wipe out the town, you know. Your patrols aren't going to be much good in a pitched battle."

"What did the Mayor say?"

Rosie suddenly sniggered "More to the point, what did Sinks say!" she shot a sideways look at the glowering soldier "In the debrief, he was raging saying we can't keep just dodging the Hordes like this. Said we should ask for outside help."

"Oh, bloody hell!" Kyle half laughed, half cringed at the thought of telling their staunchly self sufficient Mayor to ask for help "I bet she had a bit to say about that?"

"Bloody stupid woman." Sinks growled into his tankard as Rosie and Kyle sniggered.

"Anyway, he told her to send a message to the Rangers to ask for support. She told him to go and run naked through the woods covered in meat grease."

Kyle howled with laughter as Sinks muttered mutinously about 'civvies' and 'hats'.

"There was a rumour." Began Rosie but shot a look at Sinks as though sharing a silent message.

"What? Tell me!" Demanded Kyle, setting his tankard down.

"It's just a rumour" repeated Rosie "One of the traders came from London via Matwood with a load of water and he said Matwood had called the Rangers. Said the Hordes were getting too strong."

"Rangers, huh?" Kyle's eyes glowed and a grin spread across his face "Proper soldiers!" he jibed at Sinks.

The older Corporal didn't smile "If the Rangers are here then it means we're in danger too. Matwood is only fifteen miles from here. The entire reason those battalions exist is to deal with the Hordes and they don't send them out for nothing."

"I thought they, you know, 'ranged'." said Rosie "They track the Hordes and report back."

Sinks shook his head "No, they're the only unit that has a proper airborne capability – no, not that sort" he said, seeing Kyle's eyes move to the blue wings on his sleeve "I mean they have helicopters. There aren't many units who can all move by air. Choppers are incredibly expensive and the army doesn't like to waste resources."

"The trader didn't see any helicopters though?" Kyle guessed.

Rosie shrugged "Didn't say so."

Sinks scoffed "Think they might have mentioned it if they had, they aren't exactly a common sight."

"It's just a rumour." Repeated Rosie "If there was a serious threat, Matwood would have sent word."

Kyle nodded slowly. Leading the roving Hordes away from Holden was one thing but the thought of fighting one or of one attacking Holden, moving like a grey flood of death towards his home sent a shiver down his spine. Suddenly, the container walls didn't seem high enough and he wondered why the council hadn't built them taller.

He said as much to Sinks who chuckled "You don't know how lucky you are to have walls! Some places, they get overrun every night. Have to barricade their doors and shoot their way out to work every morning. Speaking of work, tomorrow we're training with the wall guards to practice our defence drills so make sure you're both there on time."

Kyle looked guiltily at his third empty tankard "Probably shouldn't have too many of these then?"

"Probably not."

Jason appeared again with another round and plonked them down on the table before the three of them.

"Oh well." Muttered Kyle "One more can't hurt."

CHAPTER 5

By the time Jason announced the meat was cooked and had begun slicing large chunks of it off, Kyle was starving. He was also more than a little drunk but he was enjoying himself. Rosie had taken to chuckling prettily at every one of his jokes and he wondered if their previously disrupted consummation could be approached in the bunkhouse later. Sinks had merely glowered at the two of them as he drank his ale, for once not making a jibing comment.

Kyle licked his fingers clean as the red dog sat expectantly next to him. As was the custom, each of them pulled a good chunk of the scorched meat off their plates and tossed it to her. Indeed, it seemed every dog in the town had appeared at Jason's shout to pick at the scraps. Dogs never went hungry in Holden.

Kyle burped in appreciation earning himself a dirty look from Rosie. He shrugged apologetically as the dog whined next to him.

"All gone, girl I'm afraid." He reached out to rub her ears but to his surprise, she looked past him towards the door.

"Anyway, Sinks says we're running tomorrow morning. Us against the guards -"

Rosie's voice was cut off by the sudden explosion of noise in the pub. Every dog, almost as one span from their position and began barking, howling, whining. A cacophony of noise that made Kyle wince.

"What the hell?"

"Move!" Sinks' voice snapped through the confusion as he shot to his feet. Kyle was dimly aware of a bell ringing outside. Quick, rhythmic gongs. If a bell was ringing in Holden, it could only mean one thing.

"Sign!" Shouted a voice as the door to the pub burst open and a woman dressed in the brown coat of a wall guard appeared "Sign! Everywhere! Christ, there are thousands of them!"

"Get to your positions! Move!" Sinks snapped at Kyle before turning back to yell at the half drunk occupants of the pub. His crisp military tone rose above the hubbub and silenced even the dogs "Move! That's the alert! All of you to your positions! If you've drunk too much, keep your fingers off the trigger until you're told otherwise!"

Kyle and Rosie turned and shoved their way to the door. Kyle mentally recapped how many beers he'd had. Probably too many. He kept his hand away from the pistol as they ran, not wanting his drinking to result in a careless accident.

The occupants of the pub surged toward the door. Between their legs, the barking, howling mass of canine fury tore with them.

*

Kyle's alert position was on the north wall, by the gate. Rosie was on the east and she vanished around the side of the pub, running for one of the ladders that were being lowered by wall guards to allow the townspeople to take up their firing positions.

There was a loud click, almost a bang and suddenly the darkened town was bathed in the glow of the powerful floodlights mounted on each tower. The bell was still ringing its rhythmic chime and a voice could be heard shouting through a loudspeaker, calling the citizens from their homes to the fight.

Men and women ran past Kyle. Despite the chaos, there was order. Everyone kept to the left of whichever path they hurried along. Doors opened inwards and occupants peered out carefully before running into the night. They had rehearsed this a thousand times. The townsfolk might all have different jobs, but defending their home was everyone's responsibility.

The first rifles cracked from the north and west towers as Kyle hurried towards them. He only had his pistol; not the best weapon for firing from the wall but he knew that even now, the children too young to man the walls would be tugging handcarts piled with weapons and ammunition from the armoury and hastening through the streets. He imagined Jane, sweating with the exertion as she emptied the shelves of guns.

Boom

The blast came from ahead, beyond the gate. Kyle couldn't tell what the explosion was, as far as he knew there were no explosives beyond hand grenades in the town and the blast was far bigger than that. He kept running.

Ten seconds more and he reached the north wall. A small squad had tugged sandbags from a cupboard by the gate and were busy piling them along the bottom of the metal entrance, the weakest part of the town's defences.

"Kyle!" He looked up to see Ali Carmichael, a man a few years older than him, beckoning him towards a ladder. Kyle jogged forward and began to climb. Ali pulled him up the last rung onto the solid roof of the container. The metal of the wall loomed before Kyle and the two of them hauled themselves up onto the wooden fire step. Kyle looked over the top into the floodlit fields that surrounded his home.

"Am I missing something?" He turned to Ali who shrugged, just as confused.

The floodlights penetrated to beyond the first line of crops which stood innocently in the harsh lights. But there was nothing. Not a soul moved in the false light and Kyle groaned.

"This better not be a drill! I've had too many beers for that."

Ali glanced at him "How many?"

"Four? Maybe five?"

"Keep your weapon away then. I don't want to get shot in the back because you can't hold your booze."

Kyle nodded seriously. A moment later Ali passed him a well dented metal flask. It was warm to the touch and Kyle opened it, sipping the bitter tea that was another of Holden's small luxuries.

"Kill or cure you." joked Ali as Kyle handed the flask back gratefully, feeling some of the effects of the beer leave his mind.

"What were they shooting at?" He asked the world in general.

"Not sure. I was on wall duty when they got sign. Came from the west wall though. Those lads up top have been shooting a bit." He gestured to the north tower with its peeing blue paint and faded collection of flags.

Kyle was about to make a comment when suddenly a burst of rifle fire came from the tower followed by another shout of warning. A heavy spotlight threw its glow across the fields, penetrating far further than the floodlights. It began a slow move across the crops, coming to rest on the wide road that led away from Holden.

"Bloody Hell!" swore Kyle.

"It's a Horde!" shouted Ali, hefting his shotgun.

"Hold fire!" came the shout from their wall commander "Don't shoot until I give the order!"

Kyle understood the sense of the command but as he drew his pistol, useless as it was at this range, he felt terror grip him and it was hard not to blast the entire clip at the approaching horror.

Walking, some running ahead of their fellows and at least one dragging itself out of the crops was a line of Wretches. Kyle saw their dead white eyes, completely devoid of humanity staring back at him. Their terrible grey rotten skin was stretched across the bones of their faces, peeling their black lips back to reveal snarling yellow teeth. The spotlight moved back across them and Kyle saw there were hundreds, maybe thousands of them.

At that moment, a burst of rifle fire came from the west wall, to their left. Kyle turned away from the horror show to the north and stared at the guards on the other wall. All of them were firing, their bodies silhouetted by the floodlights. He couldn't see over the wall and desperately strained to see what they were firing at.

"Where are the sodding rifles?" shouted Ali.

As if in response, the squeaking wheel of a handcart sounded and Kyle jumped down from the fire step to help pass up the weapons from the half dozen children that had rushed across the town with them. The armoury was at the southern end of the town so their wall was always the last to receive their weapons.

He reached down, pulling one end of a metal crate stamped with faded yellow letters reading 'PROPERTY OF US ARMY'. Someone had imaginatively crossed out the words and scribbled next to them so it now read 'PROPERTY OF HOLDEN'. He tugged it up and shoved it behind him where Ali hauled it open and began passing the M4 carbines that had been liberated from an abandoned airbase years ago.

Next came a case of loaded magazines and then boxed ammunition. Kyle seized a rifle for himself, stuffing the magazines into his pocket. Ali nudged him and he turned to see one of the children, maybe the Patel boy, mutely holding out a plate carrier.

"Thanks." he muttered, throwing it over his head. He moved the magazines into the pouches on the front and nodded to himself, loading the rifle, and resting it on the sturdy metal of the wall. Beside him, Ali had exchanged his shotgun for a similar weapon, slinging his original over his back.

"Wait for the order!" their wall commander shouted again as the south wall, directly behind them exploded in rifle fire.

"What was the explosion?" Kyle called to Ali.

"Don't know! It was in the woods..."

The wood line lay almost a kilometre in front of them, beyond the fields. The solid brush of the forest was carefully maintained by the Keepers who encouraged the thick undergrowth to stop the Wretches approaching the vital crop fields.

But the creatures that now advanced on Holden were using the road, the path of least resistance. Most of them were fairly stupid and slow, the result of advanced brain decomposition but even as Kyle watched, he saw a group of the Infected detach themselves from the rest and begin running forwards.

"Fire!"

Kyle fired. He leaned his body forward as he had been taught, trying to make his posture as flat and stable as possible. The optic atop the rifle he was using had two times magnification and the creatures were clearly visible. He breathed out, taking the first pressure off the trigger and at the natural pause of the breath, he gently squeezed the tiny metal lever.

The shots went off all along the wall, as always sounding to Kyle like a bundle of dry twigs being snapped between two hands. The rifle rocked gently and he reached down with his left fingers to grip the metal of the wall, holding the light barrel in place.

He fired again, this time following the shot through and seeing to his satisfaction the Runner go down hard. He held his breath and fired two more shots, watching them strike the torso of the figure. It lay still.

The sharpshooters in the towers were doing good work, picking off the Infected at a range of hundreds of metres. Kyle waited patiently as he had been taught, listening to the commands of the wall commander and waiting for the Infected to come into his killing zone.

The shooting paused as the tide of Wretches lulled briefly. Shots were coming thick and fast from the south and the west walls now. The east was silent apart from the shouts of the commanders there, telling their shooters to remain vigilant.

Kyle turned to Ali "How the Hell are we being attacked on three sides?"

"Dunno. I think south and west are shooting at the same Horde. It's just split up."

"Then how have we got these bastards coming at us from the north? Are they using tactics now?"

In the floodlights he saw Ali go pale and cursed himself for spooking his firing partner. Kyle turned back to the line of Wretches still slowly moving towards them "There aren't many left now." he said encouragingly and it was true. The shooters at Kyle and Ali's level had fired a magazine each and the ground was littered with corpses. The main body was still moving but Kyle could see there were far fewer than he'd first thought. Maybe a couple of hundred and the sharpshooters were now slowly but deliberately picking off the remaining few which were out of range of the assault rifles.

"What was that?" asked Ali, suddenly turning his head to the side and listening.

"What?" demanded Kyle. He'd heard nothing.

"Thought I..."

"What? What is it?" Kyle demanded again. He thought he heard Sinks' voice shouting from somewhere in the town as the fire from the south wall died and then picked up again.

BOOM

This time the explosion was not just closer, it was visible. From the woods, a thousand metres in front of them a great jet of orange fire leapt into the night. In a second, it was gone, the flash burned into Kyle's eyes as he swore and crouched behind the parapet instinctively.

"The Hell was that!" he shouted to Ali who was staring wide eyed.

Without warning, the crops ahead of them, just a hundred metres away suddenly parted and belched forth a stream of sprinting, white eyed, grey skinned monsters who leapt towards them.

"Oh shit! Enemy front! Fire! Fire! Fire!"

CHAPTER 6

On the south wall, Sinks had taken over. The commander of this section had slipped on a ladder and landed on his head. He was alright, but had been taken off to Doctor May's clinic. Sinks had assumed command.

The sight that lay before him was terrifying although if he was scared, he didn't show it. Sinks had been a soldier for more than two decades but he managed to maintain the appearance of a much younger man. He'd faced enemies, both human and Infected and met each one with a terrible calm that he tried to teach to the young men and women under his tutelage.

A spread out mess of Wretches filled the glow of the floodlights. It had begun with Runners, most of whom were now dead and then the slower ones had come. The shooters on the wall had gunned them down and were still firing. A tide line of corpses was beginning to form a dozen or so metres in front of them but the darkness was still spewing them forth.

To Sinks' right, a young man was firing his rifle too fast, the barrel twitching left and right and his teeth bared in a white snarl. Sinks stepped forward, placing his hand on the man's shoulder and body blocking him against the parapet.

"Safety! Put your safety on!" The man stared at him blankly before recovering and flicking the small catch.

"Right. Take a step back and a few deep breaths!"

The man did so, nodding a little in acknowledgement of the shock that had taken over him. To their left and right, rifles still cracked.

"We're okay, we've got plenty of ammo. We just need to keep shooting, calmly and carefully." Sinks made sure he held the man's gaze until the madness fled from his eyes and he was calmer.

The man said something but a rifle cracked and Sinks didn't hear him.

"What?"

"What was the explosion?"

Sinks turned away, pretending he hadn't heard. He glanced back towards the north wall where he knew Kyle stood and waited for the chaos to make sense.

CHAPTER 7

The first of the Wretches threw themselves at the wall. Kyle found himself leaning over the parapet and firing straight down. He looked into the blank white eyes of something that had once been a child but now reached up towards him with a terrible howling snarl sounding from the black lips and yellow teeth.

Kyle shot it. Child or not, once the Infection had taken hold, there was no curing it. The creature slumped pathetically at the bottom of the wall and he turned his sights to another.

The monsters were flinging themselves at the hard metal and Kyle's heart leapt into his mouth as one, still wearing the remnants of a filthy dress, took a running jump at the wall and managed to find a handhold on the top of the container. Kyle swore and fired down but the creature swung itself sideways, whether by design or accident he couldn't tell. The result was the same. The Infected found another handhold and began to haul itself up the metal wall.

Beside him, Ali screamed in fear and backed away from the wall, remembering only to stop as he nearly toppled back off the fire step.

"Get a bloody grip!" Kyle roared "They can't get up here!"

The figure was hanging by both hands now and Kyle fired twice, striking it in the neck and torso. It crashed to the ground and lay still. Kyle looked up and down the wall exultantly. All along, the Runners were being cut down by the townsfolk and he nodded in satisfaction. They were winning!

BOOM

This time the explosion was in the field. The sound hit his ears first, shutting out any sense of noise and giving him the feeling that someone had taken his eardrum out and struck it with a hammer. Then he was falling backwards from the wooden fire step, dimly aware that Ali next to him was also falling. Kyle landed with a thump on the metal roof of the container, the pain of the fall barely registering next to the shock of the wall, flapping like a leaf in a breeze. How could that be? It was solid iron!

Then his dazed mind caught up, recognising the terrible gash in the barrier that had been torn in front of where Ali was standing and his gaze travelled upwards, coming to rest on the blank white eyes of the Wretch as it leapt through the gap towards him.

CHAPTER 8

"Jesus!" the firers on the south wall were frightened and Sinks couldn't blame them. He could see fire burning on the north wall and hear screams from that place. Even from here he could see the breach in the iron of the wall and he cringed, hoping Kyle wasn't there.

Rifles cracked near the breach and he suddenly whipped around, roaring at his own firers to keep shooting, to cover their own stretch of wall.

"We've got to get over there!" shouted one woman.

"No!" Sinks drew his pistol "Stand where you are and keep firing! There are plans for this! Anyone who abandons their position will have to go through me!" He moved to stand in front of the nearest ladder. The message was plain and the firers turned back to their task, one by one, quickly becoming embroiled in the vicious fight.

"Come on, Kyle..." Sinks muttered.

CHAPTER 9

Rosie was starting to get a sore neck. She'd once seen a video of a tennis match. The players in their impossibly clean white clothes, the crowd of people gathered together without a weapon between them. It had all seemed so surreal as she'd watched but as she flicked her gaze for the thousandth time away from the ground before the east wall back to the terrible rent in the north, she was reminded of the rapidly turning heads of the spectators.

Before her, the floodlights reflected off the glass panes of the solar farm. Aside from the silent panels rooted deep into the ground, their section was empty. Not a single one of the Infected had come to the east wall and the guards stood restlessly, their rifles trained on nothing.

Rosie heard the wall commander, a man named Sean barking into his radio, demanding an update. Every ear in the section was straining to hear the response but he shook his head, taking his hand away from the receiver.

"Eyes-on! Keep scanning your arcs..." Rosie turned her head back to the solar farm obediently. Only the best shots were assigned to this section of the wall, their marksmanship a necessity with the fragile glass panes before them.

"Movement in the farm!" someone shouted and a second later, a dozen voices called out asking the same question 'where?'.

"Er, one half left, row four!" Rosie followed the direction, her gaze landing on a spot where a series of dark shadows were running between the glass panes. She narrowed her eyes, seeing one of them, concealed in the shadow the panel cast, turn to one of the others. The gunfire from the other walls blocked out the sound but Rosie could have sworn they were communicating.

"Zeks!" Someone bellowed and Rosie took a sharp breath as she understood. Her eyes narrowed as the figures resolved into men and women, dressed in uniform long dark coats, each with a distinctive red armband. They ran towards the Horde, now letting odd high pitched yells as they moved.

"The Hell are they doing?" Sean, the commander had moved to stand by her to watch the incredible sight.

"Trying to lead them away..." Rosie couldn't fathom the madness that would lead a human to be outside the walls in this sea of death.

"Or lead them here!" snapped the voice of a wall guard to Sean's other side "We should take them out." He sighted on one of the figures but Sean angrily cuffed him around the head.

"Leave the Zeks! It's their own lives they're wasting!"

He began to say more but his radio crackled and he listened intently before looking at Rosie who was closest.

"You - take Callum and Jess and reinforce the north wall! Make sure nothing gets through that breach! If they don't need you then get back here on the double. Move!"

Rosie needed no further encouragement. She turned and jumped from the container, landing well with a small roll, the rifle tucked against her body. She wished Kyle could have seen it and it was with his face in her mind that she sprinted through the empty streets towards the north wall.

A body lay crumpled at the foot of the wall, a man, his rifle beside him and a confused, wide eyed expression on his face. She recognised Ali. He was dead, his neck twisted at an impossible angle.

A shout sounded from above and she jerked her head upwards.

"Kyle!" she shouted, raising the rifle as she did so.

The Wretch had vaulted through the gap, careless of the tearing edges of the metal that drew black blood from the skin of its palms. It jumped and as it did so, Rosie fired.

The bullets tore into the creature's chest, ripping through the skin and finding the black organs that lay beneath it. It threw its head back and gave a terrible moaning howl before staggering backwards, both arms outstretched and falling into the gap that had been blown in the wall.

"Kyle!" she shouted again, scrambling up the ladder. Kyle lay on his back, blinking dazedly at the sky.

"Hello, Rosie." he said in a conversational tone.

"Are you hurt? Kyle! Answer me!" Callum and Jess went to the parapet, lending their rifles to the fight below.

Kyle seemed to snap out of it. He blinked a few times then swore "What happened? There was a bomb! Right outside the wall!" he scrambled to his feet and pointed to the field where a plume of black smoke was rising from the burning crops.

"What's that noise?" shouted Rosie over the sound of fighting.

"What noise?"

"That one!" her words were drowned as yet another light swept over them. This one did not come from the tower, nor from the floodlights and it was accompanied by a roaring sound that drowned out the howls of the Infected and the firing of the guns. A terrible wash of hot air sent Rosie's hair flying across her face and the whole town stopped shooting and stared in shock at the roaring thunder of the helicopter.

CHAPTER 10

It was as though a dragon had flown out of a children's story book and soared across the sky. Kyle would not have been more shocked if the monstrosity above him had breathed fire and flapped giant wings. A helicopter was something he'd seen only on grainy videos shown at Christmas or in books that Sinks had forced him to read.

He'd never expected to see one in his life, much less here in Holden!

He wondered if Sinks had called for help. After all, the old soldier was full of surprises. Now that he thought about it, Kyle realised that the explosions must have come from the chopper. It must be the Rangers, attacking the Horde and they had lost control. Now they were trying to protect the people of the town from the Wretches and in the process, they had accidentally damaged the town wall.

The people around him seemed to have the same idea. One or two were whooping and cheering. He became aware that there were still Infected on the ground below the wall and he moved forward to engage. Rosie joined him.

The creature that had breached the wall was dead and was caught in the gap of the metal, effectively forming a plug in the breach. Kyle and Rosie left it alone.

They fired and fired until the ground was littered with corpses. The stench of cordite and smoke mixed in the air with the ever present reek of death and decay. Kyle's ears and head were throbbing from the explosion and the repeated rifle shots. Too late, he remembered the earplugs that were stuffed into the top of his vest. He thought about shoving them in but the firing was dying down and it seemed too late.

The chopper moved off to cover the south tower and Kyle heard the distinct chatter of machine gun fire from the aircraft and he relished at the carnage it was unleashing on the enemy.

He gave a whoop as the last of the Wretches was shot down and scanned the ground lit by the floods. To his right, Rosie flashed him a grin and he leaned towards her, an odd kind of armless hug of victory.

"Where's Ali?" he asked.

She glanced back towards the spot where the body lay, a hard expression settling on her face "He's dead. Broke his neck."

"Shit..." Kyle closed his eyes briefly before forcing the thought out of his mind and scanning the ground through his sights. The helicopter moved back overhead, its bright searchlight scanning the fields. The sound of gunfire had died away, punctuated sporadically by shots from the towers.

"How many mags?" the second in command of the north wall moved along behind them.

Kyle patted his vest "Two. Any more coming?"

"No."

"Jesus." Kyle realised they had probably burned through most of the ammunition the town had collected since the container wall had first gone up, twenty years ago. It should have been a sobering thought but the battle joy and adrenaline was still pumping through Kyle. They had won! They had fought off a Horde! Even the army in the days after the Fall hadn't been able to stop the Hordes, being overwhelmed as they failed to adjust tactics to meet the new threat.

He turned to Rosie who was grinning at him, the same joy on her own face. To his surprise, she reached out a gloved hand and gripped his vest, pulling him close and crushing her lips to his own in a victory kiss.

"Oi! Get a room you lot!" joked someone in the section.

They broke apart and Kyle grinned at her. She grinned back and an image of her bare skin against his in the darkness of the bunkhouse burned itself through his mind.

CHAPTER 11

There was no time for romance or sleep that night. The helicopter flew away at some point and Sinks' voice could be heard later on, barking orders.

They stayed on the walls. The shooters took turns resting with their backs against the fire step, trying to sleep and failing. The temperature dropped and they shivered through the small hours as the floodlights burned, waiting for the shouts that would signal more of the Infected.

The shouts never came but as the dawn rose, grey and murky around them, the floodlights powered down with a gentle whirr.

"Movement!" called Rosie, leaning on the wall above Kyle. He jerked out of a semi-doze and hauled himself up stiffly to see figures walking through the ruin of the cornfield. Not Wretches, people.

"Hold fire! Friendlies." Called a voice although the confusion was palpable. The gate hadn't been opened and no-one would voluntarily have stepped outside the walls.

"Rangers?" someone asked the section at large but Kyle could see the black coats.

"Zeks!"

"They were here earlier –" Rosie told him "I think they were trying to lead them away."

"Are they mental?" Kyle wondered but the black coated people had drawn together and were staring at the wall. They were too far to see facial expressions but Kyle caught a distinct impression of disapproval from their posture.

However, they soon moved off, a thin, slow moving line filing into the treeline.

"Stand down!" the order came soon after the Zeks had left. The words were echoed around the walls. Kyle breathed a sigh of relief. To his right, Rosie groaned with exhaustion and rested her head against the metal of the wall.

The morning shift of Wall Guards appeared, bleary eyed in the dawn. They'd been kept back as a reserve force and Kyle wondered if they'd slept at all. At least he'd been able to see what was going on from up here. He couldn't imagine how stressful it had been, hearing the fighting but unable to see how the battle was going.

Gratefully, he stumbled down the steps of the ladder. A pair of Dr May's people had appeared and placed a brown blanket over Ali's body. Kyle looked at the scene for a moment before they carried it away. Rosie put her hand on his arm and squeezed it gently.

"Oi, you two!" Sinks' voice seemed to have lost none of its power and volume during the long night.

Kyle turned wearily. Surely, they weren't still expected to train today? He wanted nothing more than to collapse into bed.

"Clearance patrols." announced Sinks. "We're going to be out all day, linking up with the Rangers to make sure there are none of these bastards left. Get some field clothes on and get your kit!" he strode away.

Kyle glanced at Rosie who gave a wry grin and a shrug before turning away to the women's bunkhouse. Kyle watched her go, regretfully.

*

The woods may have been thick but there were deliberate paths that led through them and Kyle found himself trudging down a leaf strewn mud slick only a few hours later, his rifle clutched in both hands. He was exhausted and stared hard at everything he saw, not trusting his sleep deprived brain to translate the images into meaning.

Rosie, behind him was in a similar state. They'd covered several miles already with nothing to show for it. She was grumbling, as was her habit when nervous. The threat of the Wretches had them on edge.

"... bastard just wants us out here to show off to his army mates. Can't be a single Wretch left in the whole region after last night. Bloody noise drew the lot of them in."

"D'you reckon Major Armstrong's here?"

"Armstrong?" Rosie tried and failed to sound uninterested "Who cares?"

"Oh, come on!" protested Kyle.

Major Blake Armstrong was the commander of the Ranger Regiment and a living legend. Posters of him decorated the insides of both the male and female bunkhouses as well as more than a few houses around the town. With his startling blue eyes, dark beard and white teeth, Armstrong was the heroic face of the military, a war hero held in higher esteem than anyone else in England.

"Can't think he'll be here" Rosie said in an offhand tone "There's no way he'd have let the Horde get near us last night."

"Maybe he's arrived now to help mop up?"

"Don't get your hopes up." she muttered.

Kyle tutted but fortunately, Rosie didn't hear him. They reached the end of the track and emerged carefully into a wide clearing where Sinks stood waiting for them. He nodded as they approached, waiting patiently for them to report the all clear. The rest of the Militia were gathered around him. Apparently, they were the last patrol.

Sinks turned away from them, revealing a man behind him who Kyle didn't recognise. He was instantly intrigued. Strangers weren't uncommon in Holden, but the man was dressed in the same combat pattern fatigues that Sinks wore albeit, these looked almost brand new next to Sinks' faded uniform.

"Kyle, Rosie, this is Sergeant Fisher, First Battalion, Rangers."

Kyle stared in amazement. The First Battalion he knew was

commanded directly by Armstrong and each of its members were handpicked by the famous Major to form the elite unit.

Fisher held out a hand. He was older even than Sinks with a rugged beard on his chin, thinning hair and a weather-beaten face. Despite his years, he managed to convey a sense of extreme toughness and his lean figure betrayed his physical fitness. Kyle thought that this was a man who had seen the darkest parts of life and come out unscathed. His handshake was like a rock and his gaze held Kyle's who stammered a greeting.

"Anyway, think we're about done here." said Fisher, turning to Sinks "Our lads have found a few stragglers but we're happy the Horde is neutralised."

"How come it was here in the first place?" interrupted Kyle.

Fisher looked at him in mild surprise "We've been tracking this one for the last few days. It suddenly turned towards your town." he shrugged "It happens."

"Why did it split into two parts?" pressed Kyle.

Fisher looked mildly annoyed "What?"

"We were attacked from both sides. Most of the Horde came from the south and west but we had more than a hundred come at the north wall too."

Fisher glowered "Yeah... they got broken up in the dark. You know what the Infected are like..." He trailed off. Kyle knew that the military never used the colloquial term 'Wretches', instead simply using the clinical word 'Infected'.

Rosie piped up and Fisher turned to her, his eyes taking her in her good looks "We saw Zeks during the fight."

"Zeks?" Fisher finally sounded interested "How many? Where? When?"

"They left, hours ago." Sinks reported "Headed west, towards Matwood."

Fisher nodded at Kyle "That's why the Horde broke up. Bloody idiots probably led it here in the first place." He shook his head "Fine. I'll let the blokes know, see if we can't bring a few to justice."

Sinks cleared his throat "We're low on ammo." He told the man "Can the Major get us a re-plen? They've been stockpiling here ever since the Fall..." he let the words trail off without adding the truth of the matter, which was that without rifle ammunition, Holden was at the mercy of the Hordes. They couldn't fight off another assault like the last.

"Armstrong isn't coming here. He's in Matwood. There's been a whole load of Feral sightings between here and London and Parliament has ordered him to deal with it personally."

"Ferals?" interrupted Kyle, earning himself another filthy look from Sinks "Here?"

As far as he knew, no-one in the town with the possible exception of Sinks, had seen a Feral. The most dangerous type of Wretch, Ferals were unique in that they retained the vast majority of their mental faculties post-infection. Rumours even said that they gained enhanced abilities, able to strategize, organise and even use crude weapons. Kyle had heard it said that every Horde had a Feral at its heart, but he didn't think it was true. Wretches would follow any movement and naturally banded together.

Sinks cut across Kyle's train of thought "We'll need to speak to him. Do you have comms with your HQ?"

"No." was the terse reply "The bird might but they won't land here now. If you want to see the Major you'll have to come with us to Matwood. We're heading back in the morning."

Armstrong was in Matwood! Kyle had visited the neighbouring town a few times. At least three times the size of Holden, Matwood sat at a crossroads of trade routes through the region and made a fortune taxing and providing shelter to passing travellers. The town sat on a hill by a natural spring which, when bottled, produced the sweetest water Kyle had ever tasted. It was sold in Holden as a delicacy and he knew a bottle could cost almost a week of his Militiaman's pay.

Kyle wanted to hear more about Armstrong but Sinks began snapping out orders and they moved off through the dense forest in patrol formation. Kyle had time to shoot an excited glance at Rosie as Fisher joined them heading back to Holden. Armstrong! It was almost unthinkable that the Rangers should be so close to Holden. Kyle wondered if Sinks would let him come to Matwood the next day and resolved to force his friend to let him.

The sight of Holden threw ice water on his good spirits and all at once his exhaustion caught up with him as the sight of the hundreds of corpses littering the ground greeted them. Kyle let out a deep sigh, hiked up his daysack and set off to help clear the ground.

CHAPTER 12

The funeral was attended by the whole town, escorted by a dozen or so dogs. With an efficiency borne of long practice, the Undertaker led the residents of Holden through the front gate, past the crops and into the small clearing in the woods that served as a graveyard.

The wooden pillars that marked the final resting places of the dead stood almost as thick as the undergrowth that surrounded them. The only difference was the ordered arrangement of the posts which were aligned to appear perfectly straight from any angle.

Kyle knew that many of them did not stand above a corpse. Plenty were simply markers of family members who had vanished during the confused years of the Fall and were either wandering the country as one of the countless victims of the virus or were a pile of white bones, slowly turning to dust.

Death was a constant presence in Holden and the ground leading to the quiet clearing was well trodden, the words of the Undertaker, well-practiced. Everyone bowed their heads as the man read the words of mourning.

"... a good man, a kind man, a true Warrior and a citizen of our town"

A Warrior? Ali had fallen off the wall and broken his neck. It was hardly a Warriors' death, thought Kyle, moodily, trying not to fidget. He was vaguely sad that Ali was dead but a part of him knew that the man had died because he wasn't good enough. After all, he, Kyle had been on the exact same spot of wall and was still alive.

"... will be dearly and sorrowfully missed by us all."

Kyle wondered why no-one ever spoke ill of the dead. When

it came time for a funeral, it was always "a wonderful man" or "our darling sister". No-one ever spoke the truth. When Janis Rogers had died two years ago after eating toadstools she'd gathered in the woods, all the women had been sobbing and afterwards people had spoken for weeks about what a kind woman she'd been! Kyle still didn't understand it. Janis had been a loud mouthed snob, forever pretending she had some higher status than the other residents, all because she'd been one of the original builders of the town. To hear her speak, she'd been the one who found the old well that was the centre of the settlement and had single-handedly built the first container wall! As if she'd ever done anything useful! She was supposed to be a part of the council, responsible for overseeing childcare and the education in the schoolhouse but she'd spent most of her time wandering around interrupting people's work with her overbearing charm.

Kyle had grumbled about her to Sinks a few weeks after her death and one of the Engineers had overheard and there had nearly been a full scale riot as the Militia squared off to them in the pub. Kyle had apologised to keep the peace but every time he saw a patch of the brightly spotted mushrooms, he snorted inwardly at the foolishness of it all.

The Undertaker finished his words and Kyle let out a barely concealed sigh of relief. He pushed past the throng of townspeople to be one of the first back into Holden. Impatiently he fidgeted until Sinks approached with Rosie and a few other Militia. Of the Ranger, Sergeant Fisher, Kyle could see no sign.

"What's the 'gen'?" He demanded as soon as Sinks had appeared.

The older man scowled at Kyle's enthusiasm "Dammnit, Kyle. A man is dead."

Kyle forced a sombre expression on to his face causing Rosie to roll her eyes at him "I meant because of the ammunition and the damaged crops..." he trailed off.

It was Sinks' turn to roll his eyes "I spoke with Fisher this morning and he agreed to let Armstrong know we need a resupply. I managed to make him feel guilty for letting the Horde get this close in the first place."

"So..."

The Militia were gathering round, all of them buzzing at the sudden appearance of the Rangers and the mention of the famed Major Armstrong.

"Come on Sinks, tell us what we're doing! Are we all going?"

"No. I'm going to Matwood. And once I've got an answer, I'll be coming straight back. I'll only be gone a couple of days."

Ben, one of the newer recruits looked alarmed "What if another Horde comes at us?"

"The Ranger said there aren't any within twenty miles of Holden. If one comes this way, Armstrong and the Fist will deal with it." Sinks looked around at the suddenly nervous faces of the men and women he'd trained "I'll be back before you know it!"

"Why can't you just radio Armstrong?" this time it was Rosie who spoke. Kyle shot her a dirty look but she ignored him.

Sinks shook his head "No. I don't have enough leverage. I haven't seen the man for years. To the Rangers, I'm just another bloke from the Regular Army, they've no responsibility to provide us anything. With Fisher, I can persuade Armstrong but I need to be there in person."

"So... who's in charge while you're gone?" asked Rosie, firmly not looking at Kyle.

"You." responded Sinks without hesitation "You're in charge of training, patrols and ammunition conservation until I get back. I suggest you appoint a second in command."

Rosie nodded at Kyle "Frost."

"No. Kyle's coming with me to Matwood."

There was an explosion of indignant protest from the other Militia. Sinks held up a hand "That's my decision and it's final. Anyone has a problem with that can go jump off the north tower for all I care. We're leaving now."

Burning excitement filled Kyle and he couldn't keep the

grin off his face. A few of his fellow Militia were shooting him poisonous looks but most clapped him on the back and shoulder, begging him to bring back stories of Armstrong and the Rangers.

Sinks moved off to gather his things. Kyle grinned at his friends as they continued to congratulate him. Eventually, he pushed past them intending to head for the bunkhouse but Rosie stopped him with a firm fist on his chest. He looked down at it and then at her, meeting her characteristic grin with one of his own.

"Take it easy out there, Militiaman."

"You too, Commander." he grinned.

Her fist abruptly unclenched and took a rough hold of the front of his clothes, pinching his skin in the process. She hauled him toward her, roughly pressing her warm mouth against his. Kyle responded in kind, a grin already forming on his face.

Behind them, the Militia jeered and whistled. As they broke apart, Rosie remained close for a second.

"Make sure you come back, Frost. It might be worth your while."

Kyle grinned from ear to ear as he set off to gather his kit.

CHAPTER 13

The road to Matwood stank. The thousands of slowly rusting cars parked bumper to bumper blocked most of the available space. Efforts had been made in the past few years to clear large sections but still, the road had been narrow before it was clogged and now it was barely wide enough for the horse drawn carts of the traders to pass by.

Still, Kyle and Sinks had room to walk abreast as they strolled past the silent wrecks. A light rain was falling and the water threw up a stink from the rusting metal. Kyle could never quite forget the smell of the road, so different to the smells of smoke and mud in the town. Out here, the air smelled... dead. There was none of the vibrance of human or animal life that filled Holden and none of the wet dog smell that rose every time the heavens opened.

The dogs never passed the boundary of the woods and Kyle had watched regretfully as the trio that had followed them out the gate, turned back at this marker. Of course, he was well acquainted with the route to Matwood. They patrolled it often enough and he was relaxed enough to pester Sinks with questions along the way.

"How much ammo have we got left?"

"Not enough."

"What about the crops that were blown up?"

"The Rangers should compensate us for them. They usually do."

"How come Fisher isn't coming with us?"

"God knows. Bloody Rangers think they're God's gift to the world, pissing around in those bloody helicopters..." he muttered a few more epithets under his breath.

"What will Armstrong do if there are Ferals around Matwood? Do you think we'll see one?"

"I bloody hope not! Now stop yapping at me! Eyes on! We're supposed to be moving tactically here!"

Kyle was silent for another few paces before his excitement couldn't be contained "Do you reckon Armstrong will let me join the Rangers?"

Sinks regarded his younger friend for a moment "Is that what you want?"

"Why not? I can't be in the Militia all my life. There's more to the world than Holden. I've barely even seen the rest of the country!"

"You can't join the Rangers without being in the army first."

"You can help me join the army, can't you?"

"You've got to go to London for that."

London! Kyle had seen pictures in books of the skyline. The towering dome of St Pauls, the glass edges of the Shard. It was a land of mystery and endless promise to him. Of course, he knew the city now occupied only a tiny portion of the land that had once been the Capital. Gathered around the wide expanse of the River Thames, it remained a centre for trade and politics for the entire country.

Thoughts of the city kept Kyle silent for a few miles as the rain lessened and they passed through the ruined landscape of the south east.

"What region is London in?"

Sinks scowled at the return of Kyle's questions but answered "It isn't. The capital is its own region. It's different to all the others though. You know at the harvest we send a part of the crops and animals to Matwood? So does every other settlement in the region. Then it all gets taken up to the river and goes on a barge to the city."

"London doesn't produce its own food?"

"No. But in return, you get military support when you need it and medical supplies every now and then."

"So that's why we're stuck with you?"

"Exactly. Every town has a military liaison. Holden is only small so you get me. Matwood has Jay Paxton. You've met Jay, haven't you?"

Kyle nodded, remembering the rough looking Sergeant who organised and trained the Militia in Matwood. He didn't speak much but when he did, his accent was so strong that Kyle could barely understand one word in four. Sinks had explained that Paxton was from somewhere called New-Castle, which was in the north east but Kyle had never understood how the man had ended up down here. He mentioned as much to Sinks now who shrugged.

"I'm originally from the north too. The army doesn't care where you're from. If you've got the qualifications and experience, they put you where they need you. Besides, you need a northerner to look after you southern pansies!" Sinks shot Kyle a snide glance as he trod a wide berth around a decomposing body that had been half shoved under a faded red car with all its windows shattered.

"What about Parliament?" asked Kyle.

"What do you mean?"

"Why are they in charge?"

Sinks frowned "Because someone has to be. What type of question is that?"

"No... I mean in Holden we all vote on who gets to be in the council. I know we always vote the same people in but still, we have a chance to get rid of people who are crap."

"Democracy." murmured Sinks.

"Exactly! So who elects the government?"

Sinks walked for a few minutes in silence before answering. Ahead, Kyle could see the first of Matwood's watch towers poking above the thick band of brambles that marked the edge of the neighbouring territory.

"The government doesn't work in the same way. It's appointed, not elected."

Kyle frowned "That doesn't sound right."

"Okay, but the council controls the town, right?"

"Yeah. They teach us this in the schoolhouse you know."

"'Course they do. But the council do stuff for you, don't they? Everything the council does, affects your daily life."

"I suppose."

"So, the government mostly deals with managing the army, fighting the Infection and the like. They don't have much impact on your day to day life."

"But they control the army. The army controls the country."

Sinks gave Kyle a sarcastic look "Do we? Do I really control the town?"

Kyle frowned seriously "No. But you're at the council meetings, you trained the Militia and we do what you say. So, you might not have direct control but if you insisted the council did something, they'd do it."

Sinks was shaking his head "No. You've got it wrong. The council don't have to listen to me. I'm just an advisor. I don't have any control. The same as Parliament."

Kyle couldn't think how to frame his argument. He knew from experience that Sinks was far more skilled at framing an opinion and would more eloquent with words than he and the older man would knock his points back until he changed his mind. Instead, he threw a verbal grenade at his friend, partly out of spite.

"Isn't that what those, what do you call them… Zeks say?"

As expected, Sinks' face flushed at the mention of the word. He took a calming breath, shrewd enough to know when he was being baited "That's one of their arguments, yes. Along with not harming the Infected and letting humanity starve to death."

"But they want the government to hold elections, don't they?"

"Among other things. It depends who you ask. There's one of them, Amelia Singh, who seems to be the most dangerous."

"Why?"

"Ugh. She's nuts. She's the one who got them all riled up about protecting the Infected. Said that we should stop shooting them and put all our resources in to finding a cure. Bloody nuisance! Can you imagine what would have happened the other night if we hadn't shot them?"

Kyle grimaced at the memory "Yeah. Wouldn't have been fun."

Sinks snorted "Look, Kyle Holden is a pretty small place. You don't have the space or the time to come up with radical ideas. You've always got something else to do, patrol, farm, hunt... in London, it isn't the same. They live closer to how we lived before The Fall. Behind the walls, people don't need to fight and be scared. They don't even let you carry weapons in the city itself."

"Really? What do they do if they're attacked?"

"There are four whole regiments in London who protect the place plus the training camp for recruits. It's as safe as you can get."

"And that's where the Zeks are?"

"Right. The Zeks are a whole lot of lunatics who want to change the world. They've got a thousand ideas and most of them - I can promise you - will end up getting a whole bunch of people killed. They say a lot – they want reform but if you read between the lines, they want a revolution. A civil war."

"Right – but still, aren't they right about some stuff?"

Sinks gestured at the decay around them "Don't you think we've got enough problems? I don't see them living out here, seeing what we have to deal with every day."

Kyle considered "They were out here when we were being attacked. We stayed safe behind the walls."

Sinks stopped, turning to face Kyle "Here's some free advice, Kyle. Bravery and stupidity go hand in hand. Any idiot can put themselves in danger. It takes skill to stay alive, and if you're dead, you're no bloody use to anyone. So, just because they go running around hugging the Infected, don't think that makes them brave. Got it?"

Kyle didn't get it but he didn't push Sinks any further. Both of them were shattered from the fight and sleep deprived so he concentrated on his surroundings as they continued.

A few hours later, they turned a sharp angled corner through the bramble lined road. Ahead, the towering walls of Matwood loomed. The gates were open and a steady stream of people moved through them.

Sinks lowered his voice as a well-disciplined squad of Militia began marching towards them "And don't think I don't know you're winding me up, Kyle! Besides, you're going to be around soldiers for the next day or so, so keep your mouth shut about Zeks, elections and any other bollocks you've come up with. In fact, it's probably best that you say nothing at all."

Kyle opened his mouth to make one of his customary jokes but the look on his friend's face advised him against it and he closed his mouth, pressing his lips together tightly.

CHAPTER 14

Matwood was a bustling hub of activity. The buildings here were set out in a neat grid, each structure built in identical style, with a raised brick foundation and tightly bound wooden walls. Bars covered each window for security and as a final nod to decoration, a neatly tended moat of grass separated the buildings from the narrow streets.

The population thrived from the trade that passed through here. Of course, Holden received trade too but Matwood was crossroads for passing travellers and almost a third of the space within the neat walls was given over to feed troughs for the horses and oxen, crammed in next to sheltered market stalls and crowded hostels.

Here and there, a burst of green camouflage marked the presence of the soldiers who roamed the market. Rangers, apparently making the most of their brief respite from the constant war against the Wretches.

Kyle and Sinks were put up in a neat bunkhouse by Sinks' friend Jay Paxton, the soldier assigned to Matwood. The accommodation here was neat and orderly although dim, lacking the electric light in Holden. Kyle dropped his pack next to one of the twenty or so metal framed beds before Sinks led them out into the town.

The sky was still overcast but here and there beams of sunlight poked through. The air was heavy with moisture and Kyle felt himself sweat beneath the thick plate carrier.

Their first stop was the spring house which sold the bottled water that Matwood was famous for. Sinks haggled briefly over the price before scooping up two litres and leading the way back to the busy street outside. They both paused to tip the clear liquid into their mouths, Kyle leaning his head back and chugging it down, relishing the clean, sweet taste.

"Aaah..." he sighed in pleasure, catching Sinks' raised eyebrow as his eyes followed the swaying hips of a pretty looking redhead.

"What?"

"Your mate Rosie wouldn't be too happy about that."

Kyle shrugged in response.

"Are you going to do something about her, or what?" demanded Sinks, leading them along the street towards the town centre.

Kyle made a non-committal answer which drew a chuckle of derision from Sinks "You know, Rosie is a free woman. If you don't make a move soon, she'll go somewhere else. Women only wait for you in books and stories."

"Yeah, yeah..." Kyle shrugged off the advice, staring around him.

A woman wearing Ranger uniform walked directly towards them with a bright grin on her face. Kyle watched her warily but Sinks returned the grin and a second later had embraced her in a fierce hug with much back slapping and 'How you doing's'.

"Kyle Frost – Hannah Mitchell. Hannah – Kyle" introduced Sinks. Kyle took the woman's hand, once again finding a strong grip. She was younger than Sinks but older than Kyle and she shook Kyle's hand enthusiastically as Sinks explained that they'd served together before his posting to Holden.

"Didn't know you'd made the Rangers! Congratulations!" he enthused.

"Yeah, about six months ago now! Armstrong picked me out after a scrap near the ATR in London."

"ATR?" asked Kyle, confused.

"Army Training Regiment" supplied Hannah "It's in London. I was training the recruits there before I made the Rangers."

"Kyle here is thinking of joining." Sinks told her.

She cocked a sceptical eyebrow "You'll have your work cut

out to catch up if this muppet trained you."

Sinks laughed in response "Hah! I bet he'll finish as best recruit!"

"Alright, I'll take that bet! A case of Matwood water, twelve litres!"

"Done!" Sinks shook her hand firmly as Kyle stared in shock. Twelve litres was a vast amount of the precious water. He wondered where either of them would get the money for it.

"Why are you here, anyway?" asked Hannah "Apart from losing bets, I mean."

Sinks turned serious "Holden was hit by a Horde yesterday. Fisher and a few of your blokes helped us out but we need a resupply. Badly. They blew up half the harvest too."

Hannah looked serious "I'd heard there was a scrap, didn't know it was that bad though. Armstrong will help with the harvest, he always does. Ammo will be harder but I'm sure we can get a couple of thousand rounds sent down."

Kyle felt relief flood through him but excitement still burned at the thought of meeting Armstrong. Hannah must have read his mind because her next words echoed his thoughts.

"You'd better come and see him. He knows you're here."

Kyle raised an eyebrow at that but Sinks nodded in some hidden understanding.

"Just be warned, he might ask you to give us a hand whilst you're here." Hannah eyed Kyle's Militia equipment "We need all the manpower we can get."

Kyle nodded, his face serious but inside he burned with excitement as he swigged the last of the bottle of water. He was going to meet Major Armstrong!

CHAPTER 15

Frost

The name brought a string of memories to the mind of Major Blake Armstrong. He stood with his back to a long room filled with busy soldiers, all in the distinctive uniform of the Rangers. A window before him gave him a snapshot of the bustling streets of Matwood but the tall Major hardly saw the hurrying figures before him.

Instead, Armstrong twitched his fingers almost unconsciously, plucking and pressing in time with the thoughts that raced through his mind almost like an orchestral conductor pulling instruments and sections together at just the right moment. His face remained cold and expressionless, giving nothing away.

The Rangers behind him knew better than to disturb their boss in this mood. They completed their tasks in near silence, flinching at small noises. The dynamic of the room seemed to shift around the Major as though he stood at the centre, rather than to one side. Each of the soldiers, hardened Warriors though they were, walked like naughty children around an ill-tempered parent.

Armstrong's posture changed subtly, becoming more alert, a stiffening of the muscles at the back of his neck as he caught sight of the tall young Militiaman through the window.

Something close to a smile twitched the corners of his mouth, whether in response to the man or to the memory his name elicited, it was impossible to tell.

His features returned to their impassive state but beneath them, his mind raced. *Yes.* Armstrong thought to himself.

Kyle Frost would do very well indeed.

*

Kyle's first impression was that Armstrong seemed to be bathed in his own glow. Kyle had once been in a church. The wooden roof had rotted away but some of the images in the stained glass windows had been intact and the faces of the angels with the bright glow of light around their heads returned to his mind as he laid eyes on Major Blake Armstrong.

Kyle realised that Armstrong was standing with his back to the large window which explained the light although it did nothing to lessen the impression. Kyle wondered if the effect was intentional. Armstrong's hands were folded behind his back although as Sinks led the way forward, they dropped to his sides revealing thick, corded muscles beneath the weathered skin.

To Kyle's surprise, Sinks had tugged a battered looking beret out of his pocket and crammed it onto his head. As he approached Armstrong, he crashed to a stamping halt and threw up a glamourous salute. Armstrong returned the gesture, crisply before turning his steely gaze on Kyle. Who tried not to shiver.

"Sir, this is Militiaman Frost, of Holden."

Armstrong nodded at Kyle who returned the nod before hastily remembering what Sinks had taught him. He cleared his throat awkwardly.

"Er - it's an honour to meet you, Sir."

Armstrong did not respond. Instead, he turned to Sinks expectantly. Kyle realised that the Major had not yet spoken a word to either of them.

"Sir, I'd like to formally request that the settlement of Holden be resupplied following the engagement yesterday. We need food and rifle ammo."

Sinks held himself rigidly to attention, his eyes fixed on a spot over Armstrong's head. The Major raised an eyebrow.

"Why?"

"Er - Sir, we engaged and destroyed a force of Infected several hundred strong and no longer have enough ammunition to be an effective fighting force."

"You don't practice ammunition conservation in Holden?"

The Major's tone was ice cold. Kyle's reverence and excitement had turned to awkwardness and a desperate urge to be out of that cold stare. He wondered why Armstrong was so frigid but reasoned that a man did not become the most feared Warrior in the nation by being friendly.

"We do, sir." Sinks tone was as wooden and expressionless as the Major.

"Casualties?"

"One, Sir."

A twitch of Armstrong's brow. Was that a slight frown?

"How many Infected?"

"Initial estimates were five hundred plus."

"One casualty for five hundred Infected." it wasn't a question, it was a statement.

"Yes, sir." was there a hint of pride in Sinks' voice?

"Speak plainly then, Sinclair. What do you want?"

"Five thousand rounds of five five-six."

"Hmph."

Armstrong turned back to the window, his back to them. Kyle risked a glance sideways at Sinks but his friend remained rigid.

Armstrong's next words took Kyle completely by surprise.

"I suppose you know that I worked with your Father before the Fall?"

With a start, Kyle realised that Armstrong was speaking to him.

"I'll take that as a 'no' by your silence. How old were you when he died?"

As always at the mention of his parents, Kyle felt a shock and a clenching in the pit of his stomach. He was too surprised to speak.

"He was six, sir." interjected Sinks, helpfully.

Armstrong half turned to meet Sinks eyes and Kyle realised that his friend had spoken out of turn. After a moment, Armstrong turned away again.

"Your Father and I worked to fight the virus, back before the Fall. Obviously, we weren't successful."

There was a titter from behind. Kyle glanced over his shoulder to see the room of Rangers were stood watching them. Apparently, Armstrong had made a joke.

He swallowed.

Armstrong exhaled deeply and lowered his gaze away from the window. He turned to face Kyle and Sinks.

"The problem is, Sinclair, I've barely enough supplies to operate as it is. Frankly, these Ferals are a priority. I hardly see what you two can bring me in return for several thousand rounds of extremely valuable ammunition."

Kyle felt ice trickle through his veins. He hadn't considered the possibility that Armstrong might refuse their request. He thought of Holden, how small the container walls had seemed when the alarm sounded. He knew the town couldn't survive without the ammunition.

"Sir, with all due respect." Kyle began with the beginnings of anger in his voice "The Holden Militia destroyed an entire Horde single-handedly losing only one man in the process. I think our ability to fight and defend ourselves speaks for itself. Moreover, we removed a threat from the area, something that I understand is the job of the Ranger Battalions."

Anger flashed through Armstrong's eyes. Sinks began to speak.

"Sir, what Frost means is -"

"Shut up, Sinclair."

Sinks shut up.

Armstrong regarded Kyle with his cool stare, looking him up and down in silence. Kyle realised he had overstepped a boundary but he met the Major's gaze and held it.

"Frost by name, Frost by nature."

Kyle had heard the joke before. He hadn't laughed then,

either.

Armstrong seemed to see something in Kyle's steadfast expression that satisfied him because he gave a tight nod.

"As it happens, I need troops to support my men here in the South." Armstrong narrowed his eyes "Do you know why I'm here in Matwood?"

"Er – Feral sightings?"

"Yes. Well, that's partially correct." Armstrong exhaled deeply "What I'm about to tell you, Frost is highly secret. Are you prepared to keep your mouth shut?"

Kyle was surprised but despite his earlier outburst he wanted to impress Armstrong and so he nodded.

"Good. The Rangers are here because there are refugees on the coast."

Kyle frowned "From a town that was attacked?"

"No." a muscle in Armstrong's face twitched "From France."

France

Even Sinks had frozen at the word. The room behind them had fallen silent, lending credence to the gravity of Armstrong's declaration.

Kyle stuttered "From – the –"

"France, correct. You understand why this is so secret?"

For twenty years, Kyle knew, no-one had heard from the continent. The great landmass to the South had lain silent and dead leaving Britain as the sole survivors of the X2H virus. The idea that people, actual living people had survived there and more, were coming *here* was incomprehensible. Kyle felt a lump rising in his throat, something like a sympathetic loyalty to his species.

"That's incredible!" he finally managed to stammer.

Armstrong did not smile "There's a problem."

The silence in the room was palpable.

"The increased sightings of Ferals are true." Kyle felt Sinks stir next to him "Our estimates are that up to twenty percent of the Infected in this region are showing characteristics of the Feral mutation."

"Mutation?" the word was something out of a nightmare. Wretches were the enemy, of course but they were predictable, measurable, and understood. The thought of a change in their behaviour made Kyle's gut churn.

Armstrong glanced behind Kyle at the milling Rangers "Mutation. One that has become more prevalent as the numbers of refugees increases."

Kyle got it. He blinked several times in shock "They're spreading it, Sir? How is that possible? Are they Infected?"

Was there a weariness in the Major's eyes? He nodded once "Our task is to stop them before the virus can be spread to the population here."

"Stop them?"

"That's why I need more troops." Armstrong was all business again "Frost, if you will agree to help my men round up these refugees then I'll see that Holden is amply provisioned with ammunition and food." Abruptly, he held out his hand "Deal?"

Kyle shook it before he'd even paused to consider. He opened his mouth to ask more questions but the Rangers behind them were moving about again and to his surprise, Sinks had thrown up another glamorous salute and was pulling him backwards towards the door.

CHAPTER 16

"Sign! We have sign! Sound the alarm!"

The shout came from the sentry at the North tower. Almost immediately, the alarm bell began tolling but it was the middle of the day and the sentry's voice had been loud enough to be heard clear across Holden. Rosie flicked a wide eyed glance at the four other members of the patrol she had just led back through the gate. She saw the shock on their faces and so, pushing her own concern aside, she began barking orders.

"Militia to the gate! Form a firing line! Sentries, how many outside the wall?" she ran towards the gate as she shouted, her rifle swinging from side to side. The harvest hadn't yet started but there were still dozens of townspeople outside the walls, tending to the thousand jobs that needed doing every day. Some were hurrying back through the gate even as she ran towards it, most had pistols in their hands and were throwing furtive glances back over their shoulders.

"Report!" she bellowed at the sentry in the tower. He leaned over the rickety railing to peer down at her.

"Seven, maybe eight. They're moving fast through the corn field!"

"Firing line!" Rosie bellowed as the Militia moved to secure the outside of the gate. A pair of Keepers sprinted towards her, red faced with exertion having covered the kilometre or so from the wood line in record time. One ran past her, vanishing into the safety of Holden's four walls, the other drew up beside her, out of breath and gasping.

"Ten... ten at least, maybe more! They came out of the bushes – they shouldn't be able to do that! Three dead from my team, we only just got away..."

Rosie nodded and turned away. She shouted to the section commander of the North wall "Three down from the Keepers!"

The man nodded without speaking, adjusting the count in his head. After a moment his second in command shouted down to her "Twelve still unaccounted for!"

"Shit!" cursed Rosie as a handful of wall guards began dumping sandbags in front of the Militia outside the gate, creating a crude barrier between them and the threat.

"Spread out! Two firing points – no, not there, here." she shoved her troops into place, forming two strengthened positions in front of the gate.

"Come on... Come on!" she muttered to herself. The path between the crop fields was empty but she knew the remaining twelve townspeople would have gone into the fields, using the tall plants as cover from the Infected.

"Contact!" came the shout from the tower above and the sharpshooter opened fire

There were four of them. Four rotted, grey skinned and stinking monsters, tearing out of the line of crops at breakneck speed. They howled as they raced across the open ground towards the Militia. Rosie opened her mouth to shout a warning but at that moment the awful reek of the Wretches struck her nostrils and she gagged. Like a pile of rotten food left out in the heat of midsummer and then left to ferment in stagnant water, the miasma was terrible and unavoidable. Rosie felt her eyes water and she angrily raised her rifle, furious at her own weakness.

The shotguns on the wall behind her boomed.

The Wretches crashed to the ground almost as one.

"On the right! On the –" the shout tore itself into a wet gurgle and Rosie whipped around, staring in horror at the troops on her right. Crouched behind their small sandbag wall, she saw the terrible grey skinned monster that crouched over the corpse of a Militiaman, snarling at the three remaining troops. Even as she watched, she saw an impossible sight. The three Militiamen raised their rifles, ready to tear the monster into pieces and avenge their comrade. The rifles cracked but the Wretch lifted the limp corpse and held it between itself and the spitting death of the rifles.

Rosie stared, open mouthed.

The rifles clicked empty.

The Wretch dropped the corpse. Some of the rifle rounds had penetrated, at that range it was impossible to stop them all. But not enough to stop the creature that now leapt through the air towards the three gaping Militia who stumbled backwards in horror.

And died screaming as it tore them apart.

Rosie was vaguely aware of shouting, screaming orders at her remaining troops before she was turning and running for the safety of the gate. She felt, rather than saw, the other Militia follow her as she rolled under the gate and rose to one knee, the rifle sighting towards the Wretch which crouched, looked her dead in the eye and roared an ear splitting screech of hatred and fury.

The last thing Rosie saw before the heavy metal gate slammed shut was the terrible sight of the eyes, not white and featureless like the others but a pure black, like bottomless pools. Somehow, a terrible intelligence was hidden there, a deep-rooted loathing that was echoed in the awful screeching sound that the creature made and then it was gone and the rifle fire from the walls announced the death of the Feral as the metal gate sealed the town shut.

CHAPTER 17

"There are people!"

"Yep."

"There could be more…"

"There could."

"How are you so calm about this?"

Sinks shrugged in his usual taciturn manner. Kyle shook his head and muttered under his breath before falling silent and frowning his way around a thought.

"Did you know he knew my Dad?"

"No. You alright?"

"Yeah."

They stopped under the branches of a towering oak, around which a sturdy looking series of planks had been bolted together, forming a crude but neat bench. They sat down, watching the flow of people up and down the path before them. Kyle bent down and picked up a fallen acorn, pulling it apart absently between his fingers.

"Shouldn't we let people know that there are survivors?"

Sinks looked pained "To be honest mate, it's not the first time."

Kyle stared at his friend "What do you mean?"

Sinks gave a characteristic shrug "There's been the odd boat across the channel since the Fall. You know about the quarantine?"

"Right." Kyle nodded remembering the lessons on the brutally pragmatic policy of sinking ships and shooting down aircraft in the dark days after the Fall. Parliament had acted to prevent the spread of the virus and in the process, Kyle knew, thousands had died "But that was twenty years ago. We don't even have a navy or an air force anymore."

"Yeah, right. So, the quarantine isn't enforceable but it's still in place. Legally." Sinks explained "Armstrong and the Rangers are the only unit that has the capability to enforce it. That's why he's here dealing with it."

"Dealing?"

Sinks sighed "It's not going to be pleasant, mate."

Kyle nodded slowly "They're Infected, though."

"Yes."

"I've never heard of someone being a carrier without Wretching out."

"That's because it's a mutation. You know this was always a possibility. That's one of the reasons the Rangers are the leading unit for the army. We can manage the Hordes so long as we have supplies but we needed an elite unit specifically trained to fight the Infected. That's why Parliament spends so much on equipping them with helicopters and all that gear."

"Hmm." Kyle tried to think around the racing thoughts "Why don't people know that there are survivors? There could be other countries out there."

Sinks glanced around them to make sure they were out of earshot but there was no-one else nearby "Look mate, no-one ever claimed the rest of the world was gone. It's just practical to assume that's what happened. We can't do anything about it –"

"We've got an army!" Kyle protested "We could invade Europe –"

"And lose half our blokes?" Sinks sounded angry "No. What would we do about the Hordes back here? We can't even get rid of them, let alone the billions across Europe. I remember the Fall, Kyle. There was footage on the TV of these great swarms that you could see from space. We'd lose millions fighting them."

"We'd lose some, sure! But –"

"But? But what? Kyle, remember you want to join the army! You think you'd be the one who didn't get killed? Some tosspot General throwing you into the middle of a Horde? Besides, the mutation is coming from France so we can assume that things over there are pretty much worse than here!"

Kyle rolled his eyes, looking away so Sinks couldn't see. The idea of France, of the European continent was burning in his mind and he knew that Sinks was wrong. Arguing with the dour northerner was a sure way to be disproven though so he just shook his head.

"Speaking of which –" Sinks continued "You heard what Armstrong said, you're going out with some of the Rangers. That's your chance to prove yourself."

Kyle sat bolt upright "You mean to join them?"

"I mean they're very selective about who they take. You impress the blokes you're with though and word will get back to Armstrong. He says he knew your Dad anyway so he's not likely to forget you."

Kyle had to stand to pace up and down, so much new information was bouncing around inside his skull and he knew he needed to sit down and process it all. Probably in the Ridged Back in Holden.

Sinks stood up too "You'd better get ready."

"Now?"

"Yeah! When did you think?"

"I don't know… I thought he meant later."

Sinks rolled his eyes "You've got a lot to learn about the army, Kyle! Come on, let's get your kit."

They headed back to the bunkhouse Jay Paxton had set them up in as Kyle began to feel the first stirrings of nervousness at the thought of the Feral-infested lands around Matwood. He said as much to Sinks, wondering how to fight the new threat. Sinks snorted.

"Shoot straight, conserve ammo, get inside a perimeter at night." He grinned a wicked grin.

Kyle rolled his eyes "And try not to die on the way?"

"And try not to die on the way."

*

Four hours later, Kyle was dressed in his patrol gear, rifle loaded and ready. Three other Militia, these sporting the stitched 'M' for Matwood on their arms, stood awkwardly with him. Jaswinder 'Jas' and Kerry, were known to Kyle and the three of them had exchanged small talk as they waited for Harrison, the fourth and youngest Militiaman. Only a month past his training, the pale cheeked young man had arrived with his rucksack hanging open, spilling his water bottle over the already damp ground and earning a slap across the skull from an embarassed Kerry who, it transpired, was Harrison's aunt.

"Bloody hell! This is going to be a right laugh!" Harrison seemed oblivious to the ire he was drawing from his comrades as he enthused about the patrol.

"Just shut up and stay in formation, alright?" Kerry growled "And for God's sake, don't drop anything else!"

Harrison took a step back and Kerry rolled her eyes at Kyle "Sorry about him. His Mum– my sister was killed three years ago. I've been trying to keep the little tosspot alive ever since."

"Sorry about your sister." It was the usual response when someone mentioned a death.

Kerry nodded in thanks "Not the brightest girl in the world. Harrison's Dad was a trader who legged it the second he knocked her up and she went out berry picking in the woods by herself."

Kyle's eyes widened in surprise. No-one went out alone.

"Found what was left of her stumbling around, Wretched out."

There was a sombre pause but the sight of two Rangers approaching them made all of them, even Harrison, stand up straight. Two men, one stocky with the stripes of a Sergeant on his arm, the other tall, bearded, and solid looking were making a beeline for their group.

"That's Lynch." Hissed Jas.

"Who?" Kyle had never heard the name.

"Sergeant Lynch. Armstrong's Devil."

Kyle had no time to ask Jas what this bewildering epithet meant because the stocky Sergeant had locked his eyes onto Kyle's and a shiver had run down his spine.

At first glance, there was nothing out of the ordinary about Lynch. He was ugly, with lumpy, misshapen features but that was true of many men. It was his eyes that Kyle first noticed. An innocent, almost childlike blue they were enhanced by the muscles surrounding them which held the lids wider than looked natural. The whites were visible in a ring around the iris and as he drew closer, Kyle could see they were flecked with small dots of red.

Then, there was his mouth. Even though he was walking slowly, it hung open. His fat lips, a swollen pinkish colour were spaced apart revealing yellow teeth and a bulbous tongue. And the entire opening was too wide for his face, Kyle realised. It was as though his features had been cobbled together from a pile of spare parts with no care for uniformity.

Kyle looked back to the Sergeant's eyes. The man hadn't blinked. Not once. Nor had his mouth closed and he now came to stand before them, eyes too wide, mouth open and his gaze boring into Kyle with such force that he blinked and had to fight the urge to take a step back.

"Right, you's are with us. Stay close, don't piss about and don't argue." The taller of the two Rangers had spoken although Kyle could see he was outranked by Lynch. Lynch was still staring at Kyle.

"You're Frost. Boss knows you." Lynch's accent was atrocious. A gravelly, rasping variant of estuary English, he spoke quietly, his lips hardly moving to enunciate. The result was that Kyle had to concentrate to hear the man. That made him look harder at that awfully childlike blue gaze and a shudder of revulsion went through him.

"I'm Frost." He confirmed, unsure what else to say.

Lynch, however, said nothing. He made no signal to the

other Ranger who's name Kyle still didn't know. Instead, he strode forward, ignoring the Militia and headed for the gate.

"Right, follow the Sergeant! I'm last man, stay in sight of Lynch. I'm Corporal Gault. You can call me Corporal."

Harrison stumbled as he tried to hurry after Lynch and Gault launched into a tirade of abuse as the young man, flustered and pink-cheeked fell into step.

The great gates of Matwood were thick oak, banded in beaten iron bands like something out of a fairy tale castle. Normally, Kerry or Jas would have been ribbing Kyle at this point, labouring the fact that Matwood's walls stood almost twice the height of Holden's but the normal banter was cowed in the surprise of meeting Sergeant Lynch. Instead, Kyle nervously checked his safety catch for the hundredth time, breaking into a quick run to clear the threshold of the gate and feeling his heart beat faster as they stepped out into the wild.

CHAPTER 18

"Ferals! Ferals and Hordes!"

The council chamber was cramped and stuffy. To Rosie, it seemed that half the town had squeezed in to hear the session and the other half was standing outside the door, trying to listen. Between their legs the ridge backed dogs padded, occasionally licking hands or pressing close for comfort.

The speaker was the Mayor. Elizabeth Friend had been elected last year and was still getting the hang of leadership. Normally well respected in Holden for her calm, stoic demeanour, she was caught in a rare moment of consternation.

Indeed, the whole town was shaken. Nine of their neighbours were dead. Three bodies had been recovered and ominously, the remaining six had vanished. Four more Ferals had been sighted since the gates had crashed shut, one of them had been recognised as Luke Knight, the deputy head of the Keepers who had died in the woods. His reanimated eyes, the sentry reported, were the dark black of a Feral.

It was this turn of events that had Mayor Friend so agitated. Wretches were a fact of life but Ferals had never been seen in the region as far as anyone could remember. It didn't help that most of the younger generation had grown up only hearing about them as a horror story. Monsters, Rosie reflected, should stay imaginary.

"We've never seen such a fast infection rate. Keeper Knight Wretched out less than ten minutes after being attacked! And worse, he turned and ran off when they shot at him! How many Wretches can think like that?"

Rosie was as shaken as anyone else but she wished the

Mayor would shut up. Everywhere she looked there was fear on people's faces. No-one wanted to think about a pack of Ferals running around outside their walls. The harvest was approaching and that meant long hours in the fields for the entire town. How would they gather the crops if they couldn't go outside?

"Rosie." with a start, Rosie heard her own name.

"As the acting head of the Militia, what do you propose we do?"

"I'd like to raise a point of order -" put in Terrence, the senior member of the engineers and a prominent voice in the town council "Rosie here is competent but she's too young to be making strategic decisions like this. We need Corporal Sinclair to return immediately. Failing that, I suggest that the Militia be put under the command of the Wall Guards. Commander Mason can put together a plan for defence -"

Rosie stood up, anger burning through her "Absolutely not! *I* am in command of the Militia and I will remain so!" her voice echoed around the chamber "Commander Mason is not qualified to lead an offensive mission. Corporal Sinclair placed the Militia under my command and we will manage the threat appropriately."

"Oh, yes?" Terrence's voice had taken on a cruel tone "In one day, more Militia have been killed than in any other day since we raised the wall! How on earth do you plan to 'manage' the threat? These are Ferals! What will you do, keep patrolling as you get picked off one by one? No! We have to defend our walls, man them day and night and keep these bastards away!"

A murmur ran through the gathered townsfolk. The Mayor opened her mouth to speak but Rosie shouted over her "And then what? We ignore the harvest, stand our ground on our walls watching the crops rot in the fields? How long until we starve to death? What does Terrence think we'll do, draw lots to see who gets eaten first?"

The murmur had become a buzz. One of the dogs had begun barking at Terrence, sensing the ire of the crowd. Rosie drew comfort from the noise even as someone reached down to shush the animal.

"Perhaps the council should make sure -" Rosie continued, looking daggers at Terrence "- matters of business are addressed by those who are qualified to speak about them and not be subject to weak minded scaremongering by Engineers!"

Terrence looked furious but said nothing. There was silence for a moment. The dog whined.

The Mayor cleared her throat. As Rosie had hoped, the angry outburst had shocked the woman out of her near panic and when she spoke, her voice was rational, if not totally calm.

"Of course, we will abide by Sinks' recommendations." she looked over at Terrence "There will be no further questioning of responsibilities. That's not the way this council has ever run and now isn't the time for infighting." Terrence looked angry but didn't argue.

"Today, we encountered a new threat. We lost friends and we were all shocked. But this is Holden! The town that went to the Dogs!" A weak cheer went up from the gathered townsfolk.

"Tomorrow, we'll carry on as before. Rosie will arrange more patrols, the Militia will protect us. Every person outside the walls will carry a rifle and take a dog with them. No exceptions! Commander Mason will increase sentries on the wall as he sees fit and if these Ferals return, we'll be ready for them!"

There was a great deal of head nodding, Rosie let out a breath she didn't realise she'd been holding and felt her stress levels settle a notch.

"The engineers -" the Mayor continued, eyeballing Terrence again "- will ensure that the power remains on and the harvest equipment is ready. Let's have no more arguments! We work together!"

*

An hour later, Rosie was leading a patrol through the woods. They'd found the spot where the Keepers had been ambushed

77

almost immediately. Blood sprayed across the dark earth marked the site clearly and she had stared in consternation at the thick brambles where the Ferals had emerged from. How the monsters could have passed such a barrier was beyond her. The brambles were carefully cultivated to stop even animals from moving through.

She squeezed the pistol grip of her rifle tightly for comfort and glanced down at the dog that was leashed to her waist. She'd chosen a brute of a male, scarred from fights, and packed with muscle. Few of the dogs were willing to pass the boundary of the woods but this one seemed unconcerned, trotting alongside her with his nose to the ground.

Abruptly, he went still, the hackles rising in a long line down his back. He bared his teeth in a silent growl. Callum, her point man directly in front of her went down to one knee, his rifle pointing ahead.

A bush rustled.

The other two Militia behind her moved, standing back to back, covering them from the sides and rear. Rosie aimed her own rifle over Callum's head.

No-one made a sound.

The bush rustled again. An animal, perhaps? Rosie trusted her instinct and the hairs on the back of her neck were standing up like those of the dog beside her. She flicked the safety off her rifle and breathed carefully as she took the first pressure off the trigger.

A figure appeared on the path ahead of them.

Rosie tightened her finger on the trigger but suddenly Callum shouted, almost making her shoot in shock.

"No! Hold fire! Hold fire!"

The figure whipped around at the words and Rosie found herself looking, with no small measure of relief, into the eyes of a Zek.

"Halt!" she shouted "Hands up! Don't move!"

The man raised his hands above his head. Rosie remembered the figures she'd spotted moving through the solar farm during the attack and this man was no different. He was wearing a long dark leather trench coat and thick gloves. His head was covered in a leather hood with the sides cut out for his peripheral vision. An armband made from dirty red cloth was tied around his right arm and most curiously of all, he appeared to be unarmed.

"Don't shoot! Please don't shoot..." The man's eyes were wide with fear. He'd clearly not seen Rosie's patrol before stepping out onto the path and now he was terrified.

"Who are you?" she demanded.

"I'm Fabian! I'm not armed."

"What are you doing here? This is Holden's land."

"Holden? I'm – I'm lost. I'm with a party of Zeks, we were tracking some of the Fallen, trying to keep them away from you..."

"Fallen? What are you talking about?" Rosie wondered if the man was insane. She'd heard tales of wandering nomads, living in the woods. Maybe this ragged man was one of them. Certainly, to be out here unarmed was close to suicide.

"The Fallen! The Infected..."

"You mean Wretches?"

"We don't call them that."

Callum flicked Rosie a glance and she raised an eyebrow.

"Why don't you call them that?" Rosie's heart was pounding in her ears. This was not the place for such a conversation but she wanted to know if the Zek was a threat.

"We try to help them..." Fabian's hands were over his head and were shaking now. Rosie could see the man was grimy, covered in mud with sweat stains on the black coat. Clearly, he'd been out here for days, if not weeks.

"How can you help Wretches?" demanded Callum.

"I – there may be a cure one day."

"And I might start pissing clean water!" Rosie's coarse tone shocked Fabian. Her lip curled at his fragility.

"We try to lead them away from towns and settlements. To keep them from being harmed."

"You led the Horde to us?" Callum's voice was filled with disgust.

"No! The soldiers led them here. We tried to stop them. We didn't want you to kill them."

Callum looked back at Rosie and she saw the same confusion she felt reflected on his face.

"What do you want to do with him?" he muttered to her.

She considered. On the one hand, the man was trespassing although it wasn't a law they particularly enforced. On the other, if he'd led the Horde here then she'd happily see him hanged from the north tower. She narrowed her eyes at him.

"How many of you are there?"

"Um - ten of us. There were ten of us."

Callum spoke up "Who's in charge?"

"Zachary. A man named Zachary. I got separated."

"Rosie..." Callum muttered and she understood his warning. There were Ferals out here as well as Fabian's companions. Now wasn't the time for questions.

"Alright. Tie his hands. We're bringing him back with us."

CHAPTER 19

Lynch led the way along a well-travelled track. Kyle had never been west of Matwood before but Kerry and Jas clearly knew the paths and Lynch didn't hesitate so Kyle positioned himself between Gault and Harrison, wincing as the younger man tripped over small pebbles and waved his rifle around like he'd never sat through a safety lecture.

The empty road was lined on either side by thick hedges, their dense undergrowth providing some protection from Wretch incursions. Kerry had explained that the next town was two days walk, three for a wagon and few travellers passed alone. Most waited in Matwood to join one of the larger, better protected caravans but with the Feral sightings, no-one was travelling.

Lynch led them along a line of burned out lorries, shunted and dragged to one side. The rain that had plagued Kyle and Sinks as they left Holden had passed, but the water had dislodged accumulated mud and rust from the wrecks and Kyle resorted to tying a scarf around his mouth and nose to cover the smell. Ahead of him, Harrison gagged once or twice.

"Haven't you got a mask?" Kyle questioned.

The younger man shook his head miserably. After a moment, Kyle unwound his own and held it out. Harrison took it and covered his own face, breathing in the cleaner air greedily.

Harrison fiddled with his scarf in the process causing his rifle barrel to wobble dangerously towards Kyle.

"Oi! Point that somewhere else!"

Kerry turned at the sound as Harrison stammered an apology. Kyle rolled his eyes at the boy's aunt as they continued down the long road.

"Shame you didn't bring one of those dogs with you instead of him." called Gault from behind "They'd have been some bloody use at least!"

*

Their camp for the night was a ramshackle four walled fortification by the roadside that lay empty. Jas unlocked it with a key from his pocket and Kyle stepped in to see an almost empty space aside from a small square shipping container that reminded him of home. The walls of the fort were metal sheet, lacking any kind of fire step although ladders were placed around at regular intervals.

"It's a way station for people on the road. You pay your taxes in Matwood, we give you the key." explained Jas as he sealed the door behind them.

The container turned out to be filled with food and water of which they had plenty but Kyle saw the sense of such a fortification along the dangerous road. He pointed out to Kerry that they had seen no sign of the Wretches.

"No. We keep this route pretty clear. We don't get much Sign down here. Had a few problems with bandits a year or so ago. Tomorrow will be a different story, I reckon we'll run into more than a few Wretches."

Harrison turned white as a sheet his aunt's words and stayed silent the rest of the evening.

Lynch sat down against a wall almost immediately and appeared to fall asleep, his mouth still hanging open. Gault stopped only long enough to bully the Militia into organising a sentry roster – one that he and Lynch were not included in – before stretching out on a bedroll and closing his eyes.

Kyle laid out his bedroll next to Jas who grimaced at him, jerking his head in the direction of the gate "A lot to take in, huh?"

Kyle nodded "World-changing."

"Yeah. They must be desperate to bring us along though. Word will spread now."

"Maybe that's what they want?" Kyle wondered "Let rumours spread so it isn't such a shock when they do announce it?"

Jas snorted, casting a surreptitious glance at the sleeping Rangers "More likely Armstrong is trying to buy himself time. You know he's been saying since the Fall that we were alone?"

"He has?" Kyle remembered Sinks' declaration that no-one had ever made that claim.

"Yeah! 'Course, none of the Rangers will ever tell you that but he's been across the channel plenty of times from what I heard. Scavenging missions, spying, probably trying to carve out a little slice of hell for himself. Now he's being proved wrong about it all so we're out here doing his dirty work!"

Kyle grunted although he guessed that Jas was mostly informed by rumours. He reassured himself that Sinks was better informed than the Militiaman and tried to motivate himself by remembering that he was out with the Rangers, on patrol like a true Warrior. That brought peace to his troubled mind and he slept easily beneath the stars, relaxed in the shelter of the walls. His turn for sentry came in the small hours. He quietly paced around the interior, climbing each ladder slowly to peer into the pitch blackness.

There was movement out here, whether Wretches or wildlife he couldn't tell but the sounds of footsteps came clearly through the still night air. He strained his eyes to see but to no avail. When the footsteps receded, he forgot about them until it was time to wake Harrison for his watch.

He was woken in the morning by Gault's shouted abuse. Harrison had clearly fallen asleep whilst sitting against one of the walls and had not woken his aunt for her watch. The pasty faced teenager was mortified but his aunt joined in the insults Gault lathered the boy with. Lynch ignored the exchange, gnawing on a strip of dried meat, his blue eyes wide.

Kyle and Jas climbed the ladders to check outside the walls.

Kyle peered at where he thought he had heard the footsteps last night but the ground there was too dry and hard for footprints. He pulled his rifle from his shoulder to scan through the magnified scope but at that moment Jas's voice came from the opposite wall.

"Shit! Sign! Contact!"

Then came the unmistakeable sound of rifle fire.

CHAPTER 20

Fabian stank.

As they stood in the hastily cleared assembly hut, Rosie realised that the miasma wafting off the young man was more than the stench of an unwashed body. He smelled of death.

"What's on your clothes?"

"It's flesh. From the Fallen. We rub it on ourselves to keep them from attacking us."

"That doesn't work." Rosie scoffed.

"It does when you're up close to them... Sometimes. It gives us a chance."

"How close do you get?" the voice was that of the Mayor who stood in front of the hapless young man.

"We move with the Hordes."

"You've been inside a Horde?" Rosie was incredulous. She couldn't comprehend why someone would willingly step inside the seething mass of Wretches. She shuddered.

Fabian nodded.

"Why-"

The Mayor started speaking and then stopped, struggling to get the correct words to frame her question.

"Why do you want to help the Wretches?"

"Because - because there could be a cure. We'll use it to end all of this."

"A cure?" Rosie looked quizzically at the Mayor but Elizabeth turned to Callum instead "Fetch Doctor May."

Callum vanished and the Mayor turned back to Fabian.

"There's been rumours of a cure ever since the virus first appeared." her tone was challenging "You have any evidence?"

Fabian shook his head nervously "No, but the Rangers

released a mutation so it's possible –"

"Hold on." the Mayor held up a hand to stop Fabian. Rosie was wondering whether she should have just shot this madman and left him in the woods.

The door opened to reveal Callum and Dr May whose gaze latched onto the stranger in her typical robotic manner.

"Dr May. This young man, er - Fabian? Fabian says there is a cure for the virus and a mutation. Fabian?"

Fabian began to speak, his voice quavering with nerves "I don't know for sure about the cure but the soldiers – the Rangers have the mutation. They've released it here. The Zeks managed to find out about it and we came to try and stop it."

"What does the mutation do?" Dr May asked.

"It turns the Fallen Feral."

There was silence.

"That's quite a claim." if the Mayor sounded sceptical, Rosie didn't blame her. To Doctor May she asked "Is it possible?"

May shrugged "Possible? Yes. Unlikely though. What were you hoping to achieve in Holden?"

"I..." Fabian tailed off. Rosie suddenly saw how young he was. And how frightened.

"Where is the rest of your group?" The Mayor asked in a not unkind voice.

"I don't know." Fabian muttered "We got separated... I - I was scared..." he sounded ashamed.

Rosie surprised herself by feeling sympathetic for the young man. She'd have panicked and run if she was in the middle of a Horde, too. She wondered at the level of zeal that would encourage these people to put themselves in such danger. She wished Sinks were here to bring his perspective to the conversation. Of all of them, he was the only one who'd had experience with the Zeks and his opinion would have been worth its weight in gold.

The Mayor interrupted her reverie "Rosie? Would you take Fabian to the quarantine hut, please? Make sure he's given everything he needs. Doctor? Could you give him the once over? Thank you. Callum, please take a few of your people and ask the council to join me here."

Her tone left little room for argument.

*

"Have you ever heard such rubbish?" Rosie didn't bother to lower her voice, hoping the words carried to the pale faced Zek in the hut behind them. Her words were fuelled by a mixture of disgust at the thought of protecting the dreaded Wretches and fear at what Fabian's claims portended.

Mason, the wall commander looked troubled "We're going to get caught in the middle of this if we're not very careful."

"The middle of what?"

"Whatever's brewing between the Rangers and the Zeks."

"What, a bunch of weirdo's who want us to make friends with the Wretches? Please! There's been a thousand rumours of a cure! There's more every year! It doesn't change anything. If the Mayor had any sense, she'd put a bullet in Fabian's head, bury him out in the woods and forget this whole nonsense."

Mason looked at her seriously as they headed back to the assembly hall "Make sure you don't say that to the council. That's the sort of thing that'll wipe us off the map if we aren't careful."

"Bollocks! What are the Zeks going to do to Holden?"

"You mean aside from leading another Horde here? Did you think about that?"

Rosie was silent. She'd seen the empty boxes of ammunition in the armoury.

"This is politics, Rosie, you can't go charging in guns blazing!" Mason had stopped walking, placing a hand on the young woman's shoulder and looking intently at her "Look, there are Zeks and Rangers all over the place here. If we end up on the wrong side, we're going to find ourselves caught up in a civil war without being able to pick the right side. This is serious! If Armstrong is in the region then it means his eyes are on us. With Sinks and Kyle gone, we have to protect the town from whatever is coming. You and I are responsible for these people *and* for advising the council. So do me a favour, don't say things like that to the Mayor. She's already out on a limb with Fabian!"

Rosie was shocked at the level of emotion in his voice "Civil war? That's a bit strong, don't you think?"

Mason sighed and shrugged "Maybe. Don't forget who Armstrong is though. He isn't a politician, he's a soldier and he fights to get what he wants. If there really is a mutation - or even if there are just more Wretches turning Feral, his hand will be forced either way. More soldiers killing Wretches means more Zeks trying to stop them and that can only exacerbate things."

They slowly began walking again, watching the other members of the council arrive at the assembly hut. A pair of cleaners passed them carrying great bales of laundry, on their way to the bathhouse. Rosie forced a smile in response to their cheery greeting. Clearly word hadn't spread of the Zek in the quarantine hut.

"What do we do with Fabian, then?"

Mason sighed "The council will vote but if you ask me? We let him go. Maybe give him some supplies and a big cuddle so he doesn't tell his friends we were mean to him. Otherwise, we may as well put a strobe light on the town wall and shout 'Come and get it!' until another Horde appears and eats us."

They approached the doors to the hut and Rosie rested her hand on the door catch before opening it. She exhaled, calming herself and taking control of her emotions. She was about to open the door when a frown creased her face and she turned to Mason.

"What's a strobe light?"

"Oh, shut up. You're making me feel old."

CHAPTER 21

Kyle was down the ladder so fast he didn't recall his feet touching the rungs. Kerry had already run to check the gate was sealed and Harrison was clutching his rifle in two hands, his eyes wide with fear.

Kyle sprinted across the fort and frantically hauled himself up the nearest ladder to Jas who was firing careful shots over the wall.

Three grey skinned Wretches were ducking and dodging outside the wall. As Kyle fumbled his rifle barrel over the wall and took them in his sights, his heart came into his mouth.

The black eyes of a Feral gazed back at him.

Kyle hesitated for a crucial second and the Wretch turned and bolted into the treeline. Kyle sent three shots after it but none found their mark.

To his left, he heard Miz give a whoop and saw one of the Ferals fly back, it's chest a ruin of black gore and white bone. They both turned their barrels to the third and Kyle expected it to run for cover but to his shock, it turned and ran at the wall, jumping the height of the stacked metal and gripping the parapet, an inch in front of Kyle's face.

CHAPTER 22

Down in the fort, Harrison had levelled his rifle. He was too frightened to move and the terrifying snarls of the Wretches were turning his bowels to water.

He heard the whoop from Jas followed a second later by a shout of alarm from Kyle.

And then the terrible black eyes of the Feral appeared over the wall.

Harrison raised the rifle, squinted through the sight, and pulled the trigger. Hard.

The rifle kicked in his hands and he hastily looked back to the scene in time to see Kyle, blood spraying from his arm, spin off the ladder and crash to the ground with a yell of pain.

And the Feral came over the top of the wall, straight at Harrison.

CHAPTER 23

Kyle saw the black eyed monster vault the parapet effortlessly as his arm throbbed from Harrison's careless bullet. For a fraction of a second, a savage glee filled him at the sight of the Feral making for Harrison but a moment later that was gone and he was struggling to his feet, ignoring the pain as he brought his rifle to bear.

Bang-bang-bang-bang-bang

The Feral flew backwards as though yanked by a rope. Black blood sprayed out and covered the ground and the creature collapsed, utterly still. Kyle's eyes travelled from the quivering Harrison whose rifle lay on the ground before him to Jas who was still halfway up the ladder finally coming to rest on the awful, staring blue eyes of Lynch as he gazed that too wide gaze at his fallen enemy.

Smoke issued from the barrel of the rifle he clutched in both hands. Kyle hadn't been aware that the man had even been awake and he must have moved like lightning to be where he was now. It was hard to reconcile with the soft spoken stockiness of the Sergeant but as Lynch looked from the dead Feral to Kyle, he was aware of a profound sense of danger. The Feral, somehow, was not just dead, it was destroyed. He saw it on Gault's face too. The other Ranger was caught in a moment of silence, his eyes warily on his Sergeant before he snapped out of it and rounded on Harrison, swinging an open palm in a vicious hook into the young man's head.

"Bastard!"

Harrison sprawled, unmoving. Gault stepped forward but Lynch made a clicking sound with his tongue, the type of signal Kyle would give to get the attention of a dog in Holden and Gault stopped dead. Kerry knelt by her nephew, checking him but clearly racked with fury.

"You owes me one, Frosty." Lynch's voice was as hard to hear as ever, his accent leaning too hard on the vowels so that it took a moment for Kyle to realise what the man had said.

He nodded, awkwardly.

Lynch pointed with a stubby finger to Kyle's shoulder "Fix that."

"Here…" Jas had crossed to Kyle and was examining the wound. He frowned "Was it a bite?"

"No!" Kyle felt anger bubble up in him, a reaction as the adrenaline left him "Harrison shot me!"

"I didn't mean to!" the young man was sitting up groggily but Kerry warned him to shut up as Jas stared in amazement.

"Stupid wanker!"

"Fix it." Lynch murmured again and Jas hurried to cut Kyle's sleeve open.

"Not too bad." He examined the wound and Kyle gritted his teeth as he looked at the jagged gash in his left shoulder. It was nothing more than a flesh wound though, the bullet had grazed his skin but he could feel the entire joint throbbing from the impact.

"Stitch it." He grated at Jas and then endured, with hisses of pain as Jas cleaned it with alcohol before producing a wicked looking needle.

"Urgh."

"Man up!" Jas's voice held little sympathy. Lynch had apparently lost interest in the proceedings and had slumped back against the wall. Gault was fiddling with his kit as Kerry climbed a ladder to keep watch.

"Christ!" Kyle didn't know which he was swearing at, the Feral now slumped dead on the ground or the burning pain in his left arm.

"Talk to me, big man! How's things in Holden? How are the dogs? Is Jason still making that god-awful beer?" Jas did his best to distract Kyle as the needle poked into his skin.

"Urgh! Yeah, this batch tastes like mud with a topping of mud - ah! Christ! - the dogs are fine, better than the rest of us right now."

"Nearly done. When it gets infected and you bleed to death, what do I tell your girlfriend?"

"I haven't got - argh! - a girlfriend!"

"Alright, what do I tell Rosie, your 'not' girlfriend?"

"Sod off! You've been talking to Sinks."

"Everyone talks to Sinks."

"You shouldn't. The man's a liar!"

"If you're done whimpering like a little girl" declared Jas "That's a wrap. Twelve stitches and a strong possibility of gangrene." he began applying more antiseptic and wrapping a bandage around the arm "Well, it was nice knowing you, Kyle. Maybe you should have let those Ferals get you?"

The atmosphere sobered as both of them looked at the dead Wretch. A narrow puddle of the viscous black blood that flowed through the Infected veins was forming around the dead monster. The black eyes were open, staring sightlessly up at the overcast sky.

"Why are their eyes black?" Kyle wondered out loud.

"Probably the blood." Kerry had joined them "They're a different stage of the Infection. The blood must get into the eyeball and turns it black instead of white."

Kyle said nothing, understanding that Kerry was trying to grasp at logic to secure her own fear. Ferals were a monster out of children's stories and they were all shaken by the morning's events.

"Do we carry on?" Harrison had crossed over to them, his face swollen from Gault's blow.

"Yeh." Lynch was suddenly standing by them. Kyle had not noticed the man move and was reminded of a cat's silent movement, the ability those animals had to appear before you without you being aware of their having moved. Without further orders, Lynch led the way over to the gate which Gault swung open.

Hastening to his feet and trying to ignore the throbbing in his shoulder, Kyle hurried after Lynch, breaking into a run to clear the gate, and scanning with his rifle for the third Feral.

No sign.

No sign of refugees, either.

Lynch was already moving, heading west down a narrow rabbit path into a thick patch of woodland. They resumed their formation from the previous day, Harrison in front of Kyle. He turned to Kyle as he walked and held out a hand, a sickly grin spreading across his face as if to apologise.

"For the record" grated Kyle, ignoring the proffered hand "If you ever point a rifle at me again, I'll slit your throat."

Harrison went white and hurriedly stumbled on after Lynch.

CHAPTER 24

"Patrol's back." came the voice from the doorway.

Rosie hadn't quite been asleep but she'd wanted to be. The voice cut through her half-dream state and she blinked dully before her senses fully returned.

"Are they alright?"

"Yeah." the speaker was Ellen, one of the wall guards.

Rosie swung out of her cot in the women's dormitory and walked over to the door, tugging her boots from the rack which sat beneath a full sized poster of Major Armstrong. She looked up at the impossibly handsome features, wondering whether Kyle had met the man.

The air outside was chill but thankfully dry. She walked beside Ellen to the gate which had been closed the second the patrol had passed through it. The patrol, led by Callum was waiting for her.

"Two more Ferals." he began "Down in the south wood line. We got one of them but the other legged it."

Rosie nodded, keeping her face stoic although her heart raced with fear.

A handful of the other Militia had gathered. Their faces were creased with worry.

"We've got to do something."

"We can't harvest with those things out there."

"We've lost enough people already!"

Rosie held up a hand for silence "I know! Calm down. I -"

"Everything alright?" the Mayor approached. Rosie wondered who had told her the patrol was back.

"Yes... No. More Ferals."

Elizabeth's eyes flashed with concern "How many? Where?"

Callum relayed his report.

"More human tracks, too. All through the woods. The rest of Fabian's group are out there."

The Mayor nodded "Alright." she turned to Rosie "New plan. I want all of you out there, dogs and rifles. Find the Zeks and bring them back here."

"Bring them here?"

The Mayor blinked. Rosie realised she'd crossed a line in questioning the order so publicly and hastily turned to the patrol to cover the awkward moment.

"You heard the Mayor! Get the others, we're going out!"

CHAPTER 25

Lynch did not seem to care when the rabbit path faded out. The canopy of trees here was dense, leaving plenty of space between the trunks and their progress was unhindered by low lying undergrowth.

Harrison had settled into a subdued silence, his head down and his rifle hanging limply in his arms. Kyle tried to resist the urge to shoot filthy looks at his back every few paces. His shoulder throbbed but he could move it well enough and he did his best to put it out of his mind as they walked. He scanned the woods for any sign of the third Feral but they saw no movement beyond a fat looking rabbit that Jas felled with a skilfully thrown knife.

Kyle nodded his appreciation as the Militiaman hung the unfortunate creature from his pack. He imagined them building a fire in the middle of the fort that night and his mouth watered at the thought of roasted meat.

Whether by design or accident, Lynch led them to the remains of a small village, abandoned for twenty years. Walking down the weathered and cracked tarmac, Kyle marvelled at the handsome looking brick houses, comparing the sturdy architecture to the metal walled buildings in Holden, scowling as he realised that his home looked ramshackle and shabby in comparison. Still, the glass windows gave an indication into exactly how fragile a Pre-Fall home had proven in the face of the Wretches. He shook his head, marvelling at the naivety of a time when people thought they could live without walls.

There was movement inside some of the buildings. Half decomposed Wretches, locked in an eternal coffin surrounded by the shattered remnants of their previous lives. Some stood still, watching the Militia walk past, others knocked weakly on the windows, their blank white eyes staring and their mouths open in silent wails.

Kyle shivered, wishing they were out of the village.

They passed a road sign that read 'Thank you for driving carefully' which marked the end of the village. The road here was blocked by abandoned cars and Lynch paused, beckoning Gault to join him as the two conferred over a map. Kyle heard the distinctive crackle of a radio and peered interestedly at the taller of the two Rangers. The only radios they had in Holden were ancient and heavy, most of them barely serviceable but Gault's must have been top of the line because it fitted neatly into his daysack and appeared not to weigh the tall man down.

Kyle couldn't hear what they were saying but he saw Lynch's head snap up as Gault relayed a message. He looked at the map, then at the blocked road before making the same clicking noise he'd made in the fort. Then, he was gone, sidestepping through a gap in a hedge that Kyle hadn't seen from his position on the road. As he jogged forward to follow, he saw why. There was no gap, Lynch had just shouldered his way through, heedless of the sharp branches. Already, Kyle could see his squat outline running through the long grass of the overgrown field that lay beyond.

Kyle shoved himself through, scratching his face but ignoring the discomfort and sprinting to catch Lynch. Gault was just behind the Sergeant and Kyle managed to draw level with him, pleased to find that the Ranger was breathing hard whilst he, Kyle, was able to maintain the hard pace that Lynch set.

"What's going on?"

Gault shot him a glance but was breathing too hard for a characteristic insult "Contact, a mile away."

"Refugees?"

"Might be."

"How do you know?"

Gault panted. Behind them, Kyle heard Harrison catch up. He didn't check to see where Kerry and Jas were, they'd have to catch up if they fell behind.

"Other patrols."

Lynch drew to a halt and Kyle, resisting the urge to lean over and pant instead went to one knee, rifle facing outwards as Gault mirrored him on the other side of the Sergeant. Kerry, Harrison, and Jas arrived heaving and sweating a moment later.

"See the woods?" Lynch had not knelt, nor was his own rifle held ready. He stood, pointing a stubby finger at a thick copse of trees some distance ahead. Kyle looked but even as he did so, a flight of birds erupted, squawking out of the branches and a Wretch, slow and stupid looking staggered out of the tree line, hands raised futilely to the sky.

"Let's go." Lynch was moving again, apparently unfazed by the long sprint across the overgrown field. Kyle followed, his own breath still not recovered but his eyes fixed on the Wretch. His heart hammered and he nervously fingered his safety catch.

Bang

He hadn't even been aware of Lynch raising his rifle, let alone slowing to take aim but the Wretch spun and fell, a distinctive black spray coming from its skull. Kyle didn't have time to waste gawping at the marksmanship Lynch had just displayed, scoring a headshot from this distance whilst running because more Wretches were now spilling forth from the trees.

One, two, five and then he lost count and he raised his rifle, firing a burst of half a dozen shots earning a growl from Lynch.

"Aim, Frosty!"

Kyle checked himself, taking a Wretch in his sights and feeling his stomach lurch as it turned towards him, breaking into a fast run.

Bang

He missed the head, striking the creature in the grey skin of its neck. Black blood sprayed out and it went down, vanishing in the long grass. Automatically, Kyle averted his path so as not to accidentally tread on it and risk a bite to his legs but Lynch cut across him, shouldering him to the right and into the trees.

A blur of thick trunks wrapped in emerald ivy, a tangle of hefty roots lining the floor and then Kyle's eyes were wide with something close to panic as he desperately tried to tell brown bark from grey skin. Rifles cracked as Lynch and Gault tore into the Wretches and Kyle fired once, twice, completely unable to tell if he'd hit anything. He twisted to his right, remembering Sinks' training drills and his rifle barrel struck a tree trunk. Cursing, he flicked the safety on and dropped it to hang from the sling, drawing the Glock from his hip.

Bang-bang-bang

A Wretch was snatched backwards as Kyle drilled three rounds into its chest then moved his aim upwards firing at the neck and finally the face. A calm suddenly came over him as his confidence returned in a flash and he pivoted, remembering to push his right foot back slightly and rotating his left hand on the grip of the pistol so his thumbs lined along the barrel.

Bang

Another Wretch, this one closing in on Lynch from the Sergeant's right was flung back. Lynch saw, turning and firing a quick trio of shots into the twitching figure and then a flurry of bullets knocked the nearest Wretches back and Kyle knew Jas, Kerry and Harrison had arrived.

"Use the trees! Break them up! Don't let them cluster around you!" Gault was shouting instructions to the Militia as he and Lynch moved smoothly between the thick trunks, disrupting the Wretches line of sight, and confusing the Horde.

Kyle guessed there were no more than thirty or forty in the group, and the ground was littered with grey corpses already. He grinned savagely as he shot two more, resisting the urge to give a whoop as he caught one running in front of him, moving sideways from his perspective.

"Good shot, Frosty!" Lynch's voice was raised over the sounds of the battle but as Kyle caught his eye, the same weird wide eyed stare was fixed on his face. He turned it on a slow moving Wretch coming towards him and Kyle watched, fascinated as the Sergeant stepped smoothly to one side, sweeping the closest leg from under the beast, re-cocking his leg and then stamping with a grunt of effort onto the grey skinned forehead.

The skull collapsed in with a wet snapping sound and Kyle gagged at the sight, half laughing at his own reaction. Lynch turned a savage grin onto him and he shook his head, turning to engage more targets but there were none before him. The other Militia were still firing behind him but Gault was already ordering them further into the woods.

Light flickered through the leaves and Kyle's eyes jumped from branch to trunk to bush, spotting every flickering leaf as a Wretch and aiming the pistol. But the woods were empty and he wondered what Gault was leading them towards, suddenly becoming aware that he was panting hard.

"Up ahead!" movement again between the trees and Kyle saw a dark figure moving from trunk to trunk. Then movement above and his heart fluttered in his chest. Surely the Wretches weren't in the trees?

"Enemy front!" Gault snapped, crashing to a halt. He fired three quick shots upwards at a forty five degree angle and Kyle heard a scream that was definitely not that of a Wretch and a body fell from a tree.

A young woman, skin ingrained with filth and her hair matted with a heavy pack that bore the stains of arduous travel.

A refugee.

Kyle stared in horror at the sight but even as he watched the girl's eyes turned glassy and the twitching ceased. Kyle felt sick and turned to Gault but the big Ranger was already firing past the woman, heedless of the murder he'd committed and Kyle saw more Wretches, drawn by the sound of fighting now running at them.

The sound of their screeching hunting cry rose again under the canopy of trees.

But now, Kyle could see more figures moving under the trees, stained and filthy like the dead girl and he could hear the strange words they shouted in panicked voices to one another.

French?

But a weird whistling sound, not unlike the hunting cry of their enemy was rising and more people were moving, dark clothes mixing with the grey of the Wretches and there was a flash of a red armband as someone raised a device to their lips, blowing hard, drawing the attention of the Infected and Kyle realised in a frozen moment of fascination that the Zeks were drawing the Wretches away from the refugees, trying to stop the attack.

"Get 'em!" Lynch growled suddenly and then he and Gault were bounding forwards away from the Militia. The distance to the nearest Zeks was not far and in a few seconds, Kyle could see Gault stopped, steadying his rifle on a tree trunk. Lynch did not bother to rest his own weapon, raising it before him and firing indiscriminately into the crowd of Zeks, refugees and Wretches.

Slaughtering them all.

Kyle stared, his grin gone to be replaced by ice running through his veins. Lynch and Gault seemed completely calm, making small movements as they adjusted their aim, hot brass flying from their rifles to carpet the forest floor around them. There were human screams now coming from the crowd, mixing in with the Wretch shrieks and distinctive voices yelling at the Rangers to stop.

Kyle added his own "Stop! Stop! Those are people! They're alive!"

Lynch did not stop. Not until the survivors had fled, leaving the few slower Wretches to stagger towards Gault and Lynch.

Who gunned them down as mercilessly as they had the humans.

"Kyle!" he whipped around at the sound of his own name to see Kerry raising her rifle at Lynch and Gault.

"No!" Kyle stepped forward, slapping the barrel down as he took in Jas's shaking fury, Harrison's green face and the tears on Kerry's cheeks.

"Stop them!" he didn't think Kerry was shouting at him. It was a general declaration to the universe at large that what was happening before them was wrong, so utterly, disgustingly wrong that it had to be stopped.

But they couldn't just shoot Gault and Lynch. The world was spinning too fast for Kyle to form a rational thought but he simply knew the truth that Kerry could not gun down the Rangers.

"For God's sake!" Jas's voice was suddenly loud beneath the trees, a silence filling the void left by the sounds of battle which had abruptly vanished.

The world hung still. A small cloud of steam rose from the woman Gault had shot and Kyle found he was breathing heavily, his own breath turning into vapour. He heard Lynch's savage accent muttering to Gault and a sudden fear shot through him, making his palms sweat and a sudden deluge of saliva into his mouth making him swallow.

"Check your weapons!" Gault's voice was filled with harshness as he approached with Lynch. Kyle took an instinctive step back from where he stood by Kerry, accidentally allowing her and Lynch to face one another.

"You murdered them!" Kerry's voice broke the stillness and brought Lynch and Gault to a stop some meters away. Kyle looked at the Ranger Sergeant and his breath caught as he saw that awful, wide eyed glare locked on Kerry. He remembered those same eyes locked on the dead Feral in the roadside fort and the same instinct deep in his mind told him to run, that this monster in human flesh was a danger so profound that he must do everything to remove himself from its presence before he died.

"I said, check your weapons!" was there a hint of emotion

in Gault's voice? Kyle thought there was. The order he was shouting at Kerry, Jas and Harrison was pointless. Neither of the trio made any move to comply and Gault did not step towards them to enforce it. Instead, his chest heaved with exertion and his face was flushed.

"Bastards!" Jas had tears in his eyes which never left Lynch. His rifle hung low though, muzzle pointed at the leafy ground.

Lynch's mouth twitched as his eyes bored into Kerry's. The yellow teeth leered.

"Why did you do that? They needed help!"

"Who the bloody hell do you think you are?" Gault exploded at Jas "Some civvy, rag-tag bunch of Militia hats aren't gonna tell Rangers how to do their job! We're alive, aren't we?"

"She isn't!" Kerry stabbed her finger towards the dead girl.

"She was Infected! They all are!" Gault forced a humourless grin onto his face.

"You-" Jas stepped forward but it was Harrison, pale faced, weedy and weak Harrison who snapped. With a high pitched scream probably borne more of fear than bravery, he ran full tilt at Gault. His rifle hung from its sling and his arms reached out before him like the comedy cartoons Kyle recalled from fuzzy childhood memories. Lynch's gaze switched from Kerry to her nephew as Gault forced a contemptuous laugh, stepped to one side, and swept Harrison's legs from under him.

The young man crashed to the forest floor with a muted thump and then Kyle was aware of Kerry reaching for her rifle but the flurry of shots came from the Rangers and Kyle stepped backwards arm shielding his face as fragments of leaves and dirt filled the air.

"E-nuff!" Lynch's accented voice was as loud as the shots from his rifle that had torn the ground up around Jas and Kerry's feet. Kyle, a half dozen paces away stared in stupefied shock as Kerry, her face now pale was tugged by Jas who was muttering to her under his breath.

"What did you think we was doin?" Lynch bared his teeth at the Militia in something that might have been anger.

Kyle stared at the Sergeant, realisation dawning on him. Of course, they were here to kill them, he'd known that, really. But the reality of gunning down the helpless civilians made him feel sick and frightened. What had their crime been?

"You're a fucking monster!" Kerry shrieked, tears on her face as Gault laughed.

"You're an idiot, woman!" he snarled "This is reality! These people are threatening everything! You wear that uniform and carry that rifle, you'd better be prepared to do what's needed!"

Hands twitched on weapons. Kyle could see that Kerry was a half second away from raising her weapon and firing at Gault but the big Ranger was tense too and Kyle knew he would be able to draw and fire before any of the Militia would get a shot off.

"Stop!" he shouted, grabbing Kerry's arm "This won't solve anything!"

Kerry rounded on him, fury in her eyes but he held her gaze and he saw her fury turn to a sneer and then she turned abruptly, grabbing Jas and walking, then running off into the woods. Harrison sprinted after his aunt as Gault bellowed insults at their retreating backs.

Kyle turned back to face Lynch. The baby blue eyes snapped onto Kyle's own and the yellow toothed Sergeant stepped forward.

"Practical, ain't it." Lynch jerked a stubby thumb over his shoulder at the scene of death and carnage he had created.

Kyle opened his mouth but couldn't find words to respond. Lynch seemed to understand and nodded as Gault stared menacingly into the woods after the vanished Militia.

"May-juh says you wanna be a Ranger. Gotta toughen up, you wanna be wiv us." Lynch seemed to be sneering at Kyle who gaped.

"Go get 'em back, boy." Gault ordered "Job isn't finished yet." He pointed after the retreating Militia.

"Why ain't you run like them?" Lynch had cocked his head to one side, the too wide stare locked on Kyle.

Kyle frowned, swallowing the nausea and horror that were racking him "There's still Wretches out here." He shrugged. Leaving hadn't occurred to him.

Lynch's too wide mouth froze for a moment and then the squat Sergeant made a dry heaving sound and Kyle wondered wildly whether the man was having a seizure but as Gault sniggered next to him, he realised this was what qualified for a laugh with Armstrong's Devil. A wary smile flashed onto his own face.

"Good, Frosty. Stay on mission." He pointed after Kerry and Jas again "Go tell them that. We'll wait here." And, as though he hadn't a care in the world, Lynch sat down abruptly on the forest floor to wait.

Blinking then shaking his head in surprise, Kyle hastened after his fellow Militia.

CHAPTER 26

"Alright. Does everyone know what they're doing?"

The cluster of Militia in their patrol gear nodded at Rosie.

"Good. The second you get sight of the Zeks, I want to know about it." she tapped her radio handset.

The gate opened with a squeal of rusty springs. A section of Wall Guards lined the top, shotguns trained and safety catches off. Rosie patted her pocket discretely, hoping no-one would see the lump in the cloth. She'd been shocked when Jane MacDonald's ponderous bulk had blocked her path five minutes before. The fat woman had squeezed her into an enormous bear hug, leaving Rosie confused and awkward, never having had such an intimate moment with the armourer.

"For luck." She'd smiled, pressing the cold metal of the grenade into her hand, away from the prying eyes of the council members.

As Rosie turned to clamber under the gate to join her patrol, her mind lingered on the brief scene, wondering what lay ahead.

*

The woods were as cold and uninviting as ever. Rain had fallen overnight and thick mud now surrounded Holden. Rosie cursed as she slipped more than once doing her best to keep quiet. She was angry and stressed. The thought of the Ferals watching her every move had the hairs on the back of her neck prickling and her eyes twitching at every blowing leaf. Terrence's face floated through her mind too and she ground her teeth in frustration.

There were tracks, human by the looks of them. Wretch footprints were usually smooth and shoeless, often with distinctive limps as the tendons and muscle gradually rotted. They rarely moved alone so their tracks were easy to spot. As she squatted to look at a set left by a heavy pair of boots, she wondered what the Feral's tracks would look like. For all she knew, these *were* Feral tracks, cleverly disguised as those of the wandering Zeks.

A sudden squawk of the radio brought her head up to see Callum standing above her listening intently. He looked down and his eyes met Rosie's.

"Got them."

*

The Zeks were less than a mile along the trail Callum and Rosie had followed. Jess, another patrol leader, had spotted them and now stood with her troops in a tense circle around five miserable and dirty figures.

The apparent leader, a silver haired man was already ranting as Rosie came into view, demanding to know why he and his people had been stopped. Like his fellows, he wore a long dark coat, streaked with mud and an equally grubby red armband sewed onto the upper right arm.

"Let us go! This is against the law and –"

"You're on our land, grandpa so shut your trap before I put a bullet in you!" Rosie snarled at the man. The scarred dog trotted forward to sniff the Zek and stepped back immediately, hackles rising and a low growl in his throat. Rosie guessed these Zeks were smothered in Wretch flesh like Fabian had been.

"Take them back to Holden?" Jess asked Rosie.

"Oh yes, take us back and shoot us like you did Fabian!" the silver haired man shouted.

Rosie turned to him "You know Fabian?"

"Of course I know Fabian! He's one of our group! What have you done with him?"

"Wouldn't you love to know." Rosie's voice dripped sarcasm at the man "Where are your weapons?"

"We don't have weapons – don't be so bloody stupid! Let us go! You're nothing but bullies with guns!"

"Listen here –" Rosie rounded on the man but Jess stepped forward.

"Just tell us what you're doing here. Fabian is in Holden and he hasn't been harmed. We found him wandering alone and we took him in."

The silver haired man seemed to calm at Jess's tone. Rosie grated her teeth, knowing she could never achieve such an effect. He regarded Jess coolly for a moment before responding in a calmer voice "My name is Zachary. We were *trying* to lead the Horde away from Holden before you accosted us. The Rangers tried to set the Fallen on us –"

"Rubbish!" Rosie had heard enough. She began to snarl at her Militia to bind the Zek's hands but at that moment, the great brute of a dog she'd brought threw his head back and howled at the woods.

The Militia were in position immediately, backs to each other, forming a ring in the small clearing. The Zeks looked at them in stupefied amazement, shocked by the change in attitude.

The dog howled again and Rosie raised her rifle to the woods.

"Movement!" came a shout and she turned to the sound.

"Where?"

"North!"

"Wretches!"

"Contact!" and suddenly there were Wretches, slow ones, staggering towards the Militia. Rosie fired and one went down. A handful more shots and the others were down.

"Clear?"

"Yeah, clear!"

The dog howled again. No-one moved. The trees rustled again and this time a man appeared. Another Zek, this one dressed – Rosie had to close her eyes and reopen them to make certain = in black combat gear with a slung rifle. His hands were up, and he wore a look of cold control on his weather-beaten face.

"You there - you in charge here?"

Rosie aimed at his head, finger tightening on the trigger "What d'you want?"

"I want to talk."

"I'm not in the mood."

"Will you at least lower your weapon?"

"No."

The man sighed and his gaze flickered to Zachary and his group who were clustered uncertainly in the middle of the Militia, shocked by the sudden violence. He glanced at the dead Wretches, his face clear of emotion and then back at Rosie.

"I'm very sorry about this…"

The taser struck beneath her arm, between the plates of Rosie's body armour. It was agony, white fire burned through her bones, and she let out a piercing, inhuman shriek. The rifle fell from her hands and her vision vanished as she crashed to the ground. Around her, the other Militia were overpowered, falling to stun guns. Callum, his face red with fury backed away, rifle raised but a spray from a pressurised can struck him in the face and a second later, he was on his knees in the mud, clawing the agony from his eyes.

The woods erupted with Zeks. Clad in dark uniforms and body armour, all were armed with rifles and shotguns but these hung from slings as they wielded the yellow plastic tasers and CS sprays. Rosie had raided enough Pre-Fall police stations to recognise the equipment and could only stare as her troops were overpowered.

Rosie moaned on the floor, the electricity had stopped but she was limp, her muscles failing to respond to her mind.

The man with the weather-beaten face strolled forward as

his troops moved in to disarm the Militia. He crouched next to Rosie and pushed her rifle aside "I'm really, truly sorry that you've been caught up in all this. The last thing we wanted to do was involve civilians."

"Who the hell are you calling civilians?" Rosie spat, squirming in the mud. He pulled her pistol from its holster and covered her with it.

"Civilians... Yes, well, whatever you want to call yourselves. Unfortunately, this is bigger than you or I and I need to get my man back. I'm afraid that you'll have to do as leverage." he grimaced regretfully and made to stand up.

Rosie's arm shot out and he looked down at her in mild surprise, the pistol still in his hand "What are you -" he fell silent as his eyes travelled from the small metal pin in the mud to the grenade clutched in Rosie's hand. Her grip on his arm did not weaken.

"How about we all just calm down and play nicely?" she smiled evilly at the Zek.

CHAPTER 27

The woods seemed eerily silent to Kyle after the gunshots and screams. Part of him knew that he was in shock after the skirmish and the murder of the refugees. Another part of him was certain that Lynch had acted in the most brutally practical way possible and that Sinks, were he here, would have admitted the deaths were necessary. Still, the sight of the twitching woman as she lay dying beneath the trees filled his mind and he shook his head as he followed Kerry, Jas, and Harrison's footprints. His eyes were glued to the ground, his mind still on the slaughter behind him when he spotted the fourth pair of prints. He looked at them, looked away and then snapped his head back, staring in confusion at the flat soled shoes that no self-respecting Militiaman would wear.

"Hands up! Drop the rifle! Do it now!" the woman's voice was harsh and sudden, making Kyle jump. He reeled back, feeling a hand clutch at his shoulder. A neat twist, ducking his head under the wrist as he clapped his own hand to that of his attacker and he heard a gasp of pain as the wrist locked and something tore inside but then a foot kicked at the back of his knee and he fell, swearing.

Instantly, a body landed atop his and Kyle felt the wind knocked out of him. Doing his best to ignore the pain, he swung his right elbow across his body, attempting to lift his hips as he twisted but the figure atop him leaned forward at the exact moment his elbow connected and the blow lacked the force it needed. Still, the power in Kyle's arms was enough and his opponent gave a shout of pain as Kyle cracked him in the skull. Then, a boot swung to his left and he slapped a desperate palm out to stop the swing, clinging onto the ankle for dear life.

"Stop! Stop or I'll shoot you!" the woman's voice came again and Kyle, lying on his back blinked up at the slight figure that stood over him, feet planted firmly either side of his body with a hefty black pistol pointed at his face.

Kyle stopped. He felt like shrugging. There was nothing to be done.

"Are you a soldier?" the figure's face was hidden by the shadows of a wide hood but her voice was distinctly female. Kyle thought he could make out dark hair and nut brown skin.

He stuck his middle finger up at the woman. Someone kicked him in the ribs hard enough for him to hiss in pain.

"Enough! Answer me. Are you a soldier?"

"No. Are you?"

"I'm a Zek."

"I can see that."

The woman grunted "Not for much longer." She nodded at someone Kyle couldn't see and a moment later, a black bag went over his head. Powerless to resist, Kyle ground his teeth in the darkness as he was rolled over on the cold ground and his hands tied behind his back.

*

Kyle wasn't sure if the hours he stumbled with his captors were hard because of the distance he was travelling, or because he couldn't see nor balance his body. He stumbled over every uneven patch of ground, at first, moving slowly to give Lynch or perhaps Kerry and Jas a chance to spot him but as the Zeks dragged him along faster, simply because he could not see.

Voices came to his ears faintly, Zeks moving around him. He tried to estimate how many were in the group but few of them spoke. There was at least one to either side of him, their hands gripping his arms and guiding him. One, an older sounding male voice periodically muttered instructions to him "Watch these roots" or "duck under these brambles, now". Kyle thought the voice was not unfriendly but couldn't help remembering the words of the woman with the pistol asking if he was a soldier. He wondered what the scene might have become if he'd sported the camouflage of the Rangers instead of the dark fatigues of the Militia. After the fracas in the woods, he wouldn't blame the Zeks for not being picky with their prisoners.

The light began to change. The bag over his head was dark but there were thin patches of light poking through where the fabric had worn. Kyle had been aware at some point they'd left the cover of the trees and their pace had slowed. Wet grass soaked the legs of his trousers and the smell of moisture filled the air as he was guided, stumbling, through several turns. Kyle thought they might be crossing an overgrown pasture and tried to picture the area on a map but his memory failed him. He'd lost all sense of direction, too. The overcast sky blocked the sun and the little light he could glimpse did not help.

But it was darkening, now, surely. Kyle could hear more voices now, as though the Zeks were speaking to one another and more than once, he felt a body brush past him as persons unseen moved up and down the column of walking figures. His heart began to race as he anticipated their arrival at whatever destination the Zeks were headed for. Would they shoot him? Surely not. Kyle tried to reassure himself that if they wanted him dead, they'd had ample opportunity to kill him already and anyway, weren't the Zeks all about prolonging human life? Still, his palms, tied tightly behind his back were sweating again and he worked hard to control his breathing, determined not to show fear when the bag was finally removed from his head.

"In here, soldier-boy." A rough hand shoved Kyle forward and he winced as he rebounded off a solid structure. A cruel laugh sounded before the commanding woman's voice snapped an order and a hand firmly pushed Kyle through a doorway.

"Take him downstairs. I'll follow in a moment..." Kyle heard the commander and the friendlier man's voice fade away and then someone was roughly leading him down steps. An award shuffle, one step at a time as an older female voice berated him for his slowness. Kyle overbalanced once, almost falling forward but a strong grip held him upright.

"Here..." the same firm grip pressed him backwards and Kyle felt a chair beneath him. He submitted, lowering himself onto what felt like a hard plastic surface. He shivered slightly, the wet fabric of his trousers pressing against him.

Silence.

There was a light here, an artificial strip shining overhead. Kyle peered at it through the small holes in the fabric. It looked to be Pre-Fall technology and that was strange. The lights in Holden were usually dirty bulbs, the fittings bolted neatly but obviously to the ceiling. This strip looked as though there were ceiling tiles either side of it, a luxury that no-one, save perhaps those wealthy folk in the capital would bother installing. Were they in London then? Impossible. They'd walked for hours but not for days and Kyle knew London was many miles to the north across dangerous territory. No, they must still be close to Matwood, perhaps only a day or so from the town. A glimmer of hope went through his mind that perhaps even now Sinks or Lynch were following his tracks, readying for an assault on whatever haven the Zeks had retreated to.

Silence.

Kyle held his breath, straining his ears for sound. It seemed that he was alone in the room but he knew if he were in the Zek's position, that was what he'd want a prisoner to think. He cleared his throat, experimentally.

Nothing.

"Can I have some water? Please?" he turned his head slightly to the right, the same movement he might make if he were not blindfolded and someone was behind him, just out of sight.

"Well then, I'll just sit here and dry out, shall I?"

Still no response.

To hell with it Kyle thought and he began to flex his wrists, feeling the bonds that held him. A critical mistake the Zeks had made was not tying him to the chair. They'd assumed the cords he already wore would stop him but Kyle had been pressing and flexing his hands against them every time he stumbled and the rough rope around his right wrist was already giving.

He strained. The space he'd created meant that he could lever his fingers to tug at the knots. His arms were still behind his back though, and he could see nothing. He felt a solid knot and pulled experimentally. It didn't budge. His left arm was going numb and Kyle cursed, silently, relaxing for a moment and wiggling the muscles in his shoulders to force blood to the digits. He winced at his bandaged arm.

Voices outside, rising in pitch for a moment before falling away. One sounded angry. Perhaps they'd seen the Rangers approaching? Kyle hoped so.

Tug, strain, wiggle. The knots would not budge and so Kyle abandoned the effort, working instead to loosen the cord around his right wrist, the one that had already given him some slack. He forced the rough cord over the root of his thumb, ignoring the burning in his skin as it was scratched and pulled. The knot slipped over his thumb and he tugged, cursing again as the arm went numb and he was forced to relax for a minute. Then he pulled again and with a sudden release of pressure, the rest of his hand was free.

"Bloody hell!" he muttered before he could stop himself. His hands were free and quickly, Kyle whipped the black bag off his head. He squinted and blinked in the sudden light, his eyes throbbing. He could make out a long, low room, certainly Pre-Fall in architecture with a dusty bank of old computers down one wall and a complex array of machinery on the other. Kyle wasted no time gawping at the relics of the past but ran to the door, pressing his ear to the frame to listen.

Footsteps.

Then the door was opening and Kyle was hastily stepping backwards as the door swung inwards and a man crossed the threshold then stopped.

"Where'd-" that was as far as he got because Kyle looped his left arm around the man's neck, dragging him backwards off balance and locking his grip as his right hand scrabbled for a weapon. The man was unarmed. Instead, the woman behind him was reaching into her waistband and Kyle shoved the man forward unceremoniously, forcing her to put both hands out to stop his bulk before they both crashed to the ground in the doorway.

Kyle moved faster than he'd ever moved in his life, knowing now that everything depended on him getting the woman's pistol before she did. She'd reached for her waist on the right hand side of her torso and her right arm was now pinned beneath her fellow Zek so Kyle dived, kneeling hard on her thigh as he scrabbled for the weapon. Then, he was up, his left hand gripping the man's collar and hauling him backwards as he screwed the muzzle of the pistol behind the Zek's ear. On the ground, the woman was slowly sitting up, her eyes locked on the weapon in Kyle's hand. He flashed her his most charming grin.

"So, what do we do now?"

CHAPTER 28

The atmosphere in the damp clearing was tense enough to cut with a knife. Rosie got slowly to her feet, the grenade clutched firmly in her hand. Her body was still quivering from the aftereffects of the taser but she gritted her teeth, determined not to show weakness.

Something tugged at her as she rose and she looked down to see the twin wires of the stun gun poking out of her side. With a grunt, she bashed them away watching them tumble into the mud.

The Zek with the weather beaten face was watching her warily. Around them a ring of Zeks with their Militia prisoners had formed but no-one was moving. Rosie coughed then raised her arm to head height so the onlookers could see the danger.

"All of you, let my men go! Now!" when none of the Zeks complied she seized the leader's arm, pulling him close. Caught off guard he stumbled in the wet mud.

Shouts of protest rose and rifles were trained on her but Rosie shouted them down.

"No! All of you! Let them go! Let them bloody go!"

"Piss off!" the voice came from the Zek whose arm she clutched "What are you going to do, blow yourself up?"

Rosie rounded on him, fury in her eyes "Just sodding try me!"

The Zek's eyes widened in surprise. Rosie's hair was in disarray, her eyes still wild with pain from the taser and mud was slathered across one side of her face. She must have looked like a mad thing because the Zek bought it. He turned to his fellows and shouted for the Militia to be released.

Weapons were returned and the Militia snatched them back roughly, elbowing their captors aside. Callum came to stand by Rosie, his eyes red and angry from the spray. He coughed intermittently.

Roughly, Rosie reclaimed her pistol, the grenade still held tightly. She grabbed the Zek close and shoved her hand down under his body armour, ignoring the stench of sweat that wafted from him. Now he was stuck, the grenade pressed to his body.

"How about we have a civil conversation?" Rosie put on a falsely sweet voice "What are you doing here?"

The man grunted, a look of disgust on his face "How about you tell us why you kidnapped one of my men?"

"How about you answer the bloody question!" snapped Rosie, getting in his face "If I let this pin go, you're going to be Wretch meat in about five seconds!"

"You and me both, girl!"

Rosie looked at the plate that protected the Zek's body "That armour looks pretty solid to me, I reckon I'll get away with a bit of shrapnel. Nothing I haven't had before!" she glared at him, challenging him to defy her.

To her surprise, Zachary, the silver haired Zek stepped forward "Eric?" he addressed the man Rosie clutched "Eric, this doesn't have to lead to violence. She said that Fabian was alive and well in Holden! This isn't their fault."

Eric made a small movement and Rosie pulled him back down, gripping him hard. He looked down at her.

"You're a very dislikeable young lady."

"Bite me."

He rolled his eyes "If it interests you at all, we're in your lands trying to keep the Hordes away from your town."

"You mean the one *you* led here the other night?"

"Led here?" Eric was incredulous "Why would we lead a Horde here?"

"Probably the same reason you've brought an army into our land! Since when do Zeks carry weapons?" she gestured at the soldiers.

"Thirty men is hardly an army" scoffed Eric.

"We didn't lead the Fallen to your town!" Zachary was insistent "The Rangers led them towards us and when we tried to lose them, they headed for Holden! We were trying to draw them away when the helicopters came! They weren't helping you, they were attacking us!"

Rosie stared at the man with her mouth open. She was so surprised by the claim that she nearly dropped the grenade. Behind her, she could hear the Militia murmuring amongst themselves.

"Why would the Rangers do that?"

There was a wet sound as one of the dogs gulped.

"This isn't the time." Eric watched the treeline warily "The Fallen are all over your land. We aren't safe standing here."

"I thought you tosspots loved getting all chummy with the Wretches?" Rosie sneered, thinking furiously for a way out of the standoff.

"Not like this." Eric raised his hands "Look, here's a proposal. I leave my weapons here and come with you back to Holden. My men and Zachary stay here and we negotiate the release of Fabian. I'm sure we've both got something to offer each other."

"Shut up, will you?" snapped Rosie.

"Look - there are twice as many of us as there are of you. If we start shooting, you and I are going to go down first and then we'll slaughter each other! That's not how I want this to go!"

The Zek was speaking sense and Rosie could see the futility of labouring the point but she was damned if she'd trust these people.

"How about you and your men leave all your weapons and armour here bugger off from our land and never come back?" behind her Rosie heard Callum snort his agreement.

Eric was shaking his head "Take me back to the town and let me speak to your Mayor."

"Why?"

"Because we're on the same side here, you just need to let me explain."

Rosie snorted but she had to do something and she wasn't prepared to sacrifice the lives of half the Holden Militia in a fight with the Zeks. She gritted her teeth, making sure her grip on the grenade was firm "Militia! Back to Holden! Move in pairs, cover each other! Callum, you cover me. You -" she spoke to Eric "- you're coming with me, you and our little friend."

The grenade clutched tightly in her hand, Rosie began the slow, awkward shuffle back to Holden, the ring of furious looking Zeks watching them go, helplessly.

CHAPTER 29

Footsteps sounded behind the woman and a pair of Zeks ran into view. Kyle cursed as he spotted his own Glock in the hands of the nearest, a shrewish looking older female with a shaved head.

"Drop Graham! Put that gun down!" she bellowed at him.

Kyle screwed the muzzle even tighter into Graham's skull making the man squeak in pain. He opened his mouth to shout back but the first woman, the one with the nut brown skin had risen to one knee and shouted over the both of them.

"For the love of God! The entire world is dead and we're *still* standing here trying to kill each other! Can't we for five *fucking* minutes just talk like normal adults?"

Kyle raised his eyebrows in surprise. He had to admit that she had a point. He dropped Graham to the ground and lowered the pistol, keeping it by his side.

"Put the gun on the floor!" the shrewish woman called again but the first lady, who he thought was the commander had turned to her.

"Molly, give me the pistol. Thank you. Now-"

"Amelia –"

"Enough! You and Graham go up to the roof and keep working. No! I mean it! I'll be fine. Go!"

Molly and Graham left and Amelia turned to Kyle. To his surprise, she held out the Glock that Jane had handed to him in the armoury back in Holden.

"I believe this is yours?"

He blinked in surprise, looking down at the pistol in his own hand "I believe this is yours." He echoed.

"Swap?"

"Why not."

They swapped and Kyle checked the weapon, finding the magazine in place and a round still cocked in the chamber.

"Are you a soldier?" Amelia asked.

"Why do you think that?"

She nodded at the pistol Kyle still held "That's a Glock seventeen. Those are military issue."

"And police." Kyle pointed out, remembering that this weapon had been relieved from a constabulary armoury.

"Oh? Well, seeing as I don't think anyone's dialled nine-nine-nine in twenty years, I'll assume you aren't a copper."

The joke was lost on Kyle who just stared at Amelia, causing her to roll her eyes.

"Who are you?" she repeated.

"Seeing as you're the ones who kidnapped me, I think you should go first."

"Seeing as you were the one following us, I think we were within our rights to kidnap you." Amelia shot back.

Kyle resisted the urge to smile. He was acutely aware that Amelia was extremely pretty with a fiery intelligence behind her dark eyes "I wasn't following you. I was looking for my friends."

Amelia frowned "The Rangers?"

"No. I left the Rangers to look for Jas and Kerry. And Harrison. They're Militia, like me."

"You're from Matwood?"

"We came from Matwood."

Amelia frowned, sensing he was holding something back. Then, as though Kyle were not holding a pistol, she walked slowly into the room and sat on the chair Kyle had just vacated "Why are you out here?"

"Wouldn't you like to know." Kyle didn't think that Amelia was going to shoot him, but he saw no need to give up any information to her. His eyes flicked towards the stairs beyond the open door.

She rolled her eyes "If you want to go, then leave. We'll be gone in a few hours anyway."

Kyle looked back at the door and then at the seated Zek. Something compelled him and he carefully returned his pistol to the holster beneath his belt "I had a rifle, too."

"It's at the top of the stairs." Amelia sounded disinterested.

Kyle didn't move.

She smiled "Got your attention?"

Kyle held up a flat palm in front of him and rocked it from side to side "A little."

For some reason, Amelia laughed at that. Sometime between crossing the room and sitting down, she'd stowed her own weapon out of sight and Kyle was impressed that he hadn't noticed the movement, aware that she must have practiced the motion repetitively. She leaned back, regarding him coolly as though for the first time.

"What's your name?"

"Kyle."

Amelia sighed and forced a smile, standing to shake his hand "How do you do, Kyle. I'm Amelia Singh."

Kyle took the hand, impressed at the firm grip and eye contact. She shook once and took her hand back before returning to the chair.

"It's usually polite to introduce yourself in turn."

"It's also polite not to kidnap people."

Amelia shrugged with a small smile "You're a big boy. You'll get over it."

Kyle rolled his eyes "So, I was looking for my friends. What are you doing here?"

The smile vanished to be replaced by a weariness. Kyle noticed for the first time the dark bags under her eyes "You saw those people out in the woods?"

"Yes."

Amelia swallowed "I don't suppose you'd stand trial and tell how that bastard Lynch gunned down unarmed men and women?"

Kyle opened his mouth and closed it, the sight of the dead girl playing in his mind.

"Didn't think so." Amelia's face had lost all friendliness "You look too young and nice to be running around the woods with Armstrong's Devil. I suppose you think Zeks are all lunatics with a death wish? It's our own fault we get slaughtered? That we-"

"Before today, I'd never even met a bloody Zek so stop shouting at me." Kyle scowled at Amelia "I only met Lynch yesterday anyway. I'm only here because a Horde attacked my town and we need supplies! I had nothing to do with killing any Zeks – matter of fact, I've never killed anyone! So don't sit there with your judgemental bullshit and tell me who I am!"

There was an awkward pause.

Amelia raised her eyebrows "Well, I suppose I'm sorry."

Kyle grunted in response which earned him a well-practiced eye roll.

"Oh, get over it."

"Charming."

"I am." Amelia smiled with a hint of sarcasm.

"You're *the* Amelia Singh? The famous Zek?"

"Famous?" Amelia looked mildly embarrassed "I suppose so."

"You aren't what I imagined."

"Oh?"

Kyle was suddenly awkward, realising he was close to insulting this woman. The thought occurred to him that he owed her nothing, that she had dragged him here against his will and for all he knew, may have shot him out of hand if he hadn't freed himself. Still, there was a certain charisma to her that made him want to be polite. He changed the subject "So, what are you doing here? Where is here, anyway?"

Amelia considered him for a moment before giving a shrug "I suppose it doesn't really matter. Like I said, we're leaving just as soon as Graham can fix the satellite dish."

"What's that?"

"You know, the dishes you see hanging on the side of buildings sometimes? They can be used to receive signals. Electronic signals."

Understanding dawned. Kyle glanced at the dusty bank of computers with renewed interest and Amelia nodded.

"That one still works." She pointed and Kyle saw a monitor on the far end that had been swept clear of dirt although the screen was dark.

"There's information on there?"

Amelia nodded "We're going to send it out. Graham – the one you were… holding is – *was* – an engineer before the Fall. He's been working on the communications stuff for a week."

"Why were you all out in the woods?" Kyle wondered.

Amelia stayed silent.

"The refugees?" he guessed.

She started "You know about them?" then she sat back, a dark look crossing her features "Of course. You were with Lynch. Did Armstrong send you?"

Kyle shrugged, not wanting to give too much away.

"Sent his dog out to do his dirty work as usual." Amelia grimaced, staring out the door.

Kyle did not want to think about Lynch or the fight in the woods and a question was pressing him "What's on the computers?"

"Data."

"About what?"

Amelia gave him a flat stare.

"About the mutation?"

Her eyes widened in surprise "Why do you ask that?"

Kyle shrugged "Logic. A Pre-Fall facility which is worth getting people killed over? Data on computers that haven't been used for twenty years? It's got to be the virus. What is this, a laboratory?"

Amelia nodded looking impressed "The Beijerink Institute of Virology. The government researched the virus here in the last days before the Fall."

"And?"

Another shrug "We found some stuff."

"To do with the mutation?"

She hesitated before nodding "Yes. It's not what we hoped – or rather if it *is* then we aren't qualified enough to interpret it."

"I don't suppose you found a cure?" There was a hint of hopeful sarcasm in his voice.

She smiled sadly "No. No cure. We might have some treatments to slow the Infection though. And a test." She added almost as an afterthought.

"We can already treat it! Dr May has been doing that for years."

"Dr May?" Amelia narrowed her eyes "I thought you were from Matwood?"

"I'm from Holden. You know Dr May?"

"I trained with her before she left the city." Amelia smiled "She's probably the best doctor in the world."

"You're a doctor?"

"That's right."

"That's why you're here." It made sense. Kyle suddenly realised. His mind raced with an understanding of the complex web forming before him. Rangers, Ferals, Zeks and this clever young doctor risking her life, losing friends all to scrape data off these ancient machines "How did you find out about this place? It's been here for twenty years, you aren't going to pretend you just stumbled across it."

She watched him with the ghost of a smile on her lips, silent.

Kyle rolled his eyes "Let me guess, it's a secret?"

"These are dangerous times for Zeks. You saw that for yourself."

"Fine." Kyle shook his head "I don't know, someone tipped you off probably. Was it one of the refugees?"

The same silent hint of a smile.

A thought occurred to him "Did they release the mutation from here?" instantly he shook his head "No, of course not. That's stupid. The mutation was in France."

Amelia sat forward, a burning intensity in her eyes "Did Armstrong tell you that? That it came from France?"

"Clearly it did. Why else would they be fleeing?"

"Did he say where?"

"No." Kyle frowned, remembering Jas's words "Why would he know that?"

Amelia shook her head and rolled her eyes "Forget it. I bet you wouldn't tell me if you knew."

"Probably not." Kyle nodded.

"I bet that Armstrong didn't tell you he released the mutation?" she shot back with a sly look on her face.

Kyle gaped at her "Rubbish. Why would a Ranger do that?"

"Hah!" shouted Amelia but there was no humour in her voice "Look around, the place is swimming in refugees! People he swore for the past twenty years were dead! You know how Armstrong proved that Europe was dead? He went there! Time and again for two decades he's been zipping across the channel in his helicopters!" she was on her feet, emotion blushing her cheeks "So answer me this, Kyle! What's he been doing over there?"

Kyle shook his head "A thousand things. Scouting, scavenging, training. Who knows? That doesn't mean he released a Feral mutation!"

Amelia crossed the room to stand before him, her cheeks flushed "Do you know what we found here? They tried to treat the virus before the Fall! They tried to fix it! You know what they managed? A mutation. A mutation that sped up the rate of decomposition in the Infected! It made them die faster but, in the meantime, some of them turned Feral!"

"So the Ferals will what – burn themselves out?"

"No." Amelia seemed to calm down "No, they just linger. Whatever we found here is two decades out of date. Or I just can't read it."

"You aren't a virologist." Kyle murmured.

Amelia had turned away but looked back sharply at him "That's an awfully long word for a Militiaman from Holden."

"It's what my parents did."

"What?" Amelia stepped closed to him again "Are they in Holden? Do they know –"

"They're dead." Kyle stated flatly "Killed during the Fall."

"Oh…" she looked awkward "I'm sorry."

Kyle shrugged.

"Anyway –" Amelia seemed keen to change the subject "Armstrong sent you out to hunt refugees?"

Kyle grunted.

She looked at him measuredly "You don't look like a murderer, Kyle."

"I'm not!" he protested "I didn't think…"

She made a sympathetic face "Blake Armstrong impressed you, did he?"

Kyle looked at her stonily "I came to Matwood to get ammunition for my town. We were attacked by a Horde and shot through most of our supply. Armstrong said he'd give us some if I agreed to help Lynch."

"Help him kill refugees?"

"He said they were Infected, that they were carrying the mutation…" Kyle's words sounded foolish to his own ears.

Amelia was looking at him with a face like iron "How very naive of you."

An awkward silence. Kyle felt he should look abashed but he didn't want to concede weakness so he met her gaze.

After a moment she sighed, gesturing at the stairs through the door "Shall we get some air?"

CHAPTER 30

The gates of Holden were lined with wall guards, weapons trained on the dark clad Zeks who had trailed Rosie at a distance. The guards looked menacing but Rosie knew they didn't have the ammunition to hold off a determined assault.

Eric had been stripped of his weapons and armour although the Mayor had ordered Rosie not to tie his hands. Indeed, Elizabeth Friend looked anxious and nervous. She'd ordered Fabian reunited with Eric at once and the two had greeted each other fondly. Fabian now stood a step behind and to the side of Eric as the council and most of the town gathered to hear what his fate might be.

Rosie had recounted the events that had transpired in the woods and the council, even Terrence, were now looking mutinously at Eric as they conferred.

"Why have you brought armed men to our land?" The Mayor's voice was harsh.

"We didn't mean to threaten you. We were trying to lead the Infected away from Holden." Eric spoke clearly and met the Mayor's eyes. Rosie noted that he used the word 'Infected' instead of calling them Fallen. That was a military term and she narrowed her eyes.

"Rubbish!" Terrence growled and rose to his feet "The Wretches have been in our land ever since the Fall. We're perfectly capable of dealing with them! When Zeks have passed this way, they've been unarmed." He pointed an accusatory finger at Eric "You're leading an army here. You're here for war."

"Thirty men is hardly an army." Eric repeated the words he'd spoken to Rosie in the clearing.

"It's enough to take over a town." Rosie spoke up for the first time "You've got automatic weapons, explosives, and enough supplies to live out for weeks. You're here for war!"

"Hear, hear!" where had Terrence's voice been when he was calling for her dismissal? Now he was standing alongside her, united in the face of a common threat.

The Mayor cut across the hubbub of muttering that had broken out "You're not telling us the full truth." She accused Eric "At least have the decency to admit that."

Eric nodded "I have nothing to hide. You haven't given me a chance to tell you the full truth." He waited, looking at the Mayor and ignoring Terrence and Rosie.

The Mayor gestured for him to continue. The crowd of Holdenites had fallen silent.

"I came to the southeast with a group of Zeks. Some are my troops that you saw outside. You're right, most Zeks aren't armed. They believe in protecting the lives of the Infected in the hopes that a cure will one day end the virus. That particular aim has never been my own. I had reports of certain events in the area and I brought my troops here to determine the truth of the rumours. I didn't know that Blake Armstrong was in Matwood. He heard I was here and we were contacted."

Rosie caught the meaning in his words and she frowned "You mean 'contact' in the military sense? You're saying Major Armstrong attacked you?"

Eric nodded "The Rangers lured a Horde towards us. We managed to get away but then it turned towards Holden and we got separated from one another in the attempt to redirect its progress."

"If you know Major Armstrong then who are you?" The Mayor demanded.

"Eric Forbes. I used to be Colonel Eric Forbes before I left the army."

The muttering reached a crescendo. A soldier? The Mayor was raising her hands for quiet.

"Why did you leave the army?"

"Because what Blake Armstrong is doing is foolish. We can't continue fighting the Infected until every one of us is dead. We don't have the men or the weapons to continue. We've been at war for twenty years and our population is shrinking every year. The Zeks have worked to find a cure – or a scientific method to destroy the virus. It's the only way. I told my superiors this in the army and in response, they gave Armstrong and the Rangers more control and resources than ever. And so, I left. My troops left with me and we joined the Zeks."

People were openly arguing in the crowd now. Dogs, slipping between people's feet were whining and more than one had started barking. The Mayor was trying again for silence but no-one was listening. Rosie waited for it all to die down, her mind set on scepticism but to her surprise, Terrence rose to his feet again.

"I say, we tie these two up and send them to Matwood! We need resources! If these men have fought with the Rangers, then Major Armstrong will reward us for delivering them to him! If we let him go, Armstrong will punish us. We can't survive another attack like the last!"

The Mayor rounded on Terrence, her eyes burning "Enough! Sit down!"

Terrence sat, his face a shade of puce.

"If you send us to Matwood, Blake Armstrong will have us shot." Eric stated calmly "Please don't do that."

"What were the rumours that you heard?" the Mayor tried to take back the initiative "The ones that you came here to follow?"

Eric gazed at her "They weren't just rumours. There were reports of people crossing the channel and landing on the shore just south of here. I found some of them."

"From *France*?" Rosie's voice came out several tones louder than she'd meant. It was a mark of how shocking Eric's statement was that no-one looked at her.

Eric nodded "Blake Armstrong has been claiming for twenty years that we're alone. No-one else has been able to cross the channel to verify that. I thought if I could find evidence of this and bring it back to London then I could discredit him."

Rosie could see the Mayor was fidgeting nervously and she remembered Mason's earlier words. She swallowed the derisive retort she'd loaded and glanced from the Mayor to the wall guard commander. She sensed a danger in the air that she didn't understand. A feeling that there were powers here that were greater than those she could face with a rifle in her hands.

The Mayor seemed to have made a decision "We don't want to get caught up in a struggle between Zeks and Rangers. What do you want from us?"

"Want?" Eric looked surprised "I want you to let me go so I can find a live refugee to take back to London."

There was a titter in the gathered crowd.

Mason, the wall commander addressed Eric "You attacked our troops in the woods. What guarantee do we have that you won't attack us? We need some sort of deal."

Eric gave a small shrug "Attacking you isn't my aim. I've got – as you say – thirty men and they're well-armed. Your walls are tough but they're built to keep out the Infected, not a determined assault. I'm sure I could order my troops to attack and perhaps we'd succeed in killing most of your guards and Militia but in the process, I'd lose half my troops and these are my friends. They'll follow me but I have no desire to commit suicide nor would I want to be in control of your town! What benefit would that bring me?"

Mason leaned close to Rosie "We don't have the ammunition to keep them out. He's right, though. We'll wipe out more than half his troops. The watchtowers alone will kill a dozen. Plus, we've got those NLAW's in the armoury."

Rosie nodded, remembering the cache of military grade weapons that they'd scavenged first from the American airbase and then from police and army depots in the region. There were plenty of weapons in Holden, there just wasn't enough stuff to shoot out of them.

"I say, we take them to Matwood!" Terrence did not rise from his chair to speak.

Jason, the barman from the Ridged Back shouted out from the crowd "How are you going to get them to Matwood? His blokes outside aren't just going to stand idly by and let you take him."

Terrence blinked several times. Rosie nodded at Jason. It was a good point. The Mayor seemed to agree because she abruptly turned to the council.

"I want to set them free. We let them go and trust them to leave our lands. Then we can send our own patrols out to see about these refugees. We can vote if you like but that's my opinion. If anyone disagrees and has a better suggestion –" her eyes bored into Terrence "- speak up now."

Terrence said nothing. Jason had shown the foolishness of his plan and Rosie could see that there was no real alternative. She nodded, accepting reality and was the first to speak up "Let them go."

Mason quickly echoed her words and one by one, the council acquiesced. Eric, sensible to the conflict he was causing, said nothing, waiting patiently with Fabian.

The Mayor was staring the council down when the suddenly quiet air was shattered by the shrill clanging of the alarm bell followed by the voice of a sentry roaring so loudly his voice could be heard clear across the four quarters of Holden.

"We have sign! We have SIGN! Man the walls! It's a Horde!"

CHAPTER 31

"May-juh." Lynch's voice never rose above a calm tone, at odds with the crackling tones of his commander on the other end of the radio conversation.

"*Report.*"

"Frosty been captured by the Zeks."

There was silence. Gault shifted nervously next to Lynch. Ahead of them, the ivy covered walls of the Beijerink Institute loomed. Around the two Rangers, a cluster of half a dozen of Lynch's most trusted men crouched in the shade of the trees that concealed them, summoned by the radio that Lynch now used to speak directly with Armstrong.

"*Lynch? Clean this mess up.*"

The line went dead.

Lynch checked his rifle and without a word, stood up and began to move towards the building. The others followed, dark shadows against the ground.

*

Amelia led Kyle through the darkened corridors of the Institute. On the way, he scooped up the body armour and rifle that had been taken from him, drawing some small comfort from the familiar tools of his trade. He was impressed at Amelia's athleticism as she led him up the flights of stairs two steps at a time. Here and there, a stained window allowed a shaft of light in and Kyle, peering through the grubby glass could make out overgrown lawns surrounding the ivy covered walls of the Institute.

Ten or maybe twelve floors up – Kyle was grateful Sinks was

not there to grill him on how he'd failed to count properly – Amelia led him down a long, gloomy corridor. At the far end, Kyle could see daylight and as they approached, he could see that time or weather had caused one section of the roof to collapse inwards, opening this end of the corridor to the elements and forming a rickety if serviceable ramp to the roof.

"Watch your footing…" Amelia began to walk up the sloping roof, her own booted feet testing each section carefully before she applied her full weight. Kyle followed a few metres behind, placing his feet exactly where she trod. They emerged onto a flat, wide roof, bordered by a low parapet about the height of Kyle's thighs. Everywhere, the signs of two decades of neglect were visible.

But it was the cluster of Zeks gathered around a large, well rusted metal dish that drew Kyle's attention. Graham, the unfortunate man Kyle had threatened just a short while ago had stripped his thick coat off despite the strong wind that caught them at this height. A cluster of tools were gathered around him and the other Zeks – Kyle recognised Molly – were standing apparently as silent helpers.

As they approached, Graham glanced back under his armpit before ignoring them and continuing to twist and fiddle.

"Any joy?" Amelia called when they were just a few feet away.

"He's getting somewhere." Molly looked cold, her hands shoved firmly in her pockets.

"Good. Alright, Graham?"

Graham grunted in response before easing himself out from where he leaned against the ancient metal.

"It's alright – a couple more bits before we can test the power circuits. It *should* send the data but it'll take a couple of hours to transmit."

"Alright." Amelia sounded unhappy. Kyle sympathised. If he were her, he'd want to leave too.

Molly shivered and glanced at Kyle before asking Amelia "Any sign of the Rangers?"

"Nothing from the lookouts." Amelia turned back to Graham "What about the power source? You said that might be down in the basement."

"Oh – " Graham nodded and stepped a half dozen paces along a pair of brightly coloured electrical wires that led to a small mast at the very edge of the building. Reaching it, he tugged open a small door revealing a complex looking array of switches and more wires. Kyle gaped at the intricacy of it, impressed at Graham's ability to interpret the tangle.

"You fixed it?" enthused Amelia, seeing the pleased expression on Graham's face.

"You're bloody right I did! Found a wire that had been chewed by a mouse or something. It was sitting in a puddle of rainwater. Shorted the whole thing out!" Graham eased himself to lean back against the concrete parapet of the roof, settling in with a pensive look on his face. Kyle braced himself for what promised to be a long winded explanation but instead, he threw himself flat, dragging Amelia down beside him as the air was torn by the sound of automatic gunfire. He had a horrified glimpse of Graham's body being shredded by the bullets, his frame jerking spastically and then Kyle was pressing his face against the weathered roof, trying his hardest not to die.

*

Lynch's wide eyes stared at the figure on the roof as the gunner to his right murdered the man. Without breaking his gaze, he stabbed a finger in the direction of the Institute and the Rangers around him surged forward into the building, racing up the stairs to find their prey.

*

That same odd silence that had filled the woods after Lynch and Gault had ceased firing came to Kyle's ears. It wasn't a silence, he realised in an odd moment of understanding, simply a return to normality after the unnatural invasion of gunfire. Now that it stopped, he was aware of other sounds. Molly screaming Graham's name and trying to half crawl, half run across the roof.

"No!" Kyle roared, seizing her foot, and dragging her to the ground. As if in response, another burst of gunfire tore into the concrete parapet, spraying them all with fragments.

Next to him, Amelia had her hands over her head and had gone pale beneath her dark skin.

"We need to move!" Kyle snapped at her.

"Graham!" shouted Molly again.

Graham was plainly dead. His body was slumped against the remnants of the parapet and great chunks of flesh had been blasted from his torso. Kyle remembered the man's soft tones as he was led blindfolded and felt a flash of sorrow at the injustice of his death.

"Is it the Rangers?" shouted Molly.

"It doesn't matter!" roared Kyle as another barrage of bullets was fired. He guessed the rounds were being fired from below them, the shooter firing up at the roof from the ground. That was why Graham had been the target, the first one to present his silhouette over the parapet. He remembered the roof where he and Amelia had come up and gulped at the thought of the machine gun causing the top of the building to collapse "We need to get off the roof!"

Amelia nodded in agreement and Kyle turned, beginning a weird, awkward crawl across the roof back to the collapsed section. His knees and elbows scraped painfully but he kept moving, staying low.

Kyle slid down the makeshift ramp, rifle now in both hands. He peered into the gloom of the corridor, willing his eyes to adjust to the light.

Stillness.

Silence.

Then panting and warm bodies joined him as Molly and Amelia slid down to him.

"What about the others?" Amelia asked.

"Others?"

"There's a dozen Zeks around the building –"

More gunshots sounded, these muted by the building. Kyle's head twitched left and right as he tried to work out the source "Rifles."

"That's not from inside the building though?" Amelia was straining to listen too.

"I don't think so. Were your people inside?"

"Some. Some are in the grounds."

"Anyone armed?"

Amelia's stony expression told him all he needed to know and Kyle cursed.

"There's a second staircase. It's the far end of the building though. We'd have to pass the one we came up to get there."

"Fine." Kyle made his decision "Is there another exit?"

"The computer room – it had a fire escape."

"Let's go then!"

Kyle led the way, running whilst simultaneously trying to make as little sound as possible. He strained his ears for any sound of their attackers but there was nothing but the sound of their own breathing rebounding from the walls. At each stair, he leaned over the banister, aiming his rifle down but the staircase was empty.

Down a flight, check. Down another flight, check. Kyle's pulse pounded in his ears and adrenaline surged within him. He jumped as Amelia passed one of the clearer windows and her shadow moved in front of him. He cursed inwardly, willing himself to be calm.

"Come on!" Amelia had reached the bottom level. Kyle elbowed her back and forced his way past her, leaning cautiously out to peer over his rifle's sights down the corridor. Then, he reversed his body, checking the other direction.

"Clear!"

Amelia didn't move and Kyle resisted the urge to roll his eyes at the lack of training. How much more confident he'd feel if

Rosie or Sinks were next to him instead of Amelia Singh! She hadn't even drawn her pistol and he hissed at her to unholster it.

They reached the top of the flight of stairs that led to the computer room and Kyle, eyeing a hefty filing cabinet nodded to Molly. Together they managed to tug the furniture in front of the door, barely hiding the entrance which they clicked shut behind them. Amelia produced a key from inside her Zek coat and turned it in the lock.

Back into the computer room with its narrow yellow strip lights. Molly was fussing, caught between the computer and the fire exit that Kyle could now see in the far corner of the room.

"Leave it!" Amelia hissed.

"We can't just abandon it! The tests... Maybe we could commit it to memory?" Molly was frantic. Her hands tapped the keys and the screen lit up with the odd blueish light of Pre-Fall technology. Kyle began to examine the fire escape, seeing the metal bar. He gave it an experimental push and the lock clicked but the door stayed shut. He leaned against it, slowly pressing his shoulder into the hard surface and it moved an inch.

Daylight cracked around the edge as Amelia and Molly bickered in whispers. Kyle peered out to see the fire exit opened into a lowered section of the grounds with a brick wall forming the edge of a small walkway that surrounded the building like a moat. Atop the wall, he could see the long grass that filled the grounds of the Institute.

Stillness.

Kyle shut the door again, confident he could now force it open. He glanced once at the two Zeks and in a rush of callousness, he was furious at their weakness. Who were they to run around in Wretch territory with only a single pistol? Who were they to tie him up, imprison him and now bring their enemies to his door? He bared his teeth as anger flashed through him and just for a moment, Kyle had a burning desire to kick the door open, sprint for the woods and leave them to their fate. It was what they deserved! But, as though sensing his ire, Amelia turned to him and called his name "Kyle..."

"What?"

"Do you have any paper?"

Kyle did, a small notepad he always kept in his pocket. Before he could consider that he'd been about to abandon the two Zeks, he was unzipping the pocket, crossing the floor, and handing it to Amelia.

"Thanks..." she turned back to the screen.

"How the hell did you even find this place?" It was a rhetorical question, borne out of frustration at their predicament but to Kyle's surprise, Amelia answered in a distracted tone, hastily scribbling figures down.

"It was an anonymous message to the Zeks. It said there was data relating to the virus stored in these machines..."

Squinting, Kyle peered at the weird collection of dots and colours that filled the space behind the glass. Pre-Fall technology always fascinated him. Indeed, he and Rosie had once discovered a house a few miles from Holden which for reasons they couldn't fathom had working power and a DVD collection. They'd sat in front of the wonderfully radiant images for hours until Sinks had radioed furiously to demand they report. He wondered how it must have felt to sit and work here for hours or days at a time without having to worry about Wretches or where the next meal was coming from.

Ice flooded Kyle's veins as he saw something on the screen, something that shut down the urge to flee that had filled his mind since the first machine gun rounds had torn into Graham. He pointed at the screen with his left hand whilst his right gripped Amelia's shoulder hard enough to stop her mid-sentence.

"Why is my name on there?"

Frost

Before Amelia could answer, a sound echoed down the stairs, through the locked doors of their feeble sanctuary. The screeching of rusted metal on concrete as someone slowly dragged the filing cabinet aside to reveal their sanctuary.

*

Amelia crossed to the door and flipped a switch. The dirty yellow light went out. No-one moved. Molly pushed a button and the screen went black although Kyle could still hear the hum of the computer. It sounded impossibly loud in the sudden silence.

The screeching sound came again. Kyle could imagine that someone had pulled the cabinet partially aside out of curiosity and was now levering it fully away from the door. He and Molly had moved it silently together without much effort which meant that only one of their pursuers had discovered them.

There was a click as Kyle flicked off his safety catch. The room was now pitch dark without a single source of light. He aimed the rifle at where he thought the door had been, realising the futility of his action. If he fired, not only would he probably miss but he'd draw the attention of any other attackers. They had no idea how many there were and he shook his head at the situation.

Replacing his safety catch, Kyle groped in the dark, finding Amelia's shoulder. He gripped her head and pulled her ear towards his mouth.

"Can you get to the exit? I'll cover you both."

"Yes..." he heard the faint response in his own ear and then she was moving, gently pushing past him into the pitch darkness. He tried to see what she was doing but he could make out nothing. Not wanting to lose his sense of direction, he faced the door once again.

A stab of yellow light lanced under the entryway. The torch swept back and forth and then the door shook as someone tried the handle. To Kyle's horror, the bolt rattled loudly as though it were loose in its socket. Silently, Kyle cursed the black dressed idiots who could bring a twenty year old computer to life but couldn't fix a simple lock. He held his breath as the door remained sealed.

A click over to his right and more light, this time the white of daylight. Kyle could see Amelia by the fire exit, beckoning to him.

Molly was still hovering by the computer, clearly torn.

"Leave it!" Amelia hissed, almost inaudibly "We've got the test!"

The Zek tore herself away, finally moving to join Amelia. Kyle went last, rifle still trained on the entrance.

"Come on!" Molly had vanished through the exit and Amelia was holding it open for Kyle. He looked at the door once more, just in time to see the lock rattle again as the intruder put their shoulder to it with some force. A grunt of pain sounded from the other side.

He squeezed out past Amelia who pressed the exit shut behind her, holding the last few inches tightly with her fingers and easing the lock closed with barely a click. Kyle's rifle was pointing to the long grass above them, trying to cover any possible angle for an ambush but Amelia was already moving, aware that they were sitting ducks if they were attacked here.

"Come on! We need to get to the woods!" Amelia had the handgun out again and had pushed her way to the front. Molly crouched close behind her.

Along the narrow pathway until they reached a set of rusty rungs set into the bricks. Clearly the last of the escape route. Amelia began to climb before Kyle could insist that he went first and she paused at the top before slithering into the weeds on her belly. A moment later, her head appeared looking back over the drop at them and she beckoned them up.

Kyle followed Molly, sliding over the lip of the ladder to find they were crouched in the long grass of the overgrown lawns surrounding the Institute. Ahead, looming temptingly close were the first trees of a dense patch of woodland.

"Those woods go on for a couple of miles." Amelia was pointing "We can lose them in there."

"It's a long bloody way." Kyle pointed "Four hundred metres? That's ninety seconds on this terrain. Maybe be longer."

Amelia gritted her teeth but there was no other option. The grass was overgrown but it wasn't so long that it would conceal their movements across the entire distance. Besides, if their attackers went to the roof or looked out any window on this side of the building, they'd have a clear shot and would be able to pick them off.

"We can do it." Molly was muttering. Kyle could see no other option.

At that moment, a black coated figure erupted out of the weeds at the far end of the building, a hundred or so metres to their left. Sprinting flat out, the Zek covered the distance to the trees, weaving and bobbing to avoid imagined rifle fire.

"That's Greg!" Molly hissed.

"Bloody hell, come on! It's our only chance!" Kyle snapped and he shoved Molly and Amelia before him, breaking into a flat out run.

Kyle intentionally outstripped the two Zeks, grateful for once for the hours of running Sinks had forced them all to do. He was as fit as any other Militia and he used the extra speed to stride ahead before abruptly turning around, raising his rifle to scan the building and cover the Zeks, searching for movement. There was nothing and he mentally willed the attackers to stay inside until they reached the tree line.

Amelia was now close to the treeline and so he turned, sprinting madly after her. He caught up to Molly who had lagged behind, grabbing her by the elbow and cajoling "Come on! Hurry up!"

Amelia vanished into the trees and Kyle closed the last few meters. He turned to Molly to rally her for the last effort as she slowed, panting and gasping at the exertion.

"Come on! We're not bloody there yet!"

He was drawing breath to urge the woman again when the Feral erupted out of the woods and leapt onto him.

CHAPTER 32

"A Horde!"

The guard who had sounded the alarm was going hoarse from shouting the words over and over. Rosie, sprinting to the gate bellowed at the man to shut up. Mason, panting at her quick pace had caught up to her and was shouting commands, moving his men into position. The squeak of handcarts moving filled the air as Jane McDonald emptied what was left in the armoury. Dogs, barking and howling sprinted left and right, an unmistakable sign that Wretches were nearby.

"Rosie!" an unfamiliar voice shouted and she half turned to see Eric hurrying up, his face ashen.

"Get the hell out the way, Zek!"

"My men are out there! Let them in! They'll be torn apart!" Eric bounded past Rosie. She lurched after him, thinking he was heading for the gate but the Zek hauled himself up to the top of the container wall, jumping onto the fire step. Rosie cleared the wall a second behind him and leaned on the corrugated iron of the parapet to see the platoon of Zeks were clustered in the scant shelter of Holden's walls.

Staring at the tide of grey death that poured out of the woods.

"Christ!" it was the Mayor. She'd followed and now saw the predicament. She shook her head, either in denial that the Zeks fate was her problem or that their predicament was real. Time slowed for a moment in Rosie's mind as she registered the threat and thrust emotion aside to allow cold, hard logic to take control.

"Open the gate! Open the gate and let them in!" she roared to the guards who stared at her open mouthed and unmoving.

Rosie swore at them foully and leapt off the wall, reaching the lever and pulley mechanism that lifted the hefty gate from its concrete trough.

"Alright! I'm doing it!" the operator shoved her aside, manipulating the controls so the gate lifted two feet. Rosie went flat on her belly, rifle pointing through the space as black dressed figures began to roll, crawl and scrabble under, the terror of the Wretches driving them forwards.

"Bloody hell, Rosie!" shouted the Mayor from the top of the wall but the threat had ceased to be tribal in Rosie's mind. No longer were they Zek and Militia. Now they were human and Wretch. It was a matter of species against species and thirty well-armed allies might just sway the day in their favour.

The gate crashed down, sealing Holden against the Horde and the guards instantly began stacking sandbags against the inside, bracing the weakest point in the town's walls.

Rosie made for the wall again, where Mason and the Mayor stood. Someone reached a hand down to help her up and she saw Eric, a look of comradeship passing between them.

"Thanks."

"Don't thank me. Maybe I just gave the Horde a smaller target to get at."

Eric grimaced, turning to shout orders to his men, breaking them down into four sections, one to cover each wall. He told them to accept the orders of the section commanders and the troops moved off, as professional as any Rosie had ever seen.

"Estimate?" she called up to the nearest watchtower.

"Four hundred!" came the shout.

"Four hundred!" Eric echoed "Is that it? We can take four hundred!"

"I thought Zeks didn't kill the Wretches?" the Mayor shouted.

"We bloody do when it's us or them!" snapped the former Colonel "Where are your weapons?"

"Here they come." The handcarts had reached the north

wall, always the last to receive their arms. Rosie stared in horror at the pitifully small piles of ammunition. She couldn't help but think of the last time she'd fought here, side by side with Kyle and she felt a pang of loss at his absence.

Rifles were handed out and the Horde surged towards them. Rosie gave orders and the sharpshooters in the towers began to pick off the faster Wretches.

"They can't get over the walls. We're going to be fine." The voice was Mason's. He was wringing his hands nervously and Rosie caught his arm, squeezing him hard.

"Oi, get a grip."

He looked down as though surprised to see her holding him. He smiled, nodding although his colour was still bad.

"How about you tell them to get some tea on, yeah? Gonna be a long day." Rosie indicated the gate guards who were now standing still, unable to bring their shotguns to bear.

Mason nodded and stepped to the edge of the wall to give the orders. Rosie watched him and gave a nod of satisfaction.

She began to turn back to the wall but caught sight of Eric and, knowing his expertise may well be the difference between life and death, took a step towards him but was intercepted by Zachary, the silver haired Zek who had appeared from nowhere.

"Thank you! Thank you! Please, try to be gentle with them..."

Rosie shook him off, ignoring the stupidity of his request. She reached Eric and began to speak but he cut her off, pointing.

She stared, incredulous at the monstrous shapes she'd only been able to hear as noises in the darkness the last time they'd swept over Holden.

Helicopters! Rangers! They were saved!

Eric's face was like iron as the two choppers beat a slow path through the sky towards the stricken town.

"The Rangers!" the shout went up from all the men and women who lined the town walls. Cheers and whistles sounded as the dogs barked and howled.

"They must have come from Matwood!" Rosie babbled to Eric, filled with the utter, whole body relief that only comes from someone who has been spared a death sentence. To her surprise, the Zek seemed close to panic.

"The other night – they weren't trying to help you! They damaged the wall, didn't they? They were trying to shoot Zachary and his men!"

As Rosie began to scoff Eric grabbed her arm hard enough to hurt and shook her "You said you had heavy weapons! Get them, now! They've seen us come in, they won't hesitate to attack if it wipes us out!"

"Sod off!" Rosie snarled, pushing the weather beaten Zek away and turning as the two helicopters, squat, ugly shapes painted a drab olive green hovered above the ground. From here, Rosie could see the rearmost Wretches drawn towards the sound of the choppers and she nodded at the simplicity of the Rangers techniques.

The jubilance turned to a frown of confusion as the two birds moved closer to Holden. The sound of their engines increased and she squinted, wondering what the pilots were thinking.

Someone moved to lean on the parapet next to her and she saw Zachary, his face a mask of hatred glaring up at the Rangers.

Then the helicopters were turning, one behind the other swinging round to fly along the north wall in a slow arc. Rosie stared at them, waiting for the Rangers to reveal their motives, to see them pull a surprise manoeuvre which would see the Horde flee their land and the threat vanish.

Instead, her eyes were drawn to the side door of the first helicopter where a cluster of figures leaned out, heedless of the downdraught of the rotors. All, she saw, were Rangers, their distinctive uniform visible even at this distance. And there, in the centre, surely that was Major Armstrong? Her heart did a backflip as her eyes landed on the man whose face she'd only seen on posters. She felt an urge to wave but instantly thought that would look foolish and anyway, Armstrong was staring at the defenders on the wall with a cold, expressionless face.

"Oh – Zachary!" Eric's voice was urgent and loud enough that Rosie heard it over the sound of the helicopters. Eric lurched sideways into the silver haired Zek but he misjudged the distance and instead sprawled, one hand clutching Zachary's foot.

She didn't hear the shot although she saw the rifle flash. She heard the crack as the bullet struck Zachary and as she turned in horror to see him fall the warm, repulsive spray of blood from his neck covered her face and she recoiled in disgust.

The action likely saved her life. She was dimly aware of an enormous noise, something so loud that her ears seemed to dim the sound into a dull thump which resonated through her body, shaking her bones within her and a second later she was flying through the air, the stink of wet earth and smoke filling her nostrils as the world spun madly.

She crashed off the container wall, hitting the ground hard and landing in a heap.

The world swam before her eyes, smoke and screams filling her senses. Something flew above her, loud and roaring and spitting death from all sides. The booming of the explosion seemed to be coming from the flying beast, a continuous shuddering thump that shook Rosie's entire body.

The helicopter passed, whipping up loose leaves and grass in its wake. Someone seized Rosie roughly under the arm and Rosie looked blearily up at Eric, one side of his face soaked in blood. His lips were moving and his eyes wide but Rosie could hear nothing over the pounding din.

"...up!"

Rosie was suddenly filled with the burning need to stand and move and as she lurched the Zek hauled her upright.

Before her, lay carnage.

People, her neighbours and friends lay torn and scattered amongst the shattered remnants of the north wall. Survivors, covered in blood tried to haul their wounded comrades back. Already, someone was shouting that the wall was breached and that the gate guards should bring sandbags. But the gate guards were a tangle of such bloody horror that Rosie could hardly identify them as human. The orders were being given, but there was no-one to complete the tasks.

"The wall!" she tried to croak but her throat was dry and her voice cracked. Eric hefted her, shouting something she couldn't hear to someone she couldn't see. A dog, the great scarred brute she'd led into the forest came to her side, placing his predator's body between her and the outside.

Outside...

As Rosie's mind began to clear she could see what had happened. The second helicopter had launched a rocket and struck the gate, shattering the wall on both sides in the process.

"Why?" she croaked again but now Eric was handing her to other arms, two of his men were there, dragging her away and she struggled, the dazedness leaving her mind.

"Form a barricade!" Eric was trying to direct the survivors to block the spaces between the buildings, to stem the inevitable. Because there was no denying the truth. The Horde was out there and Holden's great walls were breached.

"Eric!" she shouted, staggering away from the Zeks. She discovered her rifle was still attached to her and moved it into the correct position, the familiarity lending some confidence to her "Eric!" she called again. The Zek turned, questioning "Use the handcarts! Block the gaps – we have drills for this!"

Eric began to direct his men, using the handcarts that had carried the rifles from the armoury to the north wall. Rosie's eyes, wide and staring rested for the briefest moment on the twisted body of a child who had pushed the cart. She turned away, knowing she could not help.

A clattering roar and every face turned skywards to see a helicopter swinging overhead in a mad turn. Gunfire burst from the chopper and a Zek, a few metres from Rosie was lifted off his feet, a great wet spray of meat torn from his side and he plunged to the ground. A second later, a Militiaman, eyes wide with shock ran over the corpse and stumbled. As he tripped, another burst caught him and tore him almost in half. The chopper swung low and Rosie could see now the man crouching behind the machine gun, firing short controlled bursts, firing *at* the people in Holden. Not the Wretches on the outside, but firing at the people.

Why?

"Where now?" Eric was asking her. Rosie looked wildly around for someone else to ask, the Mayor, Mason or even Terrence but they were nowhere to be seen. The Mayor had been on the wall next to her when the missile struck and that meant...

Rosie turned to the people around her. Holdenites or Zeks, it didn't matter "Block the streets! You! Go to the south wall and tell them we need ten more rifles here, the north wall is breached! You two – move that cart and block that street! Come on people! We're not dead yet!"

The machine gunner was out of sight, the helicopter moving out of range to set up another attack run but the second bird was now swooping along the north wall. As Rosie shouted orders, she heard a weird hissing sound fill the air and a jet of smoke shot away from the chopper, impacting in a burst of flame at the base of the north tower. Rosie heard the sharpshooter at the top let out a piercing yell of fear and she watched in horror as the tower toppled and fell. She heard the crash as it struck the ground and then stared stupidly at the empty space it had once filled.

A second hiss, another impossible explosion and then fire was burning her face again and she was flat in the mud a second time, this time with Eric sprawled next to her. This time she was on her feet again in a second, coughing against the acrid smoke and burning heat only to see the handcarts they'd shoved into crude barriers were scattered, torn into kindling and the brief sanctuary they'd provided, gone. It was then that the enormity of the truth struck her. The wall was breached, the gate had fallen. A gap in the barrier that sealed Holden. A mortal wound in the wall that had guarded Rosie her entire life.

Rosie stared through the shattered remnants of the gate, over the scene of torn corpses and dying defenders that littered the entrance to the small town. There, the last remnants of the cornfield being trampled beneath their feet, was a grey tide of dead faces, the Horde, coming to claim the town as the protection of the wall was finally removed and the inevitable happened.

Rosie felt tears well in her eyes and her stomach churn as she saw death coming towards her. She felt movement by her side and half turned to see Eric beside her. He looked down at her as she looked up at him and she saw the resignation in his eyes. The sounds of the Horde reached her ears, the terrible shrieking cry of the Wretches. Eric's weather-beaten face twisted into a wry smile at the sheer inevitability of it all and for a single second of clarity, Rosie wished that it was Kyle's face she could see as she died.

Before them, the grey wave of the dead poured like a tsunami. The dogs growled and barked their fury, ridges quivering as the Wretches moved like an inevitable tide. Overhead, the helicopters hovered, their part done. A crackling voice sounded from it, inaudible to the men and women below.

"... Mission complete... Target destroyed...."

After a few minutes, the two choppers swung away, leaving the small town to die.

CHAPTER 33

Kyle went down hard. The Feral had hit him in the chest and he was winded but he rolled quickly, snatching a look at the black eyed beast in time to see it leap forward again. He raised the rifle, thumb slipping on the safety but the Wretch grabbed the weapon and tugged and in horror, Kyle watched as the sling was torn off and the weapon went skittering away into the wild grass.

"Kyle!" he heard a shout and a brief feeling of relief struck him as he heard Amelia fire her pistol. But then the Feral was on him and he desperately flung an arm up, raising both feet to fling the Wretch over his head. It landed snarling a few feet away and rounded on him immediately.

How had Amelia not hit the thing yet? Kyle stepped backwards, allowing her space to shoot. It was only then that he heard the distinctive chatter of the machine gun and realised that their attackers had reappeared and Amelia was firing at them, perhaps oblivious to Kyle's predicament.

The Feral roared, obscene black spittle smothering its lips, razor sharp teeth bared in animalistic fury. A frown briefly took form on Kyle's face as a flicker of recognition stirred his memory. Was this the third of the Wretches he'd seen in the fort?

It charged.

Kyle went for the Glock in his waistband.

The Feral died.

He turned to the gunfire, pistol raised, a snarl on his lips.

*

Lynch stared through the magnified sight of his rifle at the young Militiaman as he gunned the Feral down and something close to a smile appeared in the pouchy mess of his face. The awful blue eyes narrowed a fraction of an inch and the tip of the tongue protruded grotesquely from between the fat lips.

Bang

The heavy shot from the sharpshooter next to him made Lynch look round, seeing the Ranger resting his weapon on the parapet of the roof next to the shredded corpse of the Zek engineer.

"What you –"

Lynch looked back through the sights.

Kyle was gone.

*

The bullet took Kyle in the centre of his chest. If the shooter had swung a sledgehammer into him, it couldn't have hurt more.

He felt himself fly backwards as though someone had yanked him with a rope and landed with a crash on his back, the sweet smell of wet grass filling his nostrils.

He tried to suck in a breath but found that he could not. Someone was kneeling on his chest and his lungs wouldn't expand.

Darkness swelled at the edges of his vision. He felt himself choke and panicked as his arms failed to move.

Dimly, he was aware of someone shouting his name and hands touching his body. A woman. Rosie? Why was Rosie here? If Rosie was here, he'd be okay. He knew she'd protect him.

With her face in his mind, Kyle sank backwards into the crushing darkness.

INTERLUDE

The line of hunters moved silently through the thick trees of the forest. The dense canopy filtered light from the overcast sky, forming deep pools of shadow.

The hunters made good use of these spots of darkness, moving slowly, careful not to be seen.

Their quarry, in contrast, moved swiftly, crashing through the forest. Their breathing was harsh and ragged as they fled.

The hunters taken a direct route through the undergrowth cutting their quarry off and now they stood, weapons ready as the first of the fleeing party came into view.

A man, dark brown skin, eyes wide with panic. He wore dark clothing and carried a military grade rifle. Behind him, ragged and dirty figures carrying their worldly possessions and then a teenager, pale faced and skinny carrying his own rifle. A woman, armed like the others came last. Her face was covered in blood.

Three shots, muffled somewhat by the soft leaf mulch and thick vegetation came almost simultaneously and the armed figures were down. The civilians did not have the breath to scream so they milled about in confusion.

The hunters cut them down.

They came forward out of their vantage point, the camouflage of their uniforms blending with the undergrowth. A few of the refugees twitched and coughed, blood flecking their lips.

A woman moved, bolting upright, rifle in her hand before two bullets found their mark and she lay still on the forest floor the 'M' of Matwood's Militia uppermost on her uniform.

The brown skinned man lay curled over to one side, hunched in pain over the terrible wound in his abdomen. The Rangers approached him warily, rifles ever ready.

In a blur of movement, the fastest of the man's life, he whipped over onto his back, a length of razor sharp silver cutting through the shadows.

A Ranger staggered back, a sharp intake of breath the only acknowledgement of the black handled knife hilt that protruded from his shoulder.

A final, muted crack of a rifle and the Ranger stepped forward, stepping over the brown skinned man as he choked on his final breath, blood flecking his lips.

The soldier leaned over the dying man, bending with unnatural dexterity to ensure his prey met his eyes, leaning closer so that only the knife thrower could see him.

The dying man choked out something close to a scream.

Lynch tore the blade from his shoulder with barely a grunt and without hesitation, rammed it down into the Jas's eye socket.

The scene was still. Birds fluttered quietly through the high branches. Darkness began to set in.

The hunters set about digging through the leaf mulch and gathering brush to conceal their crime. They worked carefully, professionally.

Hours later, as dusk fell, they left the forest, as silently as they had come, leaving death behind them.

PART 2

Winter

CHAPTER 34

Kyle moved forwards slowly, not in the trancelike dream state that frustrated so many sleeping minds but with the careful, deliberate step of one who is unsure of what lies ahead. His eyes could make out no clear discernible shape but he could sense the space around him, hear the small splashing sounds as his feet moved through the shallow, stinking water. He shuffled one foot forward, the other moving to meet it in small, careful steps. He tried to be quiet but the water was so noisy! He'd never thought water would be noisy to walk through. In cartoons it never splashed around the characters feet and it never smelled like this! This smelled worse than when Dad had been to the toilet and not used the air freshener that Mum kept reminding him about. The thought of Mum and Dad brought a cry to his lips and he clamped his mouth shut but a small, frightened squeak sounded at the memory of their faces.

"Into the tunnel, Kyle!" his Dad had shouted, shoving him roughly. Kyle had staggered forward then recoiled from the foul stench that struck him in the face. He turned, tears pouring down his face but Dad wasn't looking. He had turned back to the hundreds of grownups that were pouring past the tiny tunnel entrance, some of them screaming and some covered in blood. He'd never seen that much blood before, even when he fell over on the playground last year and took all the skin off his knees. He'd picked the scabs for weeks and every time he did fresh crimson liquid would well up and once it even dribbled down his leg, like in the war films that Dad watched and Kyle pretended didn't scare him.

The blood on these people wasn't crimson, it was a darker, deeper colour and on some people it was almost brown. And none *of them had just a drip or a graze, their clothes were covered in it and some of them had it on their faces too. Why didn't they wipe it off? He looked frantically for Mum and Dad and saw Dad shove his way into the stampede of people. He'd never seen Dad shove someone like that, it made him realise how big and strong Dad was. He couldn't see Mum anywhere.*

Someone turned and ran towards him and Kyle was frozen in a moment of horror and terror thinking the woman was coming to get him. She was a grown-up but maybe as old as Granny. She had grey hair and a lined face and she was screaming! He'd never liked people screaming, it had always hurt his ears and Mum said he'd never screamed as a baby... Mum! Where was she?

"Mum!" he cried out, taking involuntary steps backwards away from the screaming lady who barrelled towards him. She reached him and he cringed back, expecting her to hurt him but she ignored him, running straight past him into the tunnel where she vanished into the blackness like she'd been swallowed by some awful monster.

"Mum! Dad! Where are you?" Kyle cupped his hands around his mouth to yell at the rush of people. He saw kids in there too, some his own age and some bigger. One lady had a baby tied to her front and her hands extended in front of her, pushing people away. You weren't supposed to push people, he'd got into trouble for that at school once and Mrs Gaston had sat him down and told him that he was bigger than most of the other kids so he had to be more careful or he could hurt them. He hadn't meant to hurt anyone but he'd pushed Charlie Frank and Charlie had gone flying to the ground and then gone racing off to tell the teacher. Kyle wished he'd pushed him harder when he saw that. Who goes and tells the teacher?

Suddenly, he saw a figure stagger sideways out of the mass of people and his heart leapt, Dad! He hurried forward yelling to Dad but then he saw that Dad was dragging Mum backwards and she was lying asleep with blood on her face. No, not asleep. He'd done the first aid course at school and he knew the word for this... 'unconscious'. He'd had it in his spelling test and the teacher had given him a star for knowing the word. Why was Mum unconscious? Had she been electrocuted? Or banged her head? Or had a heart attack? Was she dead? He stopped as Dad pulled her closer and laid her down on the ground, kneeling beside her and shaking her shoulders roughly.

"Clara! Clara! Wake up! Clara, can you hear me? Clara! We need to go! Wake up!" Kyle saw to his relief that his Mother was awake, her eyes were open and her mouth moved but he couldn't hear what she said. His Father pulled her into a sitting position and she suddenly coughed in a spasm and vomited all over the ground in front of her. Kyle saw Dad pull back some of her hair and look at something then he hurriedly tore the rucksack off his back and pulled out a plastic bottle of water. He unscrewed the top and began to pour the water onto the spot of her head that he'd just looked at.

"Dad! You said we shouldn't waste the water!" Kyle protested.

Dad didn't look at him as he spoke "Mum's hurt her head, Kyle. I need to pour water on it to make her feel better!"

Mum suddenly gasped and Kyle stepped back, frightened of seeing her like this. She called out "Kyle? Kyle! Where's Kyle!" her hand flapped around on the ground.

"He's right here, Clara" said Dad "Kyle, hold your Mum's hand please" Kyle hesitated but Dad gave him The Look and he stepped forward and sat down on the dirty ground near Mum and held her hand. She smiled at him "Hi Kyle, sorry I lost you for a second. I had a bit of an accident!"

"Are you going to be okay?" asked Kyle with tears in his eyes.

"I'll be just fine, don't worry about me" she smiled again. One of her eyes was turning red. He said so to Dad who looked at it grimly and said nothing. Mum didn't seem to hear. Dad tied a bandage around her head tying it under her chin. It looked funny and Kyle smiled for a second. Mum saw it and laughed "Do I look funny, Kyle? Ha ha ha..." she closed her eyes and grimaced.

Dad wasn't smiling. He put the water bottle back in his rucksack and looked at the endless stream of people. Kyle could see now that some of the people had fallen over. The others weren't stopping to help them, they were trying to go around them but then someone *stepped on one of them and then the person behind stepped on them too and suddenly everyone was just running over these people that were lying on the ground.*

Dad turned to look at the black hole of the tunnel. It was small and jagged. Kyle thought it looked like it had been blown up, like in a war film where you see all the concrete with holes in it. But it was in the grass too, in an earth bank that raised up high with trees on top of it. Why was there concrete under the grass? That didn't make sense but it made the hole even more scary. He didn't want to go in there.

But Dad looked at him and said what he didn't want him to say "We've got to go in the sewer, Kyle It's the only way! When we get in just turn left and keep going. Eventually we'll come to the exit and we can get on the plane then!" he forced a smile.

"Is Aunty Licia going to meet us there?" Kyle asked.

"No... Licia isn't coming any more. I told you this." said Dad as he stood and pulled Mum to her feet. Her eyes were open but she looked like she did that time she'd drunk the whole bottle of wine at Christmas at Aunty Licia's and Dad had to carry her to bed. She wasn't bleeding that time though. Now there was red stuff dripping down her face, just like when he'd picked his scabs. Had Mum picked her scabs?

"Kyle?" his Dad said and Kyle turned to look at his Father. "It's all going to be okay, I promise." he smiled at Kyle and Kyle smiled weakly back nodding.

He was stood between his parents and the entrance to the sewer and all he could see was them. But he heard the screams behind them and the shouts and panicked cries. Dad looked behind him and then he was yelling "Run, Kyle! RUN! GET INTO THE TUNNEL!" and he was shoving Kyle forwards and dragging Mum who had closed her eyes, blood dripping off her chin now. The panic of his parent spurred Kyle forward and he ran the short distance to the sewer entrance stopping only when the black maw of the hole was right in front of him. He turned, scared and waiting for Mum and Dad.

A man dressed in a suit like the one that Dad wore to his school play suddenly appeared behind Mum and Dad and he grabbed hold of Mum's shoulder and pulled her so that she fell away from Dad. Dad turned and the man laughed at him. Kyle saw he was holding a big long gun in his hand and he pointed it at Dad. Kyle heard the man shouting.

"Back up!"

Dad said a bad word to the man. Kyle didn't think he'd ever heard Dad sound so cross.

The man was shouting something at Dad, Kyle wasn't sure what he was saying. He was pointing with the gun, like they did in the films and seemed to want Dad to move away from Kyle and Mum.

Suddenly another man and a woman came appeared from the stampede, both of them covered in even more blood than Mum was. The man grabbed the man with the gun and Kyle saw him bite into the bare skin of his neck. More blood sprayed out and covered the biting mans face. Kyle clamped his hand over his mouth in horror. Dad grabbed the gun as it wobbled in the mans grip but there was a huge BANG and it went off and suddenly there was blood all over Dad too and he had fallen onto Mum.

"Dad! Daddy!" Kyle ran forward just as the woman grabbed the man with the gun and bit into him too. The gun fell to the floor. Dad looked up as Kyle ran towards him.

"No! Kyle! Go into the tunnel!" he shouted.

"Come on! We can all go!" he saw Dad's face was turning white and he wasn't getting up. Mum wasn't moving and Kyle was scared. Dad suddenly reached out and grabbed him, pulling him close to him for a second.

"I love you, Kyle, God we both love you but you have to go in there by yourself!" he tore the rucksack from his back and pushed it into Kyles arms. "Put this on! Don't argue!".

Kyle pulled the straps over his shoulder and Dad pulled both the straps tight at the same time "You have to go Kyle! Run! They'll kill you if you don't!"

"What about you and Mum?" Kyle asked, tears pouring down his face.

Dad looked down at Mum "She's really ill" he said "I'm going to try and get help for her" there was a scream from the man who had shot Dad and Kyle tried to look past Dad but his Father blocked his view. His face was so white now, like he'd put white paint all over it and his voice was getting really quiet.

"Kyle, remember when I said that you had to be strong? And tough?"

Kyle nodded, tears pouring down his face.

"You have to do that now. Go into the tunnel, turn left and keep going. The plane will be waiting for you. Go! Go now!" he pushed Kyle hard.

Kyle stepped back but didn't turn, staring at Dad's face. Then Dad screamed as something began to pull him backwards, away from Mum. Kyle saw Dad reach over and grab the gun that the man had dropped and he saw the woman who had bitten the other man in the suit was biting at Dads ankle. He saw Dad push the gun against her head and another BANG and the woman was gone. Dad turned to Kyle and shouted "GO! GO NOW!" as more of the bloody people staggered towards him. Dad raised the gun again and fired and fired at them. Blood sprayed out of them like it had out of the man's neck and a red mist formed in the air around them.

Kyle felt a warm trickle run down his leg as he saw the people advance on his parents. Then he stepped backwards into the tunnel as Dad had said. The last thing he saw was one of the bloody people fall onto his Dad and bite him on the shoulder. Dad began hitting him with the gun, shoving him away and then Kyle saw Dad turn and cover Mum with his own body and then the terror and horror overtook him and he found himself running into the tunnel, splashing through the water.

Dad's voice echoed in his ears, seeming to follow him through the darkness.

... Turn left ...

... Keep going ...

Kyle ran and ran until the light from the entrance was gone and he suddenly realised that he couldn't see anything. He stopped and waved a hand in front of his face and saw nothing, not a flicker of light. He stopped, suddenly aware how loud his breathing sounded in the tunnel and he forced himself to be quiet as he listened.

Nothing.

He stepped forward and the sound of water splashing echoed off the walls, impossibly loud after the silence. He kept shuffling forward, his hands outstretched like the lady who had the baby on her chest. That helped, he thought about her, working through the problem in his mind of how she tied the baby to her chest. Was in in a harness? Was it comfortable? Anything to not think about the dark and the monsters that might be hiding there.

He shuffled on, the only sound his own breathing and his splashing footsteps. Nothing but that.

Breathe.

Splash.

Breathe.

Splash.

Until that wasn't the only sound.

CHAPTER 35

The dreams burned through Kyle's mind, torturing him with terrible images.

His Mother, her face hidden behind her hands wept on her knees before him while his Father held a gun to her head saying over and over *it's for the best, Kyle. We have to let her go.*

Kyle tried to bellow at his parents not to die, to stay and live with him. He railed and screamed but their expressions never changed.

Our home is gone, Kyle. The world is gone. We have to let go.

But he had a home. A place called Holden. He tried to tell them, he shouted and screamed and tried to reach out to shake his Father and make him see sense but he found his arms were trapped by his side.

The dreams changed.

Now he was afraid, more terrified than he'd ever been in his life. Something was chasing him and he was fleeing down a dark tunnel where the sound of his panicked steps echoed off dirty water and cold brick. The sounds seemed to shout at him from all angles, screaming his name.

Kyle-Kyle-Kyle-Kyle-Kyle-Kyle-Kyle-Kyle-Kyle-Kyle

Until he screamed at them to stop but all he could manage was a terrible, drawn out moan and he looked down at his body, realising with revulsion that he was Infected, he'd become a Wretch and now Rosie was before him, shouting his name over and over, begging him not to hurt her and now he was the thing that was chasing her down a reeking tunnel while he tried to scream at his body to stop but all that came from his lips was the terrible, agonising moan.

He was back in Holden, the gates were open and beyond them, he could see the Horde had appeared from the crop fields. This time they walked slowly forward towards his home. He shouted for them to close the gate but Ali was on gate duty and he just smiled sadly at Kyle, letting the Wretches walk in unopposed.

Kyle shouted and shouted until the monsters walked up and cold hands grabbed him, shaking him and screaming his name.

Kyle-Kyle-Kyle-Kyle-Kyle-Kyle-Kyle-Kyle-Kyle-Kyle

He lay on his back in the quarantine hut, Doctor May's face looming over him but instead of her usual robotic stare, her face was full of concern and worry. She rubbed his head which he only now noticed was burning as though a fire had been lit beneath his skull. She touched his skin and a wonderful cooling sensation spread from her hand.

But all too soon, she had taken her hand away and the heat built again, burning through his mind.

Now, he didn't know where he was but he was hot, burning hot. He couldn't see around him, the lights were out but he knew there must be a fire burning somewhere or else how could he be so hot?

He heard water dripping in the darkness and staggered towards it, desperate to quench his parched mouth but the closer he got, the farther away the sound went.

A flash of light, a burst of deep red and he staggered after it. A Zek? He tried to remember what a Zek was but couldn't bring it to mind.

The red light turned into red fur and a ridge backed dog was leading him somewhere. He reached out and patted the dog's muscular haunch and it turned, wagging its tail, and licking his hand.

He asked it where it was going but the dog just smiled and padded onwards. Kyle followed.

Then the sound of his own voice filled his ears and he stared at the dog, wondering why it was shouting at him but the dog was wagging its tail, trying to lead him onwards and there, through the darkness he could see his parents again, this time smiling and beckoning him towards them.

Come home, Kyle. We miss you.

He stepped forward, then stopped. The dog looked back and whined.

You're dead. Gone. I have my own home now.

Come home to us.

I can't.

Then the sound of his own voice was ringing in his ears again and a great weight was pressing on his chest. He felt the heat burning inside his head again and he screamed at the pain. The sound of water returned, a torrent of blue gushing liquid and he staggered forward only to see it sweep his parents away, their smiles never wavering.

He leapt forward, desperate to quench his thirst but the water moved around him, taunting him, always just out of reach. The red dog whined piteously and leaned in to lick at his forehead, soothing the burning again.

Then, he was in a building, a huge building from before the Fall. He recognised it. Green plants had covered the walls and hidden the brick from view but he knew there was danger inside. Still, he found himself drawn onwards, even as he tried to stop himself.

Up, up, up he went to the roof but it was empty. He spun around, confused, wondering why he was here and as he finished spinning a man in with no face raised a rifle and shot him.

Kyle-Kyle-Kyle-Kyle-Kyle-Kyle-Kyle-Kyle-Kyle-Kyle

His name echoed in his head, only this time he could hear it more clearly. A woman's voice, yelling his name. His Mother?

A face flashed before his eyes, one he didn't recognise. He felt hair brush his cheeks and smelled a familiar scent.

Rosie?

Rosie was taking care of him. Rosie who had always been there. Who loved him.

Kyle opened his eyes.
It wasn't Rosie.

CHAPTER 36

"What are you doing?"

Amelia Singh smiled at him sadly.

"Besides fixing you?"

Kyle realised that this short sentence had left him out of breath. He'd lifted his head but now he let it slump back onto a soft pillow.

"Take it easy. Do you remember what happened?"

Kyle closed his eyes. The fever had burned through him and his memory was a confused jumble of images, sounds and emotions.

"The building..."

"What building?" there was a note of steel in her voice. Kyle opened his eyes to find her looking at him intently.

"Where was the dog?"

Amelia frowned "Dog? I didn't see a dog..."

Kyle shook his head "Doesn't matter..." he took a deep breath, trying to calm himself.

It hurt like Hell and a second later his body was wracked by a spasm of coughs. Pain lanced through his chest and throat and to his surprise, Amelia leaned hard onto his shoulders, holding him still.

The spasm passed and she held a small tin mug of water to his lips. Kyle sipped, his eyes watering with the pain.

"I was shot."

"Yes."

"You're a doctor."

"Yes. Luckily for you."

"How are you a doctor? You're too young. Doctors were

trained before the Fall."

Amelia laughed at that. She sat back from Kyle and chuckled to herself until she had to dash tears away from her cheeks.

"Oh! I'm sorry. That's the first time I've laughed in a month."

A month? As she had leaned back, Kyle saw for the first time where they were. The rough yellowish rock of a cave stretched over head. A bright electric light filled the darkness in a pool around them.

"Why are we in a cave?"

Amelia stopped laughing abruptly "Yes. I brought you here. After I took that bullet out of your chest." she leaned to one side and picked up something out of view to Kyle.

His body armour.

She'd taken the ballistic plate out of the vest and he could now see the ragged hole, covered in a dark brown stain that Kyle realised with a gulp, was his own blood.

A lot of blood.

"How am I not dead?"

"Believe it or not, I'm a very good doctor."

Kyle blinked "Why aren't *you* dead?"

Amelia's face turned cold as she relayed the story. Kyle's fight with the Feral had drawn her and the Zek called Greg back out of the woods just in time to see him go down. Amelia had emptied her pistol towards the building and although the range was too great for the small weapon, it had the desired effect of stopping the shooter long enough for them to drag Kyle back into the woods where Amelia managed to stop the bleeding.

"You had a collapsed lung, massive blood loss and a bullet in your chest cavity."

"You fixed all that in a cave?" Kyle was incredulous.

"Lucky for you, the Institute had enough equipment to treat you. I managed to sneak out and recover some at night. Greg and Molly helped me carry you here."

"You just happened to run into a cave in the woods?" Kyle was incredulous.

"No. Some of our lookouts had spotted it a few days ago. They thought it might make a good rendezvous if we were attacked before we could send the signal."

"Were they bandits? The people who attacked us." Kyle asked although he frowned as he did so.

"No." Amelia's voice was cold, flat, and hard.

Kyle didn't know what to make of that. Amelia continued with her tale.

She'd returned with enough scavenged medical supplies to attempt to remove the bullet. By herself, in the cave she'd saved Kyle's life and had spent the past month waiting to see if her efforts had been in vain.

Kyle frowned "But what about the bandits - I mean whoever attacked us?"

Amelia explained that once it was clear Kyle couldn't be moved, she'd ordered the Zeks to return to London. By this point, a half dozen others had arrived at the cave and Greg, who Amelia said had been a soldier before joining the Zeks had agreed to head towards Matwood in an attempt to lead their attackers away from Amelia and Kyle. Kyle nodded at the good sense of this, it was the same decision he'd have made.

"And this was a month ago?" his breath was still coming in short gasps.

"A month ago. Give or take a few days. I lost count..." Kyle heard the strain in Amelia's voice and for the first time noticed the exhausted look she wore.

"Thank you."

Amelia shrugged, looking away from him.

"No, thank you. You saved my life."

"I'm a doctor."

Kyle frowned "Why haven't they found us? They should have searched the cave..."

Amelia's face fell "There's a lot of Infected in the woods. Some Ferals. All that shooting drew them in. I think they took the bait and followed Greg."

"A month..." Kyle was still groggy but something was

nagging at him. He closed his eyes, trying to work out what was wrong.

"We've got about another week's worth of food." Amelia told him, turning away to fidget with some boxes "I had the others leave everything they had with them." she shot a sideways glance at Kyle "We'll have to find more soon though."

"A month. They'd have made it back to London by now. Why didn't anyone come looking for us?"

Amelia's face fell and for the first time she looked almost tearful "I don't know."

CHAPTER 37

"Frost is dead, Sinclair. It's time you got over it."

Armstrong's voice was hard and cold. His face was devoid of emotion and Sinks, stood miserably in front of him could do nothing but bow his head.

"I'm promoting you to Acting Sergeant, attached to the Rangers. I'll speak to your chain of command myself. From now on, you answer to me. You need to forget about Frost and that shit-heap town. We need you here and I need you focussed."

"Sir."

Armstrong's face softened a fraction "I understand that Holden has been your home for several years, Sinclair. I'm not unsympathetic to the fact you had friends there. But this isn't the time to let their deaths into your head. You've seen the latest reports of Feral numbers?"

Sinks nodded.

"Twenty five percent, Sinclair! Those sorts of numbers will wipe out the entire region. Our duty as soldiers is to protect the civilians. The living civilians."

"I know, Sir."

"Good. I've had to request support from Parliament."

Sinks looked up in surprise, seeing the flicker of annoyance on the Major's face. He could imagine how much it had dented Armstrong's pride to admit that he could not control the Ferals with his Rangers.

"The Regular Army is sending reinforcements. What I need from you is a liaison between the Rangers and the regulars. I need someone I can trust."

"Yes, Sir." Sink's voice was miserable but he understood the sense in Armstrong's words. They'd heard about the sack of Holden a month ago and Armstrong had ordered the road that joined the small town with Matwood blocked. He'd declared Holden overrun and had forbidden the Matwood Militia from sending a scouting party to check for survivors. The threat, Armstrong declared, was here in Matwood.

"When the troops get here, I need them to follow my orders and not get caught up in the politics. Got it?"

"Politics, sir?" Sinks was confused.

Armstrong looked pained "You've seen the Zeks out in the woods. Ever since Colonel Forbes turned his coat, we've had soldiers championing their cause. You know as well as I do how dangerous the Zeks are to this fight."

Sinks nodded.

"When the reinforcements are here, I need you to tell me if there's any dissent. Any troops wearing red armbands – you know what I mean. You'll report back to me directly. Got it?"

"Sir."

"That's all, Sinclair. Go and see Sergeant Mitchell, she'll brief you on the next operation." Armstrong turned away to read through a report, apparently Sinks was forgotten.

Sinks saluted, turned, and left the building. He stepped out into the icy wind, shivering as it bit at the exposed skin of his face. The tidy streets of Matwood had transformed in the last month. The sudden drop in temperature, and a storm blown by weeks of strong winds had destroyed much of the harvest around Matwood. The town had its food reserves, but with the dozens of soldiers within the walls not to mention the traders sheltering from the weather and the Ferals, food was being strictly rationed.

The streets were busy and caked with mud. Every patch of earth not covered by artificial roads was churned into a quagmire and it was impossible to keep the paths clear. The two pubs in town were filled day and night with bored townsfolk and traders, drinking to pass the time and every few hours it seemed, the town guard were rushing towards yet another drunken brawl.

Matwood's council had erected three tall posts in the town centre and each day, three law breakers were tied in the cold air as punishment, their neighbours yelling jeering insults as they passed by. For the first few days of the new laws, rotten food had been thrown but now there was none to spare.

As he made his way along the pathways, Sinks noticed he was no longer given the usual wide berth civilians afforded to soldiers. He knew that many of the townsfolk blamed the presence of the Rangers and Armstrong for their current woes. It wasn't fair; after all, how could Armstrong have predicted the poor harvest or the attack on Holden? But Sinks understood that people were scared and angry. The destruction of Holden had appalled everyone. The strong walls, the dogs and the tea had been a constant in the life of Matwood and the idea of it simply being gone, was impossible to comprehend.

Kyle, Rosie, and his other friends from Holden made their way to the front of his thoughts again. It was hard to believe that they were all gone. Sinks had seen more friends than he could count die in the past twenty years, indeed, almost everyone he'd known before the Fall was dead. The virus had torn the world to shreds but he'd allowed himself to feel secure in the four solid walls of Holden. It had felt like a home, the first he'd had since the Infection had spread. And now it was gone and he'd been here, doing nothing.

A part of him, the rational part of his mind knew that he was experiencing survivor's guilt. It was perfectly natural for someone in his position. But it wasn't just that, Sinks thought as he drew level with the bench he and Kyle had sat on the last time he'd seen his friend. It was the cruelty with which not one, but two calamities had occurred. Lynch had returned and reported the Militia killed in a skirmish in the woods. He'd described a protracted gun battle with the Infected and a group of armed Zeks. Sinks had refused to believe the report when it came in, only giving in when reports came from the Rangers near Holden that armed Zeks had been spotted there and had fought and killed two of the Rangers.

Sinks knew Eric Forbes' name as well as any in the military. The former Colonel was infamous as a deserter and criminal. Sinks had met him, ten years previously before he was posted to Holden, back when Forbes had been a Major. He'd respected the man, finding in him a rare leader and had been as appalled as everyone when he abandoned his post to join the Zeks.

And now, some of his men had killed Kyle. The thought filled Sinks with a fury that he could not extinguish. He relished the thought of Armstrong deploying him with the new troops that would arrive from London so he could take the fight to the black coated bastards.

"Sinks!" he turned to see Hannah Mitchell, his friend from the Rangers hailing him. She was bundled up in what looked like every warm piece of clothing she owned under her combat gear.

"Alright?" he greeted her.

"Still miserable?" she attempted a jibe but seeing the look on her friend's face she softened her attitude "How you holding up?"

"I'm fine."

"'Course you are. First new troops are coming in tomorrow I hear."

"Tomorrow? I thought they'd only just left London." Sinks knew they were at least a four day march from London. Longer, if the usual cluster of problems that came with military organisation presented itself.

"Yeah, some of them are driving. Most are walking though. They scraped together all the working vehicles but it still wasn't enough."

"Wow." Aside from the buzzing Ranger helicopters, Sinks struggled to remember the last time he'd seen a working vehicle "Parliament must be taking this Feral thing seriously."

Hannah shot him a sideways glance "Sure. The Ferals are a

real problem."

Sinks caught her meaning "But if they can stop the Zeks then it's a win for everyone?"

"Right. It's getting a bit political for me. Oh – did you hear Amelia Singh was killed recently?"

"What? No, I didn't. Bloody hell." He sat in silence for a moment "I suppose that means Colonel Forbes is in charge of the Zeks?"

"Right. Now they're an army with a leader."

"Bloody hell." Sinks repeated before frowning "Wait, is that just a rumour? Who confirmed it?"

"Zeks announced it in London. She was missing presumed dead somewhere in the south east."

"Near here? Blimey, she's lucky Lynch didn't find her and slit her throat in the woods. I hope she ran into a pack of Ferals. I'd rather have that than Lynch get hold of me."

"He's not as bad as you make him out to be, you know."

"He's a fucking psychopath!"

Hannah rolled her eyes "He's a good soldier."

"There's more to soldiering than slaughtering people." Sinks shook his head "God help the Zeks if Armstrong sets Lynch on them."

"I think that's the point. If they know he and Armstrong are here, it might draw Forbes out into a full scale battle. Which we'll win."

Sinks grunted in response.

"What? I thought you wanted some payback."

"Yeah. I do."

"Well? Get your war face on then, Sinks! You can go nuts if Armstrong manages to get them to fight!"

"Yeah."

Hannah rolled her eyes "Ooh. Really scary." She elbowed him in the ribs but at that moment, Jay Paxton the regular soldier who was military liaison to Matwood approached at a run.

"Oi! You two get to the barracks. We've got a contact a mile out, need backup."

"Ferals?" Sinks was on his feet, calling as they ran.

"No." Jay called back "Zeks!".

CHAPTER 38

Kyle lay on his back. After Amelia's explanation, he'd fallen asleep, the short burst of conversation too much for his broken body. Now he was awake, not sure how much time had passed.

There was a rustle and a blast of cold air and Amelia entered the cave. Daylight followed her, quickly shut out by some shield that Kyle couldn't make out.

"Alright?"

"Yeah. Cold." she shivered. She clutched a pair of rabbits in her hand. Kyle's eyes lit up at the sight.

"Well done."

She ignored the compliment, instead drawing a hefty looking knife and beginning the grimy business of skinning. The feet went first, then a long slit down the belly before she tugged the skin away from the meat with a grunt of effort.

"Where'd you learn to hunt?" Kyle asked. He'd tried to sit up but found that the pain was too much.

"Dad taught me." she had moved onto the guts and the stench filled the cave.

"You know, for a Zek, you're pretty handy."

She scowled at him "For a dead man, you're pretty patronising."

Kyle repressed a laugh. Amelia's face was stone and it seemed the best course of action was to stay silent so he watched as she began to chop the meat into chunks.

"Did you shoot them?"

"No! The woods are crawling with Infected. I left a couple of snares out. Got lucky with these two."

"You said we still had supplies?"

"Yes, but I'm trying to save them. They're all dried food so they'll keep. Fresh food will have to do for a couple of days." she had sparked a small gas cooker and was now frying the meat in strips. The cave was quickly filled with the mouth-watering aroma.

Amelia glanced up at him briefly "We need to get you as much protein as possible. You've got a lot of healing to do still."

"Rabbit has a lot of protein."

"Yes. No fat though. We can't live off rabbit meat for long."

"Did you take the food out my pack?"

"Yes. Oh, that reminds me. What's this?" Amelia rummaged through a pile of food, tugging out a small metal pot which looked like it was filled with tree bark.

"Tea!"

"Tea?"

"Yeah. You know, hot stuff. The great British past time."

"I haven't seen tea since I was a kid."

Kyle looked at her in shock "Is it that scarce? We grow it in Holden."

"Of course. Isn't that where the water is from too? The one with the 'M' on it..."

"That's Matwood."

"Right. I've been there."

"Ever been to Holden?"

"No. I told you I knew Dr May, didn't I?"

"The Maybot!" Kyle laughed, winced, then lapsed into an amused silence.

Amelia looked at him sharply "She's one of the best doctors in the country... Probably in the world now. I learned a lot from her - including how to extract bullets from a chest cavity."

Finding himself rebuked again, Kyle instead eyed the thin wisps of smoke now rising from the frying pan "Won't the smell spread?"

Amelia looked back towards the cave entrance "I've hung sanitation strips from the hospital. They should block most of it. If not..."

"We'll have Wretches in here. Speaking of which, where's my Glock?"

"Here..." Amelia passed the pistol to Kyle, barrel first. He flinched, ignoring the pain.

"Hey! I've already been shot, point that away from me, will you?"

Amelia looked flustered for the first time. She fumbled the pistol and nearly dropped it. Kyle snatched it from her, a cry of pain tearing itself from his lips.

"Ugh!"

"Oh, no! I'm sorry..."

"It's alright, sorry. I didn't mean to give you a hard time."

"No, that was stupid of me. I didn't think."

There was an awkward silence. Kyle's chest throbbed as he checked the chamber.

Amelia turned the gas off and moved to kneel next to Kyle. Once again, he tried to force himself into a sitting position and once again, failed.

"Here..." Amelia, to Kyle's embarrassment, began to feed him the strips of rabbit meat one by one.

"You know, my hands do work." he lifted them to illustrate the point.

"As little movement as possible for the next few days."

"What if I need to piss?"

"I've got a pot..."

"Oh."

Amelia smiled "Probably best not to think about it."

"It's not healthy to repress difficult thoughts."

She smiled again "Oh, so you do have some healthy habits!"

Kyle was confused "Am I not healthy? Aside from the bullet wound, obviously."

"You've got about, what, two percent body fat? There's enough scars on your torso to be a gladiator and your feet look like they're made of leather."

Kyle shrugged "I run a lot."

"You run too much."

"I have to be fit for my job."

"For being a soldier?"

"I'm a Militiaman. I'm not in the army."

"But you'd like to be?" Amelia guessed.

Kyle shrugged "Can't stay in Holden my whole life."

"Why not?"

"There's a world out there."

"Bigger than we thought."

Kyle snorted, finishing the rabbit meat. He lay back, feeling some strength return to his battered body.

"How long until I can move?"

Amelia frowned "Until I say so."

"How long?"

She rolled her eyes "You're annoying."

Kyle shot her a winning smile "I try my best."

CHAPTER 39

The air was filled with thin snowflakes, churned by the sharp wind. Sinks shivered despite the warm layers, hoping it wouldn't settle on the hard ground. Around him a dozen soldiers, Rangers, Hannah Mitchell and Jay Paxton moved silently. The trees of the forest were thin here, allowing him to see the long extended line the troops had formed.

A bush shivered ahead of Sinks and he levelled his rifle. A second later, the Wretch stumbled forward, arms outstretched towards him. Sinks shot the creature, watching in grim satisfaction as it tumbled to the ground. A second shot went into the head before he thumbed his radio, reporting the brief contact.

"Bastard!"

The voice was harsh with a distinct northern accent. Sinks went still, searching for the Zek. A moment later, he saw the black leather of the man's trench coat and quickly called the rest of the squad. The Zek glared at Sinks with hatred as he was surrounded.

"Get your hands up!" snapped one of the Rangers, moving closer. The man ignored the order and the Ranger grabbed his wrist, kicking the back of his knee out to throw him onto the forest floor.

Sinks took a pace forward and then, with the reactions borne of long experience, flung himself flat as an explosion tore through the frigid air.

Fire lanced high into the treetops a dozen metres to his right. One of the Rangers was flung forward with a yell, crashing into the ground next to the sprawled Zek. Sinks moved behind a tree, yelling for the troops to take cover as a splintering crash of rifle fire erupted.

"There!" no time for clear directions, the Zek ambush was plain to see. Hannah, taking control, yelled at the closest Rangers for suppressing fire and ran diagonally away from the Zeks through the woods. Sinks bounded after her as a bullet whined past him in the cold air. Hannah stopped and he went down to one knee, as the Zeks in the ambush began to peel away in good order, retreating further into the woods.

"Suppressing fire!" repeated Hannah and the Rangers rate of fire increased to almost machine gun like proportions. Hannah nodded to Sinks and erupted to her feet, sprinting forward in a short, zig zag route between the trees before slamming down to shelter behind a broad oak.

Sinks was up the moment Hannah began firing her rifle. Of the Zeks, he could see no sign but he knew they were there, lying flat like Hannah or sheltering behind trees.

"Move!" he bawled at Hannah as he dropped to one knee behind a thick oak. He sighted his rifle around the tree, pulling the trigger rapidly, adjusting his aim every couple of shots to carpet the target area in rounds.

Then, Hannah called to him to move and Sinks sprinted forward, stumbling slightly on a tree root.

I'm up, he sees me, I'm down

The rhythm pulsed through his head as he stopped hard, going flat and firing.

Then, a second explosion, this one back towards the covering troops and Sinks heard a scream of pain. He cursed, risking a pause in firing to see what was happening but despite the small size of the battlefield, he could see nothing from where he lay.

"Man down! S'arnt, the enemy are retreating. We need to get Yates back to Matwood."

The radio crackled and Sinks heard Hannah curse somewhere off to his right.

"Sinks!"

"Here!"

"We're staying here!" she called before a moment later, sending an order over the radio to extract the wounded man. A pair of Rangers closed in behind Sinks, falling to lie flat behind him. A moment later, Hannah joined.

"They pulled back." The nearest Ranger told Hannah.

"Right. Give the blokes a couple of minutes to get clear with Yates and then we'll move forwards."

The Rangers nodded but Sinks gripped her arm "That was a proper ambush, Hannah. These must be Forbes' troops. Did we even hit a single one?"

Hannah hissed at him to keep his voice down "I don't know and I don't care. This is what the fight is now, Sinks!"

"Bloody hell, Hannah! We don't know how many of them there are and you just sent half our blokes away! There are four of us and they already laid explosives!"

"Enough!" Hannah snapped "Do as I bloody well say, Sinks or I'll put a bullet in you!" her face flushed red as she raged at him.

"Christ!" Sinks swore, backing down as the authority of rank overtook his objections. He shook his head at her poor decision making.

"Alright, move!" Hannah snapped and they broke into two halves, Hannah and Sinks moving as the other two Rangers covered them with their rifles and vice versa.

He came across the Zek quite suddenly, lying half concealed by a thick gorse bush. The man was middle aged, dressed in full military grade body armour and helmet. A bullet had struck the side of his neck and his skin was almost translucent from the blood loss. Sinks knelt next to him, pushing the rifle he had clutched out of reach.

"He's a goner." Hannah had approached and was looking at the man who was clearly almost dead. His eyes flickered as though he didn't really see the two soldiers.

"How many of you?" Sinks asked the man who blinked at him then stared in shock as though Sinks had only just appeared.

"Not worth it." Hannah opined.

"May as well try and get something out of him."

At that moment though, the man gave an odd sigh and went still.

"Bloody hell." Sinks turned away as the man died.

"Up ahead!"

The voice came from one of the other two Rangers, men who Sinks did not know but immediately he and Hannah dropped to the ground, turning to face the new threat.

"What've you got?" Hannah shouted but before the Rangers could respond, Sinks heard another voice, this one yelling in unintelligible French.

"Refugees!" he shouted in surprise, standing up. Ahead, a trio of filthy figures cowered amongst the trees. All were unarmed.

"On the ground!" Sinks shouted, aiming his rifle and making distinctive downward gestures. The refugees stared at him stupidly.

"Sod it –" Hannah elbowed Sinks aside and extended her arm towards them.

Bang

"What the fuck?" snarled Sinks as one of the figures was snatched back.

Bang-bang-bang-bang-bang

The other Rangers opened up, riddling the French with bullets until the forest floor was coated in their blood.

"You –"

Crack

Sinks had lunged at Hannah but she reversed her grip on the pistol she'd shot the refugee with and slammed the heavy metal slide into his face. With a yell of pain, Sinks dropped to the ground, blood covering his face.

"Don't get squeamish, Sinks!" Hannah snarled "We've got our orders. Every one of them is Infected!"

"Since when do we murder innocent civvies?" Sinks demanded, his face throbbing.

"Since now! Get a grip of yourself!"

The two other Rangers were laughing, apparently amused by Sinks' reaction. His hand twitched towards the safety catch on his rifle but he was suddenly aware of the threat three Rangers posed to him. Disgust and fury rose in him like bile but he could do nothing except spit blood onto the forest floor.

"Bloody pansy." Hannah, his erstwhile friend had turned away in disgust. The woods around them were empty, the Zeks that had sprung the ambush had fled. There was nothing else to do. She gave the order to return to Matwood and Sinks shook his head as though in denial of what he had witnessed.

Turning to follow, he glanced at the dead refugees, hesitating for a moment as though wanting to apologise but there were no words to be said. Something caught his eye and he crouched, peering at the ground beside the man, damp from the storms.

Paw prints.

A wave of grief rose in Sinks as the loss of Holden, Kyle and Rosie crashed down on him again. He knew he would feel it every time he saw a dog again. Unbidden, tears formed in his eyes and he shook his head at the miserable scene of death.

"Sinks! Get bloody move on!" Hannah's voice held no sympathy.

Sinks stood, looked away from the dead Zek and slowly began to follow.

CHAPTER 40

"I said wait!" Amelia chided Kyle.

His face was streaked with sweat and his vision was turning purple at the edges. He still lay on his back but now had managed to raise himself as far as his elbows.

"Lie down! Now!" she snapped.

Kyle hesitated for a moment before collapsing back down, hard. He gave a grunt of pain and lay, panting as his body burned.

Amelia was at his side, her fingers on his neck "What did you do that for?"

Kyle could only pant. He screwed his eyes up in fury at the weakness in his muscles.

"Calm down. Breathe." she placed a hand on his forehead, her soft skin comforting him.

"Ow." he managed to stammer.

"Yeah, I bet." her hand moved to check his pulse "That was stupid. You could have torn the stitches! You're not ready to move yet."

"I can't lie here for the rest of my life."

"You will do if you don't listen to me!" Amelia snapped. After a moment, her face softened "Look, I appreciate how hard it must be to go from hero to zero, but the more you rest now, the quicker you'll get back to where you were."

Kyle closed his eyes, willing himself to calm down. Anger and unexpended energy were making him twitchy. He couldn't remember ever being still for so long and the lack of movement was driving him mad.

"How long do I need to be still for?"

Amelia rolled her eyes at her patient "I need to change the

dressing in two more days. If the wound has healed by then, we can *start* some light physio."

"We can't stay in this cave for much longer."

"We can last another couple of weeks."

"Eating rabbits?"

"I saw a pheasant yesterday..."

"A pheasant you can't shoot without being mobbed by Wretches. We can't live off rabbit meat."

Amelia sighed, a look of desperation in her eyes.

"I don't mind if you leave me."

She snorted "If I was going to leave you, I'd have done it a month ago. Besides, where would we go if we left here?"

"Somewhere with food. Matwood."

"It's snowing outside. It's what, three days to Matwood? You can't even walk! We'd die of exposure, starvation, or Infection before we'd even cleared the woods!"

"Alright. Maybe not Matwood then. Didn't like the place much anyway."

There was silence as they both thought.

"What about the village? The one near the Institute."

"It's full of the Fall- Infected."

"You don't like calling them Wretches, do you?"

Amelia made a face "Stop changing the subject."

"No, go on. Humour me. Why do you call them 'Fallen'?"

"Urgh. It's a habit. A lot of Zeks started doing it and it caught on. It's a sign of respect."

"Respect?" Kyle was disbelieving "For what?"

"They're *people*, Kyle! Nothing more or less! They got Infected with a terrible disease!"

"Exactly! They're changed! Gone!"

"But they weren't always. I've seen people survive the Infection."

"So have I. I've seen more people succumb though."

Amelia breathed, calming the anger that was flashing in her eyes "I don't think they should be disrespected."

"How does shooting them disrespect them?"

She shook her head "No, that's not what I mean. That Feral, it attacked you and you shot it-"

"Yeah, because it was going to kill me!"

Amelia glowered at her patient "If you'll let me speak without interrupting? Thanks. What I was trying to say was it attacked you and you shot it. Fair enough. I'd have done the same. I don't want to die, the same as you."

"But the Zeks whole 'thing' is not killing them?"

The anger flashed again in Amelia's dark eyes "That's not true! There are some Zeks that are more radical about the Fall- the Infected. They won't harm them and try to stop others from harming them. That's not me. The Infected are a threat to us all. I'm a doctor, it's my job to keep people alive. But that means I look at the virus differently to you. I see a threat, sure, but I want to stop the threat entirely. That's why I'm looking for a cure!"

"Cure? Oh, you mean at the Institute." Kyle frowned. He was vaguely aware that the moments before he'd been shot were a frightening jumble of confused memories. His frown deepened as something fluttered at the edge of his consciousness. Amelia was looking at him warily.

"There isn't ever going to be a cure, is there?" Kyle asked "There's always rumours. Every trader that comes to Holden says there's one. Usually somewhere miles away, the West Country or London. Never near us, strangely."

"I've seen a few treatments work."

"Oh, sure. I've had the boosters!"

Amelia was curious "You've been Infected?"

"Suspected Infection. I got water in my eye." Kyle relayed the events leading up Dr May treating him with the vials of booster.

Amelia sat back on her heels "Huh. I didn't know that May had developed anything that effective."

"Like I said, it was a suspected Infection. It worked in the past though. We had a pair of Militia get bitten. Bad bites, too. One already had symptoms, his eyesight was going. The other didn't but we boosted them both and they recovered."

"Recovered from symptoms?" Amelia was incredulous "Wow. That's rare."

Kyle nodded proudly "Yup. Doctor May is good. Oh, you know that." he smiled sheepishly.

"Yeah..."

The barrier Amelia had hung at the cave entrance flapped briefly in the wind. A blast of cold air filled their sanctuary.

"This mutation..."

"Yes. We found data on the computers in the hospital."

Kyle frowned "Is that why there are so many Ferals?"

Amelia shrugged "We can't prove that."

"Does it matter?" when she didn't answer, Kyle pressed "Does it make all of them turn Feral?"

"No. Some it doesn't seem to affect. But the Ferals seem to decay faster than standard victims."

"That's a good thing, though?" Kyle knew he sounded hopeful.

"If we can survive it."

The 'door' flapped again. Kyle shivered. Amelia got up, crossed the cave, and fiddled with the barrier to the outside world. Securing it, she turned back to Kyle and resumed her position next to him "Better?"

"Yeah. Bloody cold out there, isn't it?"

"Good thing we're not out there, then." Amelia jibed in reference to their earlier words.

"If you can't stop the mutation, what were you planning to do with the data?"

A flicker crossed Amelia's face and, in that moment, the intimacy of the cave was broken. Kyle sensed a barrier forming between them, a line between Zek and Militia that he had somehow crossed. He looked away from his carer awkwardly, unsure quite what he had done wrong.

She said nothing and so he risked a look back to discover her brown eyes on his face "Kyle, I want to be frank with you seeing as we're going to be spending a lot of time together. I'm not the leader of the Zeks but I am important to the organisation. We have goals... Some of which other people in this country would love to know the details of. We're living in a very dangerous situation and riding a fine line. There are some things that I'm just not going to tell you. So please, don't ask."

It was her turn to look away. Kyle watched as she rose and crossed the cave, rummaging through piles of supplies that were already stacked in perfectly neat piles. Kyle lay back, letting out a silent sigh as he regarded the rough ceiling of the cave, searching in vain for answers to the mysteries that fluttered through his mind.

CHAPTER 41

The hunger was consuming. All powerful, it filled every facet of his body. His mouth slavered at the thought of warm flesh between his sharp teeth. His eyes strained for the sight of life, of skin with blood beneath its thin membrane.

Small animals fled from him. Most were quick, too quick even for his hunger fuelled speed. Some were not. Their small bones crunched in his jaw as the warmth of their lives trickled down his chin.

It wasn't enough.

It would never be enough.

He flung his head back and screamed at the grey sky, heedless of the icy flakes that landed on his black eyes.

The trees didn't move.

He stood, hands limp by his sides as the echoes of the scream faded. A bush twitched in a faint breeze and he leapt on it, tearing the scrawny branches from the trunk, and cramming them desperately into his mouth. The sticky sap was bitter on his black tongue and he abandoned the leafless wood, discarding the remnants in the snow.

A scent...

The hunger roared inside him, spurring him onwards as he ran through the trees, heedless of the branches whipping across his grey skin. He felt nothing, no pain, no cold, just the all-consuming desperation to eat, to tear, to rend and consume.

A rockface before him. He stopped, half crouched in the thickening snow, arms ready and senses scanning.

Nothing.

His black lips peeled back in a snarl and the muscles in his neck bunched to produce the howl of frustration.

The scent, again...

This time it was close.

The rock face moved.

The hunger plunged him towards it, the snarl leaping before him as he smashed through the thin barrier to reveal the banquet of flesh lying before him.

With a roar of delight, he leapt forward to the feast.

CHAPTER 42

The Feral came through the cave entrance like a typhoon.

Kyle saw it immediately, he'd been watching the entrance without seeing. Amelia half turned in time to see the monster leap at her. It tackled her to the ground with a roar, the force of the impact silencing her own scream.

They rolled across the hard ground, scattering equipment and supplies in a maelstrom of chaos.

The lantern flickered as the Feral kicked it. It was on its front now, not bothering to stand as it clawed at Amelia's feet. She screamed and kicked at the grey hands but it seized her boot and pulled, snarling and roaring.

The light went out.

Darkness filled the space for a second and then Kyle could see. A thin light reflecting off the snow that lay outside the cave entrance allowed him to see the dark shapes on the floor.

Amelia screamed again and now the two shapes were combined, rolling across the floor as they fought.

"Amelia!" Kyle shouted instinctively, wanting to know which of the shapes was her.

He saw the monster atop her, its legs pinning one arm to the ground. The other was desperately jammed under the Feral's throat.

The Feral swiped a blow at her head, a blow that rocked her and left her limp. With a howl of success, the Feral dragged her neck to its head, relishing at the feast.

Kyle shot it in the back of the head.

He wasn't stingy, either. Six bullets tore the monster into black ruin. Instantly, it slumped forward onto its prey. Amelia was crushed beneath the corpse as Kyle found himself crawling forward on his stomach with no memory of having rolled over. His feet slid and scraped for purchase as his left hand found the cold, dead foot of the Feral. He tugged, but the monster did not move.

"Amelia!" a desperate cry, a need to know he was not alone in this black hell.

He tugged again, the cold foot moving slightly but his chest burned and he saw light flicker at the edge of his vision.

"Amelia!"

"Yes!"

"Amelia! Are you hurt? Amelia!"

"I - I'm here! I'm here." she sounded dazed, confused.

"Push it off!"

Kyle tugged the heel, dragging himself along the floor. She shoved, weakly at first but with growing strength. She wiggled, he tugged and then she was out from beneath the corpse. She skittered back on her backside, away from the dead thing that had attacked her.

"Light! Get the light!"

Fumbling in the darkness. A metallic *ping.*

Light filled the cave, chasing the shadows away. Cold air blew in from the torn sheets over the entrance.

Amelia stared in horror at the feral, her breast heaving with exertion. Kyle lay on his belly, the Glock in his right hand.

"Is it dead?"

"Yes! Yes, it's dead." her eyes landed on him. In a second, the shock was gone, replaced by a rigid calm. "You're hurt."

"I'm fine." he wasn't though. He couldn't tell if he'd burst the stitches in his chest but it felt like he'd been shot all over again. He tried to roll onto his back but couldn't and he felt the cold floor against his cheek as his strength faded. Amelia gripped his shoulders and dragged him back onto his bed roll.

"Christ!"

Amelia pushed him down, deft hands undoing the bandages. She checked the wound "All fine. Don't move."

"Are you hurt?"

"No..."

"Amelia. We need to check if it bit you."

She began to protest but stopped, moving the light so Kyle could see her fully. She pulled back the collar of her coat, lowering the neckline of her top enough to make Kyle stare.

"See? All fine."

"Your face..."

Amelia frowned, the small movement enough to elicit a gasp of pain. She gingerly touched her cheek where the Feral's nails had left three deep gashes.

"Shit!" she began rummaging through the scattered piles of supplies until she found a treatment kit. Immediately, she began dabbing at the wounds, the sharp stink of alcohol filling the cave.

"It's okay." stuttered Kyle, his breath still coming in gasps "There shouldn't be any Infection in the fingers. I've seen scratches before..."

Blood trickled down her brown skin, dripping onto the black Zek coat. She flicked a glance at him "I'm fine. It just hurts, that's all." she finished disinfecting and began sticking dressings to her face.

The stench of the dead Feral was overpowering. They both looked at the corpse and Kyle knew he'd never be able to help her drag it out. Amelia stood, slightly shaky still and gripped the feet, dragging the body halfway to the entrance.

"Bloody hell!" she stopped, panting at even this short distance. Kyle empathised. The dead weight would be excruciatingly hard to move.

"Oh Christ!" he spat out, instinctively trying to sit up. Instantly, his body punished him, slamming him back down to the ground with a wall of pain.

"What? What is it?"

The light from the lantern had fallen on the face of the Feral. Kyle didn't think he'd have noticed but for the black rag tied around the creature's neck. Most of the clothes were torn beyond recognition, dirt encrusted in the folds but the scarf seemed to have survived most of the damage.

"That's mine..." he nodded to the scarf.

Amelia bent down to grip it between her fingers, examining the filthy accoutrement gingerly. The movement caused the Feral's head to lop to the side, the black eyes pointing towards Kyle.

Harrison's pale, dead face stared sightlessly at him.

CHAPTER 43

"We've got to move."

Silence.

"Kyle! We can't stay here..."

"It's Harrison."

Amelia looked at the dead face, concern in her eyes "You know him? Are you sure?"

"It's him." the pain in Kyle's chest was gone, replaced by a cold fury. He remembered the hapless teenager, pale faced and weedy. An idiot, sure but he didn't deserve this fate.

Amelia was crouching over the corpse now, her fear replaced by the professionalism of her trade. She turned the body this way and that, examining the grey flesh.

"He was shot."

The words resounded around the small space, as damning as the gunshots that had ended Harrison's existence.

"How long ago?" Kyle's mind raced as he asked the question. He'd been here a month under Amelia's care and he'd last seen Harrison fleeing Lynch's crime scene with Kerry and Jas. He assumed they'd headed back to Matwood. The thought that they'd be out patrolling so far from the town with snow on the ground was ridiculous. Perhaps the Rangers could make it out this far but the Militia?

"I don't know - we need to leave." Amelia looked towards the entrance "The snow will have deadened the shots."

It was Kyle's turn to glance nervously towards the entrance but he couldn't look away from Harrison for long "Was he shot before he was Infected?"

"I can't tell." She avoided his eyes.

"Amelia!" Kyle hissed

"He – who is he?" she stammered.

"One of the Militia I was looking for when you captured me – answer the question!"

Amelia sat back on her heels, glancing at Kyle but looking quickly away "He was shot before he turned." She held up the grey skinned wrist, peeling back a tightly fastened sleeve to reveal a clear bite mark "Looks like he was bitten but hid it from the others."

Kyle swallowed a lump in his throat at the thought of Harrison, pale, clumsy Harrison hiding the wound, knowing all the while that it was a death sentence.

"Must have been the fight in the woods..." Kyle shook his head.

"He was shot with the same bullet that hit you."

"*What?*"

Amelia nodded miserably "I've been looking at that hole in your chest for a month. I recognise the wounds."

"You can't be certain!"

She shrugged, started to speak then shrugged again "I'd bet money on it."

"I –" Kyle began to argue but the plastic in the cave entrance flapped noisily in a gust of wind, causing Amelia to spin around in terror and Kyle to point his Glock at the sound but there was nothing.

"He managed to find us. That means others will too." Amelia looked significantly at Harrison's corpse.

"Where can we go? You said yourself we can't make it to Matwood."

"Anywhere. Anywhere with shelter."

Kyle shook his head but she was right. They had to move or they'd die in this cave "Pass my map."

Amelia rummaged for the waterproofed paper, handing it to Kyle. She squatted next to him, careful to keep her body facing towards the entrance. Kyle noticed the pistol in her waistband now clearly visible and ready to draw. His own lay on his lap.

"Here..." Amelia traced a rough path from the hospital,

marked on the map in bold letters 'Beijerink Institute of Microbiology'. Kyle could see they were about two kilometres from the facility, through the dense forest. On the map it was shown as spots of sporadic trees but twenty years of untamed growth had altered the shape of the woodland. Kyle could see clearly the rock face that he presumed held the entrance to their cave.

"There." he stabbed his finger onto the wide blue expanse of a lake. A cluster of small farm buildings stood five kilometres away.

"We came past that on the way in..." Amelia muttered.

"And?"

"Overgrown but it looked safe. We can get water from the lake."

"It's not far. Let's go."

She looked at him sceptically "How? I can't carry you. You're enormous."

"Thanks. I'll manage. You take the rifle. If we see another Feral, drop me and use both hands to shoot. You've got more chance of stopping it with that."

"You can't walk, Kyle."

"Then I'll fucking crawl!" he snarled "I'm not waiting here for Jas and Kerry to show up Feral!"

Amelia said no more. She gathered up what supplies she could carry. Kyle insisted she stuff his daysack full of as much food and warm clothing as it would carry. Then, bundled up in blankets, Kyle began the laborious process of standing up.

Half an hour after Harrison's Infected body had erupted into their sanctuary, Kyle, one arm tightly wrapped around Amelia's shoulders, emerged into the wintry forest. He paused, leaning heavily on the slight woman. She grimaced, shifting his weight with her hips.

The trees grew right up to the rock face. Deciduous, the woodland had shed its leaves for the winter and the snow had fallen thickly through the branches. Kyle could only imagine how high the drifts must be on open ground. Roads would be out of the question. Travelling any distance was out of the question. Kyle began to seriously doubt that they would make it as far as the farmhouse.

"Come on..." Amelia was breathless already. Kyle's legs seemed not to obey his mind. They held his weight when he stood still but buckled under the slightest pressure. Only by keeping both knees fully locked and violently lurching his hips from side to side could he manage to move. Even then, it was at a snail's pace and Amelia was grunting with the effort.

They passed through the forest, far from silent. The woods were still and quiet, making Kyle nervous. He jumped at every twitching branch or flapping bird. The Glock was in his right hand, the other was around Amelia's shoulders. Twice they stopped to rest, Kyle leaning heavily against the trunk of a tree, not trusting himself to regain his feet if he quit them.

"How - how much further?" Amelia panted.

"Not much." Kyle lied. Amelia moved into the bushes to relieve herself and Kyle risked a look at the sky, peering through the leafless branches. An hour, maybe more before night fell and they were still hours away from the farmhouse, presuming it was even habitable. Kyle cursed softly to himself, furious at his body for betraying him. Possibilities and solutions flashed through his mind. Amelia would not leave him, he knew that and he was glad. He didn't want to spend the night out here alone. The thought of Ferals or the unknown gunman who had shot him was frightening enough, without his imagination jumping at every movement.

Amelia returned, sweat already starting to freeze on her brow "Ready?"

"Yeah. Look, we're not going to make it-"

"I'm not leaving you."

"I'm not asking you to! I'm saying we need to be practical. Make a camp with the daylight we've got left and move on in the morning."

Amelia blanched at the thought, looking askance at the woods around them "We'll freeze to death."

"Not if we're careful. We've got blankets and coats. I think we'll be warm enough. The biggest problem is if a Wretch finds us."

Amelia kicked at the snow, looking around them "There..." she pointed, striding away through the trees. Kyle lurched after her, clinging to the closely packed tree trunks.

Amelia stopped in an area enclosed by trees, roughly circular "Here. We tie rope around the trees, knee and waist height. If a Wretch stumbles on us, it'll be held back long enough for us to shoot it."

Kyle glanced around, quickly realising the sense in her words. It wasn't perfect, but it might just keep them alive. He tugged a roll of string from his daysack and tried to begin tying the knots but quickly lost his balance and nearly fell.

"Here, lie down." Amelia cleared a patch of snow, lying him down on the damp ground, a thick blanket beneath him. She worked around them, tying the knots with skill and precision. Kyle admired her handiwork.

"Not bad."

"Thanks." she sat beside him, pulling the blanket wide enough to keep her off the cold ground. She looked at the small sanctuary they'd created "Going to be snug tonight."

Kyle sniggered, despite the seriousness of the situation "It's for survival purposes only. I'm sure we can be adult about it."

Amelia lay down next to him, the light above already starting to fade. She shifted closer, her head resting on his shoulder, his arm extended underneath her. She tugged the remaining blankets over the top of them and Kyle closed his eyes, trying to relax. Absurdly, at that point, Rosie's face flashed before his eyes and he felt guilty. Reminding himself that they needed to share body heat to survive the night, he pushed the annoying thought aside.

Amelia yawned quietly next to him and to his surprise, a moment later her breathing eased into slow rhythms and he realised she was asleep. He marvelled at her calm, being able to drop off so quickly.

The light faded fast, although Kyle found he could still see some distance, the white drifts of snow reflecting the ambient light. It was quiet, and despite his nervousness, Kyle found himself drifting. He welcomed sleep, allowing the exhaustion and shock of the day to slide into uncomfortable dreams in which Harrison's face merged with that of Rosie, Sinks and the striking features of Amelia Singh.

They didn't freeze to death, nor did the Wretches discover them. In the dull morning light, they ate a quick breakfast and continued towards the farmhouse.

CHAPTER 44

The long column of marching men was disconsolate and weary. Their smart camouflage was spattered with mud and soaked from the slushy snow. They carried heavy bergans, weighing them down in the muddy ground as they approached the walls of Matwood.

For some, the towering bastion was a welcome sight, a break from the long, dangerous miles they'd walked since leaving London. For others, the rustic setting was far from homely, a desolate outpost barely claiming the title of civilisation.

Behind the marching troops, sputtering along through the churned mud, the olive painted Land Rovers trundled, laden with food, water, and ammunition.

To either side, battered quad bikes, their engines tinny and whining, scouted their flanks, the riders' eyes hidden behind thick goggles.

"Should have brought snowmobiles." observed Hannah, without looking at Sinks.

They stood atop the wide fire step that lined the top of Matwood's gate. Sinks had taken to standing here on his time off, staring out over the woods as the snow smothered the ground. Hannah had joined him, trying to reconcile with her friend.

"Surprised they got even this many working. Parliament must be bloody desperate." Hannah continued, ignoring the silence from Sinks. She gestured at a Land Rover that had broken down, the occupants now standing around it arguing "Those things were shit before the Fall. Where'd they get diesel from, anyway?"

"Ethanol." Sinks muttered.

"Oh? That's what they run on now?" Hannah tried to press him but the dour northerner would yield no more conversation. Hannah sighed, a cloud of vapour leaving her mouth in the frigid air.

The column of men spread into the cleared ground that lay between Matwood and the thick woods. The front runners, a small group of drab painted vehicles had already formed a camp but the newcomers were directed into an enormous rough triangle shape, sentries posted at each corner. Rows of barbed wire were the first defence, staked into the hard ground by pairs of soldiers with iron poles and sledgehammers. Soon, the clanging of metal could be heard throughout the town and Hannah did not relish the poor men and women who wanted only to rest after their long journey. She knew that in this weather, the Officers would abandon any attempt to dig a perimeter trench and waited, wondering if they'd attempt to throw up a wall using the snow. The speed of the work was impressive, showing the well drilled skills of the soldiers although Hannah, despite the silence of her companion, found her critical soldiers' eye falling on small details; a coil of wire not properly secured, sentry posts too close to the treeline. She cursed about them until a burst of frustration made her round on the silent Sinks.

"Are you going to sulk for the rest of your life?" she snapped.

It was the wrong thing to say. Sinks turned at her tone and paused for a heartbeat as she saw the anger rise in his eyes, still bruised from the blow she'd given him in the woods. He stepped forward, catching her by surprise and gripping her by the throat, ramming her back against the parapet.

"You think I'm sulking? You think this is me throwing my toys out the pram after I saw you gunning down innocent civilians? You're a murderer, Hannah, not a soldier."

Hannah angrily thrust his hand away from her "Leave it out, Sinks! I don't like it any more than you do!"

"Then why do it? Huh?"

"It's out of control, mate! The Ferals are everywhere and the

Zeks are only making things worse! You think I don't want to know what's happening in France? It's a bloody miracle to me too! But our job is to protect people and if these refugees are all Infected then I'll spill blood until they're all gone!"

"You don't know they're Infected! They don't look it, do they?"

"They're carriers –" she began but Sinks gave a loud, humourless snort.

"Oh yeah! Carriers! As if we've ever had a passive carrier of the virus! Twenty years, Hannah and that's never been seen before!"

"Neither have this many Ferals! The virus is mutating, Sinks! It's changing! We always knew this could happen!"

Both were breathing heavily, their breath frosting in the frigid air.

"Look, I have no doubt that some of the refugees aren't Infected but we don't have a way to test, Sinks."

"You just take Armstrong's word?"

"Yes! You know why? Because who else has studied the virus like he has? Who else has been as close to it, analysing the Infection, fighting the Wretches? If he says they're Infected then I'll believe him!"

Another pause as Sinks stared at her. Then, abruptly he turned on his heel and half walked, half ran down the stairs that led to ground level.

"Oi! Where are you going?"

Sinks did not turn. He bellowed at the guards to open the gate, ignoring Hannah's shouts behind him. Her voice echoed after him but Sinks was running, his spirits higher than they'd been since Rosie and Kyle had died as he headed away from Hannah, away from the Rangers and the glowering eyes of Armstrong. Back to the Regular Army, to men and women who, like him, had no politics, no grand aims, and designs.

Only their duty to serve, to fight and to protect the people they'd sworn to defend.

CHAPTER 45

The snow was thicker the next day. The sky was grey and the flakes matched it with a dirty discolouration that reminded Kyle of the dead skin on Harrison's face. Uneasy, he limped onwards, Amelia sweating and panting with the exertion beside him.

They stopped to rest at the edge of a wide, snow covered field. Here and there small shrubs poked through the thick white mantle but to Kyle it was a relief to see the end of the woods. A thin grove of tall pines stood at the edge of a small frozen pond and it was on the thick blanket of needles that Kyle sat.

Amelia lay on her back, eyes closed. Kyle looked at her worriedly. For his own part, he felt as though a burning hot poker was being shoved through his chest with every breath. His legs and feet were burning with cramps and he knew if he rolled up his trouser leg, his knees would be swollen from the impact. Clearly, they were almost at the limit of their endurance. Kyle risked a glance at the map. He thought that they were close now.

Amelia stirred, sitting upright. She staggered to her feet and made a beeline for the frozen pond. Carefully, she crouched on the bank and cracked the ice, dipping her hand into the frigid water and scooping a handful of clear liquid.

"Taste alright?" called Kyle.

She didn't respond, instead dipping a bottle in. The water gurgled as it rushed in before Amelia turned and came back to sit beside Kyle.

"How's the pain?"

"Fine." it wasn't, but there wasn't anything either of them

could do about it here. A gust of wind blew across them, both of them closing their eyes against the cold blast of snowflakes.

Kyle's head snapped up, the precipitation forgotten "Do you smell that?"

"Smoke."

They both looked around the field, as though the fire would reveal itself to them. Amelia picked up a mixed handful of pine needles and snow and tossed it into the air. The pile blew to their left, south. Kyle had the map out in an instant, Amelia fishing the compass from her pocket. She pressed it against the paper as they both looked, praying they were wrong.

"No. No!" gasped Amelia.

"It might not be there..."

"Where else would it be? It's hardly a forest fire, is it?"

"Who would set the farm on fire?" Kyle's question was rhetorical.

There was silence. Amelia was on her feet, staring north towards the distant smoke. The grey plume was vaguely visible against the dark sky. Clearly, it was from the farmhouse that was their destination.

Kyle slowly leaned back onto the ground. Exhaustion racked his body. He knew they couldn't carry on another day like this. It was too far to go back to the cave and they wouldn't survive out in the woods. Not with Ferals around.

"Do you think someone's following us?"

Amelia's words brought Kyle snapping to attention. As much as his injured body would permit, he twisted to look around them. His pistol came into his hands and Amelia brought the rifle uncertainly into a two handed grip.

"Christ. Could have done. We wouldn't have noticed. We made enough noise for the whole country to hear us."

The snow fell harder.

"How would they know where we were going?"

"Where else is there?" Kyle rustled the map.

"Maybe it's a coincidence? It's an old building. Maybe the snow made a roof collapse and something struck a spark."

"What, twenty years and it chooses the moment we head towards it to spontaneously combust? Not a chance."

Amelia cast a furtive glance at the woods behind them before turning back to the open field "Well? What's the point in burning the place down? Surely if they wanted us dead, they'd have killed us in the woods."

"Maybe they want to make it look like an accident? We're pretty well armed." Kyle gestured at the rifle.

"They had a machine gun at the hospital!"

"Maybe it's not them. Jas said there were bandits along the road."

"That's thirty miles from here."

"So? No-one's going to be travelling in this weather. The woods are warmer and give better cover. Where would you hide if you were a bandit? Or a refugee?"

Amelia said nothing. She raised the rifle and began to scan the trees through the sights.

"If it was the men who shot me, they'd have killed us by now." Kyle was talking himself into it "It's bandits. They moved ahead of us and burned the farmhouse. If we die of exposure, they can take our stuff without a fight."

Amelia lowered the rifle and turned to him "Well, it looks like that's what's going to happen."

Kyle scowled "No. Come on, let's figure it out. We've survived one night out here. We can do it again."

Amelia shrugged. She looked utterly dejected. Kyle began pouring over the map but there was nothing they could reach. He sat back, folding the piece of paper away.

"Look, we're both exhausted. There's water here and we've got some food left. Let's just sit down and rest. We aren't going to make good decisions when we're tired like this."

"Do you always have a plan? Is that how you get through life? Head down and charge? If it doesn't work, shoot it?" Amelia's eyes were filled with angry tears as she rounded on Kyle "You're just the same as Armstrong. All of you! I don't know why I helped you. Now I'm going to die out here, for fucking nothing!"

Kyle stared at her open mouthed. Her words cut into him and left him speechless. Amelia turned away towards the field, her body shaking with fury.

"I - I don't know what else to do. I'm not just giving up -"

She rounded on him once again "Giving up? Giving up? You think I'm giving up? I'm a doctor! I know what's going to happen! We'll get more and more tired and then we'll lie down in the snow and we'll fucking die! And for what? I came so close!" she held out a hand, fist clenched "I came *this* close to solving it all, to fixing this shitty fucking world and then you came charging in like some goddamn *soldier*!"

She slumped to the ground in the snow, sitting with her legs outstretched, the rifle discarded beside her. Her arms slumped by her sides and she leaned her head forward. She was silent.

Kyle edged himself forward, resisting the urge to grunt with the pain. He sat in front of her, his own legs crossed and looked at his companion. Her long dark hair had come loose from the thin hat she wore and covered her face. He could see the silent tears falling into the snow though, see the holes the hot liquid made in the white blanket. Kyle reached out and laid his hand on her arm, tentatively at first, then when she allowed the touch, more firmly. He shifted forward, ignoring the pain of his wound to half envelop her in his arms.

He expected her to push him away but to his surprise, she leaned her head forward and pressed herself hard against him. Sobs shook her body and he waited, muttering soothing words as the anger and emotion burned themselves out. She suddenly moved, leaning back and sniffing, embarrassed. She looked at Kyle and he saw the barrier come back up in her eyes, the defeatist anger sparking again.

"Well at least there's one thing we can do if we're going to die." she seized Kyle's head and roughly hauled his face towards hers. She mashed her lips against his, kissing him violently and knotting her fingers in his hair when he tried to pull away.

"Amelia! This isn't -"

"This isn't what? What else do you want to do? This is what soldiers do, isn't it? You fight and you fuck?" she slammed his head back towards her again, trying to bury his head in the warm flesh of her neck.

Kyle shoved her back away from him. Injured or not, he was twice her weight and she was flung back in the snow. She lay, staring at him and panting.

"Not like this." he snarled at her.

"Why? Why the fuck not?" she came at him again, this time shoving him down with a gasp of pain. She straddled him, her face in front of his. He could see the fury and hurt in her eyes, the desperate pain "What does it matter?"

"Get off!" he snarled, flinging her off him into the snow. Undeterred, she grabbed his arm and struggled with him. Now they were fighting. She slapped him hard across the face and Kyle pinned her arm, inadvertently kneeling atop her legs.

She spat in his face and he snarled at her to stop, to be still.

All at once, there was laughter.

Amelia had opened her mouth again and for a confused second, Kyle thought it was her, that her mind had completely snapped and she was having hysterics. But the laugh was low and cruel and with a sense of dread, Kyle looked up into the faces of the ring of men who stood around them, each of them laughing without humour at the scene before them.

Someone seized him from behind and he scrabbled for the pistol. His eyes came to rest on it, lying a few feet away in the snow. A foot, clad in a worn and holed leather boot came down on it. Kyle was flung onto his back and he heard Amelia scream as someone grabbed her.

"This one looks half fuckin' dead already!"

"Good! Saves us the trouble. Good tracking lads..."

"Wassup with you then, boy?" the speaker was a man whose face was hidden behind a filthy scarf. He stood over Kyle, a knife in his hand. He nudged Kyle's chest with his toe and Kyle recoiled, snarling with pain. The man crouched down and pulled Kyle's clothes aside to see his wound. He pressed the knife to Kyle's throat, the sharp edge drawing blood.

"You Infected?"

"No."

"What's this from, then?"

"Shot."

Amelia screamed again to his right. Kyle couldn't move his head far enough to see what was happening to her but he heard a chuckle of seedy laughter and could guess.

"How'd you survive getting shot?"

"I'm a doctor!" Amelia's voice was raised in a plaintive cry. The man with the knife to Kyle's throat whipped his head across at her. He snapped a terse command to someone and sounds of movement stopped.

"This true?" he turned back to Kyle "She a doctor? She treat you?"

"Yes."

"Well." the man looked up at his companions who Kyle couldn't see "Looks like we've struck the jackpot, dunnit lads? This one to play with -" he nodded at Kyle "And this one to fix us all up!"

"And to play with!" declared another man, sick relish in his voice.

The knife man, who seemed to be in charge took the knife away from Kyle's throat, levelling it at his companions "Listen 'ere. You leave the doctor alone. I don't want her nicking my kidney in my sleep! She's not for playing with."

"I'm not helping you!" snarled Amelia.

The man's response was to punch Kyle in the chest.

It was like being hit with a sledgehammer. Kyle tried to scream, to suck in breath but it was like his lungs were made of concrete. He coughed and spluttered, fighting for breath. A thin mewing sound came from his throat as he desperately sucked in air.

The world began to darken.

"Think you've done for 'im, boss." laughed a voice.

"Nah. Reckon I've just created the perfect job interview. Oi, Doctor Pretty. You make your boyfriend here all nice and better again and I'll let you earn your keep. He dies, we know you aren't any good and then we'll have some fun..."

Kyle sank back into the snow, consciousness fleeing.

CHAPTER 46

It wasn't the same as when he'd been shot. Then he'd faded into a different world made of darkness and terrible dreams. Now, the cold was still present, the glaring white of the snow all around him. Every successful breath was like a rush of cold water on a parched desert. He coughed, spluttered, and cried when his lungs would allow. When they were empty, the blackness claimed him.

He was aware that he was being dragged. Snow built up around his boots, spilling over the top and melting against his skin. He shivered.

Their captors were silent around them. No ribald shouts of victory, they moved through the forest with the skill of men well used to relying on quiet to survive. The leader walked before Kyle, the black rifle that had once belonged to the US Army clutched in his hands. The men all wore white coveralls, stained with dirt but still lending them an effective camouflage.

Kyle drifted...

Time passed, how much he couldn't tell but the group had stopped. The light was fading which meant they had been travelling for hours. Kyle heard Amelia being ordered somewhere and then someone was tugging him left and right and the coarse weave of a rope brushed against his neck. Kyle tried to struggle, thinking they were going to hang him but a gruff voice growled at him to be still. The ropes were twisted under his arms with a skilful series of knots and then Kyle found himself being hoisted into the air.

A snarl close at hand and Kyle cried out, twisting, and jerking in the air as next to him, a grey faced Wretch snapped with blackened gums. He tried desperately to swing away but then he was being lifted past the monster and it stayed, suspended by its own ropes.

His head fell back and he stared at the grey sky above him. The thin branches of the trees were moving towards him. Was he floating? He was confused, delirious with exhaustion and pain. He heard the rope creak and smelled damp wood. A woman's voice sounded and more hands caught him, pulling him towards them.

"Get him down... Into here... Yes, there."

He was lying on a bed, a soft, warm bed and he was vaguely aware of someone stripping him. A voice cackled with glee as his boots were removed and he struggled feebly, trying to prevent the robbery. A hand slapped his, a voice snapped at him and then a cold metal bracelet was on his wrist. Kyle tried to lift his hand but could not. He stared stupidly at the blurry images before him and then he heard Amelia's voice, asking for tools, for water.

Laughter.

Pain.

Darkness.

CHAPTER 47

Sinks was at war.

The hard ground before the walls of Matwood had become a churning sea of soldiers. The stink of vehicle exhaust and the constant revving of engines filled his waking hours, interspersed with blasts of icy wind or sudden snow showers. No-one had questioned him when he appeared from the walls, separating himself from the Rangers inside. Armstrong had sent no demands for him to return to his post and he'd fitted in as though he'd marched from London with the rest.

A platoon of young soldiers now looked up to him, taking their cues from the grizzled Sergeant rather than the pink cheeked London-born Lieutenant who ostensibly commanded them. For their sake, Sinks tried to calm the anger that seethed inside him. Long years of hiding his emotions for the sake of command gave him discipline and he spoke calmly to the troops, directing them when they were wrong and encouraging them when they performed well.

Every day he left the camp, sometimes in a freezing and stinking convoy of vehicles, sometimes in a line of camouflaged troops, winding their way into the woods. They encountered the Infected in droves. Ferals, their black eyes terrifying against the white snow erupted seemingly from nowhere to screams of pain and the bursts of rifle fire, sounding as always to Sinks like the snapping of a bundle of dry twigs.

Soldiers died.

Blood, both black and red stained the white snow for miles around the camp. Wretch corpses lay where they fell, the stink of death almost overpowering. The land was devoid of animal life, no birds dotted the frigid sky despite the unburied dead, instincts driving the creatures to safety.

Sinks wished he could follow.

The black mood that gripped him had little to do with the grey skinned monsters who tore his soldiers to shreds and filled his nightmares with terrible dreams of clashing teeth. Instead, it was the sneering attitude of the Rangers that made him grip his rifle tight and force his face into a cold, emotionless mask every time the elite troops passed the camp.

They shouted insults at the regular soldiers outside the walls, laughing as they passed the latrine trenches and making ribald comments. They patrolled the woods sure enough but their target was not the Ferals but the refugees. Human screams sounded whenever a Ranger patrol entered the trees and red blood stained the snow. They left the Ferals to the regular soldiers and none of the Rangers came back on stretchers, their life force pulsing through a torn neck or cold and stiff, dumped unceremoniously into the back of a rickety Land Rover.

Since leaving Matwood, the Infected had slaughtered eight of his platoon outright. Two more had been critically Infected and euthanised by the medics while a ninth, a teenager named Brown had fled the rest of the patrol upon seeing the bite on her forearm. Sinks had chased her but the shouts from the rest of the patrol had drawn him back to see another soldier, his face pale beneath the blood spattering his skin. Forced to abandon Brown, they'd raced back to the camp with their injured comrade suspended from a makeshift stretcher between them. Later, Sinks had found Brown's tracks which ended in a collection of footprints so wild it could only have been an ambush by Ferals and Brown's name was added to the list of the dead that evening.

Then there were the Zeks. Not the pacifist, Wretch-loving lunatics that wandered the wastes but battle hardened soldiers, clad in black and red who lurked between the thick trees that surrounded Matwood. But there was a difference.

The Regular Army soldiers, their uniforms distinct from the elite Rangers were not targeted by the Zeks. Sinks had lost count of the number of ambushes they'd walked into only to see the backs of the enemy, sprinting from their positions without firing a shot.

As he trudged through the thick snow, Sinks scanned the undergrowth nervously. Was there movement there? Was it Zeks or the Infected? Or was it more of the hapless civilians who'd fled their own lands, risking drowning, and storms in decades-old boats only to find bloody murder awaiting them? Sinks shook his head to dislodge the dark thoughts, hastening his pace to follow the soldier in front of him.

"Sergeant Sinclair!" the voice of Lieutenant Chard sounded in a loud hiss behind him and Sinks half turned to acknowledge his platoon commander. The younger man was jogging to catch up with him, clouds of steam emanating from his mouth.

"Sir! Stop running! Bloody Zeks could be watching us right now and put a bullet in you!"

The Officer quailed before the Sergeant, an example of the odd dichotomy of leadership that enlisted soldiers and Officers manoeuvred around. Sinks was of course under Chard's command but Chard had almost no experience compared to the decades of soldiering Sinks had under his belt. Sinks was always careful to salute the Officer when they were in camp and call him 'Sir' when speaking but he was equally unafraid of giving the younger man a hard time when he made himself a target in a hostile environment.

"Sorry..." Chard began to apologise before remembering his training and stopping "There's that clearing up ahead where Brown went missing. We've got a couple of hours of daylight left, I want to split the sections up and cover some ground there before we head back."

Sinks was impressed at the Lieutenant's compassion for the Private. Despite the fact that the missing teenager was almost certainly dead, finding her body was as important as destroying the Ferals. Sinks nodded his agreement and pressed his radio to issue the command.

Fifteen minutes later the platoon crouched uncomfortably in the snow, every soldier facing out in a ring of rifle barrels as Sinks completed the laborious process of passing orders to the section commanders. They were pleased with Chard's decision, he could see. Finding Brown would be a much needed boost to morale and Sinks made sure that every soldier overheard their goal.

"We staying out all night?" Corporal Davies, commander of two section asked. Sinks shook his head and saw Davies mask her relief. Davies was young, tough, and intelligent but being out here in the dark was enough to make anyone blanch. As she headed back to two section, Sinks remembered that she and Brown had been friendly, finding some companionship as some of the few women in the mostly male environment.

"You staying here?" Bales, commander of three section asked and Sinks shook his head again.

"No. I'm with Davies, the boss is coming with you." He indicated Chard who was kneeling in the centre of the platoon as he completed a radio sitrep with their base.

"Movement!" came a hiss from one section and every head turned towards the alarm.

"Eyes-on!" barked Sinks "Everyone watch their own arcs!" reluctant heads turned back to face the correct directions, resisting the urge to watch for a threat. Sinks met soldiers' eyes until they turned away.

There was movement – or there had been. Now there was a shaking branch, notable because the tree was an evergreen that had collected more snow than most. Having dumped a load of whiteness to the ground, it waved gently.

"Just the ice melting?" Chard had approached Sinks and his voice was hopeful.

"Can't see. Davies! Take three blokes and go find out."

Davies hissed orders and a moment later, rifle firmly in her shoulder she led a fire team under the branch and out of sight.

Crack

The rifle round passed over the heads of the kneeling platoon. Sinks wheeled around, staring at the opposite side of the clearing in confusion. Although they were kneeling or lying prone, the troops were exposed and he couldn't fathom how an ambusher would miss so severely.

Rat-a-tat-tat

The unmistakeable chatter of a machine gun sounded and Sinks swore, dragging Chard flat beside him as the rounds zipped overhead. Voices shouted 'Contact!' and the soldiers began to return fire.

"It's by three section!" Sinks pointed and Chard nodded, spilling out a stream of orders that had Bales, the commander up and directing his troops to cover and fire towards the machine gun.

"Where is the enemy?" a voice called but there was no response. From their low position, Sinks knew, they couldn't see the shooters but that wouldn't stop them firing back and applying their training.

Without warning a band of a dozen people so ragged and grimy their features were impossible to make out erupted from the treeline into which three section faced. A rifle cracked but then Bales' voice snapped out a sharp command and all firing stopped.

Save for the machine gun which opened up with a vengeance, heavy rounds tearing into the backs of the refugees and revealing the real target.

Rat-a-tat-tat

"Bastards!" snarled Sinks as two of the figures spun and vanished into the snow. The others had the presence of mind to fling themselves flat, making the hidden gunners pause in their murderous assault.

"Where's Davies?" Chard suddenly snapped and Sinks turned away from the gunfire to see the four troops that remained of two section milling about, leaderless.

"I'll take over!" Sinks snapped but Chard shouted after him

as he ran to the section lines.

"Get into the woods! Find Davies! Then get back here!"

Sinks nodded, gesturing to the four men and he led them at a flat sprint into the treeline.

Straight into the crowd of Zeks.

*

"Enemy!" the word was out of Sinks' mouth before he had a chance to stop it but, as he dodged into cover behind a tree trunk, readying his rifle for the fight it occurred to him that the Zeks were not the ones shooting.

"Sergeant?"

Sinks looked back to see the rest of two section in cover, looking past him but none of them had spoken,

"Sergeant? Over here."

It was the Zeks.

Sinks risked poking his helmeted head out from behind the tree "What?"

"We aren't shooting at you. It's the Rangers –"

"Sod off!" snapped Sinks, mind racing for what to do. He closed his eyes, revisiting the image in his memory as he'd ducked under the trees. Perhaps ten of the Zeks, all in military gear with rifles. He couldn't hope to win a firefight with them but they weren't shooting. The machine gun fire from the clearing behind him had all but stopped and there were long pauses now between bursts of firing as though the gunners were moving position.

"Sergeant!" there was urgency in the Zek's voice now. Sinks risked a second glance around the tree to see a middle aged man with weather beaten skin standing with his arms outstretched to either side, the universal sign of disarmament.

"Where's Davies?"

"Your Corporal? She went past us. We haven't harmed her. We aren't here to harm you. Please, there isn't much time!"

"Who are you?"

"Colonel Eric Forbes."

Sinks' breath caught in his throat "You're the one attacking my men?"

"Sergeant, I give you my word as an Officer that those gunners are not my men!"

"Then who the hell are they?"

"Rangers."

"Why would Rangers be shooting at my men?"

An explosion sounded from behind Sinks and Chard's voice crackled over the radio in his ear.

".., get back here! We've got another contact to the north –"

"Sergeant!" Forbes' – if indeed it was Forbes – voice was laden with urgency "Your men will be cut to pieces if you don't listen to me!"

"Alright!" Sinks was torn, half of him wanting nothing more than to gun the Zeks down and return to the platoon "What do you want?"

"The Rangers aren't shooting at your men – they're shooting at the refugees!"

"They're Infected!"

"Hah!" there was no humour in Forbes' laugh "Did you buy that propaganda, Sergeant? Blake Armstrong convinced you, did he?"

Sinks growled low in his throat. Behind him the machine gun fire was increasing in intensity. Rifles cracked in response and he heard his troops shouting orders.

"From your silence I can tell you doubt it. What's your name, Sergeant?"

"Sinclair." His admission was out before he could stop himself. Sinks couldn't have said what made him confess his name.

A sharp intake of breath "Sinclair?" Forbes started to say more but an explosion sounded behind Sinks and he turned, fear for his men overtaking his concern.

"We need to get out there!" Forbes was shouting "We need to get your men out of that clearing –"

BOOM

"Rangers!" snapped the nearest man and Sinks heard an ever increasing roar as a helicopter swung overhead.

"Sinclair! Get the fuck back here now!"

"Lads! Back to the clearing!" Sinks made his decision and turned to run. The four men around him lost no time, vanishing back under the snow covered branches. Sinks made to follow but the Zeks were with him now and he roared at them to stay.

"No! We're coming with you!" Forbes was level with him and Sinks swore, abandoning any attempt to control the black dressed soldiers and sprinting back into the clearing.

BOOM

The missile came from behind Sinks, shooting over the trees and exploding in the clearing.

Sinks froze as he realised Forbes was right. The Rangers were shooting at his men. But why? He whirled in confusion and then a hand shoved him roughly to the ground as a fusillade of bullets tore the air above his head.

"Sinclair!" Chard was next to him but it was Forbes who had shoved him down. Chard barely spared the Zek a glance, noting only that he did not seem to present a threat.

"We need to move back south, Sir!" Sinks snapped "Have we got comms with the Rangers? They're bloody shooting at us!"

"Yes, we have! We're trying to get a response." Chard was shouting as the adrenaline surged "There's a second machine gun to the north –" he pointed and as if on cue, a burst of fire came from the treeline by one section who responded in kind with a burst of fire that silenced the gunners.

"Any casualties?" Sinks saw the confusion on Chard's face that he would ask that question at this stage of the fight but the Officer shook his head.

"None."

"Then they aren't shooting at us!" Sinks shouted to be heard as the helicopter swung back overhead.

"Oh –" he heard Forbes shout beside him and then all eyes

were locked on the Ranger who crouched behind the machine gun mounted on the side of the aircraft, his face hidden behind a snow mask as he pressed the trigger and then heavy rounds tore up the snow around Sinks and two of Forbes' men were shredded into screaming red ruin by the weapon.

"Jesus wept!" Sinks looked around frantically for the signaller but the young Private with the radio simply flung his hands up in despair.

"They're ignoring me, Sergeant!"

Rat-a-tat-tat-a-tat

The helicopter had swung around as Sinks' troops began to fire on it, the rifle rounds impacting off the fuselage. For a moment, the gunner was unable to bring his weapon to bear but a second Ranger leaned out of the cabin with his rifle and fired a burst of automatic fire into one section. Sinks heard screams and shouts from there and he snarled at the airborne menace.

"Fire!" Forbes' voice snapped close at hand and a vicious hissing sound came from behind followed by a great *WHUMP* as a Zek fired an ugly, tube shaped weapon at the chopper. Sinks memory flickered and he briefly frowned as he recalled the last time he'd seen the NLAW anti-tank weapons...

BOOM

The helicopter was suddenly a raging inferno spinning out of control towards the woods beneath which Sinks, Forbes and Chard crouched.

"Move!" Sinks bellowed, noting as he did so that Chard was unmoving. He grabbed the young Lieutenant under the arms and sprinted, dragging the Officer unceremoniously behind him.

The helicopter struck the ground in a grinding of metal and shrieking protest of engines straining to turn rotors that were digging into the frozen ground and flames were lancing up, hot against Sinks back and the snow seemed too deep to move and anyway he was running east, towards the original machine gun position but now he could see Bales directing his section there, turning the ambush into an orderly attack but there was an almighty searing heat on the back of Sinks' neck and he felt himself lifted up, flung forward and he was aware of rolling over and over, cold snow pouring down his shirt collar and the odd thought.

I'm burning and freezing at the same time

"Sergeant!" he couldn't tell who's the voice was but someone was dragging him and he felt the heat on his face now. He couldn't see, he cuffed angrily at his eyes, striking himself with his rifle accidentally and the sharp pain as the metal struck his skin snapped him from the stupor he'd fallen into and Sinks stared in appalled shock at the ruin of the Ranger helicopter, burning fiercely on the far side of the clearing. Already, the trees closest to it were well alight and Sinks wondered at weapon that had felled the aircraft.

"Sinks?"

Sinks staggered to his feet as behind him the sounds of battle began to die down. He blinked, shaking his head and saw Davies, bloodstained but with her three missing men looking at him.

"I'm alright. Just flash burned."

"Bales has overrun the machine gun." Davies was staring into the woods.

"Chard?"

She caught his eye and shook her head. Sinks sat up to see Chard's wide staring eyes and the gore that splattered across the snow. He shook his head, forcing the dead Officer from his mind as Bales' voice came over the radio.

"Re-org on me! Follow the markers in to our position..."

"Did you signal them?" Sinks asked the young Private as he followed Forbes and the remnants of the platoon towards the captured position.

"They wouldn't answer. I heard them call back to Matwood though. They got an order to attack us." The young man's voice was disbelieving.

"You can't go back there, then." Forbes face was grim and

Sinks remembered that the man had led thousands of troops in his life and would well understand the losses that Sinks was feeling "You can come with us."

"Where to?"

Forbes told him and Sinks just stared at the Colonel.

"Alright?"

Bales was asking him, looking for leadership as he crouched by the torn bodies of four dead Rangers, clustered around a machine gun.

"Yeah." Sinks muttered, still staring at Forbes.

"I believe you know the way, Sergeant?" Forbes tried to smile but couldn't quite manage it.

Sinks nodded and gestured for his surviving troops to follow as he headed away from the burning helicopter into the woods, his sharp eyes spotting the tracks leading east, towards the ruins of Holden. Not the booted tracks of humans, nor the lumbering prints of the Infected but small, with sharp claws surrounding the padded feet.

Sinks straightened up, hefted his rifle, and crushed the pain he felt in his heart as he followed the dog tracks.

CHAPTER 48

"You awake?"

Amelia's voice.

He was awake, but he wasn't ready to show her yet. He lay still, listening. There was an oppressive silence around him, the dulling of sound that comes with heavy snow. He could hear Amelia's breathing beside him.

She took his hand, squeezing his palm gently.

"Kyle, I'm sorry about this. I - I was exhausted I lost it... It's my fault we got caught..." there was despair in her voice.

Kyle didn't respond. He felt stronger, his chest was lighter, his breathing easier. Tentatively, he flexed his arms and legs. Amelia's hand did not release his.

"I shouldn't have done that. I've never done that before. I didn't mean to be..." she tailed off.

"It's okay."

Kyle opened his eyes. Amelia had started and dropped his hand. She was sat on a roughhewn wooden chair beside the cot that Kyle lay on. They were in a neat, wooden walled room. Light came from a window in one wall, filled with an opaque plastic. Kyle could see snow falling outside.

"How are you feeling?"

Kyle gingerly flexed his arms and legs. He tensed his chest and core, grimacing only a little at the echo of pain "Better."

"Good."

The door thumped open. The man who'd punched Kyle in the snow was there, dressed in his white snow camouflage with Kyle's rifle hanging casually from a shoulder.

He grinned at the sight of Kyle and any relief at the receding pain faded quickly. The bandit turned to Amelia "Well. Seems you weren't full of it after all. Come on, you've got work to do." he stood aside, gesturing for her to leave.

"I'll check back on you in a bit, Kyle." Amelia seemed to be trying to tell him something with her eyes but Kyle couldn't guess at the hidden meaning. She stood, passing the man and avoiding his eyes.

"Boy - enjoy your rest. Try to leave this room without permission and we'll hang you - no questions asked. Your pretty friend refuses to help us - we'll hang you. You put a toe out of line and we'll hang you. Got it? Good. Doctor Pretty says you need another week in bed before you can get up and about. I reckon two days should do it so I suggest you think healing thoughts."

He had closed the short distance from the door to Kyle. Kyle shivered at the cold air that wafted in.

"Where are we?"

His captor slapped him hard across the face. Kyle moved a hand to block but found to his shock that it was cuffed to the edge of the bed. He stared stupidly as the lazy blow connected, rocking his head on his shoulders. He felt blood trickle from his lip.

"Speak out of turn again, boy, and I'll mess you up so bad you'll wish we'd left you out in the snow." the man took a step back, adjusting the rifle on his shoulder "As to where you are, you don't need to worry about that. Fact is, winter here has been hard. Me and my boys have got our own work to do and we need someone to do the odd jobs around here." he smiled evilly "You look like you can handle some hard work."

Kyle didn't respond. His face was throbbing with the blow.

"Oh. One other thing. You look tough and I reckon threatenin' you ain't gonna carry much weight. So let's make somethin' clear. There's a lot of blokes around here - not too many women. So long as Doctor Pretty keeps us healthy, I'll keep the boys away from her. But you cause me any problems, I'll hang you and then I'll let the boys have her. Reckon she'll keep us going until spring, don't you?" he cackled and made to leave the room.

Kyle was burning with anger at the man's words. He had no doubt the bandits would carry out the threat but there was nothing he could in his weakened, unarmed state.

"What do I call you?" he asked as the man turned to leave the hut. The bandit stopped, his hand twitching as though to strike Kyle again but instead he clenched a fist and grinned.

"Boss. That's my name. Got it?"

"Yes, Boss." muttered Kyle.

The door slammed, leaving Kyle alone with his thoughts.

CHAPTER 49

The first day that Kyle was out of bed, he nearly died.

He could walk, indeed, his recovery was remarkable. Boss met him outside the small hut with a sly grin that seemed to be his trademark. Shoving a crudely made broom into Kyle's hands he bade him sweep the snow from the paths.

It was only as Kyle stepped out the door that he realised where he was.

Twenty feet or so off the ground, the hut was just one building in a rickety but ingenious settlement suspended in the trees of the forest. Well clear of the grabbing hands of a Wretch but low enough to benefit from the shelter of the towering branches, the buildings looked carefully designed, weight evenly distributed across strong branches, even if the walls were made from a hodgepodge of corrugated iron, weathered planks and dirty plastic.

Walkways, thin wooden planks suspended from a vee shape of twisted wire and rope paved the streets of the village. It was these that Kyle was ordered to sweep and as he stabbed the bristles of the broom at a pile of freshly fallen snow, he slipped on a patch of ice and his legs shot over the side. Frantically, he grabbed at the rope, managing to secure a grip as his chest roared with agony. He gasped, the only sound he could make. The broom spun to the forest floor below as Boss roared with cruel laughter.

"Boy, you kill yourself and your pretty friend goes around the town. Get your skinny arse up off the floor!"

Kyle slowly tugged himself back to his feet, clutching the ropes tightly.

"Now. That broom ain't gonna pick itself up, is it?" Boss

gestured at a tangled bundle of wood and rope that was half buried in snow. Kyle eased himself off the walkway, back to the thin platform of planks that stood outside the front of the hut. He kicked the snow off to reveal a coiled rope ladder. He realised that the bandits must have scavenged miles of wire cable which they had twisted in with the ropes to strengthen the strands. Still, some of the cable strands were frayed and he looked at the ladder warily.

"Down you go, boy. And you learn rule number one around here - never leave a ladder hanging down. You let them Wretches into my town, I'll feed you to 'em. You go down, you get your broom and you get back up here snappy-like. Got it?" Boss kicked the rope ladder carelessly off the edge. Kyle watched it unravel to the floor.

"Get a move on!" Boss had produced a hefty looking coil of thin ropes, twisted together and knotted at one end. He lashed out suddenly, striking Kyle across the back.

Kyle hissed in pain as the whip burned even through the thick layers of clothing. Boss laughed at his pain and raised the whip again threateningly. Kyle wasted no time in scrambling to the ladder, carefully placing his feet on the wooden steps and gripping the rope tightly. Boss aimed another stroke at his hands and Kyle moved down as fast as he could.

He reached the forest floor and scanned the woods for signs of movement. The image of blackened gums snapping at him as he was hoisted into the air filled his mind.

The Wretch lumbered around a tree, arms outstretched towards Kyle. A slow one, little threat but still, Kyle jumped back.

"Boy you best hurry up and get that broom!" shouted Boss from above, making Kyle jump "Don't you worry 'bout old gummy down there! He can't get you."

The Wretch had halted suddenly, several metres away from Kyle. It's arms were still outstretched but the moan had cut off and now a faint gurgling sound emitted from the grey face.

"Get a soddin' move on!" snarled Boss, stamping on the

wooden boards.

The broom was between Kyle and the Wretch and it went against every instinct in Kyle's body to move closer but he could see now the hefty leather collar around the beast's neck. A long cable led away, behind the tree to an anchor point that Kyle couldn't make out. Clearly, the Wretch was what kept the ground beneath the treetop sanctuary safe.

"Boy you got about ten seconds 'afore Doctor Pretty gets more'n she can handle!" Boss grabbed his crotch in a revolting gesture, leering down at Kyle "You think about runnin' off, same thing happens!" Kyle stepped forward, not taking his eyes off the bound Wretch as he snatched up the broom and shoved the long handle under his clothes, leaving both hands free to climb. When he reached the top, Boss just smiled and pointed with the whip at the snow. Kyle started sweeping.

CHAPTER 50

That first day, he swept all the walkways. The snow had eased through the daylight hours meaning he only had to sweep once. He saw the sense in the task - without the regular cleaning the walkways were a death trap and he wondered how many bandits had gone tumbling to the forest floor. Sure, there was a coating of mulch beneath the trees, softened by the snowfall but Kyle didn't think anyone would be walking away from such an accident.

Boss followed him round that first day, snapping him with the whip at frequent intervals. Kyle's chest burned with pain as much as the fire in his back from the repeated blows. He saw other bandits - nearly all men watching him. Some laughed, some stared with open hostility and others merely looked bored. He counted at least thirty although when he stared at them too long, Boss would lash him.

There were more than a dozen buildings. Some were small like the hut he'd recovered in but more than a few were huge, stretching across three tree trunks with long support columns stretching down to the forest floor below. Each looked sturdy and Kyle realised that despite the ramshackle appearance, a complex design had been worked out. He presumed one of the bandits had some knowledge of engineering or architecture. Or, perhaps they had simply taken the town from its unsuspecting inhabitants, murdering the townsfolk to claim their prize.

He'd heard of similar buildings, indeed, there were at least two in Holden's lands used by the Keepers to hunt or as shelter but never on this scale. It made perfect sense, a Horde could pass beneath the town without threatening the inhabitants and nothing short of a tornado would shake the buildings from their sturdy positions. If he hadn't been a prisoner, he would have relished spending hours examining the complex structure.

As it was, he soon found that sweeping snow was the least of his troubles.

Boss soon handed the whip over. The bandits took turns following Kyle around for a few hours at a time. Each of them gave him at least one smack with the whip. Some seemed bored with the duty, others laughed at his misfortune, aiming blows at every opportunity.

For the first week, the snow eased and he had only to knock icicles off the buildings and clear the frozen patches that formed overnight. He worked all through the daylight hours and at night, he was shoved into what served as a kitchen. The bandits had a ready supply of dried meat but each day, scavenging parties would return with fresh kills which Kyle was made to butcher. Nothing went to waste, the skins being stretched to dry, the bones were run through a crusher, forming a fine powder which the bandits made into a paste, consuming it with relish.

In the kitchen that was stacked with canned goods, Kyle followed the directions of a rotund man who served as the chef, although his hands were filthy and he tended to eat a good amount of whatever they prepared.

A few berries, acorns and chestnuts made their way to the kitchen and into the bellies of the rough gang. Kyle was surprised to find he was well fed. He'd quickly come to notice that most of the group did very little throughout the day and he guessed that his enslavement was a welcome break from the tedious tasks of maintaining the settlement.

Some of the bandits went out each day, descending to the forest floor and returning as the light began to fade. Sometimes they came back empty handed. Several times, they came back heavily laden with bundles of clothes. Some were shoved into a large hut, built from corrugated iron with a hefty padlock securing it. Boss had warned Kyle not to approach this building and he reasoned that this was where the bandits stored their weapons. He filed the information away.

He was given stacks of clothes to wash, melting snow and scrubbing accumulated forest dirt from the frayed cloth. Some of the rags were stained with blood. Kyle did his best to remove the gore, trying not to think about the refugees who were surely the victims of the predatory bandits.

He slept locked into the same small hut, a generous pile of blankets helping to stave off the cold. He ate well and his chest was healing but he was exhausted. Every menial task in the town was his and the constant lashes from the whip had turned his back into a raw mess.

He saw Amelia only briefly. She was allowed to change the dressing on his chest but Boss stood close by and forbade them from speaking. She rubbed disinfectant on his back where the whip had broken the skin, but said nothing. Kyle tried not to meet her eyes.

It was at the start of his second week as a prisoner that Kyle made a mistake. It was Amelia that caused the bandits to react. It wasn't her fault but she emerged from a hut carrying a bag of medical supplies and paused, shivering in the cold air. She was wearing the thin clothes Kyle had cleaned the blood from. Nothing else would have fit her and she had not been allowed a coat to discourage her from fleeing into the forest. Kyle had been poking ice off the walkway between the kitchen and the large communal building at the centre of the town. Three of the bandits had been watching him work, two of them had been calling insults at him, trying to provoke him whilst the third lashed the whip towards him, purposely missing and laughing when Kyle flinched.

As Amelia shivered, the thin cotton stretched across her chest and the three bandits heads snapped around. Like Wretches sensing living flesh, a predatory gleam came into their eyes. Amelia noticed her mistake instantly and stepped back instinctively, her arms folding across her chest.

The bandit with the whip was about Kyle's age, a thick set man with deep brown skin. Kyle thought his name was Gavin. Gavin grinned at Amelia, turning away from Kyle.

"No need to be shy, love! Uncross them arms, let's see a little!" he laughed.

Amelia's response was to put her head down and cross a walkway, separating her from the men.

"Now don't be shy!" Gavin raced across two more walkways, cutting Amelia off. She froze, trapped. The other two had closed in behind her so the four of them were now crowding the rickety path.

"Leave me alone!" snapped Amelia, facing Gavin who was holding the whip in one hand. He slowly let it uncoil, the length hanging down over the edge of the walkway.

"No need to be so cold, love! We just wanna share a bit of bodily warmth in this 'orrible weather!" Gavin stepped forward, forcing Amelia back towards the other two.

"Just piss off! Your Boss said to leave me alone!"

Gavin made a great show of looking around, peering down at the ground, twenty feet below "Can't see no Boss here! Can you?" he chuckled "Why don't you turn round and go back in that hut? See? Georgie's even opened the door for you!" he laughed as Georgie, a gormless looking youth pulled open the door to the hut that Amelia had just exited.

Kyle moved along the walkway towards Gavin. He didn't know what he was going to do. There were three of them, Gavin had the whip and the others all carried sharp knives. He was weak, exhausted and held only the spindly broom but the three bandits were so fixated on Amelia and the promise of her warm flesh that they had forgotten him for the moment.

Georgie suddenly lunged forward, his arm wrapping around Amelia's throat. She screamed but he clapped a dirty hand over her mouth, dragging her backwards. Gavin laughed at her futile struggles.

Kyle rammed the broom into the back of Gavin's knees and kicked him in the back of the head.

There was a moment of stillness as though time paused. Georgie stared in horror as Gavin seemed to hang, his balance teetering.

Then, in a rush, time caught up with itself and Gavin slid off the walkway without a sound, vanishing to the ground below.

There was a dull thump. A shout of pain and then a gunshot sounded.

CHAPTER 51

Boss fired the shot.

Kyle whipped around as fast as the slippery walkway would allow, holding the broom before him like a spear. Boss held the rifle in one hand, the barrel pointing skyward. Kyle heard a gasp and a thump behind him as Georgie flung Amelia away from him and then the shake of the walkway as the bandit lumbered towards him. He whipped around, broom levelled.

"Stop!" snapped Boss.

Georgie continued without reacting.

Boss shot him in the chest.

Kyle flinched as the bullet cracked past him, staring in horror as Georgie was knocked backwards, a spray of blood falling behind him. He twisted and fell, one hand scrabbling for the guide rope of the walkway. He lay, choking and spluttering as he tried feebly to stand.

Boss came up behind Kyle, angrily shoving his way past on the walkway "Back!" he snarled, pointing to the nearest platform. Kyle scuttled back as fast as he could. Boss advanced on Georgie who tried and failed to back away.

Bang

Boss shot him again, this time the bullet tore into Georgie's neck. More blood spurted out before falling to the forest floor below.

Boss kicked him, once, twice and the gormless youth lost his grip. He vanished to crash onto the ground below. This time, there was no scream of pain but they all heard the distinctive snarl and *twang* of cable as the bound Wretch lumbered forward to feast.

Rough hands seized Kyle from behind and a fist crashed

into the side of his head. He shouted out and struggled but someone kicked his feet out and he fell hard, dangerously close to the edge. Someone, several someone's, knelt on him, pinning him down.

"Enough!" Boss's voice was filled with fury. He advanced on Kyle "Let him up! Do it!"

Kyle scrambled to his feet, head throbbing from the punch. He eyed Boss warily. Behind the leader he could see Amelia shivering as she watched the scene play out.

"I gave an order that the doctor was not to be harmed!" Boss roared at the bandits who had gathered at the sound of the shots "I gave a *fucking* order! Georgie, Gavin and Bruce -" he indicated the third bandit who was stood uncertainly near where Kyle had been cleaning ice " - disobeyed me." Boss levelled the rifle at the crowd who flinched "Anyone else disobeys me, anyone even thinks about touching the doctor will get what's coming to 'em."

Boss stared the men down. From below, a faint cry of pain came from Gavin.

A voice called out from the crowd "That prick killed Gavin!"

Boss's eyes rested on Kyle. Who shivered.

"Someone go and check on Gavin. If he's still alive, bring him back up. If he's dead, we'll hang this one."

A cheer rose up and Kyle began straining his ears with all his might for further sounds from the fallen Gavin.

Four of the bandits went down to the forest floor where they confirmed Gavin was still alive. They hoisted the injured man up via a sturdy looking pulley where he was immediately taken into a hut. Boss turned to Amelia and ordered her to help the would be rapist. Amelia hesitated, looking at Kyle.

"What are you going to do to Kyle?"

"None of your business, pretty. Get in there and fix Gavin."

"What are you doing with him?"

Boss fired the rifle again, the bullet smashing into the trees near Amelia. She flinched and ducked.

"Get in the bloody hut!" Boss roared at her. Amelia shot Kyle a despairing glance and fled.

Boss rounded on Kyle who was suddenly aware of how thin the broomstick felt in his hands. The other bandits began closing in, the looks on their faces promising violence.

Boss elbowed his way to the front, standing to face Kyle. He spoke, his voice carrying to all the bandits "He assaulted one of our own. He thought he could kill one of our own. He attacked one of us. If Gavin was dead, he'd be choking at the end of a rope by now but he isn't. So I want him alive."

Boss turned to the crowd "Remember he was shot in the chest. Don't hit him there. Everything else is fair game." he turned and left.

Kyle watched him go with despair. He held the broom out as the bandits, twenty or more of them closed in.

"Come on then!" he snarled as much to give himself courage as to challenge them. He swung the broom at the nearest who stepped back, then quickly forward. Kyle jabbed the man in the eyes with the bristles and the bandit reared back, swearing.

Something flew out of the crowd and struck Kyle in the face. A metal mug, or a rock, he couldn't tell. Next second, blood was streaming down his face from a cut above his eye and the broom was torn from his hands. He punched, kicked, bit and twisted. Grunts of pain came from the men as they tried to crowd him. He kicked one man squarely in the balls but a second grabbed his leg, yanking hard so Kyle fell flat on his back. He cocked the leg and kicked again, hitting the man's hands and snapping a finger. A heavy kick slammed into the meat of his thigh, deadening the muscle. He tried to kick out again but the strength had gone from the limb.

Someone stepped past him and tried to pin an arm. Kyle reached up with his free hand and jabbed his thumb into the man's eye, watching him reel back. A second later, the man swung a hammer fist and broke Kyle's nose.

His vision gone in a flood of bloody tears, Kyle went mad. He gnashed his teeth like a Feral, kicking and punching with abandon. Several meaty thumps gave him satisfaction but then blows began to rain in, heavy boots hitting with careful aim below the ribs, sending bursts of agony through him. He screamed, curling into a ball to protect himself but the blows only intensified, the sound of heavy grunts accompanying them.

He faded, the pain overwhelming him. After a while, a sharp order shouted at the men to stop. Kyle lay still, curled into a ball of agony. His chest was on fire, his limbs numb and throbbing. Someone tied a blindfold around his head and then the cold metal of the handcuffs bit into his wrists. He felt his clothes being cut away and the knife biting into the flesh of his back.

Then, they were dragging him away, along slippery walkways, laughing cruelly. His hands were hauled above his head, a squeak of metal telling him that a winch was hoisting him. Up, off his toes so his entire bodyweight was suspended from his wrists. The pain was intense and he desperately tried to grip the metal with his fingers to take his weight but he slipped and fell, the cold steel tearing into the soft skin of his wrists.

Someone grabbed his foot and Kyle lifted a knee, hearing the clack of ivory as he connected with a chin. A man swore and then hauled down on the limb, jerking his wrists again.

The cold air burned his exposed skin, still raw from the whip. He hung, swinging gently although the man holding his legs stopped him from fully turning.

There was an ominous silence. Then "This is for Gavin, you skinny little prick!"

The whip was like burning lava on his skin. Kyle bit his tongue as he tried not to cry out. His mouth filled with blood as the whip whistled through the air and lashed him again. The bows before had hurt but they'd been softened by the layers of clothes. Now there was no such protection and the men around him grunted in satisfaction and he heard the whip passed to someone else.

Thwack

The pain burned through him, an awful, white hot agony that refused to fade. He scrunched up his eyes, jaw clenched only to realise that his shattered nose was blocked with blood. He choked and spluttered, hot, salty liquid splattering his mouth.

Thwack

A grunt escaped him, torn from his mouth without intent. Someone laughed.

Thwack

Another grunt. Kyle clenched his jaw, his whole body tensing for the next blow.

Thwack

Something began to burn in Kyle. A deep, fiery feeling that kept his mind focussed. He heard the laughter begin to die as the whip landed again and again.

Thwack-thwack-thwack-thwack

Not a sound escaped Kyle's lips. The pain was beyond words, beyond thought. In his mind, Kyle focussed the face of Boss, the bandit lying before him, bloody and begging.

Thwack

Boss's face exploding under Kyle's fists, blood and teeth flying.

Thwack

Kyle's knife cut through Boss's throat, his blood soaking Kyle's laughing face.

Thwack

Kyle dangled Boss upside down from a rope. Below the walkway, a sea of Ferals roared and jumped at the bandit as Kyle, laughing, slowly lowered the man.

Thwack

He shot Boss in the face, advancing forwards and firing until the man's skull was shattered, his skin unrecognisable.

Thwack-thwack-thwack-thwack

The men had stopped laughing. Stopped talking. A savage satisfaction filled Kyle. He wouldn't let them hear his pain, wouldn't give them the pleasure. They could do what they liked to his body, he wouldn't let them win. They couldn't kill him without provoking Boss and anything else, Kyle could survive.

The strokes fell again and again, the pain worse with every blow. Kyle's teeth were now bared in a silent snarl, the blood from his nose soaking his teeth so to the bandit holding his legs, he looked like a Feral.

"Enough!"

The voice cut through the snow dampened woods. The whip fell silent.

"Let him down a bit. Bit more, stop there." Kyle's feet landed on something solid and for a moment, he stood upright, forcing his knees to hold his weight.

A heavy blow to his knee and he fell, landing on a solid surface, surprisingly warm. The roof of the kitchen, perhaps?

He heard footsteps approach and then stop near him. A brief argument.

"That's enough! Boss wants him alive."

"So? It's sterile, innit? Can't see how this'll kill him!"

Someone laughed in response and then a second later, hot liquid splashed across Kyle. He didn't move, didn't react as the man pissed across his face, soaking the blindfold.

More laughter, more feet and it seemed like every one of the bandits came to relieve themselves on him.

He fought back the bile in his throat, his lip curled in a permanent snarl of fury. In his mind, Boss was the one begging for his life as Kyle pissed on his fallen enemy. He lay in the snow, blood pouring from every orifice as Kyle gloated at his destruction.

Eventually, the humiliation stopped. Kyle was on his knees, the stinking liquid soaking every inch of him. He shook, not with cold but with fury. A desperate need to be free of his bonds, to tear, to destroy, to obliterate his oppressors filled every fibre of his being. He forced it down, choking on the fury, burying the beast inside him until it could be let free.

They left him on the roof, still suspended from the winch

so that he could not lie down. The best he could manage was a kind of awkward half sit, his hands stuck at chest height. The blindfold remained as the sound of the bandits faded and he was left with the blackness.

That suited him fine. Black thoughts matched what his eyes could see as Kyle's mind burned.

CHAPTER 52

Night had fallen by the time the blindfold was removed. Kyle kept his eyes down. He didn't fight whoever was removing the bonds but he stood, silent. When he was told to move, he moved. When they told him to wash, he heated snow and cleaned the stink from his skin, ignoring the agonising sting in his back.

Amelia came, ordered to silence. She cleaned the wounds on his back, wrapping bandages around his torso. Kyle felt her eyes on his, saw the concern on her face but he ignored it. He dressed when he was told to and picked up the broom, sweeping the freshly fallen snow as ordered.

The bandits seemed to give him a wider berth now. A few had shot cruel comments at him when he'd returned to his tasks but the lack of reaction had quickly bored them. It was only Boss that still followed him around, the whip an ever present threat.

Kyle was re-tying a cable that formed the handrail of a walkway leading to the forbidden supply hut when he felt the twisted cable snap at his heels. A casual blow from Boss to get his slave's attention. Kyle turned, finding himself face to face with the bandit leader who was taken aback by the deathly stare from Kyle.

A strange kind of competition arose. Boss had inadvertently stepped too close to Kyle who now towered at least a head above the bandit. His blue eyes stared into the brown of the bandit's and both men stood, unblinking.

Boss tried to sneer his way through the intensity. He half-heartedly raised the whip but Kyle didn't flinch. Snowflakes passed them like silent spectators. Somewhere, outside the small bubble of their struggle, the world continued, unaware. Boss found he could not look away, could not raise his hand to strike the younger man, as was his habit. A dark magnitude seemed to have settled over Kyle. A looming threat that imparted itself through the cold, unyielding blue eyes.

Kyle seemed to swell over the bandit as he straightened his back, standing fully upright for the first time in weeks. The pain in his chest and back seemed dulled as though it existed on some distant plane that could not touch him here as he towered over his tormentor. A cruel smile formed on his lips, white teeth bared as though some bestial instinct had taken over his mind, invigorating him to rip, to tear and to kill.

His gaze, to the suddenly fearful bandit, looked like that of a Wretch.

Boss took an unconscious step back, away from his slave and Kyle leaned forward. What would have happened next was impossible to tell because the voice of another bandit, one of Boss's many minions shattered the spell.

"Boss?"

The bandit half turned, muttering some mundane set of instructions before he turned back to Kyle, whip held threateningly in his hand but the young man was tying the cable again, bent over to see his task more clearly. Boss stood looking at him in shock for a few seconds, watching the silent snowflakes settle on Kyle's back. Then he cleared his throat awkwardly.

"Make sure you don't go near that hut. That's the supply hut."

"Yes, Boss."

Boss turned on his heel and strode away, trying to push the memory from his mind. A bandit, one of the few women in the camp was carrying a bundle of scavenged goods towards the supply hut. She stepped aside as Boss approached her, beginning a casual greeting but the bandit leader snarled at her, lashing out with the whip and sending the pile of booty cascading from her hands to the forest floor below.

"Pick it up! Pick it up, you ugly bitch!" Boss's fury broke free in a shower of spittle as the unfortunate woman scuttled down the nearest rope ladder, wondering what had brought her leader's ire upon her.

"Kyle!"

He turned at the sound of his name. Amelia was beckoning him from the door of the hut opposite the supply store. After a moment, Kyle walked over and she tugged him inside. To his shock, it was the room where Gavin lay sedated on a thin wooden bed. His leg was bound and set and his face was bruised but otherwise, he seemed not to be badly injured.

"He's out of it..." Amelia pulled Kyle into a fierce embrace, hands carefully avoiding his injured back. She held him tightly for a moment before leaning back, her hands still on him "How do you feel?"

"Fine." Kyle stared back at her concerned gaze.

She blinked at the fierce intensity she saw there. He was standing straight, his body tall and stronger than she'd seen it since he was shot outside the hospital. She wondered at the effect the brutal whipping had taken on him.

"We need to get out of here before they kill one of us."

"Got any ideas?"

"A few. They're starting to trust me more now. I'm not being followed everywhere." she glanced back surreptitiously at the sleeping Gavin "There isn't much more I can do to keep them distracted. Most of them are in good shape. A few broken bones and a couple of infections." she frowned "Have you thought about where they get their supplies from?"

"They scavenge."

"Yes... But they're a bunch of bandits with no-one to rob. The trade routes past here are all guarded by the Militia and no-one has been travelling for weeks in this weather. Yet they've got enough food to make sure you aren't hungry."

"Makes sense they'd feed me." Kyle had thought about this "They want me to do all the boring jobs. And they want you to hang around and fix them. Keeping the two of us alive and healthy is in their interests. I die, you stop helping them as much. You die, I tear them to shreds."

"It's not all about revenge, Kyle. We need to get out of here."

Kyle's eyes froze at her words "I want them to pay."

She nodded, reaching out and taking his hands in a surprisingly intimate moment "I know. I know what they've done to you. But we have to focus on getting away. We can't do anything if we're stuck here. We need supplies, weapons and warm clothes. Otherwise we'll freeze to death first night we're away."

Kyle's jaw flexed as he ground his teeth together. Amelia squeezed his hands "Hey, stay with me here. You go all medieval on them and they'll kill me. You're not getting me killed. You do that and I'll be bloody livid."

The joke brought something of a thaw to Kyle's expression. He nodded briefly.

"Yes? I know you want revenge. You might get it, too. But the best revenge on these bastards is to get away and survive. Then you can come back with your Militia friends."

The images of Kyle arriving at the head of an avenging army brought some peace to him and he nodded again, meeting her gaze fully.

"Okay? Promise you won't do anything rash?"

"Promise."

She leaned in suddenly, wrapping her arms around his chest and pulling him close. After a moment's hesitation, Kyle returned the embrace, smelling the scent of her warm hair against his chest.

"Look after me, Kyle." she murmured.

CHAPTER 53

Lurcher was one of the smaller bandits. He was older than Kyle, although not as old as Sinks. He clearly held some standing among the ragged band because he'd managed to claim Kyle's pistol. The Glock now hung from his hip in a poorly fitting holster. He pulled it out at intervals as he stood watching Kyle. He'd fidget with the pistol, ejecting the magazine, pulling back the slide and field stripping the weapon.

Kyle ignored the man, carrying out whatever task the bandits piled on him next. He carried food from hut to hut, chipped ice from the walkways, cooked meals, emptied the stinking latrine buckets and melted snow into water. Always, one of the thugs followed him and he'd noticed that more often than not, it was Lurcher.

"Where you from, boy?" the man would snap as he rammed the magazine of the Glock home.

"Holden." Kyle would respond.

"Where's that?"

"East of Matwood."

"Matwood! You tried the water?"

"Yes."

"Not as good as whisky, but good stuff!" Lurcher would roar with laughter at his own poor jokes. The other bandits seemed to avoid him, never standing with him and at mealtimes, in the communal hut, the seat next to him was the last to be taken.

Snow was falling again, piling up on the walkways and Kyle, the same tattered broomstick in hand continued with his thankless task.

"Bet you want this back, don't you?" Lurcher brandished the

pistol, watching to see if Kyle's eyes followed it. Kyle ignored the man.

"Bet you'd love to get a hold of it... Love to pop me!" Lurcher grinned, showing surprisingly clean teeth "You wouldn't get anywhere near. I was in the army before all this - a sniper! I killed people for a living." when Kyle didn't react, he snorted in disgust "You're as weak a pussy as I've ever seen. Wouldn't last a minute as a soldier!"

"Lurch?" Boss had appeared. Boss was the only man who Lurch seemed to respect. His tone changed instantly as the leader approached and he pasted a sickly grin onto his face.

"Boss."

"All quiet?"

"Yeah. Just watching this mong."

Boss laughed at that "He is a mong. Reckon we broke him with that whipping." both men laughed at Kyle who ignored them, brushing a pile of snow over the edge.

"What you two talking about?"

"Home. Says he's from - oi! Boy! Where you from?"

"Holden." muttered Kyle, not looking up.

"Holden!" Boss sounded as though the word was familiar "With all the dogs?"

"Yes."

"Maybe that's why he's such a pussy -" laughed Lurch "Too much time with the dogs, now he's been heeled." he whistled a few times, laughing at Kyle.

"Nah, they were a bunch of pansies down in Holden" Boss jibed "Whole town got wiped out. Bet that's where these two came from."

Kyle carried on sweeping, his head away from the two men but he felt his blood turn as cold as the snow he swept. Holden had been attacked? His heart pounded in his ears as he searched for meaning in Boss's words. There were often tales of towns being wiped out, very few of them were true. Surely this was just an overdeveloped rumour after the Horde that they had fought off. After all, the bandits were hardly in regular contact with reliable sources. No, Boss must have heard a rumour and was now using it to taunt Kyle.

"Yeah, I heard the Ferals tore the whole lot to pieces. By the time the Rangers came to help, there was nothing left. Nothing to do but bomb the place to hell and back." Lurcher gave a cruel snigger.

"Maybe we'll ransom this one to the Rangers? After all, they always want grateful survivors to spread the good word of their work. Maybe the boy here will, what do they call it, evangelise for them?"

Both bandits laughed heartily at Boss's joke. Kyle's hands gripped the broom handle so tightly it was a wonder the wood didn't snap. His teeth gritted together and it took all his self control not to turn and attack the two men.

'Look after me, Kyle.' Amelia's words played through his mind, bringing a sense of calm. He carried on sweeping.

An alarm sounded. A high pitched whistle blown by one of the sentries down on the forest floor. It sounded twice, two long blasts followed by silence, then another two long blasts.

The good humour of Boss and Lurcher evaporated. Both twisted around to look through the trees in the direction of the sentry's whistle. Kyle looked but could see nothing. He was still staring when Boss suddenly whipped around and glared at him.

"Boy! Get them paths swept, now! They aren't done 'time I get back, I'll whip you! Now get sweepin'! Lurch, watch 'im!"

Boss hurried off towards the sentry post at the far end of town, Kyle's rifle on his shoulder. Kyle tried to see what the sentry had spotted but a metallic click announced Lurcher cocking the pistol and he hastened to sweep faster, remembering Boss's threat.

His heart thumped painfully in his chest. Surely, Holden couldn't have been overrun? The Rangers, Armstrong himself had been only a few miles away! Even if Sinks hadn't managed to return in time with the ammunition, Kyle knew it would take a lot to breach the sturdy walls! His heart sank as he thought of the Ferals and their uncanny speed and aggression. No! He couldn't give in to despair. Rosie, Jane, everyone he'd ever known was there and he couldn't imagine them dead. He gritted his teeth and clenched his fists as below him, Boss's voice called out a greeting.

Kyle shoved the thoughts of Holden from his mind and held his breath, trying to make out what was being said.

"... Come up... Stay here tonight?" Boss sounded almost polite. A male voice responded, a short, brief answer given to the question. The speaker sounded bored. Boss, on the other hand, sounded like a nervous teenager and his voice carried as it rose in nervous volume "Good to see you! ... couldn't come? Weather's shit, innit?"

There was general patter from the bandit to which the guest gave monosyllabic replies. After a while, Boss lapsed into silence. Kyle heard the distinctive *ting* sound as a ladder was climbed, a grunt of effort sounding as someone pulled themselves up.

"Back, lad!" Lurcher sounded apprehensive and his grip was firm but not rough as he pulled Kyle away from the nearest platform where the ladder was creaking ominously. A gloved hand appeared over the top as Kyle watched, a tough looking, narrow fitting gauntlet, the sort that might be worn by the Militia...

Kyle blinked stupidly as he found himself staring into the eyes of the Ranger, Gault.

If it had been Lynch himself, Kyle could not have been more shocked. He'd last seen the man weeks ago in the forest as he'd mercilessly gunned down human and Wretch alike and the memory of the dead refugee Gault had shot out of the tree returned and he blinked, heart racing.

Gault hauled himself up onto the platform and looked away from Kyle without recognition, turning to offer a hand to a second Ranger, this a woman Kyle didn't know.

"Lurcher!" Boss was calling from out of sight "Show our guests into the communal hut!"

Lurcher directed the two Rangers as Boss, panting came up to the platform and hurried after his guests, following them into the communal hut. Kyle found himself alone on the walkway and paused, uncertain of what action to take next. A second later, his ear was pressed against the door of the hut.

"... Think you and your boss will be happy with... Promise you we've got the real thing!"

Kyle frowned, wondering what Boss was selling to the big Ranger. A narrow gap had formed between the doorframe and the door itself and he pressed his eye to the crack.

Next second, he was lurching away, his broom frantically sweeping as the door swung inwards to reveal Gault.

"I know you." He stabbed a finger at Kyle who froze. Behind Gault, Boss was trying to lean around to see Kyle.

"Boy! Get out of here! Men are talkin'!"

Gault ignored Kyle "Frost! The Militiaman." He nodded to himself, a realisation settling over him. Filling the walkway in front of the door with his bulk, Gault strode forward, stopping when he was face to face with Kyle "Two birds with one stone, eh? Hope you ain't too comfortable here. I reckon I know someone wants a word with you." He grinned conspiratorially, the expression doing nothing to reassure Kyle.

"Boy!" I said –"

"I want him too." Gault interrupted Boss.

"What? The boy? He's no-one!"

"So you wont want much for him?" Gault grinned and Boss swore.

"Lurch! Get Doctor Pretty over here now!"

"And the boy." Gault prompted as Lurcher scurried over to the hut where Gavin lay injured.

Kyle stepped inside the hut, grateful for the warmth. Absurdly, he still clutched the broom in his hands and he kept it tight, looking at the two Rangers and the bandit, wondering if this was his opportunity to escape.

Boss glowered at Kyle but said nothing until Lurcher arrived with Amelia just moments later. She stepped in to the room, looking in confusion from the Rangers to Kyle.

"That's her." Gault spoke before Lurcher could even shut the door. He turned to the bandit leader "How much?"

Boss seemed to consider "S'been hard keepin' her alive all this time. Lady eats more rations'n you'd think. She –"

"She's a doctor. Probably did more good than the rest of your sorry bunch of goons ever did. How much?"

Boss grinned for the first time "Oh, so she's worth more then?"

Gault did not grin "Lynch wants her. Now."

Boss's grin faded and his colour went bad "Lynch?"

"Yeah. Want me to call him to come here?" Gault made a show of reaching for his radio.

"No." Boss's humour had evaporated. He rounded on Kyle "Boy – out. Lurch, take him and lock him in a hut. Don't care which." To Gault he said "You can have the boy. All I want is a fair price and Amelia Singh is worth her weight in gold. Let's not play games."

Kyle saw Amelia's eyes widen in shock and he felt his stomach lurch. Of course Boss knew who Amelia was! He should have realised the threat. A Zek doctor by the name of Amelia was obvious even to the bandits! And Lynch would pay to have her in his control – he'd shown his opinion of Zeks in the woods outside Matwood. Kyle cursed himself for not thinking to give Amelia a fake name but Lurcher was shoving him out of the door and Amelia was watching him go wide eyed. He tried to silently tell her *I'll help you. Let's get out of here* but he didn't know what he could do.

As Lurcher slammed him into his sleeping hut, shooting the bolt on the outside, her voice played in his memory *Look after me, Kyle.*

CHAPTER 54

Immediately, Kyle looked around the hut. Since he and Amelia had been taken, he'd barely looked at his surroundings. He'd been exhausted each night they'd brought him back here and he'd wasted no time in collapsing asleep. Each morning, he'd been woken by the door being thrown open and more often than not, a boot in the ribs. Now, he took stock.

The thin blankets might serve as a rope to lower him to the ground but he grimaced at the thought of a knot slipping or the frayed cotton tearing and leaving him broken on the forest floor, at the mercy of the Wretches. The door was locked though, the only window, a sheet of dirty plastic overlooked a twenty foot drop without a branch to land on.

The window...

Ten seconds later, Kyle had levered the flimsy plastic out of the frame. Up close, the design was shoddy, a weak channel of wood gripping the sheet in place. It was surprising the glass hadn't been blown out by the wind or snow. Laying it carefully on the floor, Kyle leaned his head out, whipping it back instantly.

Two of the bandits were stood outside the door to his hut. They had their backs to him or they'd have seen Kyle but his heart raced as he thought through what he'd seen. All around the village, the bandits were spread out, facing the communal hut. Kyle realised that Boss was taking no chances, surrounding the Rangers as he struck whatever price he was asking for Amelia. Kyle wondered what the cost of a human life was. To Boss, probably not much.

Leaning out carefully, Kyle peered again. The bandits were

facing intently towards the centre of Treetops. He leaned back inside, shivering at the cold. The window was big enough for him to climb out but the side of the hut was smooth, with nothing for him to climb on to. If he was going to climb out, he'd have to go up. He closed his eyes, trying to remember what lay on the roof of the hut but couldn't recall seeing anything. Hopefully, he'd be able to grip onto the roof.

Otherwise, he'd fall.

Thinking quickly, Kyle rolled the blankets into tubes and tied them diagonally around his body, ignoring the burning agony in his back and the lingering pain in his chest. Then, he leaned out again. The two bandits had moved away from the hut, still close by but now on the nearest walkway. From the communal hut the sound of arguing voices came. Clearly, the negotiations were not going well.

Kyle seized the moment. He lifted one foot onto the windowsill, flinching as the wood groaned under his weight. He glanced at the bandits. They hadn't noticed. He gripped the top of the window frame, fingers scrabbling for purchase. Then, he pulled himself up so that he crouched in the window frame, facing out.

He didn't fit. Sure, he could have scrambled through but he needed to stand in the frame, rotate back to face the inside of the room and then climb up onto the roof. He swore, thinking. He tried to twist around but could only turn half the distance he needed. He realised that he'd turned the wrong way so that his back was now to the bandits, meaning he had no idea if they could see him or not.

Shit

Gritting his teeth, Kyle pushed up, hoping to stand on one leg and grip the top of the hut but his foot slipped on the icy wood and shot out towards the ground below. He flailed frantically and gasped as the bulk of one of the rolled blankets caught on the rough wood of the window frame.

Kyle froze.

He was now held in place by only the thin cotton of the

bundled bedsheet. He hardly dared move. But now, he was in a perfect position to see up, his whole body overbalanced out the window. A thin plastic gutter ran along the edge of the roof.

Before he'd given his mind time to hesitate, Kyle had lunged for the plastic and caught it. Next second, he pulled himself up, now standing on the windowsill, facing towards the roof.

Sweat beaded along his brown and he tried not to think of the drop behind him and how close he'd come to falling. He glanced left, to where the two bandits were still watching the hut. The voices had lessened in tone and the watchers seemed to have relaxed. Kyle swung his right leg up, over the gutter and then followed with his left, repressing a grunt of pain as he pulled himself onto the roof.

He was free!

He lay flat on the roof, watching. Not a moment too soon because the two bandits moved back towards the hut to stand on the platform. They moved back closer to the hut and Kyle bared his teeth. But there was nothing he could do. Injured and unarmed, he'd never overpower the two men, much less silently and he could hardly charge in to the meeting with Boss and Gault without getting shot.

Instead, Kyle turned to the back of the hut, sliding silently across the surface. Here, a tree branch extended beyond the building, rising into the heights of the forest. Kyle gingerly stepped from building to bough, gripping the cold wood hard. Below him, the forest floor yawned and carefully, desperate not to make any noise, Kyle began to climb down the tree.

CHAPTER 55

The forest floor was cold and snow stood ankle high. A lone Ranger, left by Gault as a sentry, was bored throwing spiteful glances up at the warm lights of the treetop village. He'd watched his fellows vanish into the hut and heard the first argumentative negotiations but then silence had fallen with the night.

Now, he kicked moodily at a snowdrift, cursing softly as his boot struck a concealed tree root. He rubbed his toe on the back of his leg ruefully, glancing back up at the warm huts as voices sounded from a walkway. A snatch of conversation floated down.

"... Bloody well hurry up and pay us!"

"Bastard will be haggling for all he's worth."

"Boss'll get a good price for the bitch. She's the one they're looking for, alright."

"Don't mind what he gets for her s'long as I don't have to freeze my bollocks off out here much longer."

"We could go in the hut..."

There was silence. The Ranger repressed a sneer as he imagined the two men looking furtively around, like naughty schoolchildren. A moment later, the walkway creaked and damp door hinges moaned as the bandits snuck into the warmth of the hut. Half hoping a voice would cry out in recrimination, the Ranger was instead disappointed and a moment later, jealous as he shivered in the darkening air. He consoled himself that tonight at least, he'd sleep in a warm bed with a roof over his head. If Gault let them, of course. It wouldn't be a surprise if they found themselves ordered to march with the prisoner through the night. She was a prize, after all and they'd want to waste no time in securing her.

Or, the Ranger considered, turning to peer through the gloomy trees, perhaps they'd come back in the night and massacre these tree-pikeys. After all, loose ends were loose ends. The bandits were a useful pawn in the dangerous political game the Rangers were playing but their usefulness may have run its course. He relished the thought of going door to door, the surprise on the thug's faces as they realised that they were nothing more than overgrown playground bullies, after all. No match for the Rangers.

With these bloody thoughts, the sentry consoled himself as he turned back to check the ground behind him.

Movement.

He froze, eyes flickering from side to side in the rapidly fading light trying to spot what had drawn his gaze. Most likely an animal but there were still Wretches in the woods. He was calm as he flicked the safety catch off his rifle and rested the butt more snugly in his shoulder.

"Hey! We need help!" the voice was faint, not from distance but from weakness. The Ranger's brow furrowed as two figures appeared through the gloom. One appeared to be half dragging the other who was swathed in threadbare blankets.

"Please! I - I saw your lights... My friend is cold - I - I think he's dying... Hypothermia."

"Stop! Hands where I can see them!" it was clear the two men were unarmed. The speaker was thin, pale and drawn, all the signs of surviving in the wild through this abysmal winter. The other was barely visible through the blankets over his head. The man was twitching towards the lights as though desperate for the warmth.

"Please!" the cry was desperate.

The Ranger considered. On the one hand, Gault would have his balls if he risked their mission, on the other, he didn't want to leave these two to die on the ground in front of him. Death was plainly staring the pair of them in the face and he had a terrible feeling that if he threatened them with his rifle, they'd simply bow their heads and accept the quicker end.

"Alright! Over there... There's a ladder."

"He can't climb... Can you help?"

The Ranger instinctively walked closer as the blanketed figure stumbled and fell against the base of the tree. The speaker tugged his friend upright, staring hopelessly at the length of the twisted rope and cable of the ladder.

"Here, I'll give you a leg up. No! Watch your footing!" the Ranger was too far away to grab the blanketed figure as the man tripped over the same root he'd caught his toe on earlier. The soldier winced in sympathy, letting his rifle barrel go and gripping the upper arm of the stumbling man. The flesh was ice cold, even through his gloves and he drew a breath in shock, realising just how close to death these refugees were. This one stank, too and he wrinkled his nose as the waft came from beneath the soiled blankets.

The smell...

Too late, the Ranger tried to stagger backwards but the blanketed Wretch had seized his arm and was pulling his flesh towards its mouth. He tried to backpedal but the pale man moved like lightning. An blow from the heel of his palm flashed at the edge of his vision and landed in his throat. Next second, the Ranger was on his hands and knees in the mixed snow and leaf mulch, choking desperately.

Kyle shoved the toothless Wretch away, knocking it to the floor where it writhed stupidly, caught in the tangles of the blankets he'd brought from his prison. The plan had been simple enough, he'd realised his moment when the two bandits above had snuck indoors. The blow to the Ranger's throat had been to keep him quiet and he now checked the man, satisfied that he hadn't killed him.

The next move, was a savage blow to the head with the rock he'd scooped from the forest floor. Blood spattered from the Ranger's scalp and Kyle raised the stone again, but the man lay still.

Moving quickly, Kyle began to strip the fighting gear from

the prone soldier. The plate carrier was of the highest quality, each magazine pouch filled. Kyle took all of it, wrapping the last blanket around his body beneath the tightly fitting rig to stave off the cold and wasting precious seconds adjusting the pistol holster. Carefully, with wary glances above, he covered the man in the soiled blankets he stripped from the Wretch, reassuring himself that the stench would keep any wandering Infected from attacking. He bound and gagged the Ranger before turning his attention to the toothless monster.

The winch hook dangled just out of reach but Kyle managed to manipulate the controls, wincing only slightly at the faint squeak.

Roughly, he shoved the Wretch under the cable and began to tie it around the monster's chest, wrapping it round tightly. Finally, satisfied that it was secure, Kyle began to winch the Wretch up. When it was just below the level of the nearest walkway he stopped, listening for any sounds of alarm. There were none.

Taking a moment to collect himself, Kyle gripped the first rung of the rope ladder firmly and began to climb, his face set in grim determination.

CHAPTER 56

Boss was gritting his teeth. Gault made him nervous but he was doing his best to haggle. Amelia sat on a rough chair, her hands bound behind her back and her mouth gagged. So far, the Ranger hadn't budged an inch and Boss had a sinking feeling he was going to lose the negotiation. He'd had known the man would drive a hard bargain but this was intolerable. He'd thought Amelia would be an end to his isolation in the woods. He'd have enough money to sneak away from the gang of cut-throats and start a new life, maybe up north. But the intimidating pair of soldiers before him were dashing those dreams.

He scowled, realising as he did so that he had almost no leverage over Gault. Of course, he had far more men surrounding them but if he tried violence, he'd be the first to be shot. Besides, most of his men were armed with knives or rusty hunting rifles. These soldiers were dressed for war and carried enough ammunition between them to win one. He suspected that even if they overpowered the two men, the next day would see a helicopter overhead and a full out assault which would destroy the treetop sanctuary.

Boss was not a stupid man but he was brutal, rather than subtle. He didn't have any idea what to say to these men to get more out of them and he realised that pushing his luck with their tenuous alliance was a poor idea. Perhaps, he thought, he could take all the money for himself and run? He'd tell Lurcher, of course, the man was as loyal as his namesake. The two of them could flee into the night and he could quietly murder the lapdog in the woods, leaving his body for the Wretches. It wouldn't buy him much in a town but it was surely better than living here.

Boss shrugged to himself and the Ranger seemed to sense that the deal was done. He ignored Amelia and didn't offer a handshake. Instead, the other soldier banged a bag of paper money down on the table. Boss nodded tightly, scooping it up and making it vanish beneath his jacket with all the speed and skill of an illusionist. He felt Lurcher stir beside him but ignored the man. He'd explain later.

He was about to speak when a wailing scream sounded from outside the door.

"Shit!" Lurcher was already moving towards the door. Boss threw the Rangers a suspicious look but they were staring at the door plainly as surprised as he was.

Lurcher was through the door, Kyle's appropriated pistol already drawn. Boss waited a heartbeat before he too moved to the exit. A burst of gunfire came and Boss leaped back inside the communal hut, throwing the door closed. He heard Lurcher wail in pain but ignored the man.

The Rangers had taken up defensive positions, covering the entrance to the hut. Boss rounded on Gault, indignant "What is this? What have you done?"

The Sergeant ignored the bandit, turning instead to stare at the empty chair which had held Amelia Singh, only moments before. From outside came another burst of gunfire. Shouts of panic were sounding all around them and a bullet slammed into the building, making Boss flinch.

"Where the fuck did she go?" snapped Boss, seeing his prize vanish.

The Rangers eyed him suspiciously and Boss suddenly felt a cold shiver down his spine. He panicked, conciliatory words spilling out of him as Gault fixed him with a baleful stare "No! This isn't me - isn't my idea! Look! You can have the money back, keep it until we find her! I don't know what's happening..."

His voice trailed off as Gault drew his sidearm and casually pointed it at him.

"No! Please! I didn't do anything!"

The big Ranger shrugged and opened his mouth to argue but then seemed to change his mind. His finger tightened on the trigger as he shot Boss.

CHAPTER 57

The darkness was punctuated by screams of panic and the cries of injured men.

Kyle moved along the towering walkways like a vengeful demon. He drove the Wretch before him, shoving the beast into the bandits who screamed and twisted in panic.

He ducked into the pools of darkness between the artificial light, adding to the uproar, yelling warnings.

"Wretches! Wretches on the walkways!"

bandits ran to and fro in panic. Some yelled their own warnings. Kyle hauled himself atop the kitchen, turning to yell into the darkness.

"They're attacking us! The Rangers are attacking us!"

A gunshot split the night, the bullet snapping into the wood of the hut, close to Kyle's head. He rolled back away from the edge, coming face to face with another winch system which stretched upwards into the dark treetop.

Black anger flashed through Kyle's mind. The memory of the lash, a firebrand against his skin burned through him. This was where they'd hung him as they brutalised him. A rational part of his mind told him that this was irrelevant to his escape.

The other part of his mind roared for vengeance. More bullets struck the roof and Kyle, heedless of the danger wheeled around, the stolen rifle firm in his hands. Lurcher stood on a walkway, the Glock held in one hand. He fired again, his eyes locked on Kyle.

Kyle sighted along the rifle and fired, squeezing the trigger but Lurcher twisted, running full tilt along the walkway, and ducking behind a building. Kyle cursed, making to follow the bandit but another door to the communal building swung open and Amelia stumbled out. Her hands were tied behind her. She staggered towards the nearest walkway but Kyle saw her falter as her feet encountered the icy wood.

A shot from the communal hut and she lurched forward in panic, staggering and slipping. Then, she fell.

"Amelia!" Kyle roared her name, seeing her half turn towards him as he stared in horror. But the twist saved her and she stayed on the walkway, feet finding a precarious purchase on the slippery plank whilst her body fell against the twisted cable handrail that ran either side.

She balanced, just. The gag muted her scream but Kyle saw her eyes desperately lock with his own. He scrambled to the edge of the roof, leaping onto the wooden platform below just as Lurcher ducked around the side of his shelter and fired.

Kyle twisted, the rounds passing him in the darkness. He flung himself flat, bringing the rifle to bear as Lurcher emptied the magazine.

Bang

Kyle returned fire, watching as Lurcher vanished back behind his shelter. How had the man missed? Kyle put the thought out of his mind, stumbling to his feet, and hastening towards Amelia.

The walkway he was on was parallel to hers so he had to move to the far end, turning onto the adjacent path, all the while snatching glances at her precarious position. A bandit loomed before him and Kyle shouted to confuse the man.

"Wretches behind me! Run!" the man half turned but must have recognised Kyle because he paused, sideways on. Kyle hit him at a run, body-slamming him and flinging him down onto the walkway. He tried to snatch at the nearest handhold but Kyle was already moving, clearing the man at a jump and his flying foot knocked the bandit's hand aside. The man's legs rolled off the walkway and he hung for a second, teetering off balance.

Kyle was already over the man, one hand on the rifle, one on the cable handrail but he stared down, under his feet as, almost in slow motion, the bandit pitched headfirst off the walkway.

Kyle heard the wet snap as his neck broke, even from twenty feet up. The sound was sickening, bringing bile to his throat. Cold shivers seemed to run down his spine in sympathy.

He tried to force the sound from his mind as a second later, he reached Amelia, tugging her upright. He snatched the fighting knife from the front of his stolen plate carrier and slashed the bonds around her wrists. She tore the gag from her mouth as, without wasting time for words, they ran, putting as much distance between themselves and the communal hut as possible.

They ran down a walkway, the shouts of alarm beginning to fade behind them. Ahead, Kyle could see figures milling but they were hunched in the darkness, cowering from the gunfire.

"What happened?" called Amelia from behind him.

"The Wretch they had below, I winched it up. Took this from one of the Rangers." he hefted the rifle.

"You killed him?"

"No, just knocked him out." Kyle tried not to think of the wet snap of the bandit's neck. Revulsion flowed through him but his back burned as if in response and a savage glee flowed through him at his victory.

The crowd of bandits ahead moved out of the light. Kyle pointed the rifle at them but did not fire and they scattered, slamming doors behind them. He raced ahead, Amelia close behind.

"Over here!" they reached a platform between walkways, bolted to the trunk of a towering oak. Amelia elbowed her way past Kyle and led the way. Kyle saw what she was aiming for. The supply building was ahead. The padlock gently reflecting light from the village.

Jamming the knife under the loop, Kyle struck it once, twice with the butt of the rifle and the brass lock snapped open. Amelia swung the big door inwards and they both half fell inside. As they slammed the door shut, panting and sweating Kyle pressed his ear to the door, listening for sounds of pursuit.

Amelia's hand gripped his arm, listening.

"Nothing..."

"Okay. Come on. Let's get some supplies."

There were no windows but Amelia had found a small electric torch although it flickered as she switched it on. The weak beam faintly illuminated a few crates. She found a pair of rucksacks and began stuffing dried food in along with several plastic bottles of water.

"Here..." she directed his hands in the dark towards piles of clothes. Guided by touch, Kyle picked out several layers of warm clothes for the two of them as well as some waterproof shells.

"Shine the light a sec?" Amelia obliged as Kyle checked a few details "What size are you?" he asked, innocently.

Amelia prodded him hard in the side "None of your business. Here, let me do the clothes..." she shoved him unceremoniously aside, handing him the small torch. Kyle grabbed the rucksacks and began checking the food, switching a few heavier canned goods out for some of the dried military rations he'd seen being brought through just days before.

"Where did they get these?" he shone the light to Amelia, to direct his voice.

"Huh?" the beam landed on her, frozen in the artificial light, a pair of different sized bras hanging from each hand. She flushed as the beam landed on her and quickly shoved the undergarments out of sight.

Embarrassed, Kyle muttered something and continued stuffing the bags with food.

"That'll do."

"Yeah, let's go."

Kyle hung a rucksack across his back, gritting his teeth at the pain. Amelia moved past him to the door, reclaiming the small torch.

"Give me the pistol."

Kyle unstrapped the stolen weapon, handing it to her where she held it expertly. He readied the rifle as she carefully opened the door, peering out.

A series of gunshots startled her and she leapt back inside, backing into Kyle who instinctively pulled her down into a crouch beside him.

Rifle shots, distinctive in the snow dulled air sounded. But they were not from outside their hut nor aimed at them as Kyle had initially thought.

"Back by the communal hut, I think." Kyle was impressed at Amelia's ability to judge the gunfire. He stepped carefully over to the door and peered out again.

"I think it's clear... Boss was trying to sell me to that Ranger!"

"Gault – he's one of Lynch's men."

"You *know* him?"

"I – we can figure it out later! We need to go!"

"Yes... Come on!" She swung the door open again, this time pulling it sharply to.

"Lurcher is outside."

"Shit."

"He's got your pistol."

"I think he's out of ammo. He shot the whole mag at me and I didn't hear him reload."

"Did he hit you?" Amelia was concerned, looking Kyle up and down.

"No. Some sniper he was!"

"We can take him."

"And draw the others with the sound? No, wait for him to pass by."

Amelia leaned in to open the door again and suddenly jumped to the side, spinning away from the entrance and raising the stolen pistol but it crashed inwards, knocking her off balance and into Kyle.

Lurcher stood in the doorway, looking as surprised to see them as they were him. His face split into an evil grin as he saw the rifle, pinned behind Amelia and her own weapon, pointing uselessly at the floor.

Lurcher grinned as he raised the pistol, single-handedly. He opened his mouth for a smart final word and Amelia kicked the gun out of his hand.

He swore, clutching at broken fingers as the Glock clattered uselessly onto the wooden floor. Kyle raised the rifle, fully prepared to murder his oppressor but instead Lurcher turned and bolted.

Kyle scooped up his Glock, shoving the weapon into his waistband as Amelia watched Lurcher flee "Think he's gone."

"Nice kick."

"Thanks. Come on."

Amelia led the way, stopping at the nearest rope ladder which she dumped unceremoniously over the edge. Holstering the pistol, she began to descend as Kyle knelt above her, covering the walkways with the rifle.

If the bandits noticed them going, they stayed away. Kyle could hear more gunshots coming from the far end of the town now and wondered what confusion he'd sown with the Wretch he'd set loose. A grim smile played over his lips at the torment the brutal group were now suffering.

Amelia called up to him and he turned, descending the ladder carefully, hearing the sounds of havoc fade as he lowered himself down.

A few seconds more, and he was free.

He turned, jubilant to Amelia only to freeze as he saw Boss, Kyle's stolen rifle held in two hands, aimed at Amelia's head as he grinned evilly at them.

CHAPTER 58

"Drop it! Drop it or I'll fucking shoot you both!" Boss's voice was drawn and strained. Kyle only now noticed that the bandit leader was holding himself hunched over. Was he injured?

Kyle slowly placed the rifle on the floor where Amelia's stolen pistol lay. Boss kicked them both away, into the darkness. Kyle raised his hands, furious at himself.

"Move over there. Yes. Stop now." Boss covered them both with the rifle and sidestepped, peering through the trees to where the sounds of fighting still came.

"What did you do?" Boss's voice was weak. Kyle wondered how badly the man was hurt.

Kyle shrugged, there was nothing to hide "I winched the Wretch up and set it loose."

Boss snarled in fury "Bastard!" he looked at Kyle's gear "Where's that from?"

"Took it from the man they left on the ground."

"Cleverer than you look, boy. Too fucking clever. Who are you, anyway?"

Kyle was confused "What do you mean?"

"You aren't a Zek, are you?"

"Do I look like a Zek?"

Boss gave a strained laugh "No. You're someone though…" Boss's voice faded.

There was silence. Kyle could feel Amelia, beside him shaking with frustration at their predicament. He heard the long breath she drew in as she tried to calm herself "Boss, you're hurt. Let me take a look at it."

"Stay there!" snapped the bandit, trying and failing to gesture with the rifle. He was still looking past them to the sounds of fighting. A burst of gunfire sounded and the bandit swore, something close to a sob filling his voice.

"The bastards! I nearly had enough, you know, enough to stop living in this shit hole! Stop shivering my arse off in the woods like a damn pikey! You were supposed to be my lottery ticket!" he pointed at Amelia "Amelia Bloody Singh! They were paying a fortune for you!"

"What went wrong?" Kyle, for all his fear, was curious.

"Bastard shot me when she legged it." Boss seemed to diminish in size as blood loss began taking its toll. He was still watching the town, straining to see something.

And then he leaned forward, slightly too far. At full strength, the bandit wouldn't have noticed it happening but his legs were weak from lack of blood. He stumbled and almost fell, managing to recover himself in time as the rifle barrel dropped.

Kyle didn't hesitate. He drew the Glock he'd recovered from Lurcher in a smooth, practiced movement. Boss tried to react but the rifle barrel was still pointing at the snow covered forest floor when Kyle fired the first shot, hardly aiming the weapon in his haste. He pulled the trigger over and over as Boss staggered backwards and fell, the rifle falling aside.

Kyle moved forward, kicking the weapon away and leaning closer but the bandit was dead. The bullets had torn into his neck and face. His tongue lolled out of a shattered jaw and his right eye was missing. Kyle bared his teeth savagely at his victory.

He half expected to feel guilt, but instead, he found himself becoming surprisingly calm. That the man had been about to kill them, he had no doubt and he felt no regret at pulling the trigger. Instead, he felt only disappointment that the brute had got off so lightly. The pain in his whipped back made itself known, as though it had dulled through the evening's fighting as it anticipated revenge, only to now make its appearance as Boss died.

Amelia had knelt beside the bandit but didn't even bother

checking his pulse. He was dead.

"Let's move! We need- " her words were cut off as it became apparent what Boss had been waiting for.

A bright geyser of orange light flung the shadows back like a sweeping broom. Kyle felt hot air on the back of his neck and staggered forwards as the shockwave hit him. Amelia flung up a hand to shield her eyes but the blast was already fading, the shadows leaping forward to reclaim the woods.

"Jesus!" he swore, staring at the raging fire the explosion had left. Where the centre of the treetop village had been was now a giant bonfire, quickly spreading through the treetops. Embers and chunks of timber rained down onto the snowy floor. The destruction was appalling, the village almost completely gone.

"Boss...?" Amelia gasped.

"Must have been. Didn't trust his men..."

They stared in morbid fascination as the inferno increased, the trees lending fuel to the blaze.

"Kyle..." Amelia gestured. She'd recovered the fallen weapons and Kyle now found himself reunited with the rifle and pistol that he'd carried since he and Sinks had left Holden. He wondered again at the bandits' claim that his home was gone and tried not to dwell on it as he and Amelia stepped into the forest.

"Where are we heading?" he asked as they slowed their pace, surrounded by shadows.

"Away. We'll find somewhere."

"Do you know where we are?"

"I mean... Roughly." she muttered "We didn't come far after they took us. I think if we head north, we'll come onto a trade route. Then we find a town."

"Not Matwood. Armstrong's there." Kyle pointed out.

"Fine. Let's get as far away from here as possible. We can camp and figure it out in the morning."

Seeing the sense in her words, Kyle nodded and followed her into the darkness.

PART 3

CHAPTER 59

The night had faded into a dull dawn before they felt secure enough to stop. Snow was falling again although instead of the fat, gentle flakes that had characterised the past two weeks, these were small, hard pellets of ice whipped through the trees by a vicious wind that burned Kyle's cheeks and reddened his lips. He squinted through the blizzard, cursing as a hefty gust made him flinch, causing him to stumble into Amelia.

"We need to stop..."

"You think we're far enough away?"

"They aren't going to be chasing us..."

Neither of them stopped walking although their pace slowed. They threw surreptitious glances back over their shoulders but the driving snow reduced visibility to just a few metres.

"We can't keep going in this."

"Are you cold?"

"No. You?"

"No."

The lies kept them both trudging forwards stubbornly for a few minutes until the ground began to drop sharply away through the trees.

"There..."

Amelia led the way towards a giant dirty yellow protrusion of rock. Kyle was reminded of the cave they'd left far behind them, Harrison's Infected corpse rotting inside it and he shivered, although the hard stone was the only shelter they'd seen.

He reached it a half step ahead of Amelia, kicking the powdery snow aside with his boots. The trees had broken the worst of the drifts and it was only a few inches before he found the mulchy needles of the forest floor. He glanced up, grateful that the trees here had gradually turned deciduous, the towering pines revealing glimpses of the dull grey sky.

Without speaking, they tugged a battered army issue basha out of Amelia's stolen rucksack, pinning it into the ground with scattered pine branches. A trio of sticky but sturdier pieces of timber acted as loose poles, raising the shelter off the ground. Amelia took some string and secured it to the ground as Kyle scattered snow across the top, hoping it would give them some semblance of security should any of the bandits have pursued them.

Finally, they clambered into the pair of grubby sleeping bags they'd appropriated and lay down, shivering. After a few minutes of chattering teeth, they hastily zipped the two bags together, clinging tightly to one another until their exhausted bodies found the peace of sleep.

*

Kyle jolted awake as Amelia twitched, her body pressed against his. His hand went to his pistol as the image of Boss, dressed in a Ranger uniform and wielding a whip of roaring fire faded slowly from his mind. He looked at Amelia's sleeping form, pressed against him and realised with a rush of pleasure that he was warm. The snow had died down and the light looked to be fading.

The dream faded and practicality returned. He peered as far under the shelter as he could but saw nothing. His slight movement disturbed Amelia who stirred, then woke abruptly, looking around.

"How long were we asleep?"

"Most of the day by the look of it."

She rummaged in the sleeping bag for a moment before drawing out the map they'd taken from Treetops, quickly pinning the loose folds of the bag around their bodies, trapping the heat.

"Here..." she pointed at the machine printed map, now twenty years out of date. Someone - a careless bandit perhaps - had drawn in crayon across several of the routes and features, obscuring much of the useful information but Amelia's finger pointed towards a clearly visible line of a small cliff, in the shelter of a deciduous patch of trees.

"Yeah?" Kyle couldn't have pointed to Treetops on a map if he'd tried and so he was reliant on Amelia's navigation.

"There's buildings here, houses maybe, not far from this - what's that, a railway?"

"Yes." Kyle recalled Sinks repetitive lessons on map reading, something he'd zoned out of without fail. He wished now he'd paid closer attention to the old soldier but he thought Amelia was right.

"Can't be too far. We can have a look at least?"

"Don't we want to get further away?"

"What, in case they follow us?"

Kyle shrugged, thinking "I s'pose the snow will have covered our tracks. Sounded like the Rangers pretty much wiped them out, too. Only thing they might come looking for is you." he finished by holding her gaze, seeing the flash of fear on her face, quickly controlled. He marvelled at her self-control.

"Well, if they find us, they find us. We can't keep walking in this weather. One of us will die of exposure or an Infected will find us while we sleep." she shook her head "I say we head for these buildings." she stabbed her finger on the map "The railway is always another option. It's not far from there and it might be easier to walk along at least."

"Alright." Kyle nodded and made to get up but a spasm of pain tore through him and he gasped, hand clutching his chest.

Amelia was looming over him immediately, gently but firmly pushing him down to the ground "Steady... Let me check your dressings before we move." she gingerly peeled back the bandages, her face coldly professional at the mutilated ruin of Kyle's back and the nearly healed scars on his chest.

"What's this?" she was pointing to his arm, the flesh wound where Harrison's hastily fired bullet had scored his flesh.

"Oh... It was an accident." the memory brought back images of Harrison's Infected face and he didn't share the details.

"It's infected."

The words were like a gunshot to Kyle's already overburdened mind. He whipped around, staring at the injury which was red and inflamed "What? How did I get Infected? It was weeks ago! I wasn't bitten! How -"

Amelia interrupted him "No, bacterial infection. Not Viral."

Kyle blew air out his mouth in something approaching relief. He settled back, suddenly feeling weak.

Amelia pressed her hand to his forehead "How do you feel?"

"Shit."

"Seriously."

"Not ill. Just tired."

Amelia looked grim "We need to get somewhere safe. If we move now, we can make those buildings by nightfall. Then I can see about cleaning the wound. We don't have any antibiotics..."

Kyle swallowed, suddenly nervous "You can treat it, can't you?"

"Yes." Amelia glanced at the light "We need to go now if we're going. If we don't make it by nightfall..."

She helped Kyle to his feet and they set off casting nervous glances at the rapidly darkening sky.

CHAPTER 60

It wasn't a collection of houses, it was a farmhouse. A red bricked, four walled farmhouse and to Kyle, trudging slowly through the snow, it was a vision of Heaven.

"Come on!" Amelia led the way around the weathered wall, her mouth set as she stared up at the sturdy looking building "What are the chances?" she shot a look back at Kyle, excitement burning in her eyes. The emotion was well placed. The wall, although weathered, stood well above Kyle's six foot five inches and rough patches of brambles had forced their way up close to the base. Kyle was reminded of the container wall in Holden and he nodded approvingly, casting a professional eye over the wall.

"What's it for?" Amelia was confused.

Kyle shrugged, then realised that Amelia couldn't see him "Dunno. To keep the animals in?"

Amelia began to voice her own opinion as they reached a corner and turned onto an overgrown road that led to the front of the house but as she cleared the corner, she stopped abruptly.

Moving quickly, Kyle brought his rifle into his cold hands, moving to cover Amelia but it was not Wretches that greeted him as he leaned around the corner. Instead, a huge, rotted tree trunk leaned across the road, the top third smashed like a hammer blow into the roof and upper floor of the farmhouse.

Amelia did not speak but she began to weep at the sight, not breaking down but tears spilling uncontrollably down her cheeks.

"Let's have a look, anyway." Kyle tried to encourage her. When Amelia didn't move, he took her gently by the elbow and led her forward, towards the peeling black paint of a gate. They passed under the tree trunk which looked as though it had fallen several years ago. It had smashed the roof and some of the wall of the farmhouse but had mercifully left the perimeter unscathed. Kyle, trying to ignore the almost catatonic state his companion had fallen into, viewed the building practically. Despite the damage, it was in mostly good order although what years of exposure to the British climate would have done to the inside was anyone's guess.

He approached the black metal gate cautiously, pushing Amelia into the shelter of the wall. She leaned against the brick and stood, staring into nothing. Her stolen rifle hung from its sling and her arms hung by her side. The tears ran down her cheeks as Kyle glanced worriedly at her.

"Wait here..." he needed to get her inside and get them both out of the wind but first, he needed to make sure the small compound was safe.

The gate was locked with no mechanism obvious. Kyle shoved it with his shoulder but the great black iron didn't budge. He looked up, but a tight coil of razor wire ran across the top and there was no way for him to even grip the edge. Not that he thought he could have pulled himself up with the ever present throbbing of his injuries.

He glanced back to Amelia who had slid down the wall and was now sat, knees bent in the snow, staring into nothingness. She had begun to shiver. Kyle made up his mind and jogged back, passing her without a flicker of recognition from her face.

He reached the fallen tree and moved down the length of the great trunk to a point where it stood only waist high on him. He reached out and knocked the wood with a gloved hand. It was only then that he realised how cold his hands were. How long had it been since their shelter in the woods? Long enough. A shiver rocked his body.

Kyle took a step back from the log, drawing in a deep, long breath. The cold air filled his lungs and his vision brightened for a second. He could almost hear Sinks' voice in his head, repeating the endless lessons on survival and concentration, telling Kyle to focus, to use the environment around him.

Don't give up

Kyle pushed his rifle behind him and tugged the knife from the plate carrier. He chipped away at the fallen log, scattering small shavings of rotted wood. About six inches deep, he found white, sticky timber and his heart leapt. Stowing the knife, he placed two hands on the trunk and hauled himself up, ignoring the scream of protest from his chest and back. Gritting his teeth, he forced himself onto his hands and knees, edging slowly up the length of the trunk towards the wall.

A blast of icy wind whipped around, turning his head to the left. Amelia had fallen sideways and now lay flat in the snow which was beginning to settle on her.

"Amelia!" Kyle shouted her name but she didn't move. Heart pounding, he leapt from the log, landing hard and slipping on the icy road. He recovered and bounded the short distance to her prone form.

"Amelia! Can you hear me? Wake up! Come one! You've got to wake up!"

Her eyes flickered open and she murmured something indistinct before they slid shut again.

Kyle slapped her across the cheek. Hard.

Blinking and stuttering she rose onto one elbow. Blood trickled from the corner of her mouth and she stared at Kyle in shock. Her mouth opened and vague gibberish sentences emerged.

It was enough.

Kyle stood, hauling the slight woman to her feet roughly. He half led, half dragged her over to the tree trunk. She didn't protest, seeming unaware of what was happening but at least she was compliant. He pushed her up onto the trunk before he clambered up in front of her.

"Come on!" he began to move. Amelia stayed put, blinking in confusion and looking around her. Kyle swore and turned around, still on his hands and knees. He grabbed her arm and pulled her towards him. She came willingly but then stopped as soon as he turned around.

Kyle swore at her, shouted, and threatened but she only stared at him in confusion. He guessed that whatever funk she'd fallen into was being compounded by the early stages of hypothermia and, gritting his teeth, Kyle began the excruciatingly slow process of edging backwards along the trunk on his hands and knees whilst he tugged her forward towards him.

Minutes passed and he risked a glance backwards. The snow had picked up again and he slipped more than once on icy patches on the smooth wood of the trunk. It groaned beneath them and Kyle tried to concentrate on the unspoiled timber at the centre. Surely it would hold their weight!

Halfway along and they were both shivering. Kyle's stolen scarf had pulled up, leaving exposed skin at the back of his neck where snow was now settling and melting, sending rivulets of icy water down his body. His teeth chattered and his hands were numb. Amelia's eyes were locked on his, she seemed incapable of independent thought. He shuffled backwards, his weight on one arm, his injured body screaming at him. He pulled her forward with the other arm and she shuffled too. It was like a terrible mockery of some child's game. Crawling and being led along a path, any error causing them to fall.

He risked a glance over the side. They were now at least the height of the wall. Eight feet? Nine? Kyle didn't know but he guessed that if either of them fell from this height then they'd break something. If Amelia fell, he did not have the strength to retrieve her and if she broke a bone, he could not carry her back up here.

The log suddenly groaned alarmingly and the wood shifted under him. Kyle froze in place, holding his breath.

The wood settled and he began the slow crawl again. Shuffling backwards. Tugging Amelia forwards.

Shuffle.

Tug.

Shuffle.

Tug.

Then, he was over the wall and for the first time he could see clearly into the rectangular shape formed by the red walls. A neat, tidy courtyard filled only with snow. Lean-tos were built around the interior, some stuffed with snow covered logs, one with rusted farm equipment. The gate was barricaded from the inside, two hefty looking bolts securing it to the ground. The walls of the farmhouse were drawing closer and Kyle began to worry about how to get down from their precarious perch.

The trunk began to thin as it approached the smashed house but it was still thick. Thinner branches had mostly fallen away, rotting as the seasons passed and Kyle could see clearly that a sturdy section of the trunk continued well into the building. It looked secure.

He looked down. Of course, the tree had to fall where there were none of the lean-tos for him to step on! Instead, the ground was now frighteningly far beneath him. He could probably reach onto the wall itself, but there was still a big drop down and Kyle didn't feel like risking it. He looked back to Amelia who was staring at him as though he were the only thing in her world.

Shuffle.

Tug.

Shiver.

Then the trunk snapped.

CHAPTER 61

Kyle fell.

His feet landed on something solid.

His hands caught the trunk and his gloves found purchase.

He felt every stroke of the bandit's whip, every fibre of the unknown gunman's bullet in his chest and without a shred of shame or self-pity he roared out in an impossible agony.

The air left his lungs in a bellow. It felt as though he'd been shot with molten lava and the fiery rock was burning its way into his torso. His hands slipped and his face smashed forward against the wood. The blow shook him and his feet scrabbled for purchase.

Slowly, Kyle became aware that he was standing on something solid and that meant he was on the wall. His arms were clutching at the trunk and every fibre of his being was screaming at him but he was not seriously hurt. He moved one foot experimentally and almost fell as his foot slipped into space.

He looked down.

The wall was a few inches thick and as his mind focussed, Kyle managed to position his feet so that he could stand. Gingerly, he released his grip on the log although he kept his hands close, balancing precariously. A sob of agony tore itself from him and he didn't care. His breath came in sharp bursts, thick clouds of mist pouring from his lips.

Amelia

He looked at the broken trunk. The wood had partially snapped close to where it had smashed into the house. The head of the fallen tree was still attached but jagged splinters showed where the log had broken. It now rested on the wall which was how he was able to stand. Amelia was still atop the log, now several feet above him. How she had not fallen was a mystery.

And how she was going to climb down in the state she was in, was another.

"Amelia?" Kyle called up. To his relief, she peered over the edge at him although any chance of the shock having cleared her mind was quickly removed as she did nothing but stare.

"Climb down!" he called.

Nothing. She didn't even blink. She just gazed at him.

"Shit." He looked frantically from left to right. They had a rope, but it was in the pack on Amelia's back. He cursed at himself for not thinking of it earlier although he couldn't see how he'd use it in this situation anyway. Furiously, Kyle slapped both hands against the log, roaring his frustration.

There was a faint wobble.

Kyle didn't dare move. Had the trunk shifted again? He wasn't sure. Then he felt the wobble again and he realised with horror that the bricks in the top of the wall had been knocked loose by the falling tree and were now moving beneath his feet.

He stayed stock still. Furiously, he tried to think around the problem. They needed to get down or they'd just freeze to death up here. But if he jumped, he might break an ankle and then he'd freeze on the ground. Amelia would stay on the trunk and die too.

Death up here.

Death down there.

There was only one thing to do.

Kyle slapped the trunk again, careful to move his feet as little as possible.

The wall gave a wobble.

He began to shove against the trunk, feeling a small give in the bricks. Kyle let a rocking motion build, pushing the wood back and forth a few inches as momentum built. He didn't look up at Amelia. She'd either hold on, or she wouldn't.

He pushed and rocked and the wall moved.

Then it collapsed.

Several metres of the sturdy red bricks fell inwards, moving in a slow, deliberate tumble. Almost a gentle movement, the collapse sped up as it reached the ground and the weight of the trunk dragged it harder.

The tree hit the frozen ground in a puff of snow.

Kyle crashed down a ball of agony. He landed badly, smashing his shoulder into the ground but almost immediately, he was up again.

"Amelia!" he dashed forwards, peering through the dusting snow. He cast about frantically for her but could see nothing. He called her name, over and over and finally, he saw her leg sticking up over the trunk. She lay on her back on the far side, the rucksack having cushioned her fall. Her rifle hung from its sling and her eyes were open but staring vacantly up at the snow. Kyle reached her and shook her, pressing his frozen fingers into her neck, checking for a pulse.

She blinked. Then stared at him and smiled, vacantly. She was alive.

Wasting no more time, Kyle lifted her bodily and dragged her inside the farmhouse and finally out of the snow.

CHAPTER 62

The door to the house was unlocked and Kyle pushed it shut behind them. He dumped Amelia in the hallway and doing his best to ignore the pain and shock in his body, he moved through the house, room by room until he was certain it was clear. The top floor was where the tree had come crashing in and Kyle stood, staring at the damage, looking out to the wall they had just crossed. There was nothing to be done about the damaged perimeter and he hoped the trunk would block the hole enough to keep out any curious Wretches.

There were four floors, an enormous house to Kyle who was used to one-roomed huts in Holden. The upper floors had their windows blocked by sturdy wooden shutters, reinforced with metal bands which had kept the interior preserved to a level of almost Pre-Fall cleanliness. Dust was evident everywhere but someone had taken the time to put protective sheets over the beds which were neatly made.

On the second floor, in the white metal bathtub, a man had killed himself.

He was almost completely decomposed, the remains of his clothes hanging off exposed bone and dried sinew. He'd taken the trouble to leave the window open so the bathroom smelled almost clean. His final words were scrawled in a leather bound notebook he'd carefully placed away from the window with his name embossed in gold letters across the front.

Kyle shut the door, finding a key in the lock, and securing it from the outside. The house contained no other surprises and so he returned to Amelia who was shivering in the hallway. He moved a table and a set of heavy chairs in front of the door and hauled her up to the nearest bedroom. Gathering the thick duvets and blankets from the neighbouring rooms and barring the door, he took her weapons and gear from her un-protesting hands. She stared blankly at him all the while as he filled the silence with a nervous chatter, trying to hide the fear he felt at her mental state. Her clothes were wet through and she was shivering violently. Perhaps the Kyle of a few weeks ago, the young man who had left Holden with Sinks would have scoffed at the idea or been at the very least embarrassed but it was almost without thinking that he stripped her sodden garments off, exposing her damp skin before he wrapped her in a thick towel from the adjoining bathroom. He did the same to himself, trying to control the painful shivers that wracked him before he shoved her unceremoniously onto the luxuriously soft bed where she fell and lay, watching him with that strangely vacant expression.

He tucked her in, wrapping her arms around her thin body and pulling the duvet under her. Then, he rushed under the cover on the opposite side and pulled her skin close to his, wrapping his arms around her and shuddering at the awful shivers.

The warmth of the thick bedding worked wonders and he felt her shivering slow, then stop and her breathing began to settle. The blank stare slowly began to fade from her face and her eyelids drooped once or twice as he watched. Finally, her eyes closed fully and a moment later, the reassuring sound of rhythmic breathing began to issue from her mouth. Kyle felt a great wash of relief. He didn't know the medical reasons for her catatonic state but at least they were now as safe as they could be. The house was a miracle, the warm bedding a boon they could not have imagined. Kyle felt the trauma of the past few weeks begin to whir through his mind and he braced himself for the onslaught of terrible nightmares but before he knew it, he was asleep.

*

For once, Kyle was spared dreams. His exhausted body and mind fell into a warm, dark pit of comfort, peace flooding through him.

He woke hours later. Was it hours? The light that had crept through the shuttered window had faded and he thought it was full night. Amelia's breathing was easy against his chest, both their bodies warm and relaxed. He listened, seeing if he could detect any danger but the house was silent. The wind was audible outside and at the thought of the driving snow, he shivered and once again felt his eyelids droop.

*

He felt movement and woke in something close to a panic as arms struggled against him. There was a moment of pressure and then he relaxed as he heard Amelia's voice in the darkness.

"Is that you?"

"Yeah. Are you with me?"

"Huh?" Amelia sounded groggy "I'm right here."

"Okay."

His sleep filled mind struggled to make sense of the words and there was silence for a period of time. Perhaps they both slept again because his voice shocked him when he spoke "How are you feeling?"

"Hot."

A few seconds later a light snore sounded and Kyle let sleep and warmth claim him again.

CHAPTER 63

Daylight was streaming around the edge of the shutters when Kyle awoke with a full bladder. He shoved the covers aside and stumbled into the bathroom. There was water in the toilet cistern and he operated the flush, watching as the cistern refilled. He wondered at the source of water and reasoned there must be a tank somewhere in the house, probably nearly empty. He spun the tap in the sink and after a few noisy air bubbles, a stream of dirty water issued forth.

Movement in the bedroom and Kyle padded back towards the covers. Amelia was half out of bed, hastily wrapping the towel around herself. Her eyebrows shot up at the sight of Kyle and he blushed, suddenly aware that he had left his own towel somewhere under the sheets. He stumbled forward and snatched it up as Amelia vanished into the bathroom.

She emerged a moment later, the towel securely fastened under her arms and went back to the bed, pulling the covers back over her. Kyle also returned beneath their warmth. Despite the shelter, the air in the room was still cold and he shivered briefly.

"Not exactly how I pictured you undressing me for the first time."

The joke took Kyle by surprise and he turned to see Amelia staring forwards, the ghost of a smile on her lips. Relief at her apparent return of awareness flooded him and he forced a chuckle at the joke.

"You pictured me undressing you?"

She snorted "Yes, you're nice to look at, Kyle. Don't let it go to your head." her face turned serious "We're in the farm house, aren't we?"

"Yes. Do you remember getting here?"

"No... I remember being cold."

Kyle carefully relayed the story of how they'd crossed the wall. He began to leave out the parts where she'd frozen but she pressed him and he found himself holding nothing back. When he finished, she sat in silence, digesting the words.

"Thank you."

He grunted.

"Do you reckon we're even on keeping each other alive yet?"

"I reckon I'm winning." he sniped.

They both found that very funny for some reason and dissolved into helpless giggles which helped to warm them both up. Kyle felt a sense of peace, a security he'd not felt in weeks. He knew they needed to eat, drink and secure the broken wall but those concerns seemed a long way off, far outside the warmth and comfort of this room and these heavy covers.

After some time, they were both hungry and Amelia leaned out of the bed to grab her rucksack. She began tugging clothes for both of them out, flinging some towards Kyle who pulled them on under the covers. To his surprise, she dropped the towel away and stood, her naked back towards him as she dressed. He caught himself staring and hastily averted his eyes but found them drawn back to the sight of her smooth nut brown skin.

"Kyle?"

"Yeah?"

"Stop staring."

He tried not to laugh as he finished dressing.

Clad in layers of warm, dry jumpers they explored the house together at a slower pace than Kyle had initially moved through. He warned her of the dead man but she insisted on seeing the tragic scene. She glanced coolly at the body and announced that the man had died by driving a knife into his own head. She pointed at the rusted handle of a sharp blade that lay on the white metal of the tub beneath his head where it had dropped from his decomposing flesh. Kyle wondered aloud what could drive a man in such secure settings to such an action.

"Let's find out." Amelia scooped up the gold embossed notebook and led Kyle back to their bedroom, locking the bathroom door behind them.

"Arthur John Cooley" she read from the front page "Look... It's a suicide note." Amelia began to read the dead man's words as Kyle pulled the duvet around his shoulders.

"I, Arthur John Cooley do hereby leave this final message to ~~whoever~~ whomever should find my house and my body. I was born on the twelfth of May, Nineteen Seventy Eight in this very farmhouse. My Father died when I was a baby and my Mother remarried. My stepfather's name was Cooley and we took his. They're buried in the garden out the back. Perhaps whoever you are will be kind enough to bury me next to them if you have the energy and the time. These are hard times, ever since the Collapse. The Zombies are all over the countryside. I went into the village just a day after they announced the virus and I saw the vicar attacking some of the families who sheltered inside the church. A couple of the local lads saw me and tried to get me but the Beast was too high for them. If only there was someone alive to say 'I told you so' to! All those snooty old women who told me I was a menace driving the Beast on our narrow roads. Well, that truck got me this far and if it weren't for my own carelessness, it would have got me a lot further.

I'm rambling a bit, sorry. The mind tends to wander in the face of imminent death. Even if it is on my own terms. Whilst I remember though, there's a couple of important bits I need to let you know. Hopefully, the four walls are still standing although if you're reading this you must have managed to get over them. They'll keep out the worst of the zombies but if a big group of them or a bunch of thieves come through, I've installed shutters on all the windows. The second floor is the best to shoot from, it's mostly cleared of furniture so you can move from room to room quickly and the windows give the best cover of the whole farm. Also, the basement is full of food - long life stuff too. All my guns are down there, I oiled them and unloaded them but the combination to the safe is my date of birth.."

Amelia looked up at Kyle, her face shining "The basement!"

Kyle led the way, both of them with their pistols drawn. The door to the basement was in the kitchen, under the stairs. Kyle had missed it before because the hefty kitchen table had been pushed up against it but now they hauled the table aside and opened the door to reveal a dusty but dry looking low-ceilinged basement. As Arthur Cooley had promised, it was stacked with food. Emergency rations, tins of beans, packets of freeze dried drinks. A medical chest, racks of boots, clothes, batteries, fuel and jars containing some complicated looking gear that Kyle couldn't identify were stacked in neat piles.

"Was this bloke mental or something?"

"He's a prepper." Amelia picked up a box of rations marked 'British Army'. She tossed it aside back onto the pile "Went out of date fifteen years ago."

"Not a very good prepper then."

"These are still good... To be fair, some of the out of date stuff might be alright. There's not much real food in it to go off..."

Kyle found a pyramid of tins stacked in a corner. They all bore the words 'Survival food - thirty years' on their metal fronts and indeed, they appeared outwardly to still be good. Kyle pointed them out to Amelia and together they manoeuvred half a dozen over to the bottom of the stairs.

The gun safe was filled with a collection of shotguns and small calibre semi automatics. A couple of large bore hunting rifles piqued Kyle's interest but ultimately he left them alone. Spare clothes in a variety of sizes were of more interest. Kyle pointed out the quality of some, marvelling at what in Holden would have been considered the height of luxury.

He turned to Amelia to hold up a pair of well stitched walking trousers only to leap back in shock as she leered at him from behind a gas mask.

"Bloody Hell!" he laughed, jokingly pushing the mask away from her face. She tossed it to him and he pulled it on to his own face causing Amelia to roar with laughter.

The rest of the morning passed the same way. They tried on ill-fitting clothes, Amelia pulling on a vastly oversized hat and boots and stomping around the basement and Kyle trying on a women's 'hiking' t-shirt and held out his arms in mock pride.

"I can see your soul through that!" Amelia snorted.

The rest of the house was far colder than the basement and so after sealing the door, they retired to their second floor bedroom where they tentatively opened one of the military issue rations, finding to their surprise a brightly orange mixture of sauce and beans.

"Is it supposed to look like that?" Kyle wrinkled his nose as Amelia used a plastic spork to taste the food.

"'fink so." she chewed for a moment, before shrugging and swallowing "It's not bad." she held out the spork to Kyle who took it and chewed with a disgusted expression on his face.

Amelia laughed and then laughed harder at his indignant expression until he threw the spork at her and she shoved him and then they both collapsed laughing onto the soft pillows.

Well fed, they found exhaustion was lingering just out of sight and soon they were asleep again. When they woke, it was dark and after a brief but unsuccessful search to locate the source of the water in the bathroom, they returned to the basement to explore further.

To their combined surprise, under a tarpaulin that they assumed covered more stacks of food, they found a well-equipped gymnasium. Kyle stared in shock at the cleanliness of the racks and shining chrome of the weight bars. Clearly, Arthur Cooley had believed in personal fitness. Kyle openly compared it to the rusty gym in Holden where the Militia trained under Sinks' watchful eye.

"Here..." Amelia had found a handful of brightly coloured rubber bands and she instructed Kyle to take his shirt off, talking him through several movements which she said would help restore the muscle strength he had lost through the injuries.

"Shit! I forgot!" she half shouted, clutching his arm and pulling the infected wound down to her eye level to inspect "How does it feel?"

"Fine. I'd forgotten about it." Kyle looked at the gash which was in fact looking puckered and red. As Amelia began to examine it he became aware that it stung intensely and he did not protest as she led him towards the crate of medical supplies. She checked the names of several packages, tossing more than one aside contemptuously until she found antibiotics and rubbing alcohol. Kyle was then subjected to her shoving him down into a sitting position while she cleaned the wound.

"Who stitched this?"

"Jas."

"He did a bloody terrible job. You should have told me at the hospital."

"Well, I was too busy being shot at."

"There was that." she conceded "I'm going to take these out. Hold still."

Kyle tried not to wince as she snipped Jas's handiwork out of his arm. He felt the final stitch go and there was a moment's relief before she tipped rubbing alcohol into the half healed wound. He hissed in pain and pulled away from her but she told him not to be such a baby.

"You tip that on a bullet wound, then!" he protested.

"I just did." she pointed out.

"Oh, very funny..." he grumbled to himself.

She worked in silence for a few minutes as Kyle sat with his thoughts. Eventually, she announced that she was done and they both made their way slowly through the house. There were plenty of bedrooms. Kyle was surprised that they were the first to discover the house and he said as much to Amelia.

"Who would come here though? It's not near a settlement and it's too far for the bandits." she shrugged as they made their way back to the bedroom "There must be a thousand places like this throughout the country. Throughout the world."

"The world." Kyle tasted the words as he lay back on the bed, hands under his head. Amelia lay down next to him, elbowing his arms off her pillow.

"What about it?"

"It's just... I never really think about what it means. All those different countries. There used to be so much."

"There still is."

"Yeah, but the Wretches are all over it, aren't they? When was the last time we heard from France? From Germany? From America?"

Amelia was silent for a moment "I suppose Holden was your world?"

Kyle nodded slowly "I suppose so. Do you really think Boss was right?"

Amelia sighed "I hope not."

"Me too."

Kyle let his thoughts whirl for a moment. The image of Holden destroyed lingered in his head but he forced himself not to dwell on it. There was nothing he could do. He tried to focus on positive memories, the sight of a red dog wagging its tail, Sinks' surly face ordering him about and Rosie's welcoming smile. But when he tried to bring her face into his mind, all he saw was Amelia's dark beauty.

CHAPTER 64

The snow was still falling the next day and they were both still exhausted. Amelia dragged Kyle down to the basement and made him work the atrophied muscles in his chest and back. She changed his dressings and they both ate themselves full, regaining their strength.

A stack of well worn books was uncovered behind a box of anti-bacterial wipes and together they perused the titles by the light of a gas lamp. Amelia was impressed that Kyle could read, more impressed when he told her of the titles he'd covered back in Holden. One of the great appeal to new Zek recruits, she explained, was that the group taught literacy and basic mathematics to all its members. Kyle was surprised but shied away from the subject, still unsure of how to relate the image of the shrewish Amelia Singh, figurehead of the Zek movement that he'd cultivated in his mind with this young, attractive woman who was the sole reason he was still alive.

They carried a stack of books back to their bedroom where they huddled under the covers. Kyle knocked Arthur's diary aside as he clambered in and, ignoring the wealth of literature he'd just painstakingly selected, began exploring the pages of the leather bound journal. He began to read on but Amelia demanded he read out loud and she wrapped a blanket around her head like a shawl and listened, enraptured.

"Zombies. Of all the apocalypses we knew would come, that's the one I most suspected. After that rubbish with COVID in the early twenties we knew it was just a matter of time before something else came. COVID knocked the world into a panic, but it hardly scratched the surface. Doctors and politicians told us that it was a good thing, that it prepared us for a real threat but they

did nothing to prevent another virus. Didn't bother boosting the Health Service, didn't even create a proper vaccine. Luckily, I long stopped believing in the government. Bunch of posh-boy idiots, no real experience of life. You can tell that from the laws. All the paperwork I had to go through just to get a shotgun! And then I had to pretend it was for hunting, not for self-defence. Meanwhile across the pond the Yanks could buy an arsenal in the corner shop."

"Anyway, everyone thought I was mad, repairing the walls on the farm, shuttering the windows and spending all that cash on supplies. But they're all dead now and - well, I suppose no-one wins in an 'I told you so' contest here."

"Zombies. That's what I was writing about! Of course, the fiction was there, plain as day. Films, books, and everything in between. We all knew the drill, slow, hungry, and undead. Corpses that were reanimated. Of course, you can't reanimate a corpse. A dead bloke is a dead bloke. But there was precedent for a virus that made you crazy. Rabies, mad cow disease. It wasn't such a leap to see a virus that made zombies."

"Shoot them in the head."

"Walk away, don't worry, they can't run."

"Well, they bloody can! The only thing I didn't really work on was my cardio. That was a mistake. I relied too hard on the Beast but these bastards are fast. I suppose that should have been obvious, you can't spread a zombie virus if the infected can barely walk. It's only transmitted through bites so all you have to do is not get bitten. Anyway, if you're reading this then get fit and stay fit. All the walls in the world don't matter if you get bitten."

"Why are you stuttering?" Amelia asked.

Kyle looked up with a grimace on his face "It's the word, 'Zombie'." he spat it out as though it tasted bad in his mouth.

Amelia gave a half smile "You know, that's what they call them in the west country." she shrugged "It was a common name during the Fall."

"I know what it was. We had the books in Holden. Even saw a couple of films once." an angry look passed over Kyle's face "It's mental. All these rules they had. You had to shoot them in the head, they bite you and that's it, they eat your brains - Wretches don't eat brains! Urgh!"

"It's just stories." Amelia shrugged.

"It's stupid." Kyle muttered darkly "People wanted something that scared them but they put all these rules in place. This magical idea of an undead zombie."

"They aren't that different from the Wretches." Amelia pointed out.

"Wretches aren't 'undead'. They're people Infected with a virus. You lock a Wretch in a house and it'll starve to death, I've seen it happen!"

"Put enough of them in there together and they'll eat each other to survive! You've seen that, too! Besides, trauma to the brain is the most effective way of killing them."

"Same as you or me!" Kyle gestured to his bandaged chest, out of sight beneath the covers "I'm living proof of that, I was shot, I'm still here."

"You mean they don't always get stopped by bullet wounds?"

"Give them enough and they do."

Amelia rolled her eyes at him before shaking her head in gentle exasperation "This really pisses you off, doesn't it?"

"Oh, it doesn't matter." Kyle picked absently at the leather binding of Arthur Cooley's diary "It's just ridiculous. All these rules for your monsters. Monsters are monsters. They're scary for a reason."

Amelia nodded slowly and Kyle looked at her. Their gaze met for a moment and held as neither of them said anything. To his embarassment, Kyle felt blood rush to his cheeks as he blushed, noticing even as he did that the same effect was taking place beneath Amelia's darker skin. They both looked away quickly and Kyle began reading again.

"Sorry about all the rambling. It's hard to concentrate. The bite is pretty severe, I can feel a fever coming on. I can't have long left now. I think I recognised the one that got me. The lad who used to work behind the bar in the pub. I think he did Saturday nights and the odd night here and there throughout the week. He was a good

looking boy, I can remember a few of the younger girls having fits of laughter when he asked them what they wanted. Poor bloke don't think he knew what had hit him. Anyway, I was doing a run in the Beast when I saw him and... Well, it doesn't matter. I thought I could get into the Beast before he got me but the little wanker was quicker than I thought. Still managed to get him though, tomahawk to the head. Hah! That felt good. But he got a good nip in at my ankle and I suppose that's it. I didn't even bother cleaning the wound at first but old habits die hard and now it's cleaned and bandaged. I wonder if people ever dressed a wound after a snake bite? That's what they're like, these Zombies. Snakes. One bite and it's all over."

"Oh, for God's sake." Kyle tossed the diary down onto the bed. Amelia had drawn her knees up to her chin and wrapped her arms around them. Her face was pale "He killed himself, didn't he? Little bite to the ankle and he bloody thought it was all over."

He fumed in silence for a moment as Amelia leaned forward to put a hand on his. She squeezed his fingers "He didn't know."

"It's just so stupid!" Kyle gestured around "It's a bloody fortress, he could have survived here for what, ten years? And then he gives it all up. He had antibiotics, that's all it takes! Instead, he killed himself."

"It's frustrating."

"It's stupid."

Amelia squeezed his hand again and Kyle put the journal down. He breathed, calming himself. There was nothing to be done for Arthur Cooley now and he pushed the leather bound book aside, not wanting to read more.

"Come on, let's see what else is down there."

"We've been through everything!"

"Fine. Stay here by yourself then!" Amelia hopped out of the bed, scooping up her pistol and headed for the door. Kyle ground his teeth for a moment before following her.

*

When Amelia drew his attention to a single dusty cardboard box, Kyle realised that she must have spotted it before and said nothing. Inside, six bottles of golden yellow liquid stood on the cold concrete of the floor, their blue labels intact and smooth.

"Scotch!" Kyle beamed. He scooped up a bottle and held it up to the light. Excitedly, he pointed out to Amelia the label babbling about a time that Sinks had bought a bottle with his army pay. It had been well out of the price range of the meagre wages of the Militia but Sinks had taken Kyle to the wall and together they'd polished the bottle off resulting in the most catastrophic hangover of Kyle's life. The thought did not put him off one bit though as he led Amelia via the dining room, retrieving a pair of round spirit glasses from a dresser.

"You spotted those quickly."

He shot a grin over his shoulder as they hastened back to the warmth of the bedroom "Priorities!"

Cocooned once again in the huge double bed, Kyle poured them both equal measures and gently clinked the glasses together.

"Cheers!"

"Cheers."

He then watched in stupefied amazement as Amelia threw the glass back in a single shot. Immediately, she gagged, retching, and dropping the empty glass onto the duvet. Her eyes streamed with tears as Kyle, still with shock on his face began to laugh heartily.

"Wh - what the - urgh! What *was* that, ethanol?" she began to cough and splutter. Kyle, barely able to stand as he howled with laughter fetched a water bottle from their pile of gear and handed it to her. She washed her mouth out, grimacing at the terrible effect.

"You're supposed to sip it!" he chortled "It's scotch!"

"I thought you were supposed to down it!" she began to laugh too, despite the discomfort.

Kyle refilled her glass and sipped at his own, wiping tears

away from his face. She laughed at the ridiculousness of the incident, raising the glass to sip but dissolving into helpless giggles.

A few sips later and she was over the shock. They sat, working their way through the scotch although neither of them had much tolerance to the strong alcohol. They talked, Kyle regaling her with tales of Holden, long nights spent in the Ridged Back with the dogs pattering between the tables.

"Dogs?"

"Yeah. Holden - the town that went to the dogs!" Kyle grinned then sipped more whisky "There were what, fifty of them? No-one ever bred them or anything. They weren't a pack as such, more just general pets. Some slept in houses, some slept outside. There was always one around if you needed one."

"Needed?"

"Yeah. You know." Kyle shrugged "If you'd had a bad day you took a dog and kind of curled up together. It made you feel better."

"You didn't talk about a lot of stuff in Holden, did you?"

He shrugged again "Not really. We made jokes a lot, a kind of 'get on with it' type thing. We probably drank too much too." he looked guiltily at the quarter empty bottle, realising that the same was probably true of this situation.

"It worked, though?"

"Yeah. No. Oh, I don't know. I was happy, but I wanted to leave. Always wanted to."

"To go where?" Amelia's questions were frank and gentle. The conversation flowed easily and Kyle felt she understood everything he was saying.

"The army. Always thought that was the place to be. Get to travel, see the rest of the country. Train, be better at what I do."

"Is that important to you?"

"Being good? Yes. But it's not like... It's not that I want to be better than other people. Well, I do, but only because I want to be better for myself, not because I want to beat them. I s'pose it's the same result in the end. We all use each other to set a standard."

"I think that's true."

The conversation lulled. Amelia refilled their glasses, draining her own with a bold flourish. Her cheeks were flushed and Kyle could feel his own face was reddened. He was about to direct the conversation towards Amelia, to hear more about her past but she moved off to the bathroom, a slight wobble in her step, or was it a sway in her hips? It was only when she closed the door with a snap that Kyle caught himself staring after her.

"We need some music!" she announced as she returned.

"Music?"

"Yeah! You do know what music is, don't you?"

"'Course I do! It's just not - I dunno, safe?"

"Why not?"

"The noise? Attracts Wretches."

Amelia gave a dramatic pause, cocking her head to listen to the silence. Below the sound of their voices, the howl of the wind outside the shuttered window filled the background.

"I think we'll be alright." Amelia declared with mock seriousness. She tottered over to the bedside table, removing to Kyle's eternal surprise an ancient, silvered plastic CD player.

"Where did you find that?"

"Here. Arthur must have put it there and forgotten about it. Here..." she handed him her glass of whisky, thumbing the controls. A moment later, a heavy beat tore from the casing and Amelia gave a whoop, flinging her arms in the air and beginning to twist and writhe in time "Come on!" she beckoned.

"I don't dance." Kyle declared flatly, sitting down on the bed with both glasses in his hands.

"Yes you do!" Amelia lurched forward, seizing his wrists and ignoring his protests. Trying to balance the glasses and resist her surprisingly strong grip at the same time, Kyle over balanced, lifted up and then fell back onto the soft mattress, immediately falling over backwards.

Amelia fell onto him with a shriek, whisky spraying over both of them. Kyle caught a face full and spluttered, twisting his head from side to side as Amelia still pinned his wrists. He felt her shaking on top of him and forced his eyes open in shock, thinking she was sobbing, that he'd injured her somehow but instead her eyes were screwed up with silent laughter.

"What?" he demanded, a slow smile spreading over his own face.

In response, she shook her head, unable to speak. A guffaw erupted out of her mouth, startling her for a moment before she laughed even harder at the shock.

"Oi!" Kyle tried and failed to keep a straight face as she still clutched his wrists. She howled with mirth for a minute or more, tears dripping off her face onto his own even as he protested, laughing himself.

"Oi! Stop dripping on me!"

She opened her eyes, giggling at the sight of him below her "Oh! I'm sorry. How did we get here?"

"You tried to make me dance!"

"Oh, what a crime!" she snorted "Well, you should know to dance when a lady asks it of you."

"I don't dance." he repeated.

"Everyone dances." her eyes flashed mischievously "Especially when they're covered in whisky."

"It's all over my face." he pointed out, wriggling his wrists futilely. He was very aware of the warmth of her body pressed against his and the closeness of her face. He could smell the whisky on her breath.

"Yes."

"And all over the bed."

"Oh dear." she'd locked her legs around his, pulling the two of them closer together.

"We should clean the whisky up." he muttered huskily as her hair fell down, tickling the side of his face.

"Yes, we should." murmured Amelia, her dark eyes boring

into his own.

"But I suppose that can wait."

"I suppose it can." came the response and then Kyle tasted the warm softness of her mouth as she pressed her lips to his.

CHAPTER 65

The morning light streaming around the edge of the shutter woke Kyle with a start. At once, a stab on pain lanced through his head and he wrestled for a moment with the oppressive weight of the bed covers to place a futile palm on the offending body part. Nausea welled in him for a second and he made to stagger to the bathroom but a feminine groan followed by a distinct wet noise sounded close at hand and then a quick pattern of feet dashing across the room followed by an awful sound of sickness and retching. Seeing little choice, Kyle flopped backwards onto the bed and pressed both hands over his sore eyes. A moment later, he heard the bathroom door open as Amelia returned.

"Not the worst reaction I've ever had the next day." he joked.

There was a groan in response followed by the bed lowering as her weight landed on it. Kyle remained in his fragile position, wondering if he'd ever move again.

"Are you..." he began tentatively.

"No." was the terse response.

"Okay then. How about some water?"

"Yes."

Gingerly, Kyle removed his hands from his eyes, flinching at the pain. He found that he was capable of movement after all and, with an effort of will, swung his legs out of bed. He glanced down at his nude body, the memory of last night returning in a flash. Suddenly shy, he glanced back at Amelia's prone form. Her head faced away from him and he hastily pulled his discarded underwear on. Scooping up a water bottle, he brought it round to her face, handing her the open bottle. She took it and wriggled into a more upright position, chugging the water down as though it were like nothing she'd ever tasted. The duvet fell down as she did so and Kyle averted his eyes, embarrassed for her.

She lowered the water bottle, regarding him with some amusement "No need to be shy, Kyle. You certainly weren't last night."

He coughed, awkward but not sure why. He made to turn away but Amelia reached forward and grabbed his hand from behind "No. Don't do that. Here..." she pulled him to sit next to her on the bed, pulling the duvet back up against the cold. She rested her head against his shoulder, groaning at the pain in her head "Tell me." she insisted.

"Sorry..." Kyle muttered, feeling foolish "It's just, we were drunk and..."

"Oh, what. You think I can't make decisions when I'm drunk? Well I can and I can promise you there's nothing to regret."

He looked down to find her grinning in that lightly mocking way she often seemed to regard him. He smiled tentatively and she grinned in response, making to pull his head down to hers but halfway through she baulked, backing away.

"Maybe I'll brush my teeth first though."

"Oh, yeah. Good idea."

*

The morning passed in a flurry of excitement, as though an invisible barrier between them that neither had been consciously aware of had been removed. Through the appalling headaches they lay beneath the covers, warm skin to warm skin talking of anything and everything. They ate the strangely yellow coloured military rations stockpiled by their host and forced cold water through their lips. When movement seemed possible again, they stopped talking and let their bodies speak, moving carefully and closely together beneath the covers, exploring each other in ways that had previously been barred to them.

As the effects of the whisky began to subside, Kyle found himself filled with a buzzing energy. Amelia groaned at his suggestion they venture outside to see the damage to the wall.

"We've got to do it at some point."

"God, and you thought I reacted badly this morning! Wait until I'm out in the snow!"

"Come on! I want to go for a walk."

"Oh, alright. Go and find my clothes first though."

Kyle rooted around the collection of thick winter gear they'd carried up from Arthur Cooley's basement. It occurred to him that the two rucksacks of gear they'd stolen from Treetops had barely been touched, indeed, they'd stacked the proceeds of their new windfall carelessly atop them. He turned to point this out to Amelia but she was sat up, watching him with a narrow eyed smile and she'd allowed the duvet to slip aside down the smooth brown skin of her arm, revealing just enough to make him drop the clothes and cross the room in three quick strides to pull her mouth to his.

It was early evening by the time Amelia agreed they should venture outside. This time she fetched the clothes, tossing them to Kyle on the bed. He was impressed and attracted to the confidence she showed, totally comfortable standing fully naked in front of him, joking all the while.

The smiles faded as they opened the shutters on the windows, peering out across the four walled farmyard. The snow was piled high on the ground, indeed, Kyle didn't think he'd ever seen such a deluge. The red walls were just visible beneath caps of white and high-piled drifts. The lean-tos surrounding the inside of their perimeter were snow covered, hiding their contents from view.

They made their way to the front door, slinging their rifles over their shoulders to remove the hefty table and chairs Kyle had used to seal the entrance. Then, glancing carefully to the left and right, they made their way out into the snow.

The trunk had knocked the wall inwards and the fallen

bricks were now buried in the snow, showing just how much had fallen in the short time they'd sheltered here. Some height still remained, perhaps two feet of red brick now supporting the weight of the half rotted trunk. In a quiet voice Kyle relayed some of the detail of their entrance to Amelia, pointing out a few minor details that she looked at in silence.

"We'll have to block the damage up."

"Yes..." Kyle ducked under the log to look at it from the other side as though this would give him a better perspective. The thick trunk was immovable, clearly and even if they found saws and axes it would take energy and time to chop through. He pointed this out to Amelia who nodded seriously. They moved around the side of the house, passing through a small garden which in summer would probably host a smooth lawn but was now a blanket of virgin white. They spotted two stacks of white stone on which were the names of the Cooley parents and they stood for a moment, reading the names.

"I'd like to bury him." Amelia announced.

Kyle nodded in agreement although he pointed out that the ground was too hard to dig in at present.

"We've got time. I don't think we're going anywhere soon." Amelia said, moving to stand close to Kyle.

He looked down at her, feeling his heart leap at her words. She smiled up at him and he saw the same excitement in her brown eyes. It filled him with an unexplainable warmth despite the frigid air.

The yard at the front of the house was clear and the gate, on inspection was as secure as any entrance either of them had ever come across. The lean-tos, they discovered were filled with carefully stacked firewood with bundles of smaller sticks arranged in neat rows. Clearly, Arthur Cooley had gathered and maintained the supply and they hurried back to the house, discovering a hefty cast iron range that after some time spent tracing the complicated network of pipes, they guessed would heat the house and water tank.

With a little daylight remaining, they discovered the

remains of Arthur Cooley's 'Beast'. Kyle had never been in a working car and he'd held little anticipation that they'd find anything more than a rusted shell and indeed, the 'Beast' was, rather like it's owner, a sad remnant of former glory. A hefty off road vehicle, its monstrously outsized tyres and barred windows were evidence of Arthur's 'Prepping'. A dozen canisters of fuel were covered in a tarp but Kyle and Amelia left them as they were, finding little use for the ruined monster.

Back inside. They explored the shattered loft of the house, finding the source of the water in the bathrooms. A weathered looking tank had survived the blow from the tree and was filled with water. An examination of Arthur's diary gave some explanation on how it functioned and so, as darkness fell the two of them relaxed in a house now filled with warmth from the roaring fire.

They settled on the sofa downstairs in the living room after once again barricading the door and checking the shutters. The rifles lay on a dusty coffee table that probably once belonged to Arthur Cooley's Mother. Amelia propped an elbow on the high back of the sofa and leaned her head onto her hand. She curled one leg beneath her and stretched the other out onto Kyle's lap, smiling at his attempted foot rub.

"It's supposed to feel nice!" he protested as she winced.

"It's a foot, not a wrestling partner!" she objected "A bit gentler. That's it. Yes." she closed her eyes in pleasure. After a moment she asked a question that made Kyle blink in surprise.

"Was there anyone in Holden? You know, someone you were close to?" the question asked, she opened her eyes to see his response. Kyle's brow flickered in a semi-frown but he took a moment, still rubbing her foot before he answered.

"There... Was. Rosie. We kind of grew up together. Both orphans and we joined the Militia together." he looked up at Amelia, suddenly feeling absurdly guilty.

"Did you ever..."

He sighed "No. It was strange. I cared - *care* - a lot about her. It's almost like we were friends though but the option was always there. We just never got around to it, I s'pose." he stared off into the distance, Rosie's face suddenly clear in his mind instead of Amelia's.

She smiled at him and leaned forward to take both his hands in hers "I don't think you've anything to feel guilty about."

He shook his head "No. I don't. It's just... I can't think of Holden being gone. It just doesn't sit properly in my mind."

She nodded seriously and lifted his hands to her mouth, kissing them gently.

"What about you? Any boyfriends I should be watching out for?"

She laughed "Plenty! But none recently."

"Plenty?" he probed, gently.

To Kyle's surprise, a flicker of annoyance crossed her face. She leaned slightly back away from him "Yes. I've no shame in that. I've had boyfriends, flings and even some you might call lovers."

"No - I didn't mean it like that." Kyle quickly interjected, seeing the misunderstanding "I'm not into that anti-promiscuity thing. Some of the older people in Holden were, used to grumble about how girls these days are all 'slags'. I never got it. What's the point in being a bloke if you pretend you want women to be chaste and virtuous? Pretty much all we want is sex." Amelia smiled at him until he added as an afterthought "And food."

She chuckled at that, leaning back towards him "That's probably the most honest thing I've ever had a man say to me. Sex and food!" she laughed and shot him a cheeky look "You've got those in abundance."

Kyle leaned forward and kissed her. She sat back with a smile on her face.

"So, what about you? How did you end up with a name like Amelia Singh?"

"Hah! I suppose it's not that common. My Father is Indian, moved here as a young man and my Mother is British. I suppose I would've had a pretty multicultural upbringing if it wasn't for - " she gestured around as though to illustrate the apocalypse that surrounded them.

"Where are your parents?"

"London." she smiled "Safe and sound, as far as I know and awfully shocked at the little political upset their only daughter has become." that mischievous grin was back, something that Kyle realised she habitually wore when talking about herself "Dad is a doctor, Mum works with him. Not that any of us have anything even approaching formal qualifications."

"Why did a doctor know how to hunt?"

"Hah! London isn't the land of plenty, you know. We still have to scrounge and scrape. Dad spent lots of his spare time out on hunting trips and he took me with him a few times."

"And he taught you to be a doctor?"

Another shrug "It's just what you fall into. Doctors are more in demand than soldiers since the Fall and I was brought up in hospitals, there was nowhere else to leave a little girl. It's what I know. And in answer to your question, no. Dad learned from Doctor May, same as I did. Oddly enough, we learned alongside one another."

"But now you're a Zek?"

"Yes. Or, I was. I don't know what the Zeks are anymore." for a moment she looked so forlorn that Kyle wanted to put his arms around her, to comfort her "It started out as people arguing against the government. Against the military having so much power. It was popular in London, all of us were members. It's what they always say, isn't it? Socialists in your youth, conservative by middle age and a liberal in between."

"How did you end up joining?"

"Like I said, all my friends were in it. I went to a few meetings and before long, it was where I went to socialise, to drink and learn." she frowned "It wasn't so serious at first... Or at least I didn't think it was. I'm good at public speaking, always have been and so people naturally listened to me. When they voted to make me the spokesperson for the London Zeks, I was flattered. But then I met the rest of the organisation, the ones spread around the country and suddenly it was very real. It was quite frightening really."

"Why?"

She paused, thinking for a while. Kyle remembered her reticence, way back when he'd woken in the cave, before the Feral that had been Harrison had destroyed their sanctuary. She began to speak a few times, stopping and thinking.

"You don't have to tell me. I'm not trying to pry." he leaned back.

"No... Sorry, I suppose the last few years have just made me cautious. I don't trust people easily." she smiled apologetically.

"You don't seem worried around me."

"We've been through a lot."

Kyle nodded seriously "We haven't really talked about anything that happened to us."

"No."

"We probably should."

"Yes."

There was silence for a long few minutes. Kyle fidgeted with his fingernails and Amelia stared into nothingness.

"Maybe later?"

"Maybe later."

CHAPTER 66

The next day the snow had eased and a bright sun was shining off the packed white carpet. Leaving the sanctuary of the warm house, they trudged out into the snow to begin repairing the wall. Kyle quickly found that he was in poor physical condition, a result of the many injuries his body had suffered. He tired easily, the cold not helping and found his breath came in sharp bursts. Amelia forced him to slow down and stop several times, warning him of the dangers of over exerting himself.

In the same lean-to that held the ruin of Arthur Cooley's Beast, they found several sheets of rusted sheet metal. Together, they dragged them across the snow covered yard and stood, breath coming in clouds as they tried to determine how best to patch up the rent.

Amelia saw the Wretch first, clutching Kyle's arm in that surprisingly strong grip and pointing. Across the narrow lane, walking slowly past them the Infected was a morose sight. What was driving it onwards, Kyle could not see but even so, he slowly unslung the rifle and began to raise the barrel.

Amelia pushed it down, turning to him with a pleading look in her eyes. Through the hole in the wall, Kyle could see the monster ambling past without a glance in their direction. He did not take his eyes from it.

"It hasn't seen us..." Amelia's voice was almost silent, barely discernible.

Kyle gritted his teeth, his finger resting snugly on the trigger guard. Still, he watched as the Wretch continued on it's slow way, passing behind the wall and out of sight.

"Thank you."

"What if it comes back in the night? It only takes one of them to kill you."

"Just... Thank you. One day we might be able to cure this thing. Then we'll regret every one we killed."

Kyle kept his thoughts to himself.

They managed to patch the wall up. It was a poor job and they both knew it but it was the best they could do. They found a long saw but the blade was rusted through and it snapped the second Kyle tried it on the dead trunk. If Arthur Cooley had kept any more tools, they didn't find them. Exhausted and frozen, they gathered armfuls of firewood and returned to the house to eat.

"Tea." Kyle complained "If I had a cup of tea, everything would be alright."

"Tea? There's tonnes of it!"

"What? Where?"

"In the ration packs we've been eating... Here." Amelia vanished, returning a moment later with a handful of wrapped paper bags.

"I thought they were wipes!" Kyle leapt to his feet and boiled some water. Minutes later, he was sipping the twenty year old brew with a grimace of distaste "Ugh. Awful." he took another sip.

"But you're drinking it?"

"It's tea, isn't it?"

She laughed and shook her head at his stubbornness.

He sipped his way through the scalding liquid and at the end, smacked his lips in feigned delight "That's another one I owe that bastard Boss and his goons. They took the last of my tea leaves. Might have been the last in existence for all I know."

Amelia's smile was brief and humourless at the mention of Boss. She cleared her throat awkwardly, not meeting Kyle's eyes "I'm glad he's dead. I'm glad they're all dead. I never thought I'd be grateful to see anyone die but they were evil."

Kyle gently rocked his head from side to side, the empty mug clutched in both hands "No. They weren't evil. They were just bastards." he looked up at her, for once no joke to hide behind "They were just men who had a choice to do the right thing and chose not to." he shrugged "Once they made that choice, there was no going back."

A tear formed in Amelia's eye and she let it fall down her cheek "Aren't you glad?"

"That they're dead? I'm glad." Kyle's gaze returned to the empty mug but he saw none of the smooth whiteness of the china "It's more than that. When they... When they hung me above that hut and whipped me I stopped being scared. Ever since I woke up in that cave and felt weak... I'd been scared. I felt useless, like I couldn't fight anymore. And when they took us, I just did what they said. Didn't fight back."

"There wasn't a chance for you to."

"No." agreed Kyle "There wasn't. But when that whip started to land, I started seeing them all dead - you know, in my head. It made me happier than I'd ever been but it's hard to describe... Normally when you think of the emotion you think of smiles and laughter."

"Happiness?" Amelia questioned.

"Yeah. But this was different. It was still happiness - I mean, it made me happy so it must have been but instead of smiles, it was me baring my teeth. Like a snarl. And I was laughing at Boss. Laughing at him being hurt. It wasn't funny to see him hurt but it made me laugh with happiness to see that I'd won. To feel like I was in control again."

Amelia watched him in silence.

"And then, when he fell in the woods and I - I killed him, it wasn't like that. I thought I'd be... I dunno, howling like a wolf but instead I was just cold. It was almost like the training drills or like shooting a Wretch. He was a threat, I stopped him." Kyle shrugged to himself and seemed to finish speaking.

"I felt like howling when you shot him." Amelia spoke up, her eyes not leaving Kyle "I wanted to see him hurt, too. When I watched them all hurt you there was nothing I could do. You were my patient and I couldn't stop them. So when you killed him I was happy. I was jealous, too. I wanted to be the one to kill him but I knew that you wanted to more. So I was happy, like it was our victory." a sob shook her and Kyle took her hand.

"We won." he said simply.

"Yes." she responded, thickly.

"Yay for us."

"Yay for us."

CHAPTER 67

Their shoddy attempts at a repair blew over in the first breath of wind. They put the sheets of metal back up, this time stacking timber against them to jam them in place. That seemed to hold.

The weather turned cold again although some days sunshine seeped through. In the evenings, they rested. They read books, curled together on the sofa. They made love, they ate food and drank more of Arthur Cooley's whisky and they talked endlessly about each other, their plans for the future, their fears and their loves.

Amelia had a habit, Kyle had noticed, of bringing up difficult subjects without a moment's warning. It was an odd trait but as yet, he couldn't find fault with the method. They both had a lot to discuss. They lay in each other's arms in their shared bed, the sweat still drying on their skin. Kyle felt himself drifting off, his thoughts spiralling into dreams when Amelia suddenly piped up, her head nestled on his chest.

"You never asked why your name was on that computer."

Kyle felt as though a jolt of electricity had been pumped through him. His heart beat faster and his mind began to race.

"Are you alright?" Amelia sounded worried.

"Yes. It's just… It wasn't my name, was it?"

"No."

"My Dad's?"

Amelia nodded "I didn't know that when I met you."

Despite the shock, Kyle felt excitement flush through him "Did you find anything about him?"

Amelia looked hesitant "It was all twenty years old, Kyle. He hasn't been there since the Fall."

"I thought he was dead."

"I know."

"Maybe he's alive. Maybe my Mum is too."

"I don't know." Amelia squeezed his hand "I hope so."

Kyle let out a breath, sipping from a canteen of water that sat beside the bed as he tried to process his thoughts. Amelia was watching him with concern and to distract her, he shot a half thought through question "What did you say you found there?"

"A few things – there was a lot that I couldn't interpret but the main thing was a test for the Infection. You know we've never developed one of those?"

"I thought there were machines in London?"

She scoffed "They don't work. Apart from the blindness there isn't any real way to tell if someone has the X2H virus."

"But my Dad made a test?"

"Yes." She smiled "It needs some equipment to set up but I could do it in most towns. That's a real game changer for medics."

Kyle nodded slowly "You said you got an anonymous message about the Institute? Who do you think it was from?"

She watched him carefully, understanding the meaning behind the question "I... I have a theory about it. I only really worked it out once I met you though."

"What?"

Amelia sighed "I'll start at the beginning. The Zeks got an anonymous message about the Institute. We –"

"How?"

"How what?"

"How did you get the message?"

"Er – it was a coded radio signal. We have an intelligence network and they picked it up. Anyway, it told us that there was documentation at that Institute which related to the Feral mutation. It was a government facility before the Fall and that's why no-one knew about it."

"There was nothing else in the message?"

"No. It was very short – I got the impression that it had been sent in secret."

"By..."

Amelia made a face "This is just a theory, you understand?"

Kyle nodded.

Amelia took a deep breath before speaking rapidly in a small voice "I think it was sent by Dr Frost. I think Armstrong has him under control somewhere and is making him release the Feral mutation but it got out of control. It's probably in France and that's why the refugees are flooding here. When you came to Matwood he saw an opportunity to manipulate you into his control. If you helped Lynch murder refugees then he'd have you over a barrel and if he controlled you, he could use you to blackmail your Father." She stopped and watched him warily.

"What?" Kyle was surprised by her expression.

"I – I thought you'd be upset. Or angry. Or something."

Kyle cocked an eyebrow "No? I don't know. It makes sense."

"That's it?"

"What else do you want?" he half smiled "It's a logical theory. Right now, all the clues point to my Dad being alive somewhere in France. That's where the mutation came from and that's why the refugees are everywhere." Kyle shrugged.

"Do you believe me?"

"Believe?" Kyle shook his head "It's not about belief. Either it is or it isn't. We can't tell."

She smiled nervously and Kyle reached out to pull her back to him "I suppose we can't tell. I want to find out though. At the very least I could show people how to do the test. That, along with the treatment we found would save a lot of lives."

Kyle nodded, images of his parents filling his mind. They lay in silence with their thoughts for some time as the world spun outside the window. It seemed such an isolated slice of paradise that Kyle never wanted to leave but finally, his train of thought broke and a different idea occurred to him.

"You never said what it was that scared you about the Zeks?"

Amelia grunted "Mmm. Scared is the wrong word. I just

didn't want to be caught up in a war between the Rangers and the Zeks. That wasn't what I joined them for."

"The Zeks aren't at war with the Rangers!"

Amelia's eyes flashed as she leaned back to look at Kyle "They bloody are! What do you think you saw out in those woods? Was Lynch handing out Matwood spring water to us? No! He was murdering Zeks! That's what happens out in the wilds! And who cares if another Zek goes missing?"

Abruptly, she stopped, drawing in a breath, and blinking rapidly.

Kyle took her hand and she leaned forward, giving him a surprisingly intimate kiss "Sorry. I don't mean to get angry."

"It's okay."

She nodded and smiled at him "Thank you for saying that. Thank you for not dismissing me. I know you don't agree."

"It's okay for us to disagree, I think."

"Oh yes? Is that in the rule book for lovers?"

"'Lovers'?" joked Kyle "Is that what I am? Your lover?"

Amelia leaned back, regarding him with that strange little smile she wore. She propped herself up on an elbow and looked at him for a long minute. Then, as abruptly as she'd stopped speaking, she leaned forward and kissed him, hard. Kyle responded in kind, pulling her close and feeling her hair on his face.

They leaned back and looked at each other, seeing the same look of joy reflected on the others face. They said nothing, didn't try to spoil the moment with words that weren't yet ready but the silence spoke volumes for them.

CHAPTER 68

The snow eased, leaving in its wake a freezing wind which blew in from the east. The ground froze hard each morning although they had little reason to venture outside. They lived in an idyllic cocoon of warmth, nourishment and intimacy which seemed to Kyle as though it would never end. They talked endlessly, avoiding the subject of Armstrong, the loss of Holden and the other topics that made Kyle's face twitch and his hands fidget. Of course, they were waiting for something, a sign that their paradise would come to an end. Amelia thought out loud about it one evening in front of a log fire which Kyle had built after discovering and removing a blockage in the chimney.

"Where would we go?" she asked, lying back against Kyle, a blanket tucked around her legs.

"London? To your parents?"

"Maybe. The Zeks are there though. And the Rangers."

"Another town, then. Maybe the west country?"

"What about France?"

Kyle craned his head to see her face. Her expression was serious "You mean to find my Dad?"

She shrugged "Maybe. Like you said though, we don't know anything about that. That wasn't what I meant."

She sounded put-out and Kyle tried to revitalise her enthusiasm "What would we do in France?"

"Explore. Find a home."

"We could do that. Find a big house like this one, somewhere with a wall."

She laughed "We could go south! Find somewhere sunny and hot."

"Ugh."

"You don't like sunny weather?"

"Makes me all sweaty. Besides, wouldn't you want to find other people there?"

"Maybe." Amelia pressed closer to him "I like you all to myself though."

"You've got me all to yourself here."

"Mm-hmm." she seemed to be drifting off.

"So, what are we waiting for?" he breathed, not wanting to hear the answer.

"Mm-hmm." her eyes were closed.

Kyle stared down at her, drinking in the sight and the scent of her, never wanting to shatter the sanctity of this utopia they'd found. He stayed like that until the fire died to embers and finally a faint glow in the ashes and Amelia woke shivering. He led her, half asleep to the bedroom and held tightly to her as sleep finally claimed him.

CHAPTER 69

The man appeared out of the driving wind, weeks after they'd fled the ruins of Treetops.

Kyle was outside, checking on their handiwork in repairing the wall when he heard the voice and the clang of metal as someone tried the gates.

Quickly ducking under the fallen tree, he moved silently along the wall, rifle in two hands until he reached the gate. He peered through the thin gap between the post and the wall and saw a wild faced man, hair and beard long and matted bashing on the metal. He was terribly thin, shivering in the brutal wind and carried no visible pack nor weapons.

"Please! Please let me in! I need help..."

Kyle's instinct was to back away, to let the man succumb to the death that was clearly hovering over him but he knew Amelia would never accept such an action. Instead, he shouted to the man to wait and hurried inside to fetch Amelia. Together, they ran up the stairs to the top floors from where they could survey the area surrounding the farm. The ground was clear and free of any marauding force. Kyle's instinct told him that the man was alone, that he was just what he appeared to be, a ragged refugee.

"What do you want to do?" it was a mark of how close they'd become that she did not simply demand they let the man in. As too, was his decision to tell her.

"I think the two of us can handle him. He looks half dead anyway. We're both armed and a lot stronger than him." the weeks of good food, rest and hard hours in the gym had put muscle back on both their frames, filling their gaunt faces out. Amelia looked at him and nodded, retrieving her own weapons before they made their way out to the gate.

Kyle scrambled to the top of the wall, giving the lane outside the farm a long look. On the ground, the man shivered in the wind, a threadbare blanket wrapped around his shoulders.

"Where have you come from?"

"A village... We were attacked, weeks ago. I've been living in the forest."

"Who are you with?"

"Just me! There were three of us but the Ferals..." the man tailed off.

"Are you Infected?"

"No! No! I promise!"

Kyle hesitated a moment longer, his rifle trained in the man's general direction but not threatening him. He glanced down to Amelia who nodded.

"Take the blanket off!" he ordered and the man complied, unwrapping the rags from his torso. He was stick thin, emaciated and his skin filthy. Kyle believed his story, that he had indeed been living in the forest through the terrible snow. He ordered the man to turn around and from his vantage point could not make out any weapons. Finally, he nodded to Amelia to open the gate although he made a point of obviously flipping off the safety catch and firmly taking the man in his sights.

The gate swung open, Amelia stepping smartly to the side. In a burst of energy that Kyle wouldn't have thought the man capable of, the refugee lunged forward into the shelter of the four walls. He slipped on a patch of ice at the edge of the road and careened off the gate which swung into Amelia, catching her off balance and knocking her to the floor. She landed hard and Kyle roared at the man to back away from her.

Instead, the refugee gave a shriek and ran towards her. Kyle's first shot missed the man by a hair, whipping past his shoulder and ricocheting off the gravel of the courtyard.

"Kyle, no!" Amelia shouted, her own rifle now retrieved. The refugee stopped in front of her, his hands held out to the side in a pacifying gesture.

"I'm sorry!" he shouted, backing away and hunching over pathetically "I'm sorry! I didn't mean to!"

Amelia was back on her feet, rifle in her hands and backing up quickly, putting distance between herself and the man. Kyle snarled at their guest to lie down on his front and put his arms behind his back but the man seemed unable to comply, repeating his pathetic apology and begging them not to kill him.

Kyle climbed down from the wall, a small part of his mind revelling in the new strength his body had earned and the lack of pain from his injuries. Quickly, he crossed the ground between him and the emaciated man and with a quick twist of his hips, floored the unfortunate fellow, kneeling so his legs straddled his opponents and he could control the skinny wrists.

"Shut the gate!" he snapped at Amelia who hastened to secure the entrance. Beneath him, the man moaned and whimpered until Kyle told him to shut up.

Amelia hurried over, handing him a pair of plastic cable ties which Kyle used to secure the man's hands. Then, he frisked the stranger, finding a small but wickedly sharp black knife which was so at odds with the man's appearance as to be completely remarkable. He pocketed the blade and then, under Amelia's watchful eye, frogmarched the bound man into the house.

They tied the stranger to a chair in front of the fire and Kyle fed him military rations on a plastic spork. The man dribbled sauce down his chin and panted heavily between chews. Amelia examined him with a professional eye, lifting his ragged clothes and questioning him although he did not answer many of her questions.

He was shivering hard and Kyle fetched a pair of blankets, wrapping them tightly around him as Amelia asked him where he'd come from.

"A village."

"Where?"

"I don't know... I'm lost."

"What was it called?"

The man gaped at her for a moment before answering "A - Alton."

Kyle flicked a glance at Amelia who caught his gaze and nodded minutely. She too could tell a lie when she heard one.

"How many of you escaped?"

"Four. One died in the fire."

"Fire?"

"Yes. The attack caused a fire."

"How?" demanded Kyle.

"I don't know..." the man was lying again. Kyle considered slapping him and demanding the truth but he thought a good blow might kill the poor fellow.

The stranger's eyelids began to droop and he was clearly spent. Amelia nodded to Kyle and together, ensuring their guest's hands were securely bound, they moved him to the sofa, covering him with blankets. Kyle took the liberty of tying his ankles together loosely so that he could still walk, but not very fast. Then, they stepped out of the living room into the kitchen.

"What do you think?" Amelia crossed her arms and spoke quietly.

"I think he's about dead."

She nodded, seriously "He might not make it through the night. He's got mild hypothermia, severe dehydration and he looks like he hasn't slept in days. The food might just make him sick, too..."

"We can't trust him. We have to keep him tied up."

Amelia nodded her agreement then her expression changed "That thing you did at the gate, where you flipped him on the ground. Can you teach me that?"

"What, you've never done martial arts?"

"I'm a doctor, Kyle. Remember?"

"Vividly. You seemed like you knew your way around a firearm when we met."

"That's different. Anyone can learn to shoot a handgun. We all had pistols in London."

"I thought you couldn't carry them in the city?"

"Not legally but no-one cares. So you'll teach me?"

"Of course. I can teach you to use the rifle, too. We've got those hunting rifles in the basement..." he broke off as their guest in the next room gave a frightened yelp. They both hurried to the door.

"I can't see!" the man wailed, still hog-tied on the sofa.

Amelia pushed past Kyle, moving to the man's side. She waved her hand in front of his eyes and he blinked.

"There! I saw that!"

"Torch." she snapped at Kyle, tersely and he fished the small electric device he'd taken from Arthur's collection out of his pocket, handing it to her.

She shone the light carefully into both eyes, watching the pupils dilate and then said some soothing words to the man who almost immediately began to fall asleep again. She placed a hand on his forehead, feeling his temperature before checking his pulse, counting the beats in her head.

After a moment, she stood, satisfied that the man was asleep and led Kyle from the room by the arm, pulling the door closed carefully and muttering to him.

"He's Infected."

"Oh... Shit." Kyle looked back at the man, wondering how tightly he'd done the ropes up.

"His eyesight is starting to go. That's advanced Infection." she looked grim "We don't have Dr May's booster and I've never seen someone recover with antibiotics at this stage."

"Poor bastard." Kyle tried to think from the man's perspective.

"He said he was chased by Ferals. They killed the others in his group."

Kyle nodded.

"From the Infections I've seen, the chances of turning Feral are significantly higher when the infection comes from one of them." she shushed Kyle when he tried to speak "It also makes the whole process much quicker. What's the quickest you've seen?"

"Er... A couple of hours. That was multiple bites though. Usually it's a few days."

"I didn't see where he was bitten. Presumably he kept it hidden..."

"What can we do?"

She shrugged "Restrain him? I can't see that we have much choice when he turns..." her voice trailed off.

"I'll shoot him when he does. I don't mind." Kyle set his jaw, firmly.

"No. He's my patient." Amelia looked him in the eye, showing her determination. Kyle didn't argue.

They stepped back inside the room where the man lay succumbing to the virus. Kyle had seen people Infected before, of course but Wretching out, as it was commonly known, was morbidly fascinating.

A person did not die when the X2H virus moved into its final stages, but they appeared to. Their sight was the first to go, the irises dissolving into a milky whiteness. The skin turned grey and pallid and the lips, tongue and gums started to darken, eventually turning to black a few days after the victim had Wretched out.

Manic bursts of rage were common, people commonly threw punches or bit at those close to them only to suddenly go calm, reduced to tears at the shock of what they'd done. Eventually, they lapsed into a twitching feverish coma, lying still as their breathing slowed, their skin greyed and they appeared, outwardly, to die. Amelia explained that even when fully Changed, the Infected still retained a low heartbeat and breathed although their entire metabolism was significantly reduced.

"Can't you give him something now? An injection? Like an overdose." Kyle suggested as they watched the twitching figure.

"Don't have anything that would do it quick enough. It would be painful too." she shook her head.

To their surprise, the man opened his eyes and looked across the room at them. A feverish cackle broke forth and even from here, Kyle could see the beads of sweat on the man's brow.

"I know you!" he shrieked, delirious "I know you...!" he trailed off, eyes dropping shut.

"Hallucinating." Amelia said sadly.

They both stood in the room, unable to tear themselves away or unwilling to leave the man alone. He twitched and sweated as they watched. Amelia moved to sit on the arm of a nearby armchair, still watching. Kyle stood next to her and put his hands in his pocket, his brow creasing as he found the small knife he'd taken from the man. He pulled it out and examined it absently, turning it back and forth in his hands.

It had a surprising weight to it and he guessed that it was a high quality blade. It was clearly Pre-Fall, with a manufacturer's name printed in machined type on the small black metal blade. He flicked his wrist, simultaneously pressing the blade with his finger and it snapped open with a metallic click. That brought Amelia's attention away from the patient as she looked to see what Kyle was doing.

"Nice."

"I like it." he closed the blade and flicked it open again, nodding in approval at the smooth action.

Amelia frowned suddenly, looking back at the patient.

"What?"

"I..." she sat back, frowning "I'm not sure. Hang on."

Kyle lost interest and began flicking the blade open and closed, admiring it. He clipped it to the inside of his pocket, nodding at the secure feeling. He drew it and flicked it open, practicing the motion until the knife felt comfortable in his hand. He was vaguely aware that the sound of it opening was likely to be annoying to Amelia but was engrossed and so when she leapt up with a start, her hand flying to her mouth he jumped, leaping backwards in expectation of her ire.

"It's him! That knife! That fucking knife!" she pointed from the man to Kyle to the man again.

"Who? Who is it?" he demanded.

"Lurcher!"

Kyle stared. He looked at the emaciated man, in the late stages of infection and before he knew what he was doing, his feet had carried him across the room. He grabbed the man's chin roughly and twisted his head this way and that. He hauled the beard down, pulling the hair so that it looked as though the man were clean shaven and bald. Was it him? He felt Amelia at his side, he expected her to protest his rough treatment but instead she shook the man, hauling him back to consciousness.

"Are you Lurcher? Answer me!"

The man woke and wailed, cringing away from them. Kyle could see to his revulsion that the irises of his eyes were ragged. He must be almost blind.

Without warning, the man who may have been Lurcher lunged at Amelia, His teeth snapped and he jack knifed his body in an explosive movement that Kyle would have been willing to be their entire food supply, he wasn't capable of. As it was, Kyle reacted instinctively, his left palm crashing into the man's forehead, knocking him back hard onto the sofa, his teeth snapping an inch from Amelia's hand.

They both stepped back, hastily. Amelia was rubbing her hand.

"Did he bite you?"

"No." she covered her fingers. Kyle seized her hands, tugging them up and checking the skin frantically. There were no bite marks, no punctured skin. He sighed in relief, meeting her gaze before they turned back.

"Are you sure its him?"

She began to speak but stopped, thinking "No. It looks like him and he had a knife like that."

They both stood watching as the man thrashed against his bonds before lapsing into silence.

"If it is." Kyle spoke carefully "I can't think of a worse fate. If anyone deserves this, it's him."

"If it's him, what about Boss? Maybe he's alive too." Amelia's voice was panicking. She turned to Kyle, eyes wide "What if he follows us here? What if he finds us?"

"He's dead." the image of the bandit leader's shattered face was a sight that Kyle thought would never leave his mind. He shook his head at Amelia "You know he's dead. This bastard can't hurt us and there's nothing else we can do."

"Yes, there is." she snatched the knife from his hand, flicked the blade open and stalked across the room. Without a pause, she raised the blade above her head and stabbed down, viciously into his eye socket.

Immediately, the struggling and snarling stopped. The man was totally still, the black handle of the knife protruding from his eye socket.

Kyle stared in shock. Amelia stood over the corpse, her shoulders heaving as she stared. Slowly, carefully, he moved up behind her, putting his arms around her waist and leaning close. She allowed him, placing a hand over his own.

"That's all we could do."

"Yes. That's all we could do."

In the end, they dragged the corpse outside and poured Arthur Cooley's fuel supply over it. Kyle flicked a match and they turned away, letting the flames consume what may or may not have been a bandit named Lurcher.

Kyle tossed the small knife into the flames with a grimace as they returned to their sanctuary, sealing the gate behind them.

CHAPTER 70

As it turned out, Amelia was excellent with a rifle. Both the military rifles and Arthur Cooley's hunting firearms came naturally to her and soon, Kyle was trudging into the bitter wind, estimating distances around the farm and setting up sturdy targets. She knocked them down with impunity. She showed the same skill as he ran through the fundamentals of military rife drills learned from the endless training with Sinks. Her footwork through close quarters drills was impeccable and soon she was changing the magazines almost as quickly as Kyle.

Her martial arts prowess however, was terrible. Of course, Kyle was not a perfect partner for her being nearly twice her weight and strength. He tried to repress a smile as she ducked and twisted out the way of his carefully thrown punches, her feet planted like tree roots to the mats.

Her groundwork was little better. Her locks and choke holds barely brought a flush to his face and she grew easily frustrated. Using a pair of sticks in lieu of training knives, Kyle smartly stepped through her guard, slashing at her face and knocking her over repeatedly.

"I'm bloody awful at this." she snarled, losing her temper one afternoon and lobbing the piece of wood towards the side of the gym. Unfortunately, she missed, instead striking Kyle in the face.

Half laughing, half furious he staggered back as she rushed forward, showering him with apologies. He took his hand away to see blood covering his face and swore in surprise. She pulled him upstairs, making a great deal of fuss about cleaning and dressing the small wound.

"It's fine! Honestly, I don't mind." he reassured her.

"I just get so frustrated." she grumbled "I'm terrible at it."

"You're great with the rifles." he pointed out.

"Yes, but when am I going to need those?"

He rolled his eyes "Let's take a break for a bit. Why don't we do something else?"

She grinned mischievously "What did you have in mind?"

What he had in mind ruined any chance of productive training for the rest of the day although neither of them felt any regrets. The next day Amelia awoke reinvigorated in her desire to train harder but Kyle insisted they begin patrols of the area, emphatic that it was as important a skill as any martial art. Amelia grumbled but allowed him to lead her out the gate and into the open ground that surrounded the farm. They explored together, Kyle showing her the hand signals that Sinks had taught the Militia. She kept too close to him as they walked but he didn't press the issue, enjoying the sense of exploration together as they wandered across pastures now filled with undergrowth.

Amelia cursed at her wet trousers, giving Kyle a long lecture on the practicality of the black coats the Zeks wore. The leather, she said, kept the rain out and protected against bites while the ankle length skirt kept water off your legs unlike these bloody weeds - she kicked at the long grass with a heavy boot, ignoring Kyle's exasperation and repeated exhortations that they were not to leave any sign that they'd come this way.

Rolling his eyes at her obvious peevishness he led the way back across the field that led to the wall opposite the gate. He fancied she had finally taken the lesson on board, standing a safe distance away from him and keeping her head on a swivel when suddenly she dashed towards him and he dropped to one knee, scanning the area for danger.

"I've just thought! Those bags we took when we left Treetops, I'm sure there are some waterproof trousers in there. We haven't been through them, have we?"

Kyle agreed that they had not, Arthur Cooley's supplies had

been more than enough and the bags had been buried in an untidy pile of clothes for weeks. He pleaded with Amelia to remain quiet until they had finished their patrol but the second they were back in the gate, she rushed up to the bedroom leaving him shaking his head in amazement at what would excite her.

He moved into the kitchen, boiling some water on the range and setting out two mugs with the stale, army issue tea bags. He glanced out the un-shuttered window, noticing the first touches of spring - buds on the trees and the slight change in temperature. His brow creased as he wondered what the warmer weather would mean for Amelia, would she want to stay now they were no longer entombed by the elements? His inner insecurity told him to be ready for rejection whilst his head told his insecurity to shut up.

The door to the kitchen banged open and he turned with a smile, the light from the window momentarily affecting his ability to see into the darker kitchen. Amelia seemed to be laughing and he smiled in response, raising a quizzical eyebrow.

She moved forward away from the light, something clutched in her hands and held out towards him.

"You alright?" he asked, confused.

Wordlessly, she thrust something into his hands. Something heavy and smelling of damp. He realised that one of them must have thrust it into the rucksacks in those last, dark moments as they readied themselves to flee Treetops.

"There were crates of them..." Amelia's voice was barely above a whisper. When he met her eyes, her face was streaked with tears "They - they were selling them. Like a - a bounty." her voice cracked.

"I..." Kyle didn't know what to say.

Amelia shook her head, stepping forwards and laying a tender hand on the object, stroking it gently as though it were a living thing. It suddenly felt as though it weighed a thousand tons and he felt Amelia's world pivot as the realisation landed.

They both stared at the thing Kyle held in his hands.

The bloodstained black coat of a Zek.

CHAPTER 71

Hours later...

Amelia sat with a cooling cup of tea in front of her. Kyle had tried embracing her but she barely responded. She stared at the table, emotionless. Kyle remembered the almost catatonic state she'd been in when they'd arrived at Arthur Cooley's farm in the snowstorm. At least then he'd know what to do, to get her warm and in shelter. With this emotional schism, he had no idea.

"Are you hungry?" he asked, tentatively.

She blinked. Looked up at him in surprise, then shook her head.

"We don't know-" he began but she held a hand up, cutting him off.

"You don't." she emphasised the 'you' and Kyle was taken aback "There have been rumours about this. Zeks always disappear. People say that it's the Infected, it's just the nature of our work but we found the coats, bullet holes and bloodstains."

She went on, relaying horror stories from the depths of her memory. Every rumour, every whisper that Zeks lives had been sold to the Rangers played out.

Kyle listened. There was nothing else he could do. He didn't speak, offered no opinion. He felt helpless to comfort her but realised the best thing for her to do was to talk. She spoke as though he were not there, unloading her conscience without looking at him.

"It was all Armstrong."

"But why?"

It was the first thing he'd said in almost an hour. The question was filling his mind and it slipped out, almost unbidden. Amelia looked up and he almost flinched as her eyes met his but there was no anger in her expression.

She smiled humourlessly "Because that's what he is. A killer. Zeks have been calling him out for years. Armstrong isn't a subtle man, Kyle. When something gets in his way, he kills it. Look at what he did to those refugees! For twenty years he's been ruler of his own little kingdom of war. No-one questions him, no-one tells him what to do and no-one holds him to account for his crimes. Except the Zeks."

Several thoughts came to Kyle's mind but he knew this wasn't the time so he said nothing.

Amelia forced a smile, for his benefit and Kyle was suddenly aware that she wanted to be alone. Clearing his throat, he muttered about checking the perimeter and left the room.

*

Amelia came and found him out in the garden where Kyle was rearranging a stack of timber. She came up behind and slid her arms around him.

"Sorry."

"What for?" he put his hand on hers.

"Don't know. Sorry for overreacting."

"You didn't."

She squeezed him and he squeezed her hand in response.

"I never really understood what the Zeks do." He prompted "I know you said they were at war with the Rangers…"

He felt her grip loosen for a second but then it came back, stronger.

"You don't have to -"

"No. I want to." she cleared her throat but stayed behind him "In London, it was different. There it was all speeches about developing a cure and helping *people*. We talked about changing Parliament's approach to the virus but it didn't go anywhere. Did you know there hasn't been an election since the Fall?"

"Yes." Kyle remembered his conversation with Sinks on the road to Matwood, a lifetime ago "The politicians are appointed now, not elected."

"No." Amelia shook her head against his back "Well, they are but they shouldn't be. During the Fall, an emergency session of Parliament was approved which removed a lot of the faff that came from democracy. It was supposed to be temporary but it's still in place."

"Because the virus is still everywhere."

"Right. But Parliament now appoints new Members of Parliament. They aren't elected. Sure - a nationwide election isn't the main thing in everyone's mind but most of Parliament are now soldiers - or former soldiers."

"What? Why?"

"Because they're the most successful people in the country! The ones with the most power. People like Armstrong."

Kyle couldn't argue with that. Amelia released him and they began to walk slowly around the inner walls.

"So, what scared you about that?"

"That? No, it's what the Zeks wanted to do about it. I was all for elections and curing the virus – most people would agree with that. But some of the Zeks are radical. They'd overthrow the government to get what they want. Plunge us into a civil war which only the Infected would win."

Kyle stopped, turning to face her. It was ridiculous and he told her.

"Yes, I know. Black coated hippies taking over the country?" her face was deadly serious "Did you know there are soldiers in the Zeks? A few thousand of them, actually."

Kyle did not and his surprise showed on his face.

Amelia nodded as though she'd expected his reaction "A former Colonel named Eric Forbes resigned from the army and joined us about six years ago."

"Forbes..." the name was familiar.

"You've heard of him. The Battle for London? He was there. Got covered in medals. He was tipped for promotion - could have even become a Field Marshall but then he left. That was about the time that I started to meet other Zeks, not just the people in the city."

They carried on walking, turning around the corner back towards the farmhouse.

"Eric thought – *thinks* - that Armstrong is the key to everything. He said he holds too much power and if we can stop him, Parliament will be forced to negotiate."

"But Armstrong is just a Major."

"Yes, but he's the head of the most ruthless fighting force in the country. All the Rangers are loyal to him. Essentially, he's a gang leader with the biggest gang."

Kyle frowned "So, how does that make him the key to Parliament? If his strength comes from the Rangers..."

Amelia nodded "Right. Eric and I disagreed over that. He was all for starting a guerrilla war against the Rangers and trying to kill Armstrong. We managed to change his mind and he backed down but Armstrong has plenty of spies in the Zeks and he decided to strike first. That's when Zeks started to disappear."

"So where is Eric now?"

"He came south with me but he went to the coast. He thought that if he could find a few refugees and prove to Parliament that Armstrong had been lying about France being overrun then we could discredit him. I don't know how that went."

"Could it have been Eric's men who attacked us?"

"What? No." Amelia shook her head emphatically "If Eric wanted me dead, he'd have killed me years ago. We disagree but we're on the same side. No, I think that was Lynch."

"Why would Lynch want you dead?" Kyle held up a hand, answering his own question "Because you found the Institute. And if Armstrong has spies in the Zeks then he probably intercepted the anonymous message."

"Right." Amelia stopped turning to him and taking both his hands in hers "Can we go inside? I want to be distracted."

without waiting for a response, she turned and began tugging him towards the house.

Obediently, Kyle followed.

CHAPTER 72

The next day, they buried Arthur Cooley. Kyle retrieved a bed sheet from one of the unused bedrooms and together, they carefully wrapped the skeletal remains of their host and carried him down to the garden. Kyle swung a pickaxe at the ground and before long he was streaming with sweat. Although the temperature had improved, the ground was hard and unyielding but he persevered. The wounds on his back and chest ached but he ignored the pain, digging and scraping until a hole, several feet deep lay in the ground.

They lowered the sheet down with ropes, tugging the cord back up from the grave and standing together, arms wrapped around each other.

"Thank you, Arthur." Amelia murmured.

"Thank you." echoed Kyle.

"This has been the best time of my life."

Amelia's declaration was said in a small voice, her eyes fixed on the grave. Kyle looked down at her in surprise, suddenly very aware of the warmth and feel of her next to him.

"The same for me."

They stood there as time passed and the world spun on it's axis.

"Okay?" Amelia turned and smiled at Kyle and he nodded. Together, they began to cover the grave, carefully spreading the earth at first so it didn't fall onto Arthur's corpse too hard but then as the sheet vanished beneath the brown dirt, faster until the grave was filled.

"I think he'd have liked that." Amelia observed, standing and leaning on the shovel.

"Shit!" Kyle suddenly swore, turning back to the house "His

diary! I was going to bury it with him..." he looked back at the filled grave.

"Why don't we leave it in the house? Then if someone else comes they can see what happened."

Kyle nodded slowly. The idea sounded right to him.

"Maybe we could add something at the back? A memory of our time here?" suggested Amelia.

Kyle agreed and so, after a final moment of silence at the foot of Arthur Cooley's grave, they returned inside. Amelia found a pencil in the basement and she flipped the pages until she found a clean one.

"What date did we get here?" she asked Kyle, the pencil already between her teeth.

"God, no idea. I don't even know what month it is."

"March, I think. Maybe late February?"

"Just put 'winter'."

She complied, beginning to write. Kyle marvelled at her neat handwriting, so much cleared than the untidy scrawl he'd perfected in Holden's schoolhouse.

"You're good at this."

"What, writing?"

"No, I mean you're telling the story better than I would."

"That's because you communicate in grunts and shrugs."

"No I don't!" he prodded her in the side. Amelia shrieked and jabbed him with the pencil before he mock wrestled her until they lay flat on the sofa. Amelia began to write as Kyle pulled her close. She stopped for a second, glancing back towards him and he peered at what she'd written.

"We healed here, graciously accepting Arthur's wonderful hospitality. These were the happiest days of my life. It felt as though the world had never been destroyed, had never died around us and that this was the life we'd chosen to live. If reality had never intruded again, I'd have been happy to spend my days here with Kyle."

Kyle swallowed a lump in his throat and tried to kiss her but she continued writing.

"If it wasn't for this house, we'd both have died in the cold. Instead, we lived and fell in love-"

His sudden need to see her face caused the pencil to draw an uneven line across the page but it didn't matter. He looked deep into her dark eyes, marvelling at the smoothness of her brown skin.

"I love you."

"I love you."

The world passed them by, leaving them in peace for a time.

The next day, Amelia told him she wanted to leave.

CHAPTER 73

"I don't want to go."

"No, neither do I."

Kyle breathed deeply, calming the rising emotion inside him. He felt betrayed and hurt but he understood.

"Zeks are dying, Kyle and I might be able to stop it. This test we found…"

"We could just stay here and ignore the world." he protested weakly.

"We could." she nodded.

They were entwined in bed. In typical fashion, Amelia had dropped the metaphorical bombshell on him, announcing that she thought they should leave the sanctuary of Arthur Cooley's farmhouse.

Amelia took a deep breath and looked into his eyes "Kyle, if you ask me to, I'll stay here with you forever."

He looked at her and knew that she meant it. He also knew that he'd do the same.

In a perfect world.

"That isn't us, is it?" he smiled sadly.

"No." she smiled too "I'm not going anywhere without you though. Who knows, maybe you'd make a good Zek?"

"Hah. Everyone needs a hobby, right?"

She squeezed him and some small semblance of relief settled over him that wherever they were going, they'd go together.

"That's a good point, where should we go?" he asked.

"London?" she was thinking out loud.

"Armstrong might have gone back there by now."

"You could join the army, though." Amelia pointed out.

"Mmm." He grunted "Not sure the idea of serving alongside men like Lynch and Armstrong appeals anymore."

Amelia kissed him hard at that.

"Maybe London is too dangerous." She murmured after a while "What about my people?"

"Zeks? Where?"

She smiled conspiratorially "We have a few little hidey-holes."

"Will they let me in?"

"I'm not going in without you."

They dressed slowly, neither of them wanting to hasten the end. Kyle found a map from the basement and they puzzled over it. It surprised Kyle how close they were to Matwood and Holden. In his mind, he'd imagined them being separated by a gulf of impassable distance but he supposed they'd only been able to travel so far given the conditions they were moving in.

"Here..." Amelia pointed to a small village, the Pre-Fall shapes of houses gathered haphazardly around a road.

"That'll take us... About two days?" Kyle guessed "Look, there's that railway we saw on the bandit map." he traced a finger along it "It might be easier to follow that. I know it isn't direct but we can leave it here -" he pointed to a marked level crossing "- and just follow the road."

Amelia nodded her agreement, still looking at the map.

"Better pack for five days. If there's nothing there..." Kyle glossed over the awkward moment, not wanting to bring Amelia back to the state of emotion she'd fallen into when they discovered the Zek coats "We'll have to come back. That could take a while."

"Fine."

They packed, taking their time again. When the heavy rucksacks were positioned in the kitchen, they arranged the house carefully, checking the windows were barricaded and leaving notes to guide any future guests to the caches of supplies. Then, they wrote their final message in Arthur Cooley's diary and left.

CHAPTER 74

The railway was an hour's walk from the farm. Kyle found it easily enough but the sight of the sturdy chain link fence running along it was enough to make him stop in his tracks.

"Climb it?" suggested Amelia but Kyle pointed mutely to the rings of barbed wire at the top. They moved on, walking along the fence hoping to find a tree that had fallen, like with the farm wall but there was nothing.

"Didn't you bring those pliers?"

"Oh, yeah. Here you go." Amelia unpacked the rusty tools and handed them to Kyle. He began to snip the wires, trying to make a hole big enough for them to get through and he made progress but Amelia suddenly shouted a warning and he looked up in time to reel back in horror as a Wretch lunged at him.

"Jesus!" he swore, scrabbling for his rifle but the fence held the monster. The gap he'd cut was barely big enough to fit an arm through and the beast snapped and snarled at them futilely.

"Sorry, Kyle!" stammered Amelia "I was looking the other way!"

"Doesn't matter... No harm done."

They both watched the Wretch for a moment longer. The blank white eyes seemed to twitch after them. They left it alive and carried on, fortunately protected from the Wretch by the thick undergrowth that sprang up along the fence.

An hour later and they found an open stretch of railway line. Quietly, Kyle cut a hole and moved through carefully. The tracks were up a steep bank and he slithered up on his belly, rifle in hands. A careful look left and right and he signalled for

Amelia to join him. To left and right, the great rusted metal stretched in a straight line. Kyle thought he could see the Wretch they'd seen earlier but couldn't be sure.

"Alright?" Amelia hadn't paused and now led the way down the tracks. Kyle glanced back towards where the Wretch had been and shivered.

"What's up? Shall we try another route?" Amelia's face was serious. They'd both learned to trust their gut instinct in the past few months.

"No, it's just very open. We need to keep watching our backs."

They set off, turning every few minutes to look behind them, a spot between Kyle's shoulder blades beginning to itch.

The feeling continued until the track began to bend and rise before them, vanishing out of sight around a corner. They moved slowly, keeping to the inside of the track, and checking both ahead and behind until Amelia who was in front suddenly stopped, quickly stepping to the side and ducking beneath the cover of the steep bank.

"How many?" Kyle muttered, kneeling behind her, and looking backwards.

"None. Train." was the quiet reply.

It was absurd but the possibility of coming across a train had never occurred to him. In his mind's eye he'd seen nothing but the empty tracks stretching off into the distance.

"We could go around, cut another hole in the fence." she suggested.

They both looked at the thick undergrowth along the track boundary. Kyle shook his head "The last spot that was clear was twenty minutes ago."

She looked wary "Better to be safe than sorry."

Kyle chewed the problem over before shrugging "Shall we take a look?"

In response, Amelia rose and moved forward, her rifle held at the ready position as though she'd carried it her entire life. Kyle followed, peering around the corner as the train came into sight.

There was no movement, no crowd of half rotted Wretches waiting to greet them. Instead, the great metal snake stood forlornly on the tracks, weeds and decay covering it. They approached the rear carriage carefully and peered underneath but the foliage was too dense to allow them to see. Still, they moved slowly, creeping up the side of the rear carriage and stepping carefully away to see the windows, covered with grime and moss, built up from two decades of neglect.

The doors of the train stood at Kyle's shoulder height, smooth metal pressed tightly together.

"This wouldn't be a bad place to shelter." He hissed to Amelia.

"What?" She stopped, leaning her head back to head him, all the while watching forward for danger.

"I said, this would be a good - *Jesus shitting Christ!*"

This last expletive was torn from Kyle and staggered backwards as a terrible moan and a series of cavernous thumps sounded from overhead. Amelia stepped back from the train, her face pale and her rifle barrel scanning the filthy glass. Kyle moved to her side, safety catch clicking off and his finger tightening in the trigger guard. He saw nothing, but the glass seemed to bend and vibrate with each thump.

"Inside?"

"Jesus..."

"Come on."

Amelia began to jog, placing her feet carefully on the edge of the sleepers. As they moved along, the awful moans and the thumps seemed to chase them, rising in a fever pitch of longing until they were both moving at a dead sprint, terror driving them onwards.

"There!" Kyle gasped breathlessly and unnecessarily as the end of the train loomed. They ran forward, glass knocking and decades old voices moaning for their flesh and then they were past, out into the overcast glare but free of the trains shadow.

They didn't stop.

Kyle risked a glance over his shoulder, his imagination conjuring Hordes of black eyed Ferals but instead, the front of the train stood abandoned and forlorn, a bramble sprouting from the shattered windscreen. He called to Amelia and she slowed then stopped, leaning over to place both hands on her knees and heaving with exertion.

"Nothing coming." Kyle gasped, putting a hand under her arm and pulling her onwards.

"That was -"

"I know."

"Those people..."

"We can't help them."

They moved on, faster than before and with frequent glances back, both of them shaken to their cores. Kyles eyes scanned the overgrown hedges to either side of the tracks, checking for danger and relying on his instinct more than a conscious action.

Instead, his mind saw only that which his eyes had been spared by the grime encrusted on the inside of the glass. The interior of a tomb, hundreds of people packed together, dead and rotting as the summers and winters of twenty years baked and froze them. He imagined how it had happened. A packed train, maybe fleeing the same virus that had finally caught them. Just one Infected person, smuggled onto the train by a loving relative and then the snarling, the white eyes and the yellow teeth sinking into flesh. He imagined the screams and the dread as the virus passed up the train, slowly spreading as people, crammed in together were unable to escape.

"Why - why didn't they break the glass?" he stammered "Why didn't they get out?"

Amelia was pale beneath her dark skin "I read about these. They were evacuation trains. They strengthened the glass so the people inside would be safe..."

"Oh God."

"The driver must have escaped. That's why the front was smashed. He left them."

Try as he might, Kyle could not fault the driver for fleeing. After all, he'd done the same.

They spoke little the rest of the day, only brief sentences to decide where to shelter for the night and quiet agreements. They stopped beneath a towering oak with branches as thick as Kyle's torso. Together, they suspended one of Arthur Cooley's survival hammocks between two branches and scrambled in, ten feet off the ground. Kyle stretched out and reached for Amelia as the light faded and was relieved to find her close. They wrapped themselves around each other, each drawing comfort from the warmth of the other's body. He breathed in the smell of her hair and the musk of her skin and tried his hardest to force the thought of the terrible iron tomb out of his mind.

They slept safely, beneath the towering oak. The next morning, they found the Horde.

CHAPTER 75

The level crossing was another mile up the track, the barriers permanently lowered. They turned left, leaving the rails and heading onto a tarmac road so overgrown they were forced to slow their pace and navigate great patches of weeds and brambles.

They smelled the smoke ten minutes before they saw the blackened beams. Amelia froze, pointing with horror on her face but there was nothing to be gained by standing in the open and they moved on, learning from yesterday and hugging the hedgerows with rifles at the ready.

Approaching the Zek house, Kyle stepped carefully, scanning over his rifle sights for anything, his finger on the trigger. A rough stone wall bordered the road but as he took another step, he could see the feet of a corpse hanging over a shattered breach.

"Oh my God!" Amelia hissed, rushing past him. Kyle cursed but she had thrown caution to the wind.

"Back!" he hissed at her "We have to move back!"

"No!" she was already crouching by the man and Kyle stepped past her, aiming his weapon into the front garden and catching a glimpse of a middle aged Zek, dried blood still flaking his chest with his eyes pecked out by crows. He gulped down the nausea that rose in his throat.

"A few days ago." Amelia murmured and Kyle nodded in agreement, looking at the cooled ashes.

Amelia led the way over the wall, aiming her rifle as Kyle hastened to keep up with her. As they approached the house it was plain to see they could not go inside. The upper storey had collapsed into the lower leaving scorched beams poking skywards. Another body, this one a woman of a similar age to the man had been shot near the front door. Amelia saw a handful of brass glinting dully in the obscured sunlight and bent down to pick them up.

"Military ammunition."

"Same as we have." He pointed out but it was a weak argument. The wall behind them was well mortared flint which must have stood for over a century. It was plain to see where the explosives had blasted the bricks apart and the bullet holes that marked where the Rangers had fired automatic weapons at the couple.

"That bastard!" he knew Amelia meant Armstrong and he shared her fury but he still hissed at her to keep her voice down.

"You there!" a crisp man's voice sounded from the road and Kyle whirled around to see a face topped by a camouflage helmet leaning around the hole in the wall. As he raised the rifle it whipped back out of sight.

"Back!" he shoved Amelia behind him, moving to stand in the doorway to the house.

"Who are you?" Amelia shouted.

"Corporal Dodds, British Army!" came the response and Kyle's heart hammered in his mouth. If the Rangers found Amelia here, they would kill them both. He stared frantically at the ruined house, wondering how much protection it would give them.

"What do you want?" he shouted.

"I'm on patrol." Dodds called back "You know it's illegal to be out here without a pass?"

Amelia and Kyle exchanged a confused glance. The land they were in was between territories and certainly wasn't policed by any town "What do you mean?" Kyle called back.

Dodds leaned out cautiously to show his empty hands. Then he stepped through the gap in the wall as a full section of soldiers appeared behind him. Kyle felt himself relax as he saw the uniform of the Regular Army, distinct from that of the

Rangers.

"I mean that since the troubles around Matwood it's illegal to travel without a pass." The man was about Kyle's age and had an apologetic expression on his face. He looked them up and down "Where have you come from?"

"We – we were sheltering for the winter in a ruined house."

Dodds raised his eyebrows "Really? Where was it?"

Kyle nodded to the railway "Miles away up there."

Dodds nodded but Kyle could see he wasn't interested. He nodded at the rifles "You aren't going to use those on us, I hope?"

"Not unless you make us." Amelia shot back.

Dodds rolled his eyes "Look, do you have a pass or not?"

"No. We've been away from the towns all winter."

The soldier nodded slowly "Right. Look, be that as it may, I have to take you to my commander. You aren't allowed to be out here."

Amelia gestured around "What about this? Did you kill these people?"

Dodds looked shocked "No! Did you?"

"Of course not!"

"We came to inspect the ruins. The fire was pretty intense. We could see the smoke for miles."

"And you didn't bother to come and check anyone was hurt?" the derision in Amelia's voice was plain.

Dodds shrugged "Not my call. Look, it's a three hour walk back to our camp. I'm afraid I have to insist that you come with us."

"I'm not giving you my weapons." Kyle grated.

Dodds held up both hands in mock surrender "Fine. Bring them with you. Just promise not to shoot me in the back, alright?"

CHAPTER 76

Kyle could feel Amelia chafing at the slow patrol pace of the soldiers but Dodds and the other troops seemed content to ignore them as they moved along a complicated route of winding, narrow lanes that could have been anywhere in England. They saw no Wretches nor refugees and Kyle wondered at the lack of movement in the landscape. He mentioned it to Dodds but the Corporal held a finger to his lips and left Kyle in a frustrated silence.

He could tell when they were close to the soldier's camp because their demeanour began to relax as they approached the security of home. Still, nothing but overgrown hedges hung on either side of the cracked tarmac until Dodds came to a halt at a seemingly random spot.

"Kilo Foxtrot." He called.

"Alpha Sierra." Came the response from a hedge to the left and Kyle jumped as an entire section of thick undergrowth peeled back. He remembered the hedges the patrols in Holden had moved to conceal their own position and nodded at the simplicity of the barrier.

A cluster of armed soldiers greeted them along with a machine gun position built up with sandbags. Kyle could feel curious eyes on them, taking in their weapons and full rucksacks but no-one made a move to stop them as Dodds led them into a camp filled with soldiers.

Long, drab coloured tents stood in four neat rows with random branches and leaves strewn across their surface for concealment. Kyle could see that they were in a field that prior to the Fall had probably held crops. In any case, it was now a dry, flat surface and the camp was bordered on two sides by thick hedgerows. The third was a diagonal row of deep trenches and barbed wire that ran from one corner of the field to the other, forming a triangular shaped camp. Along the wire at intervals were dead Wretches and a small party of soldiers dressed in protective gear was outside the wire, removing them.

"Corporal!" a voice called and Dodds turned to an Officer who was waiting nearby. The woman held the three pips of a Captain, wore a bright red beret and looked tired. Her uniform was clean though and the pistol holstered on her right leg looked serviceable.

"Ma'am." Dodds greeted her "Two civvies out without a pass. Found them in the ruins of the burned out house."

"Very good." The Captain turned to Kyle and Amelia "Who are you?"

"Who are you?" Kyle returned evenly, his rifle still held in his hands.

The woman frowned slightly but the exhaustion in her eyes was plain and she simply shrugged at Kyle's stubbornness "I'm Captain Albright, Royal Military Police. This sector is under my command and under the Declaration of Imposed Quarantine under..." she frowned, patting her pockets but not finding what she was looking for.

"Under Compensatory Direction of the Ministry of War, Ma'am." Dodds supplied.

"Yes." Albright nodded at Dodds "That. It's an offence to be out without a pass."

"So?" Amelia shrugged.

Albright blinked in surprise "Er – well, you're under arrest."

Kyle glanced past Albright at the scanty row of tents "Where do we go, then?"

"Maybe we should have a chat with them ma'am and see what they're up to?" Dodds suggested. Albright nodded and led the way to a small tent in which a long, low table was covered with a collection of military and civilian maps printed in the smart ink of Pre-Fall technology.

"Sit down." Albright gestured "Coffee?"

Kyle accepted a hot black mug and rested on a plastic chair that showed the signs of heavy use.

"What are your names?" Albright had produced a notepad and a pencil and was now sat opposite them, resting the paper on the table.

Kyle felt Amelia squeeze his leg under the table and he nodded. Giving up Amelia's identity to a soldier was foolhardy and as he felt her stir, an idea sprang to his mind "My name's Jason Mitchford." He stole the name of Holden's pub owner, hoping the dead man wouldn't mind "This is Jane MacDonald. We're both from Holden. We got separated from our group months ago by the Ferals and we've spent the winter holed up."

"Holden?" Albright looked pained "You've heard the news?"

Dejection washed over Kyle, followed by resignation "We heard rumours. What happened?"

Albright sat back with a sigh "Bloody awful. They were attacked by a Horde and overrun. The whole town was wiped out."

Kyle felt tears in his eyes and shook his head, looking down.

"Did no-one get out?" Amelia asked.

Albright shook her head "The whole area is heaving with the Infected. There are Ferals everywhere. My men and I have just come from Matwood. Spent three weeks there." She rubbed her eyes.

"What about the Rangers?" Kyle suddenly asked, "Armstrong was in Matwood before the winter."

"You mean when Holden was attacked? They tried to help but by the time word got to them the town was already overrun. Armstrong had to bomb the place to try and reduce the Horde numbers."

Kyle shook his head slowly in numb disbelief. He felt Amelia's hand on his but resignation was dawning on him. He realised he'd known the truth since Boss's jeering words but a part of him had held on to the possibility that it was a lie. Hearing Albright's words was like a knife blow to his already battered flesh.

"What about Sinclair? Corporal Sinclair? He was our military liaison. He was in Matwood when I left!" joy rushed into Kyle's mind at the thought that Sinks had perhaps survived "He –"

"I know who Sinclair is." Albright looked serious for once "He's why I was sent down here from London." She indicated her regimental insignia. Kyle felt his blood run cold. What did a Military Police Captain want with Sinks?

"What did he do?"

"He deserted. Along with his entire platoon. Killed some of the Rangers, too."

"What?" Kyle half laughed at the ridiculous suggestion "He didn't even have a platoon! We only came to Matwood for supplies!"

Albright shrugged "The only reason I'm telling you this is that every soldier in the region is on the lookout for Sergeant Sinclair. He's now part of an insurgency fighting against us."

"Rubbish." Kyle sat back his eyes like iron "That's not Sinks!"

"Ugh." Albright sighed and glanced to the far end of the tent where a messy cot with a crumpled sleeping bag lay. She looked regretful "Look, I'm sorry about Holden. Really, I am. But don't go mentioning Sinclair's name around here if he was your friend. The man is the reason all of this is happening. Well, at least in part."

"All of what?"

Another sigh "I suppose the Ferals are to blame really, maybe that's what drove Sinclair over the edge but the Minister for War deployed half the army to this region."

"Surely that was to deal with the Ferals?" Amelia sounded confused. Albright stared at her for a moment with a small frown.

"What did you say your name was?"

"Jane."

"Hmph. Well, it was to do with the Ferals, yes. But the Rangers are dealing with them. The bigger problem is the refugees. There are thousands of them now."

"They were here before the winter." Kyle pointed out.

"Not this many." Albright shook her head "Cunningham has ordered them all eliminated to stop the spread of the Feral mutation and –"

"*What?*" Amelia's voice was filled with such disgust that Kyle forgot his grief for a moment "You're murdering them?"

Albright's face was resigned "Don't think we're happy about it! There's no other way! If there were, Armstrong and Cunningham would have tried it!"

"Who's Cunningham?" Kyle was confused.

"The Minister for War –" Amelia muttered before rounding on Albright "You don't know they're Infected! They could be healthy! These people came here looking for help and you're gunning them down in the woods?"

Albright held up her hands "These are tough times, lady! What else do you suggest we do? We can't afford another Holden! The Ferals are everywhere! If we don't act then it'll be the Fall all over again! You think Cunningham will let that happen?" Albright rose to her feet, the fatigue vanishing from her eyes "Our job here is to protect civilians! If that means firebombing the entire region then I'll light the flames myself!"

Amelia did not back down an inch, she had risen to her feet too but when she spoke her fury was controlled "What if there was a test? A way to tell if people were Infected?"

"What if we had a pizza oven running twenty four seven?"

"I found a test! In the Beijerink Institute near here we found a test that can guarantee a positive result if someone is Infected with the X2H virus!"

Albright wanted to rubbish the suggestion, Kyle could see but the same frown had returned to her face and she leaned back as though looking at Amelia from an alternative angle "I know you!"

Amelia let out a small, frustrated grunt "Of course you do! I'm Amelia Singh!"

Kyle rose to his feet, hands reaching for his weapons but

Albright just looked at him in surprise "What are you doing?"

Kyle opened his mouth to speak but found himself blinking in surprise instead "I –" he lowered his hands as Albright made no move to attack Amelia.

Albright dismissed the threat and turned to Amelia "The Zek?"

"The Doctor." Amelia's eyes burned with a feverish light.

"And this test…"

It took some explaining. Both women sat back down and ran through the story of the Beijerink Institute as the fatigue returned to Albright's face. Her mouth hung slightly open in disbelief as Amelia glossed over details of Treetops, Arthur Cooley's farm, labouring the point that the test was real, producing the page from Kyle's notepad she'd taken as they hid in the computer room.

"Alright." Albright took a deep breath and raised her mug of coffee, scowling when she realised it was empty. Kyle pushed his own half-drunk mug across the table to her "Say this test is real. Can you prove it?"

"Yes." Amelia was emphatic "I could make it out of equipment you have here."

Albright's eyes widened in disbelief before she nodded "Fine. Maybe you can, maybe you can't. I don't know." She stared into the mug of coffee for a moment and Kyle wondered if she'd finally fallen asleep. Suddenly her head jerked up as she looked at Kyle "You say you know Sinclair? You're friends?"

"Yes."

"Look, my job out here is to arrest him. Maybe you can help me." She held up her hands as disgust coloured Kyle's face "I'm not asking you to betray your mate. I know he's in the area, patrol saw him yesterday. What I want you to do is negotiate him surrendering to me."

"Why would he do that?"

"Because –" Albright leaned forward, suddenly energetic again "Because, I'm not a Ranger. My job here is to see that justice is done. If the Rangers get hold of him, he'll get a bullet in the head. I told you he shot down a helicopter? Right. If he comes to me, I can guarantee his safety. Trouble is, he won't come near us. Every time he sees our troops he scarpers. Now I don't really care what he's done, I'm a police Officer, not a judge. But he can't keep running around in the woods like this. He's got his own troops to think about and between the Ferals, refugees and the Rangers, people are going to get killed." She rapped her knuckles on the table as though underlining her point "You go out and talk to him for me and then you –" she jabbed a finger at Amelia "- can make your test. Maybe we can sort this mess out if it works."

"You're just going to let us wander off into the woods?" Amelia was suspicious and Kyle nodded in agreement.

Albright shrugged "To tell the truth, I've got nowhere to put you even if you don't have passes. It might be an offence but this is an operating base, not a prison and I'm not risking sending you with an escort back to Matwood or somewhere else." She lifted her hands and let them drop in a gesture of futility "You may as well be out doing something useful."

CHAPTER 77

Albright passed them back into the hands of Corporal Dodds, closing the tent flaps behind them and a moment later, Kyle heard the distinctive creak of her lying down on the cot bed. He and Amelia followed Dodds out the concealed gate and turned left, away from the direction they'd arrived from.

Now that they were not prisoners, Dodds seemed more willing to chat telling them of the awful battle being waged around Matwood against Ferals, deserters and Zeks.

"Zeks?" Amelia snapped "Zeks are fighting you?"

"Not us." Dodds shook his head "They've finished off a few of the Rangers though. They aren't the normal nutters –" Albright had not bothered to tell him who Amelia was and she ignored the slight "These are soldiers – or something like that. They've got military grade kit anyway and they move as well as our blokes do."

"And they're fighting the deserters?" Kyle was confused.

"No. Nothing like that. They've joined Sinclair and his men. Basically, got a small army running around the woods."

Amelia mouthed the word *Eric* at Kyle and he remembered her description of the former Colonel. He wondered at Sinks, that his friend would have joined forces with such a man but his excitement at seeing Sinks alive filled him with energy as Dodds led them an hour's walk north of the small outpost, leaving them in the shadow of a thick patch of woodland.

"Patrol got sight of Sinclair here yesterday." He reported in a gruff voice "We'll be down the road a little ways. They er – they tend to leg it when they see us." He gave a half smile, half grimace before turning and leading his small patrol away.

Kyle glanced at Amelia who took a deep breath "Are we going

to bring them back to the camp if we find them?"

Kyle considered. Albright had let them go but as she said, there was little else she could do. Then again, she had been receptive to Amelia setting up the test and Kyle did not want to think of Sinks fighting and dying out here in the woods if there was an alternative "If we can prove that Armstrong was wrong about the refugees then maybe Parliament will arrest him. Then we could free my Dad..." he stopped himself before excitement could overcome rationality.

Amelia smiled and took his hand "I hope so. So we'll try and convince them?"

"Movement." Kyle looked past her, seeing the dark shape in the treeline. He brought his rifle up to bear, eyes staring to make out the figure.

"Infected?"

"Animal, I think."

A dark shape, low to the ground broke between the shadows cast by the trunks. A patch of spring sunlight glinted and the creature raced through it, a thousand colours brilliant in the light as a lolling tongue, grinning teeth and red fur raced towards Kyle...

Amelia shrieked in terror but Kyle gave a great roar of joy, dropped his rifle, flinging himself down to envelop the dog in his arms.

Next second there were barks and a howl and a pack of four legged, grinning canine bodies flung themselves at Kyle, licking and whining and rubbing themselves all over him as he roared with delighted laughter, heedless of the heavy paws that trod on him and wet noses that rubbed him.

"Kyle! KYLE!" and there she was, Rosie, alive, pale and thin with the stink of weeks spent living rough but she was elbowing dogs aside, wrapping Kyle in a bear hug before punching him in the shoulder.

"You're alive!" he was beaming, his face already aching with joy.

"You southern poofter!"

"Sinks! You miserable tosspot!" the two men hugged fiercely, slapping each other's backs with gusto and then all pretence vanished as more figures emerged from where they had hidden. Black dressed Zeks, filthy civilians and children. Kyle swept the Patel boy who'd handed him his plate carrier on the walls of Holden a million years ago into a tight hug, seeing the same joy reflected on the boy's face. Jason Mitchford, a heavy bandage around his head slapped Kyle on the shoulder and Dr May, somehow spotlessly clean gave him a tight lipped nod which was almost a hug.

"Amelia?" a middle aged Zek with a weather beaten face had approached Amelia and the two stared at each other in shock. Kyle suddenly guessed that this was Eric Forbes and he looked from the man to Sinks then to the survivors of Holden and the ragged band of soldiers in dirty uniforms that watched the reunion with raised eyebrows.

"Where have you been?" was the question on both sides and for the second time in as many hours Kyle and Amelia related their story. Rosie looked from one to the other as they spoke and Kyle saw a thoughtful smile settle onto her features.

Sinks raised an eyebrow and made a grotesque motion, his body concealed from Amelia's view behind Jason and Kyle shot him the finger, earning a beaming grin in response.

"But you've been killing soldiers?" Kyle had a thousand questions but that was uppermost.

A nearby woman wearing the stripes of a Corporal started in anger "We've been defending ourselves from the Rangers!" she snapped "Those bastards have been hunting us for weeks! Between them and the Ferals it's a bloody miracle anyone is left!"

Sinks caught her eye and Davies blinked, lowering her eyes. Kyle could see the exhaustion on all their faces and understood the outburst.

"It's Kyle, isn't it?" the man he assumed was Eric Forbes stepped forward to shake his hand formally "It's a pleasure. Thank you for keeping Amelia safe."

Kyle raised both eyebrows "It was the other round. I was shot outside the Institute and she saved my life."

"You made it then?" Eric turned to Amelia with excitement in his voice.

"Yes." She held up a hand to stem his enthusiasm as the other Zeks muttered to one another "We didn't find everything. A lot of it was beyond me. There were two things, a treatment to prevent the spread which Kyle tells me Dr May –" she nodded at her erstwhile teacher "- has already perfected an –"

"Produced, not perfected." The Maybot grated out in a flat tone of voice "Do you have the research?"

"No." Amelia shook her head "But there was a test that they'd developed which can be done in the field to determine if someone is Infected."

Every voice could hear her and the buzz of excitement set the dogs who had mostly calmed to whining and running under everyone's feet again. A pair of the wheaten canines were leaning against Kyle's legs, forcing him to adjust his balance every few seconds. He didn't mind in the slightest.

"We met an army Officer, she sent us here to speak to you…"

Amelia relayed the last part of the story, up to the point where the dogs had emerged from the woods. Sinks and Eric exchanged serious looks at the offer to surrender. Kyle could see the soldiers looking to Sinks with hope in their eyes. He wondered at the hardships they'd endured.

"What was the Officer's name?" Eric asked.

"Albright."

"Albright…" Eric tailed off, looking around as he peered into his memory "I think I remember her. RMP?"

"Yes."

"Yes, I think I've met her at least." Seeing Kyle's look of surprise, he continued "There aren't that many Officers in the army these days. Most of us know each other, at least by reputation. She'll know who I am." He turned to Amelia "Look, if you and Dr May can set up the test then this could change everything."

"She wants you to surrender. That's the condition for proving that the test works." Amelia looked at Sinks who nodded, before turning to his soldiers.

"Everyone hear that?"

Nods and murmurs of assent.

"Any questions for the lady?"

Silence.

"Anyone here who doesn't want to go back in and surrender?"

Silence again.

Sinks turned back and nodded "We're in."

It was as simple as that. Sinks bullied them all into some semblance of a tactical formation as they headed back towards Albright's outpost. Dodds met them with a wary look at Sinks but the dour northerner shook his hand and the tension eased. Kyle shook hands and swapped hushed jokes with the Holdenites who had survived, noting all the while those who hadn't made it. Rosie stayed close.

"The Mayor? Jane?"

She shook her head and Kyle felt a lump in his throat.

"You and her, huh?" Rosie nodded at Amelia.

He owed it to Rosie to be honest and he owed it to Amelia not to apologise and he held Rosie's eye as he told her the full story.

To his surprise, she smiled "I'm happy for you."

"You are?"

"'Course!" she elbowed him in the ribs "We're still mates, aren't we?"

"You mean now I'm not dead?"

"Exactly!" she grinned then cursed as she tripped over a dog in front of her that was excitedly trying to rub against Kyle.

"The dogs all made it?" he leaned down to pet the wheaten ears.

"Yeah! They were what got us out. They got between us and the Wretches..." Rosie tailed off, her face falling and Kyle squeezed her hand.

"I'm sorry I wasn't there."

She shrugged "Nothing you could've done." She relayed the story of the attack and Kyle felt a surge of burning anger at the Rangers.

"How can they get away with it?"

"You listen to Eric talk and he'll tell you Armstrong has been getting away with it for years. Apparently he's done this to other towns too. Anyone who questioned or disagreed with him... That's part of why Eric left the army in the first place. You know most of his men came too? That's who they are." She pointed at the armed Zeks and Kyle nodded in understanding.

Approaching Albright's camp, Dodds brought them in and Albright appeared, rubbing sleep from her eyes but looking more alert than when Kyle had left.

To his surprise, she recognised Eric and even saluted "Sir."

"Captain. We're here to surrender."

She nodded as though that were expected "I'm not planning on handcuffing you, Sir. Would you have your blokes unload their weapons though?"

It was an odd sight, the mass arrest of the deserters and Zeks who stood with their weapons looking no more captive than they had upon entering the camp. Kyle could see that dozens of prisoners unable to defend themselves from the Ferals was utterly impractical and Albright was happy to make sure her charges could defend themselves when needed. Amelia and Dr May vanished inside the command tent to begin setting up the test as Eric approached Kyle.

"You're Dr Frost's son?"

"Yes. Do you think he's alive?"

"I don't know for certain. You thought he was dead?"

Kyle relayed his final memory of his parents in as brief an explanation as possible, the pain of the experience grated into his mind.

"He seemed to have been Infected?" Eric frowned "I'd imagine if anyone was able to treat an Infection then it was your Father." Seeing Kyle's face light up he gave a small smile

"We'll do our best to find out."

Amelia emerged from the tent as the light was beginning to fade. She looked tired but a bright energy was glowing in her eyes as she approached Eric and Kyle "We need to test it."

"It's ready?" Kyle was surprised.

Albright approached "Ma'am? I've held off contacting higher command until you've completed the test. I can't hold for much longer though. Are you nearly ready?"

"We need test subjects."

"Test subject? Oh…"

Amelia gave a grimace as Kyle reached for his rifle.

CHAPTER 78

Full dark had fallen by the time Kyle, Sinks and Dodds along with a cluster of Albright's soldiers wrestled the Wretch back into the camp. Kyle was sweating badly after the hunt and fight. Fortunately, they'd not encountered a Feral and the Wretch that they'd restrained and hooded was slow and dumb but surprisingly strong and they struggled to drag the dead weight as the creature stumbled and fell.

"Ugh." The guard at the entrance to the camp grimaced as he shone a red torch on the small group "Sure you don't want to just shoot it?"

"It needs to be alive." Dr May had appeared, her characteristically robotic face making the guard step aside uncomfortably.

They dragged the creature to the tent where Amelia, her hair dishevelled, leapt from a chair to usher them over. A small syringe lay on a white cloth before her and as Kyle bound the Wretch to the chair he stared at it in surprise.

"That's it?"

Amelia nodded "The blood test goes in this liquid –" she held up a small vial "and that's it. It was designed to be done in the field."

"Simple."

Albright bustled into the tent to watch. Her fatigue had passed and she was now as wide eyed as the rest of them, the full gravity of this moment not wasted on her.

"Ready?" Amelia asked Dr May who ignored her, jabbing the syringe into the grey flesh and extracting a sample of black goo.

"The colour coding is different to what it should be." She explained "The test was designed to be blue for negative and red for positive. This will be yellow or orange. We didn't have quite the right compounds in the camp."

She dripped the Wretch blood into the vial and shook it vigorously before placing it on the table.

Every eye stared at the liquid as seconds ticked by like hours.

"Nothing's happening." Albright put her hands on her hips.

A minute passed.

"Should it have done something?"

Amelia didn't answer but Kyle could see the disappointment on her face.

"We –"

"Do it again." Dr May turned and began to fill a new vial as Amelia ran over a series of notes on paper. More blood was extracted and dropped into a new vial.

"There!" Kyle had been sitting reversed on a chair, leaning on the plastic back but he leapt to his feet, tripping slightly.

"Red!"

Indeed, the liquid in the vial was turning red and Amelia clapped her hands together.

"Excellent!"

"Again." Dr May had already gathered more needles and vials.

Red. Red. Red. Finally, the Maybot pronounced herself satisfied but Albright was shaking her head.

"That doesn't prove anything. Anyone can tell that's a positive." She pointed to the thrashing Wretch "What about someone who hasn't gone through the change? Someone who's a carrier?"

"Like the refugees." Kyle understood. He groaned "How are we going to find one of them?"

"It doesn't have to be a refugee to prove it works." Eric was saying "We need a human with a suspected Infection."

"Someone who was bitten." Sinks nodded.

"Exactly." Before anyone could stop her, Dr May ripped the

hood from the bound Wretch and thrust her bare forearm into its snapping jaws.

The scene slowed before Kyle's eyes. Every person moved at the same time, all leaning forward to grab the woman and protect her but the yellow jagged teeth had already bitten down hard and Kyle could see the spill of crimson blood as the Wretch gave a muffled howl of delight.

Dr May's only response to the pain was a swiftly stifled hiss and a tightening at the corners of her mouth.

Amelia was the first to reach her mentor, frantically tearing at the Wretch's head but Albright was a step behind her, swearing futilely as she tore her pistol from its holster.

Bang

Everyone flinched as the shot echoed from the canvas of the tent and the Wretch went slack, Dr May's arm falling from the jaws.

"Bloody hell!" Albright was already moving past the dead Infected to see where the bullet had gone. Kyle remembered the camp full of soldiers around them and winced but Eric was already pointing to the groundsheet where a neat, round hole showed. Albright breathed a sigh of relief but next second May was in her face.

"You had better hope the Infection took or you'll be out there looking for a new subject!"

It was the most emotion Kyle had ever seen the robotic woman convey and he froze awkwardly, holding his breath as Amelia grabbed some gauze to clean the wound.

"Leave it!" Dr May snapped, apparently unconcerned about the deadly virus now surely travelling through her veins "We need a test subject! I will do."

She began to gather yet another needle and vial and drew a sample of her own blood as the dead Wretch dripped black goo onto the floor.

Red. Positive.

"Another." Dr May had sat down and was directing Amelia.

"The booster, Doctor!"

May shook her head "Another test. Prove it works."

Kyle wondered at the selflessness of the woman. Death now surely had her in its grasp but she insisted Amelia test her a total of five times, each as red as the last. Finally she looked up at Albright as calm as ever.

"Satisfied, Captain?"

Albright, white with shock just nodded as Amelia injected a double dose of the booster into May's arm.

"I need to be quarantined." May stood up and allowed Amelia to lead her out of the tent.

A shocked silence hung over them. Kyle caught Sinks' eye and the dour northerner simply shook his head in amazement. Albright stared after the two Doctors, guilt clear on her face. Finally, Eric broke the silence, clearing his throat gently.

"Captain? I think you had better contact London."

CHAPTER 79

Kyle expected the next twenty four hours to pass in an anxious knot of tension but instead, he found himself exhausted. Collapsing next to Amelia under a hastily erected basha, a soothing silence fell and Kyle felt the familiarity of home as a pair of dogs curled up next to them.

"Kyle?"

"Hmm?"

"I love you."

"I love you."

"I'm worried." Amelia murmured in a small voice.

Kyle nodded in the darkness.

"What if the army supports Armstrong? What if they arrest us? What if Armstrong gets hold of us?"

"Shh." He pushed his forehead against hers "We'll deal with it."

He knew it wasn't the right answer but it was the best he had. They lay in silence beneath the basha which moved in the faint breeze. She opened her mouth to speak several times but closed it again. He heard the intakes of breath each time but she stayed silent. He felt sleep beginning to take him. Finally, she spoke and he heard the fear in her voice.

"Look after me, Kyle."

"I promise."

The early morning light didn't wake them and it was almost midday before Kyle rolled out of the sleeping bag.

A faint thunder met his ears and he blinked stupidly, staring around.

"Chinook." Sinks' voice greeted him and Kyle glanced to see his friend, still filthy but looking far more rested. He held out a mug of steaming tea, the survivors of the bag the Holdenites had managed to scavenge. They stood together watching the horizon.

"The big one?"

"Yeah." A bright morning sun was shining and Sinks shaded his eyes to stare "Two of them. With an escort."

Albright appeared, barking a series of orders which had her troops scurrying around. Someone produced a series of flares which were spread around the half of the field not occupied by the camp. Soldiers ran to and fro stacking unused equipment away in tents and the buzz of energy woke the last of the sleepers who squinted in the light.

"What's happening?" Amelia emerged to stand by Kyle.

"Helicopters."

"Rangers?"

"No." Sinks pointed and now the flight of four aircraft was clearly visible, driving through the sunlight towards the small camp "Coming from the north. From London."

The helicopters slowed as they approached and Kyle could make out that there were two different types. One, the unmistakeable double rotor of a Chinook which he recognised from Sinks' lessons back in Holden whilst the other two, sleeker looking and smaller, Sinks told them were Apache gunships.

"See the roundel on the side?" the northerner pointed and Kyle saw a red and blue device painted on the side. Sinks explained that these were air force aircraft, whilst the Pumas that the Rangers flew in were operated by the army.

All conversation was drowned out as the din of the approaching helicopters began to beat at their eardrums. Kyle pulled his scarf up over his mouth and nose as the downdraught began to reach them. A terrible gust of stinking hot air smote him and they all stepped backwards as the two Chinooks began to slowly descend into the field. Above them, the Apache escorts flew a wide ring.

Kyle expected the aircraft to open and disgorge the

occupants but instead, the rotors began to die down and a minute later, the Apaches landed too and he felt an odd ringing in his ears at the sudden silence.

An electronic whirring and the rear doors on the Chinooks finally opened, lowering to the damp grass of the field. A bullish looking woman in her fifties with pale skin and dark hair in a tight bun led the way, dressed in a civilian suit.

Kyle stared. He'd never seen someone in a suit outside of a picture. Up close, the clothes seemed wildly impractical and out of place. What was the point in a jacket that didn't cover your chest? Why did they have ties on when a Wretch could grab the scrap of silk and pull you into their jaws? There were no visible pockets on her trousers which looked far too thin for any serious use and those shoes were polished brightly enough to be seen a mile away...

"That's Cunningham!" Amelia hissed and Kyle started, looking from the bullish woman to the cluster of mixed suited civilians and senior military Officers who had emerged from the Chinooks.

"Minister!" Albright had stepped to a small gap in the wire to greet her guests and seemed as surprised as any of them. She flung up a salute, her hand meeting the corner of her red beret.

"Captain." Cunningham looked around, her eyes landing on Eric and then Amelia. A small twitch crossed her mouth.

"Colonel Forbes!" she called, stepping past Albright as the other politicians and Officers crossed the wire.

Eric nodded and crossed to shake Cunningham's hand "General."

General? Kyle wondered but remembered Amelia's complaint that most of Parliament was made up of former military Officers. Looking at the bullish Cunningham he could well believe she'd been a soldier.

Albright turned and beckoned Kyle, Amelia, and Sinks towards them. Sinks moved stiffly and Kyle sensed the apprehension in his friend.

"Who are you?"

Albright introduced them. Cunningham's eyes lingered on Kyle and then lit up when Amelia's name was mentioned. To Kyle's surprise, she shook the Zeks hand.

"It's a pleasure, Dr Singh. I know your Father."

Amelia nodded although the worried expression never left her face.

"I understand there is a field test for us to see?"

Amelia turned without a word and began to lead the way to a small shelter the soldiers had built as a quarantine. The guards saw her approaching and pulled apart the entrance way, allowing Dr May to emerge, blinking in the strong light.

"Dr May!" a surprised voice sounded from behind Cunningham and Kyle turned to see one of the accompanying Officers, a grey haired Colonel was staring at Holden's Doctor in surprise. A second man, this one in a suit was nodding to May in greeting too.

"Well?" Cunningham's voice was impatient and Kyle realised that no more than a few minutes had passed since she'd exited the Chinook. Clearly the Minister for war was not one to waste time.

"Minister." Dr May looked none the worse for her Infection and night spent in the quarantine shelter "I can confirm the test works. It shows positive results as soon as a few minutes after Infection."

Cunningham looked from the doctor to the quarantine shelter and frowned "You tested it on yourself?"

The Colonel who'd recognised May stepped up beside Cunningham "Minister, I can vouch for Doctor May as can others here." He turned and a few voices called out in assent "She's probably the best doctor in the country. If she says the test works then it's true without a doubt."

Cunningham seemed to pause for thought. She eyed May with an unreadable expression which the Maybot was equal to, meeting her gaze without a flinch. Finally, Cunningham gave a sharp gesture and stepped several paces away from Kyle and out of earshot. A handful of her fellows joined her and they had a brief, whispered exchange.

"Here we go…" Sinks muttered, watching them warily.

"It'll be alright." Kyle muttered, reaching out to take Amelia's hand.

Tense silence. Cunningham glanced over at them, briefly meeting Kyle's eyes.

"Come on…"

Eric fidgeted with his hands. A dog whined near Kyle and he petted it absently.

"Alright!" the harsh word came from Cunningham who straightened up abruptly. She turned, striding quickly across the ground towards Albright and leaving the others jogging to catch up with her.

"Captain? You are to escort Sergeant Sinclair back to London to face a court martial." She looked Sinks full in the face "The charge is being absent without leave."

"Ma'am!" Sinks nodded, the relief on his face palpable.

Cunningham raised a finger to him "I'm not unsympathetic to your situation, Sinclair but I have to take some action. Your punishment will likely be reduction in rank and a fine. I'll make sure there's no prison time."

"Thank you, Ma'am. What about my men?"

"There won't be any punishment!" Cunningham raised her voice so it carried "But you will return to Matwood with us –" she pointed at the Chinooks "- for a full debrief. After that you'll re-join your units."

Mutters and grins amongst the soldiers as Sinks turned to Albright, formally surrendering his weapons. Kyle watched as a pair of her troops in the distinctive red berets bound his friend's hands.

"See you in a bit!" Sinks was escorted to one of the tents. Kyle wondered if they were going to fly back to London but it seemed Cunningham was not finished.

"Colonel Forbes." She turned to Eric who watched her with interest on his weather beaten features "I'm concerned that you are in a dangerous position." Cunningham looked uncomfortable "You've become something of a figurehead and if things continue this way, then more troops will leave to follow you."

Eric nodded "I have a proposal."

Cunningham narrowed her eyes "Go on."

"As the test has proven viable you must determine whether or not Blake Armstrong was lying about the refugees. If they are not Infected as appears to be the case then he must be removed from his position and the Ranger Regiment given a new commander."

Cunningham regarded him for a two second count before snapping her next sentence "Do you think the refugees are Infected?"

"No."

Cunningham nodded as though she'd expected this. One of the uniformed Officers behind her tittered but both she and Eric ignored him. She seemed to come to some decision, taking a slow breath before speaking.

"I'm going to offer you this once, Forbes. I suggest you take the deal. Full reinstatement at your previous rank with all benefits and pay in absentia. *If* Blake Armstrong is determined to have lied to Ministry of War, he will be removed from his post and command of the Ranger Regiment will be given to you."

"No." Eric shook his head vehemently. Kyle stared at him in shock.

Cunningham simply cocked an eyebrow and waited.

"I'll accept only on the condition that you contact the Rangers immediately and tell them the truth which is that the refugees they've been murdering at Blake Armstrong's command are *not* Infected and he is immediately to be removed from command."

Cunningham looked away for a moment before turning back to Eric "You want me to willingly push the Ranger Regiment into a mutiny?"

"I demand it."

"Minister, I –"

Cunningham held up a hand, cutting off the protest from behind her. Kyle held his breath, watching the exchange and sensing the weight of the powers at play. Everything hung on a knife's edge and he could feel Amelia shaking beside him.

"Fine."

Kyle's legs almost collapsed as Cunningham stepped forward to shake Eric's outstretched hands. Almost immediately she turned to the group behind her, snapping orders and a junior Officer ran back to the silent Chinooks to radio Matwood.

"I hope you know what you're doing, Eric." Kyle heard Cunningham mutter as the Zeks with Eric began to cheer and slap each other on the back.

"I know how to deal with Blake." Eric murmured back "If his own men don't kill him then I trust I can rely on you?"

Cunningham let his hand go and held his gaze. Kyle felt the ferocity pass between them as her lip curled.

"Fine."

Eric smiled in victory and stood stiffly to attention "Thank you, Ma'am."

PART 4

CHAPTER 80

Kyle closed his eyes and prayed for a swift death as the Chinook struck a pocket of air and plunged downwards. Across from him, two of Eric's men stifled grins at his discomfort and he wished the interior of the cabin was quieter so he could explain he'd never been in so much as a motor car, let alone flown.

But that wasn't true... He remembered a blurry childhood memory, the details vague and indistinct. There was his Mother, smiling as she pressed him into a booster seat and his Father driving and he was aware of movement, of songs playing on the radio.

Amelia grabbed his hand and he started, realising the helicopter was descending rapidly and he peered through one of the small, round windows to see the unmistakeable sight of Matwood emerging from the forest like a desert oasis.

Thump

The wheels touched down and the pilot lowered the rear ramp immediately, not waiting for the engines to die down. Kyle tensed, uncertain of what to expect but Cunningham, Eric and a handful of his soldiers left the helicopter, indicating that the others should remain aboard.

Not a chance Kyle thought, relishing the thought of escaping from the metal coffin with its roaring voice. He and Amelia hurried out, their feet clanging off the metal ramp until they splashed through mud.

Kyle stared. The ground outside Matwood was a quagmire of filthy, churned up earth. Instantly, Kyle looked around for a dry spot to stand, wary of his boots but there was none. An inch thick ooze covered the ground, wet enough that even the thousands of boot prints that had surely caused the mire were obscured. In front of him a Land Rover, tilted to one side was abandoned in the mud and its side spattered with filth. Kyle stared around, noticing the stink in the air as he walked clear of the Chinook's rotor wash.

"Look!" It was the first time they'd been able to speak after the roar of the engines and Amelia pointed frantically. Kyle remembered Sinks' description of the camp the soldiers had built and he followed her gesture to see the rows of wire and drab coloured tents expecting to see an orderly and functional setting but instead soldiers stood around in disarray, staring in confusion.

Some looked at the helicopters but most stared towards the walls of Matwood from which a great roar of voices was sounding. Even as Kyle watched, the gates swung open to emit a crowd of men and women, all shouting furiously and some throwing objects.

A trio led the way, two men carrying one between them and all three ducking to avoid the missiles the entire town seemed intent on hurling at them. A handful of people had made it to the fire step atop the wall and were hurling abuse down as the trio made a beeline for the helicopters.

"That's –" began Kyle but a shout of recognition from the massed soldiers came and a moment later they were joining in the fury.

"Armstrong!"

The figure was not being carried, he was being dragged and as he came closer, Kyle could make out the bloodied features of Major Armstrong. One eye was swollen shut and his nose was surely broken. Kyle wondered if it was his own men or the townsfolk that had beaten him up so badly. He shook his head, remembering Cunningham's words about a mutiny.

"Bring him here!" Cunningham was waving at the two other men who Kyle could see were both soldiers. One was in Ranger uniform with their face to the ground and the other was Jay Paxton, Sinks' opposite number in Matwood.

"Ma'am!" Sergeant Paxton greeted Cunningham, clearly recognising her.

"Does he need a medic?" was Cunningham's only question at which Armstrong shook his head, pushing away from Paxton and the other soldier who Kyle could now see was Sinks' friend Hannah Mitchell. She shot Armstrong a poisonous look as the Major managed to stand although he breathed heavily and blood dripped from his nose.

"Major Blake Armstrong –" Cunningham began formally and Kyle saw the Ranger sneer at her words "You are charged with murder, wilfully deceiving your chain of command and concealing intelligence for your own benefit." She gestured behind her "These aircraft will take you to London to face your court martial. You are relieved of your command."

Armstrong spat blood and looked at Eric, a small smile on his face "Eric."

"Blake."

The two men stared each other out before Cunningham made a small gesture and two of the senior Officers approached, helping Armstrong into the aircraft. He shot a look at Kyle as he passed, surprise registering on his face before he saw Amelia and his eyes widened.

"Frost."

That was all the time he had before he vanished. Cunningham turned to the soldiers who were gathering from the camp, demanding a senior Officer who appeared in the form of a Major in a muddy uniform who hastily saluted.

"Major, Colonel Forbes is now in command of this region. You're to report to him for orders." Ignoring the surprise on the Officer's face she turned to Eric "Colonel? I expect a report by this evening but some idea of your immediate intentions would be helpful."

"Deploy the Rangers to reopen trade routes then use the regular troops to round up the refugees. I want to speak to them and find out what is happening in France."

Cunningham nodded but Hannah Mitchell strode forwards

"You don't need them, Sir. I know what he's been up to."

"Who are you?"

"Sergeant Mitchell, Second Rangers."

"Well?"

"There's a place in northern France, Sir. A research facility that the Major knew about before the Fall. He has a team there that created the mutation."

Kyle stared at Hannah, feeling Amelia tense beside him "Who? Who is in the team?"

She looked at him in surprise as though just recognising him "I don't know, I've never been there. The other Rangers talk about it though."

"That's my Dad!" Kyle didn't care that his voice was too loud "It has to be!"

Cunningham was looking from Kyle to Mitchell and finally at Eric "Colonel?"

"Minister. I'll send you a report tonight."

Cunningham turned and vanished into the Chinook which rose in a screaming roar before it and the three other helicopters vanished, the sound of their rotors fading slowly.

"Sergeant?" Eric beckoned Hannah over away from the watching eyes as the Major commanding the regular troops began to shout his soldiers back into some semblance of discipline.

Kyle and Amelia followed.

"The mutation –" Amelia spoke over everyone "Did Armstrong release it here?"

"I don't know. I think so." Kyle could see that Hannah's eyes were filled with grief "He told us the refugees were all Infected. I can see how stupid that was now." A tear formed in her eye and she dashed it away angrily.

"What about this Facility in France?" Eric wanted to know, his voice was low and fierce "We *have* to know where it is!"

Hannah shook her head "Only Lynch and a couple of his closest have been there. I've heard them talking about it."

Eric looked at Amelia "Can you help with the refugees?"

She nodded and he looked grim "Alright. Sergeant?" he addressed Hannah "I want the Rangers out engaging targets around all the trade routes. Clear them all, understood? Pass that along. See if anyone is willing to identify the French Facility. Go!"

"Sir, what about Lynch?" Hannah asked.

"What about him?"

"He's still in Matwood. He'll be looking to get revenge for the Major."

"Lynch is just one man." Eric shook his head "He's my problem now."

"Sir." Hannah nodded and turned back to Matwood.

Eric moved off to brief the Major and Kyle turned to Amelia "What did he mean 'help' with the refugees?"

She looked surprised "Oh, I speak French. I can ask them if they know where the Facility is."

Kyle stared "What, thousands of them? She said it's a Pre-Fall Facility!"

Amelia stared "So?"

"So, it'll be on a Pre-Fall map!"

Amelia gaped "Oh."

Kyle rolled his eyes "Right?"

CHAPTER 81

In the end, it was no more complicated than that. Matwood, like all towns had a store of Pre-Fall maps, both military and civilian and Eric, dressed in a fresh new Ranger uniform located the Facility as night was falling. Kyle found he was exhausted, blown out by the day's events but the thought that his Father could be near and the answer to the curse of the virus could be within their grasp kept him wide eyed and enthusiastic.

"Here." Eric jabbed the blunt end of a pencil at the map. They were crowded around one of the rare electric bulbs that Matwood allowed. Kyle thought longingly of the solar farms and turbines that had graced Holden, only now recognising what a luxury it had been. They were in a small hut which Jay Paxton had accommodated them in. Eric, Amelia, Kyle, Hannah, and two Rangers from the second battalion named Cole and Williamson who'd given them the location that Eric was indicating. A pair of dogs who seemed unwilling to leave Kyle made up the party.

"Hardelot." Kyle read the unfamiliar text earning a scowl from Amelia.

"Château d'Hardelot."

He stared at her.

"It means Hardelot castle! It's just south of Boulogne…"

"There are beaches." Eric was pointing out "Plage d'Écault." He looked at Amelia "Plage means beach, doesn't it?"

"Why do we need a beach?" Kyle wondered imagining the helicopters of the Rangers swooping over the coast.

Eric hesitated "It's an idea…" he tailed off but looked up to see the whole room watching him expectantly. He sighed "This is an idea, not a plan. If – and I stress *if* – we find Dr Frost and God willing, a treatment for this plague then we'll need to fight the Infected in Europe. We can't keep hiding on our island forever." He shrugged "If we're already landing at Hardelot then a nearby beach is a good route for supplies." He paused again, adding almost as an afterthought "For an invading army."

Kyle glanced at Amelia but Williamson, a middle aged man who had joined the Rangers only a few months prior from the Regular Army spoke up "First things first, boss." Kyle flinched at the use of the bandit leader's name but he'd come to learn that was the informal term of respect for an Officer amongst the soldiers "The place might have a stupid name but if it's a castle then we can assume the place is fortified."

Kyle gulped at that. Everyone was silent for a moment.

"We can assume that any place that has survived the Infected for twenty years is fortified." Eric broke the silence "Chateau often means stately home. It may not be a true castle." As Williamson began to disagree he held up a hand "I know, plan for the worst. We'll make sure we have breaching charges on the aircraft. Happy?"

Williamson nodded.

"Fine. Now, there's forest shown on both sides." Eric traced the tree line on the maps "We can use the trees for cover, fly low over them and attempt a landing on this area here." He pointed at a wide open expanse.

"How many aircraft?" Hannah asked.

"The Pumas can carry twelve?" he confirmed, reminding everyone present how little time Eric had spent as leader of the Rangers.

"Twelve with full kit." Cole, the second of the two Rangers confirmed.

Eric thought for a moment "We can request a Chinook, too. Four loaded helicopters, one Chinook. If we can't do it with that then we don't deserve to get in."

The details began to blur in Kyle's mind, the minutiae of

military planning and the complex slew of acronyms fading out of his understanding. Amelia made an excuse and led him out of the room, standing on the step outside.

"Pretty intense."

Kyle nodded "Yeah."

"I'm going with Eric." Amelia declared.

Kyle had thought nothing less and he nodded "I'm coming with you." He was silent for a moment "Eric thinks that there could be a cure there. My Father could have made one."

"It's possible." Amelia sounded sceptical "I think it's more likely that if we can free your Father from Armstrong's control then we can work on *making* a cure."

Kyle nodded, aware that a thick knot of tension was forming in his chest "I wish we weren't going with Armstrong's men."

"They handed him over, remember?"

Kyle nodded, remembering the tale of the furious Rangers who had turned on their leader, beating him to a pulp. He wondered at the betrayal they'd felt.

"Besides, they weren't all fanatical. Lynch was the worst –"

"Eric says he's taking him."

Amelia nodded slowly "He doesn't have much choice. Lynch is the best Sergeant and he needs competent men."

Kyle grunted but at that moment Eric opened the door and bade them come back in.

"Alright. I think we're ready. I'll assemble the troops tomorrow if we can get the Chinook. We'll take a mixed force of Rangers and my Zeks." Eric glanced at Hannah "Do we have spare uniforms?"

"Oh, loads!" she nodded "The Major had just ordered a whole bunch of new kit. He was expecting to recruit a whole lot of blokes to meet the Feral threat."

"Excellent." Eric suddenly looked keenly at Kyle and he felt the stares of the other Rangers "Frost. I understand from Sinclair that you had an ambition to join the Rangers?"

Kyle gaped at the man, feeling Amelia's surprise next to him "I – I did. That was before…"

"Before all of this, yes." Eric nodded in understanding "I can't promise that Blake Armstrong is no longer a threat but I intend to keep my position as the commander of the Rangers. Things will change under my watch." He cleared his throat, a little awkwardly "Would you like to join, Frost?"

Kyle stared at the man, his world seeming to shrink to the words as they came from the weather beaten man's mouth. Would he like to be a Ranger? The Kyle that had set out from Holden would have killed for the opportunity. That was before watching Lynch murder innocent civilians with that awful stare on his face, before Gault had haggled with Boss for Amelia's life and before Armstrong had changed from a face on a poster to a monstrous psychopath. The vision he'd held of the elite Warriors had been so utterly removed from their reality that he'd come to see them as his enemy.

Eric frowned "You're concerned?"

Kyle blinked several times "It's – It's not what I thought it was, Sir."

"No." Eric nodded slowly "I understand that. From what I've heard and seen of you, you'd be a good fit. You'd have to learn on the job of course, there won't be time to send you on the training cadre until the Feral threat is neutralised but that's the same for me." A faint smile creased his lips.

Kyle nodded and suddenly he realised he was fed up with choices being taken from him. For months he'd been chased, beaten, tortured and forced to flee from every threat. He felt as though he'd been on the run for half his life and the only solidity was Amelia. He glanced at her, seeing the small smile on her face. He knew how she felt about the Rangers – how *he* felt – but Eric was right, this was a Ranger Regiment without Armstrong and with a new purpose. He could see himself in the uniform, riding in the doorway of their helicopters as a true Warrior and he thought of the alternative, perhaps joining the Matwood Militia with Rosie, struggling to follow Amelia around as she campaigned for the Zeks or scratching out a dull living as a guard on a trade caravan. He mentally shook his head. There was more to life than that.

"I'll do it, Sir."

"Excellent." Eric gave a measured smile "Welcome to the Rangers, Frost."

CHAPTER 82

"Stop!" Amelia turned to him the moment they were alone, pressing her finger to his lips.

"What?"

"I know what you're going to try and say. You made the right decision. You're still my Kyle and doesn't matter to me what uniform you're wearing."

Kyle sighed, feeling a surge of relief "You aren't angry?"

Amelia cocked her head on one side as she looked up at him. They were in a small room they'd commandeered in a mixed bunkhouse "How could I be? It's what you want. My problem with the Rangers is all because of Armstrong. Eric is right, with him in charge, things will be different. The Rangers will be what they should always have been."

Kyle grinned and kissed her, relieved.

"Now, get that off –" she tugged at his dirty shirt "- and let me see what you look like in this!" she threw the new Ranger uniform at him and he tugged off his clothes. Midway through, she ambushed him and he was forced to wait until morning to tell if it fitted.

*

"Check out the fresh meat!"

The Rangers were filled with nervous energy. The Chinook Eric had summoned from the air force had landed half an hour ago and had been refuelled from one of the Ranger trucks. Around the great double rotored beast sat the four other helicopters that would carry the Rangers. Kyle had been run through a hasty lesson on their characteristics, learning that they were a now ancient model of aircraft known as a Puma, serving as a troop transport, gunship, and reconnaissance craft. He'd been assigned to C Platoon under a cheerful Sergeant named Ross. Williamson, the middle aged man from the briefing was with him as was Hannah Mitchell. The rest were strangers apart from Gault who was heckling him from the doorway of the Puma Ross had been leading them too.

Kyle hesitated at the jeer but Gault had spotted him and sauntered over.

"Frost." Gault approached and jabbed a gloved finger into Kyle's chest "You reckon a shiny new shirt makes you one of us?"

"Hello, Gault."

"*Corporal* Gault, new boy. Time you showed some respect to a real Ranger."

"I am a Ranger." Kyle was not intimidated by the sneering man but he was aware of the rank on Gault's uniform and was keen not to blunder so early in his new career.

Gault laughed "Ain't been through the cadre, have you? Got here because you're friends with the new boss." He grinned, flicking a knowing eyebrow "Hope he's better than your last one, eh?"

A flash passed across Kyle's vision at the mention of the bandit camp and what might have happened next was anyone's guess but a soft voice sounded behind him.

"Take a look, gents." Lynch's voice was as unusual as the rest of his appearance, too soft and gentle for the wide staring eyes and fat lips "This 'ere is Gault. Reckons he's hot shit. Ain't bad in a scrap, are you Gaulty?"

Although he was a full head taller than the Sergeant, Gault seemed to wilt in Lynch's presence. Warily, he nodded.

"Ain't like you and me though, Frosty." Lynch's voice had dropped and Kyle got the distinct impression he was speaking only to him as though it were just the two of them, not the increasingly uncomfortable crowd of Rangers.

"Sergeant?" Kyle didn't understand.

"Look at 'is eyes. 'e's scared now. 'e's the same with the In-fect-ed." Lynch drew the word out into its component syllables "Not like you. They don't scare you, eh?"

It was something Kyle was slowly coming to realise about himself. The thought of battle did not fill him with fear like it used to. Even now, as they prepared to land in the unknown and Feral infested lands across the channel, he was filled with something approaching excitement, rather than concern. The thought of the Ferals made his hand twitch to his weapons but it was a desire to fight rather than a fear he wanted to destroy.

"No, Sergeant." Kyle met Gault's eyes, seeing the man flinch away from his gaze.

"We's predators, you and me. Not like 'im."

Abruptly, Lynch shoved past them both and swung himself up into the cabin of the Puma. Gault seized the opportunity and vanished towards another aircraft as Ross led Kyle into the cabin, showing him how to fasten the buckles of his belt.

"What was that all about?" Williamson hissed to Kyle from the next seat but Kyle could only shrug.

"Right!" Ross's voice crackled across the radio in Kyle's ear. He frantically tried to remember the brief introduction to the communication equipment but Ross continued speaking "Pin your ears back, troops! We're going across the channel and getting stuck in. Proper stuck in!"

Kyle saw heads nodding.

"All I want from you is your best. All of you know how to do your jobs, even the new ones." His eyes lingered on Kyle "Give Frosty here a pointer if he doesn't know our drills but trust me, you can rely on him. He's one of us now."

More nods.

Ross regarded the small cluster of troops for a half second, meeting their eyes before grinning "Let's do this!"

A violent cheer and fists pumping.

The rotors began to turn.

Williamson flicked onto a private channel with Kyle so they could talk "You all good, Frost?"

"Yeah." Kyle hefted his new rifle, a very similar pattern to his old US Army M4. The Glock Seventeen at his side was a familiar weight "Still can't believe we're going to France."

Williamson laughed "Blowing your mind?"

Kyle nodded with a wry grin and the man laughed again.

"Trouble with you, Frost is that you're too damn clever. The rest of us don't have to think as much as you do." He hefted his own weapon, a dull black metal general purpose machine gun with a brightly coloured belt of ammunition hanging from it "This sort of thing simplifies it. Make sure you keep it simple on the ground, yeah?"

Kyle nodded and Williamson switched back so they could hear Ross's voice over the rapidly spinning rotors but Kyle tuned him out as the aircraft began to stagger into the air. How on earth was this ever going to be simple?

CHAPTER 83

The Puma whipped across the churning waves below them, seeming to Kyle to almost skim the white crests. His seat faced outwards, back to back with the opposite side of the cabin and for the thousandth time, he checked his seat belt as the pilot banked gently to the left.

Williamson caught him doing it and laughed leaving Kyle looking sheepish. They'd been flying for an hour, taking a slow route to the coast and Kyle had stared in fascination and not a little fear as the green forest ended abruptly in white cliffs, looking as though the land had been carved by a giant cleaver. Then the sea! A great shining mass of roiling water. Kyle had seen video of the waves before but nothing had prepared him for the stench of salty air permeating the downdraught of the Puma. Then the pilot had dipped lower across the waves and he'd flinched as spray caught him. Kyle had licked a drop on his lips, grimacing at the salt taste.

"Coming up on the coast!" Ross called over the radio and Kyle leaned forward eagerly, wanting to fix in his mind the first image of the dead continent.

To his surprise, yellow sand met his eyes, lashed by breaking waves. All too quickly the Puma sped inland and the sand gave way to forest identical to that on the English coast behind them. Kyle frowned in disappointment but then Eric's voice crackled from the command aircraft.

"All callsigns, two minutes to landing. Repeat, two minutes to landing."

"Kit check!" Ross snapped and Kyle patted his magazine pouches, checking they were sealed shut. His safety catch was applied and he released the inner lock of his pistol holster, allowing for a quick draw if needed. He drew the fighting knife on his chest, checking the keen blade before returning it to the sheath.

"There!" Williamson pointed a gloved hand and Kyle leaned forward but there was no need. From their height, he could see where the forest ended and what looked like a seething grey carpet began.

Wretches.

Thousands of them.

Tens of thousands.

Kyle gaped, hefting the rifle in his hands. No-one spoke. There were no words.

"Alright, it's just a few Infected!" Ross's voice was harsh, snapping their attention away "We've got the Pumas to draw them away, they aren't our problem! Stay on the mission and remember your jobs!"

Kyle nodded, trying to ignore the awful sight. He wrapped his left arm through the strap of his daysack, preparing to swing it onto his back the moment they touched down.

"Remember, Frosty! Out, duck, and run twenty metres!"

Kyle nodded at Williamson, feeling an odd calmness take over as the helicopter slowed and the pilot began to lower them. He looked at the ground below them with interest seeing tangled brambles. He grimaced.

"Stand by, all callsigns stand by." Eric's final message came over and Kyle braced for the touchdown although they were still twenty metres in the air.

Flac-flac-flac-flac-flac

He turned, looking for the source of the odd sound but seeing nothing.

"Incoming fire!" Ross called and Kyle felt his heart race as he realised they were being shot at.

The pilot made a swift turn, moving them out of the line of fire and Kyle saw the Chateau for the first time. Rising out of the green undergrowth in a gleam of white stone, the place looked like something from a fairy tale. Kyle could well imagine knights riding out on quests or great pageants being held in the wide, central courtyard but instead he flinched at the sight of men firing rifles from the tops of the walls and then the vision was lost behind towering trees as the pilot descended rapidly.

Thump

The Puma touched down, Kyle released his seatbelt and swung the daysack onto his back, sprinting forward and racing through the ankle high undergrowth.

Rat-tat-a-tat-a-tat

Machine gun fire, louder the further he got from the Puma sounded in his ears and Kyle swore, flinging himself flat. He wriggled his arm through the second strap of the daysack, cursing as his unfamiliar gear caught and he flapped his arm, trying to get it through.

"Here!" Williamson wrenched his arm clear before bounding past him and going flat, vanishing from sight in the undergrowth.

"Target indication?" Kyle called, seeing nothing.

"To your front, Frosty. See the tanker?"

Williamson's voice crackled and Kyle rose up on his elbows, stretching to see. Ahead, a rusted metal tanker sat abandoned and decayed. From the top Kyle could see the small flash of rounds being fired. But not towards them. Instead, the machine gunner was aiming at the other aircraft as they touched down in the makeshift landing ground and Kyle had a sudden surge of fear for Amelia but Ross was bellowing at him to fire and he aimed his rifle at the tanker, pulling the trigger and smelling the stench of burning powder.

A section of Rangers was up and moving on Kyle's right, using the covering fire to close on the enemy position but as they moved, a voice shouted a warning and Kyle saw the small, dark shape lobbed over the tanker and the Rangers twisted, flinging themselves flat before the grenade exploded.

Someone screamed in agony.

"Friendly!" shouted an unmistakeable voice and Lynch

arrived beside them "Frosty, Williamson, with me!" he bellowed and without waiting for an answer he sprinted forward. Kyle staggered to his feet, ducking instinctively as another burst of fire came from behind the tanker. Lynch was keying his radio ahead, directing the other platoons to suppress the shooters by the tanker even as he sprinted towards it. Kyle stretched his stride out, remembering how fast Lynch had moved the last time he'd followed this man.

Lynch went flat and Kyle crashed to a halt behind a row of small shrubs providing scanty cover. A panting sound from behind and Williamson joined them, his machine gun held in both hands.

"Got to get closer!" Lynch pointed at the left hand side of the tanker where no gunfire had sounded but as he pointed, a face leaned around the side of the rusted cab and fired a single shot.

Kyle ducked as did Lynch but Williamson was too slow. Kyle turned, sensing the man was hit even before he heard the grunt of pain. The Ranger dropped the machine gun and went still.

"Man down!" he turned and roared before turning to the tanker, seeing the figure step back out.

Bang

Lynch fired and the figure vanished. Kyle raised his rifle but Lynch snapped at him to take Williamson's weapon. Hastily, he slung his own rifle, grabbing the gun.

The blue eyed Sergeant turned his terrible gaze on Kyle "Ready?"

Kyle nodded and Lynch lurched to his feet. Kyle sprinted forward, the gun barrel focussed as tightly as it could be on the cab. No movement showed and he heard the gunfire from the Rangers slow as they approached.

Kyle reached the tanker before Lynch and made to move around but a gloved hand caught his shoulder and Lynch held up two silent fingers as the awful blue eyed stare held Kyle's for a moment and then he counted down and the two men erupted around the side of the trailer, Kyle moving wider with the machine gun held in his shoulder.

There were four men behind the tanker. Dressed in the odd camouflage of the French Army, they were taking it in turns to lean around and fire at the Rangers. Even as Kyle watched, one of them was throwing a grenade which left his hand before he ducked back into cover.

Kyle and Lynch fired at almost the exact same moment. The man in Kyle's sights twitched and bucked appallingly as Kyle killed him and then he fell forward, lying still without ever looking back at Rangers. Lynch killed another who managed to twist around as the bullets took him and he dropped, falling across the two others, knocking one down and blocking Lynch's next shots so suddenly there were two of the Frenchmen and two Rangers and Kyle was filled with a sudden, primal need to kill the men before him before they could react and kill him.

One of them turned and let out a savage roar and ran forward, closing the short distance. Kyle fired, but missed and he heard Lynch return the war cry but then the man was on top of him and he could see nothing but the snarling face of his enemy.

The Frenchman gripped the machine gun barrel and tugged. The weight of the weapon was already extreme and Kyle simply let go. His enemy overbalanced and Kyle tore the fighting knife from its sheath and swung it in a vicious overhand plunge.

The Frenchman blocked it with a bent wrist and sent a tight blow with his left hand towards Kyle's throat. Kyle dropped his chin and twisted his hips, driving his own left hand across his body to block the blow and it glanced off his chin, hurting, but doing little damage. The Frenchman grabbed his knife hand, trying crush the blade from his grip and Kyle snarled, kicking out and ramming the hard toe of his boot down the other man's shin. The Frenchman grimaced in pain and for the briefest moment as their eyes met Kyle was struck by the absurdity of the scenario. Twenty years of blood, Infection, and death and here they were, not celebrating the survival of their species against all the odds but instead locked in a primal battle to the death.

Then his opponent backhanded him across the face and the moment was gone. Kyle roared in fury and wrenched his knife hand free of the man's grasp. He saw the soldier's eyes widen in fear but then he twisted a short chopping blow and the blade bit deeply into the soft skin of the Frenchman's neck. He fell backwards but he had a grip on Kyle who found himself landing atop his enemy, snarling, and twisting to free himself. He wrenched the knife free in a spray of gore and slammed it down, again and again into the Frenchman's throat, roaring his fury and hatred but then Lynch was there unceremoniously kicking his hand aside and shoving him off the dead man.

"He's had it."

Kyle lay on his side, chest heaving as he stared at Lynch who was crouching by the body, seeming to admire it. Kyle pushed himself up to one knee, staring aghast at the red gore that spattered his hand up to the elbow. He heard a strange sound like a tree creaking in a strong wind and looked up to see Lynch, his expression its usual bared teeth and wide eyes but now with the creak emitting from his mouth as he laughed.

"You a fuckin' savage, Frost." he reached out and clapped Kyle on the shoulder.

Then there were voices of command and the rest of the Rangers were closing in. Kyle felt the stares of the experienced soldiers and saw the approving nods they gave. Ross gave him a thump on the shoulder and bade him collect the machine gun which Kyle did.

"Medic!"

The dreaded cry brought any grisly celebration to an end and Kyle followed Lynch around the tanker. Already, Amelia was crouching by the prone figure and Kyle raced to see if he could help.

She shot him a fearful glance, taking in his gore soaked

figure but he shook his head "Not my blood."

She turned back, tightening a tourniquet as Lynch came in beside them, glancing at the casualty who was bleeding profusely.

"The grenade." Amelia explained as the mixed force of Rangers and Zeks began to form a perimeter around them "I can patch him up but he needs to be extracted." She stared around and Lynch grabbed his radio, summoning a medivac helicopter.

"We're nearly there." Kyle murmured, wondering a second later why he'd said that. She knew where they were.

"Kilo one-two, *not* kilo one-three." Lynch was arguing with a voice on the other end of the radio. He listened for a second "You come down 'ere like that and I'll slot you. Kilo one-two."

Eric knelt next to them, looking expectantly at Amelia "T One." She nodded and he glanced at Lynch, happy the Sergeant was summoning help.

"Frost?"

Ross's voice. Kyle turned to see the Sergeant and the other troops from their Puma.

"You got Williamsons jimpy?"

Kyle hefted the machine gun.

"You're keeping it."

Kyle stared, looking past the Ranger to where two figures were carrying a stretcher slowly towards their position. That pace could only mean one thing and he felt his head spin at the man's death.

"Sergeant?" Eric called to Ross who knelt beside his commander "It's just beyond these trees. We'll need the breaching –"

That was as far as Eric got. The sharp crack of the rifle sounded long after the Colonel had pitched forward. Kyle went flat, dragging Amelia down with him as Lynch raised his rifle and fired a long burst in the direction of the white walls.

"Man down!" Kyle shouted, crawling to Eric who was groaning in agony.

"Where's he hit?" Amelia shouted, joining him.

"Thigh!"

"Tourniquet!"

Kyle wrapped the black strap around the man and wrenched it tight, screwing the pressure on as Eric clamped his jaws over the pain.

"Hit it!" Lynch shouted and Kyle heard a thump and a hiss as a mortar began firing and then the first big explosion blotted out the sight of the walls and the deafening sound of the evac Puma sounded, beginning a rapid descent. Kyle could see figures leaning out of the cabin, watching and he helped Amelia roll Eric onto a stretcher, ready to lift him into the cabin. He shook his head at the bad luck of the injury.

"Go!" the Puma touched down and they ran through the downdraught, hefting the injured Zek onto the cold metal floor where the crew pulled him inside, a medic already attaching an IV. Kyle was vaguely aware of a figure exiting the cabin on the other side but then he was ducking, running with Amelia out of the rotor wash as the Puma climbed, turned, and was gone.

Taking Eric with it.

"What now?" he turned to her but she had gone pale beneath her dark skin and he turned to see what she was staring at, realising who the figure he'd seen exiting the chopper was and why Lynch had requested the specific callsign.

Major Armstrong grinned back at Kyle as though this were a fine game to be playing.

CHAPTER 84

There was no time to ask how the Ranger was here, no space to pause and rationalise the chaos. Instead, Armstrong slipped into the role Eric had vacated, assuming command.

"Move forward! Close in, use cover! Keep those mortars firing!"

There was the faintest hesitation. The Rangers looked from Armstrong to Lynch, the Zeks stared at Amelia but then the *zip* of rounds passing close by returned everyone to the reality of their predicament and suddenly politics were thrown aside as the basic needs of survival became paramount.

"Come on!" Kyle grabbed Amelia by the arm and they sprinted forward, edging along the tanker to see the white walls of the ancient Chateau. Rising between them and their target were what had once been a row of neat trees but was now a thick growth of shabby trunks, one or two fallen and rotting. Kyle immediately saw the passage the French had cut through to access the car park they'd landed in and already a small mixed group of Zeks and Rangers were bounding towards it as the mortars behind them lobbed explosives over their heads.

Zip

"Bloody hell!" Kyle snatched his head back as a series of high calibre rounds passed through the air. He glanced at Amelia "Stay low."

She nodded and they broke cover, uniformed bodies moving around them, hardly bothering with any pretence at tactical formation. This was just a mad dash to close in with the enemy and get themselves out of the killing zone.

"There!"

A natural rise in the ground topped by trees offered cover and Kyle slammed hard into it, keeping his head low as Amelia crashed down next to him. A thump and a muttered curse announced Ross with a trio of Rangers who included Hannah.

"The gate is just ahead." Ross was pointing and Kyle risked raising his head, ducking back down immediately.

"At the end of the wall?" Kyle analysed the split second image in his memory.

"Yeah." Ross rolled over and tapped another Ranger "You got the charges?"

A nod but then Ross raised his head and rifle rounds tore the ground above them and Kyle went flat, small flecks of mud and grass landing on his face as Ross cursed.

"How are we going to get close?"

"Boss'll have to call the Pumas. A couple of missiles should do it – oh!"

Everyone stared, risking poking their heads above their makeshift parapet as the now familiar sound of aircraft engines sounded.

"That's not one of ours!" Hannah shouted as the mortar fire stopped for a moment. Over to their right, Kyle could hear Armstrong's voice shouting orders. The attack seemed to have stalled.

"On the roof!" he called and pointed to the crenelated battlements of a squat, square tower that rose just above the ramparts. A cluster of figures, too far away to see properly were huddled.

"Anyone got a shot?" Hannah called but no-one was risking exposing themselves. She cursed but the noise of the helicopter was growing louder and Kyle rolled onto his back, seeing two of the Pumas were now approaching at a rapid rate, clearly on an attacking run.

BOOM

He flinched, then ground his teeth as the same noise that had blasted him backwards in the darkness atop Holden's wall sounded and a jet of fire leapt up from the gates to the Chateau.

Unbidden, an image of these same aircraft destroying his home flashed in his mind and a moment of disbelief gripped him as he tried to rationalise how he was lying here in France in the uniform of his enemy.

"Everyone up!" Armstrong was yelling and he had stood to lead the charge "The Horde is closing in, we have no more time!"

Again, tactics were hopeless. Kyle fired the machine gun he'd inherited from Williamson in short, angry bursts at the top of the brilliantly white wall with its ancient bricks and every other soldier there echoed the noise, hundreds of rounds impacting the stone in a desperate bid to keep the defender's heads down long enough for the Rangers and Zeks to cross the open ground.

"Right! Push right!" Ross had kept his head and was directing them, moving them diagonally across the open ground to the gate around which a fierce fire was burning. Kyle bared his teeth as the heat reached them but a gust of wind blew black smoke in his face and he choked, before seeing an opening the missiles of the Pumas had blasted, the twisted remnants of the chateau gate lying between fire blackened walls.

And then the first men were through, Rangers and Zeks breaking past the cover of the walls and the professionalism of the soldiers became apparent because Kyle could see them firing short, disciplined bursts back up at the walls they had breached and now there were bodies, falling from the ramparts and someone was screaming an awful cry.

"Medic!"

Amelia was gone, sprinting to help the wounded but now there was open ground before Kyle leading up to the ancient walls of the fortification and he was sprinting forwards, seeing movement, and knowing that to stay still was to be shot.

"Here we go!" Hannah was beside him, a cluster of unfamiliar faces around her and the soldiers were firing as they ran, shattering the glass in the windows and then they were up a short flight of stone steps and Kyle slammed against the side of the building as Ross pushed him back, stacking Rangers and Zeks into a tight group and then the door was open and they vanished inside.

"Stay here!" Hannah snapped at Kyle and he nodded, understanding that he was not trained for this and would risk lives by breaking formations. Instead, he slammed a new belt into the machine gun, training it around the circular walls but the defenders were dead and Armstrong was closing in on the door, directing men to cover the damaged gates and was that a Puma overhead?

"Kyle!" Amelia was pointing, shouting and Kyle could not see the top of the tower where she was indicating but he stepped back, stumbling on the stone steps and craning his neck to see a helicopter, distinctly not one of the Pumas but a blue, civilian aircraft hovering above the building and a trio of men, ragged and dressed in civilian clothes were being forced in at gunpoint...

BOOM

This time the explosion was outside the walls and Kyle whirled around to see a Puma flying past, the gunners firing their weapons in mad bursts at something outside the walls and he realised with a gasp of horror that the vast Horde he'd seen from the air had reached them.

"Amelia! Inside! Get inside!"

She was crouching by a casualty, one of the Rangers was bleeding and Amelia was covered in red gore. She ignored Kyle and he swore, running towards her even as Hannah Mitchell appeared at the door, yelling for them to come in.

"Come on!" he reached her, grabbing her and hauling her roughly to her feet.

"I can help him!" she snarled but the smoke at the shattered gate had parted and Kyle could see the first grey skinned figures running – no, *sprinting* – towards them and he ignored her protests, hauling her away from the dying man and towards the doors where Hannah was gesticulating wildly and

Lynch was shoving the last of his men into the shelter of the fortified building.

"Come on!" Hannah roared and Kyle flung Amelia before him, flinching as she fell on hard flagstones but Hannah had slammed the door behind them and Lynch was roaring at his men to move forward, pushing them through a set of vast double doors and Kyle stared around at a vast and ornate atrium as the unmistakable howl of Wretches came from outside.

"All in, Sergeant!" Hannah snapped formally at Lynch but there was no response. Kyle turned in confusion, adrenaline making his movements twitchy and he saw Hannah standing with her back to the door staring at Lynch who had his rifle in his shoulder, the awful, wide eyed stare locked on Hannah.

"Traitor."

BANG

The rifle shot sounded impossibly loud in the echoing space and Kyle flinched, staring in disbelief as Hannah was flung back against the doors, gore erupting from the terrible wound Lynch's bullet had torn in her neck.

Amelia had got to her feet from where she'd stumbled, her own pistol now in her hand and she made to run towards Hannah, her instinct to help overriding her self-preservation for the briefest moment and Lynch's awful blue stare locked on her and there was a second, a long, drawn out second in which Kyle *knew* that Armstrong's Devil was considering his options, making the choice and then his fat lips twitched and he fired and Amelia fell.

Rat-tat-a-tat-a-tat-a-ta –

The machine gun jammed and Kyle flung it away, ripping the Glock from the unfamiliar holster but he'd forgotten to press the release and the weapon caught and Lynch was sprinting away, moving further into the building and Amelia hadn't moved and Kyle abandoned the blue eyed Sergeant and ran to her side, rolling her over, shouting her name, screaming it, shaking her, begging, pleading and crying but his protests were as futile as any mere words in the face of stark reality because Amelia did not hear him, could not respond and the dark eyes stared sightlessly up at the ornate ceiling above.

CHAPTER 85

What did it matter that his own name was being yelled in his headset? Who cared that the Ferals were smashing at the door, making Hannah's bloodless features jump and bounce with every pounding blow? The Horde had come to wipe any trace of Kyle Frost from the earth, to tear flesh, rend bone and obliterate the naïve young man who'd dared to believe that he could play at being a Warrior. He welcomed his fate, wished with all his might that this tide of grey skinned death would wash over him and bathe the entire world in its majestic slaughter because how else could life continue when Amelia Singh lay dead on the floor before him? Her eyes were wide with fear and a messy puddle of grey matter lay beneath her, staining his hands as he tried to lift her, to kiss her face and tell her he would help her.

Kyle

He heard her voice and it spurred him into action. He laid her head down, drawing his knife and slicing through the cotton of her shirt, placing his hands one atop the other over her chest and leaning down hard.

One, two, three, four...

Her eyes stared up. She did not move.

"Come on!" Kyle roared, leaning to press his lips to hers, blowing air into her lungs, giving his own life force to bolster hers, pressing those features he'd kissed and loved in the sanctuary of Arthur Colley's farm...

"Frost!"

Hands were grabbing him and he snatched up the knife, slashing at them and then slammed his hands back down onto her chest, willing her heart to beat.

One, two, three...

"Bring him!"

"Get the fuck off me!"

"FROST!" it was Ross with one of the Zeks. Kyle raved at them but they ignored him, dragging him backwards by his arms and he cried out as Amelia moved further and further away. He thrashed and struggled and threatened but Ross swung his fist, crashing into Kyle's jaw and his vision dulled for a moment.

The door crashed down crushing Hannah's body under its weight and the Wretches burst through. Kyle wrestled his arm free of the Zek who dropped him and gripped his body armour instead, tugging him backwards as Kyle finally managed to draw the Glock from the holster, emptying the pistol into the tide of grey death that surged at him.

A pebble thrown into a breaking wave.

"Come on! Upstairs!" Ross seemed to care keenly whether they lived or died. Kyle wanted to tell him there was no need but his head was bumping on the cold steps as he was dragged upwards and he couldn't frame the words in his mouth.

Surely they needed to go back to Amelia? Someone, Dr May perhaps could patch the wound in her head and give her a blood transfusion and...

He couldn't see her anymore. The Wretches had covered her, trampling her face with their cold feet and he yelled out, lunging back towards them but Ross didn't understand and he bawled at Kyle to keep firing.

Who cared what Ross thought?

He was aware that they'd stopped moving. He was still on his back and there were other figures around them. Bodies lay on the ground, French soldiers who'd met the ferocity of the Rangers and died. Armstrong was shouting orders somewhere, telling them to get to the roof and Kyle remembered the civilians climbing into the helicopter. Surely that was his Father? He had to tell Amelia! He lurched to his feet but Ross was shoving him backwards, snarling in his face and Kyle tried to get around him but Rangers were bullying him backwards, blocking him with their bodies and forcing him up a narrow, twisting staircase as Ross shouted in his face.

"Frost – Frost! Listen to me – she's gone. She's dead!"

Look after me, Kyle

"I need to go back –"

"No! We need you here – we need you, Frost! We need you to fight or we're all going to fucking die! There's a Horde down there – a Feral Horde! You understand me? She's gone!"

"Where's she gone?"

Was it a joke? Was he trying to be funny? Kyle wasn't sure. He didn't remember deciding to speak the words but they came from his mouth anyway and he grinned at Ross, seeing the fear on the Ranger's face and hearing his tone lower as they climbed.

"She – she's dead, mate. She's dead."

A single word seemed suddenly very important to Kyle, a name that held all the meaning in the world. It sat in his mouth with a bad taste and he abruptly jerked forward, vomit spewing forth. He stared at the bile, unseeing. His eyes landed on the Glock, still in his hand. As though in a dream, he began to reload the weapon.

"That's it, Frost!" Ross encouraged "Here, take my spare mags." He shoved pistol magazines into one of Kyle's pouches.

"Here they come!" someone was yelling and Kyle saw the Ferals burst around the bottom of the staircase and the Rangers unleashed a storm of death, appallingly loud in the confined space and the Ferals sprawled, black gore spattering the pristine white walls of the Chateau.

Kyle did not fire. He did not even register the Ferals. Instead, he turned to face the stairs, moving upwards now faster and faster.

At the top, he stumbled over a pair of French soldiers who lay in their own blood and he wondered vaguely why they had been waiting here but a moment later there was a soft *bing* and a pair of double doors slid open.

A lift.

They piled inside, crammed into the confined space as Kyle's jaw worked trying to frame the word.

"Stay with us, Frosty!" Ross called, shooting him a concerned glance.

The lift arrived and they hastened up another short flight of stairs, emerging onto the roof of the Chateau in a shock of daylight.

A voice was yelling orders, screaming to be heard over the din of a Puma that hovered a few metres away, the edge of the cabin level with the ornate crenelations. The wounded were being carried over to the side of the building as the pilot lowered the aircraft and Kyle nodded as he saw stretchers being passed aboard. The voice was still bellowing orders and Kyle frowned, the word becoming more conspicuous in his mouth. He wondered if he was going to vomit again.

The roar of the Puma took his attention as the aircraft pulled away, climbing into the sky. A second Puma was there, this one taking the healthy soldiers. Ross tried to pull Kyle across but he shook the man off, shoving him away. Someone had barricaded the door and now turned, running to board the chopper. Kyle could see Ross was already aboard and was gesturing but the cabin was full and there was no room for him.

The Puma left.

The voice was shouting again as a third Puma swooped down and Kyle saw Armstrong, his entire right side covered in blood shoving the last of his troops onto it. A Zek, the same man who'd barricaded the door, climbed aboard and gestured to Kyle but something had happened to the word and it was no longer just a bad taste in his mouth. Now it was an awful, burning pain in his chest, as bad as the bullet that had struck him down, worse than the bandit's lash because the word was *Lynch* and as the helicopter hovered Kyle realised that the terrible blue eyed devil had taken Amelia from him and he was going to get away.

The funk that had gripped his mind vanished and Kyle raised the Glock in the two handed grip that Sinks had taught him a lifetime ago. He roared the word, bellowed Lynch's name across the rooftop and saw Armstrong's gaze land on him, his eyes narrow and a savage smirk spread across his face.

With a crash, the door to the roof burst open and Kyle whirled around with the pistol, expecting that the Ferals had found them but instead, the bloody and ragged remnants of the French garrison spilled onto the roof, as surprised to see the Rangers and Zeks as the latter were to see them. There was a pregnant moment and then the Zek, crouching in the cabin of the Puma, opened fire.

Next second, Kyle was firing too, gunning down the soldiers before him as they shouted and twisted to bring their weapons to bear. None of them managed. They fell to the roof and lay still.

Something rolled gently away across the roof down the slight slope the builders had left to drain rainwater into the gutters.

BOOM

The grenade detonated a metre away from the Puma. The ornate parapet did nothing to protect the aircraft. As the smoke rose, Kyle saw the Zek had been flung back into the cabin, his torso a bloody mess but the shrapnel had passed higher, striking the rotors of the helicopter and it lurched sickeningly, tilting away from the building. The pilot tried to compensate but as the helicopter rocked back towards the building, it struck the white stone parapet, lost power and plunged down out of sight.

There was a faint *whuff* as something exploded but it was different to the concussions of the grenades. Kyle flinched back as a wall of heat shot up the side of the tower, black smoke washing over the rooftop from the roaring inferno that was the Puma.

"Frost!" came a terrible cry and Kyle saw Armstrong emerge

from the smoke. He looked barely alive. His weapons were gone, as was his helmet and blood covered the right side of his head where the blast had burned his scalp. He staggered, his eyes fixed on Kyle and there was movement behind him as Lynch emerged from the smoke to catch the Major under the arm.

Kyle raised the pistol. Too late, he realised that the magazine was empty and as he fumbled for one of the spares that Ross had shoved in his pouches, Lynch shot him.

The bullet took him in the chest, flattening itself against the ceramic plate of his body armour. The protection saved his life but the sheer force of the bullet was not lessened and Kyle hit the ground, old pains burning through him as he fought like a demon to suck in even a tiny scrap of air.

"Fuck you, Frost!" Armstrong was screaming and the two Rangers had closed in "You and your fucking Father!" there were tears in Armstrong's eyes as he spoke "You were my safety net! You! In that shit-hole town for all these fucking years! I knew if I had you then I could make that lab-coated idiot do what I ordered! And instead, look what happened!" he gestured wildly around as Kyle choked and gasped. He could barely understand Armstrong but the Major didn't seem to care.

"We thought this was going to be it! We'd have a cure! Stop all this bloody madness..." Armstrong was leaning heavily on Lynch, his entire side soaked with blood. Kyle wondered if the man was dying "Instead, your bastard Dad had to release the mutation! Look at the mess he's made!"

As if in response, the cry of a Feral rose above the crackling roar of the burning helicopter and Kyle's eyes turned to the now open door that led onto the roof.

"We had it all worked out! You in Holden, the Zeks to distract everyone and no-one would have seen what we were achieving! But you had to fuck it all up, didn't you! Stopped us from killing that bitch, Singh! Stopped us getting her from those bandits but now we've got her!" Armstrong showed his teeth in an animalistic snarl of victory.

Kyle spluttered but found some air to speak "Where's my Father?"

"Gone!" Armstrong spat the word at Kyle "Flew away like a coward! Those bastards in London must have warned him I was coming to clear his mess up..." Armstrong's head lolled then snapped upright "I should've known he'd run! Should've just grabbed you years ago instead of having Sinclair watch you all that time..."

"Sinks?" Kyle felt ice run through his veins.

"Hah!" Armstrong tried to laugh but he didn't have the strength. Lynch hoisted him more upright "Sinclair was watching you every minute of every day! Sending me reports..." Armstrong spat blood onto the roof. Lynch was looking up at the sky for something but Kyle couldn't see what. Blood was dripping steadily from the Major and Kyle wondered how much longer the man had left.

"May-juh." Lynch warned and Kyle heard the distinctive sound of the final Puma's rotors as it swept towards them. It was moving slowly, the pilot no doubt watching the plume of smoke of the other aircraft warily.

"The thing is, Frost." Armstrong seemed to hitch himself upright as though the sound of the helicopter was an injection of hope "You're just like us!" he smiled "You're a natural born killer - a savage! But you control yourself, you reign it in until you need it and that's what this was all about. The strong leading the weak!"

Kyle didn't understand what Armstrong was trying to say, the man seemed delirious and was rambling but he didn't care. He could see the Glock beside him, still linked to him with the retention bungee. He tried to reach it but his hand seemed to weigh a thousand tonnes. Lynch was looking at the approaching helicopter and didn't try to stop Kyle.

Armstrong had seen though and he shook his head "What? What makes you want to kill me so badly?"

Kyle showed his teeth "Amelia!"

Armstrong looked confused "What? Oh. The Singh woman?

You fell for that?" he shook his head "You poor little idiot. You think you were the first one to fall for her? She was a liar, Frost, a politician who did whatever it took to get her own way." he chuckled ruefully as the rotor sound grew louder "I'm sorry she got to you before I did. You'd have made a wonderful Ranger."

The Puma drew close, the hot stink of the exhaust fumes overwhelming them and the noise overpowering the sound of the crackling flames. Lynch hauled Armstrong towards the aircraft as a Ranger inside the cabin reached down to help the Major.

"This was always bigger than you and I, Frost!" Armstrong bellowed, one hand on the chopper "Bigger than men like you and I could ever imagine!" for a moment, he looked scared and Kyle wondered what on earth it was that could frighten such a man.

He never found out. The hard polymer of the Glock touched his hand and Kyle snatched the pistol up, rolling to one knee and firing at Armstrong. He saw the first bullet strike sparks off the Puma and then one found its mark, biting into Armstrong's flesh.

A snarl close at hand and Lynch was there, a heavy boot kicking Kyle back to the ground and the terrible, blue eyed stare was fixed on Kyle and he knew that Amelia's death would go unavenged, that Lynch would kill him and then the roar of the Feral sounded and Lynch turned to see the cluster of grey skinned, black eyed beasts erupt from the shattered remnants of the door onto the roof.

The next few moments blurred for Kyle. He was aware of shooting, firing the Glock shot after shot at the Ferals, watching their black blood spray into the air. Lynch turned and grabbed Armstrong who had collapsed on the roof, one arm outstretched towards the Puma. The Ranger in the cabin raised his rifle and fired at the closest Ferals, chopping them down but he was too slow and Kyle watched as a grey skinned monster still wearing the remnants of a French soldier's uniform passed Lynch who fired and missed, fired and missed and the Feral leapt at the dying form of Armstrong who had staggered to his knees and then their momentum carried them onwards as the two of them, arms interlocked, fell over the edge of the building.

There was a moment where they hung in plain sight and Kyle could see the snarl of fury on Armstrong's face and then they were gone, plummeting down to the burning wreckage of the Puma, a dozen floors below.

Lynch ran to the edge as the Ranger in the Puma, oblivious to Armstrong's fate fired short bursts, nailing the Ferals that dared to venture onto the roof.

"May-juh!" Lynch was shouting, staring down, his head turning left and right as he searched for some sign of the fallen body "May-juh Armstrong!" and Kyle heard something he'd never heard in the man's voice, an emotion he wouldn't have thought Lynch capable of.

Fear.

He bared his teeth, lined Amelia's killer up in the pistol sights but an animalistic snarl to his left revealed a Feral coming to tear his flesh and he had to pivot, to waste the bullet meant for Lynch on this innocent Wretch. Lynch saw Kyle turn and made his decision. Without taking a run up, he bent his squat legs and leapt through the air, landing with his torso half in the Puma cabin. Kyle wished with all his might that the man would fall to join his master in death but Lynch was safe and Kyle could not fire from this angle. He turned as the Puma began to circle away and Kyle saw that terrible blue-eyed stare, the too wide mouth and the yellow teeth fixed on him and then the pilot completed his turn and Lynch was gone.

Kyle turned to greet the mass of Ferals that erupted from the door. He dropped the magazine from the Glock, discarding it on the debris strewn floor and calmly replaced it with another. Lynch was gone and Amelia would have no justice. Instead, it was just him, no Sinks, no Rosie, no dogs, and no help.

The Ferals were pouring through the door now, some screaming their terrible cry, others silently running towards the bloody, shattered remnant of a man that squared his feet and leaned slightly forward from the hips. Kyle's chest seared with pain where Lynch's bullet had struck him but the trivial needs of the flesh seemed a world away. Only one thing seemed important to Kyle and that was to fire and to kill.

Bang

Bang

Bang

Click

Kyle dropped the magazine and replaced it. He heard noise from behind him and pivoted to see Ferals clambering over the lip of the building. He didn't pause, pivoting on both feet to see three more Ferals behind him.

Bang-bang-bang

"Come on!" he roared as something in the burning wreckage of the helicopter exploded. Smoke was flung into his face. He coughed, then roared in anger, furious at the weakness of his body.

Bang

Bang

"Come and die!" Kyle roared at the Ferals and they did. Mindlessly, thoughtlessly, unable to comprehend the snarling beast encased in human flesh before them, they ran at him. Some leapt for him, some tried to roll and grab his legs. More yet sidestepped and tried to flank him.

All died.

"Come on!" Kyle shot one between the eyes, feeling the magazine empty. He ejected it, missing it with his left hand and dropping it to the ground. He slapped the next in, releasing the slide and slamming his left palm forward, twisting his hips and stopping a Feral dead in its tracks.

Bang

The monster fell backward, tripping one of its fellows who paused long enough for Kyle to shoot it, pressing the barrel against the grey skin of its forehead.

Behind the beast, empty space. But the Ferals clambering

over the lip of the building were coming faster than before. Some had crushed limbs and dragged themselves and Kyle realised they were scrambling over each other up the side of the Chateau and he remembered the endless sea of grey flesh that they'd flown over.

"Come on!" he roared again.

BOOM

The ammunition on the burning Puma must have exploded. The blast slammed Kyle into the ground, crashing his helmet against the hard surface. Pain lanced through his skull but he staggered back upright. Dimly, he was aware that his whole right side was burning with pain, covered in blood which was dripping onto the ground. It didn't seem to matter.

The Ferals had paused.

Not stopped, not left. They'd paused.

They were looking at him.

Black eyes stared into blue. Kyle's mouth hung open as he sucked in breaths, the last he'd ever take. The moment stretched, an eternity of time, an impossible delay as he looked into the eyes of the monsters. Why had they stopped? Was it the pile of their dead fellows that surrounded Kyle on all sides? Was it the explosion? Or had the blow to his head robbed him of his sense?

Kyle snarled in disgust. He looked at the pistol in his hand, knowing that it was empty. He'd shot his last magazine. Did the Ferals know that? Could they tell that the man before them was dead? Well, he wasn't done yet and with a grimace, he abandoned the pistol and pulled the fighting knife from its sheath.

"Alright then." he muttered, an acceptance of fate.

The nearest Feral twitched, then another.

Kyle raised the knife to his temple, his empty left hand mirroring the right in a clenched fist, preparing to drive the blade down into the rotted skull of the first to reach him. He snarled, an animalistic sound of pure hatred and venom, inviting them to the knife.

"Come and die with me."
The blade slammed down as the grey wave broke over Kyle.

CHAPTER 86

Acrid smoke mixed with sea spray filled the air in the camp. Four towering walls stood in a strict square shape atop the sloping sands that led down to the waves. Thousands of men and women, most in military uniform and some in civilian garb jostled and filed along the metal road surface the engineers had laid. In contrast to the security of the fortification, the great double gates on both sides of the square stood wide open allowing the constant stream of soldiers and equipment to head for the distant sounds of war.

Patrolling overhead like a great swollen eye was an airship, a true relic of a bygone era. Sporadically, a rifle would crack from the drab painted gondola and nervous eyes would flicker to the gates, hearts racing at the thought of the Wretch the sharpshooters had just gunned down.

Officially, the camp was designated Boulogne Amphibious Staging Post or BASP for short but even the newest arrival knew it by the common name 'Camp Seaside'. On the sandy shore, small landing craft braved the breaking waves to offload the stream of traffic to and from the dark grey shapes of larger ships out in the channel, the same vessels that had carried this invasion force to the dead continent.

The clatter of a helicopter still drew a curious look from the new arrivals, all of whom had heard the rumours of Major Armstrong's death. Sceptics dismissed the news as hearsay but the newfound synergy between the elite Rangers and their Regular Army counterparts was evidence of the wind of change that had swept through their ranks.

Still, confidence was rare in Camp Seaside as the towering column of black smoke on the horizon illustrated the distant sound of artillery and rifle fire. The sight of filled body bags passing back against the tide of soldiers gave credence to the warnings the Officers and Sergeants drilled into their troops. Stay in formation, wait for the helicopters, don't waste your ammunition.

As the troops covered the miles to the front line the sounds of the Pumas clattering rotor blades reached their ears and soon, they could see the aircraft hovering above the great mass of Ferals as the soldiers on the ground fired volley after volley into the massed ranks of the enemy. Futile hands reached for the warm flesh inside the cold metal but the skilled pilots kept their craft out of reach, staying low enough to distract their enemy as brave Rangers leaned out of the cabin, firing calmly into the hellscape below them.

The tactics were working but from the glass cockpit of a second airship, hanging over the battlefield the commanders could see the endless swathe of the Infected and their faces were grim, constant reports being sent back to London expressing the futility of their presence here. They trusted their men and praised their actions but every soldier in France knew they needed an edge, some new tactic to destroy the innumerable enemy.

Dogs howled in Camp Seaside.

"Hush." Rosie chided the scarred brute that had lifted its voice into the smoky air. The dog complied but continued to whine as the latest procession of body bags passed them by.

"Eight." Sinks observed from beside her "That's the third lot we've seen in an hour."

"Day isn't done yet."

"No." Sinks grimaced "Are you ready yet?"

Rosie nodded and clicked her tongue for the half dozen dogs she'd 'borrowed' from the survivors of Holden. The rest had stayed in England and Eric, when he'd asked Rosie to cross the channel had tried to protest but she had flatly refused to go without Sinks or the dogs and Eric had been too weak to argue.

"Get to the Chateau and find what's there. This could be the

answer to everything."

Rosie closed her eyes briefly at the memory of Eric's words. She shook her head slightly, finding herself once again fiercely denying that Kyle was dead. But the Rangers that had escaped the Chateau had seen the building overrun, swearing that no-one could have survived the Horde.

"Come on. We need to link up with the second battalion." Sinks was trying to distract her, to get her to focus on the mission and Rosie nodded miserably, following him towards the camp exit where they forked off from the main column of troops. A mile of muddy ground followed, the dogs picking their way through with their tails low as they shot poisonous looks at Rosie for making them wade through the muck. Small clusters of troops moved in patrol formation and one of them, led by an Officer stopped Sinks, directing them towards a tall woodblock nearby.

"What did he say?" Rosie jogged to catch up, grateful to be out of the mud.

"Second are camped in that woodblock. They haven't cleared the Chateau yet."

Rosie nodded, grateful that Eric's orders seemed to have preceded them. They approached the trees, seeing the uniforms of the sentries who beckoned a Ranger Officer to meet them.

The Lieutenant was named Fortis and he didn't seem to care that his mission had been delayed for a civilian and an ageing Private. He warned them that the Horde had indeed moved on but the area was far from safe.

"Lynch's report said they had to get into the building and extract from the roof. We lost a Puma up there and there's half a dozen dead Rangers including the Major." Fortis led them under the trees where a platoon of Rangers were waiting, looking tense.

"Are we going in by air?" Sinks asked but Fortis shook his head.

"No. As quietly as possible. We know there's a entrance on

the southern wall so we infill through there. Plan is to get into the main building and onto the roof. We gather as many bodies as we can and *then* we extract by air." Fortis looked at the dogs "Can they stay quiet? Have they ever been in a Puma?"

"They'll be fine."

"Good."

An hour later they were moving quietly along the small rise that, unknown to Rosie, Kyle had crouched behind as he prepared to storm the Chateau. Ahead, the white walls loomed and a faint pall of smoke still hung in the air.

"Here we go!" Fortis made a series of complex hand signals and four of the Rangers led the way to the breech. Here, the first of the Wretch corpses lay, their grey flesh at odds with the green grass their blood had stained. The dogs pressed close to Rosie and she swallowed grimly, stepping carefully through the gates into the courtyard.

Pale skinned corpses lay here and the Rangers loaded their own dead onto makeshift stretchers, laying them in a neat row and covering their faces as they cleared the yard of threats. A small group warily approached the base of the tower, peering into the ruins of the crashed Puma. Two of the occupants had been thrown clear and their bodies were easier to recover but the pilots were unrecognisable and had to be carefully placed in a heavy body bag, piece by piece.

"Any sign of the Major?"

Heads shook. But they weren't finished yet.

Rosie could see the once ornate doorway to the main building had been torn from its hinges. Kyle had admired the fairy tale quality of the Chateau when he had stood here but now, blackened by soot and battle it looked to Rosie no different than any Pre-Fall building, ruined and dead.

She could see edge of the tower had been gutted by the flames and exploding ammunition and she wondered if the whole thing was at risk of collapsing. Fortis seemed not to care because he continued.

Inside, brass bullet casings crunched underfoot and the first fresh blood was spilled as a pair of Ferals, rendered immobile by gunshot wounds to their legs snapped at the Rangers. Both were dispatched with blades, the soldiers doing their best to stay silent.

"Oh..." Rosie's hand covered her mouth and she knelt beside a figure that lay on its back, the dried blood beneath her flaking. Tears filled Rosie's eyes, not so much for the dead woman but for Kyle. Her emotions at seeing him with Amelia Singh had been tempestuous but ultimately, she'd been glad to see her friend happy. Now, the jealousy she'd felt left her feeling sick and unclean as she looked on the terrible sight of Amelia's dead face.

A sound behind made her turn to see Sinks kneeling with one hand on Hannah Mitchell's chest. He caught Rosie's eye "Shot."

"Maybe they were Infected?"

He indicated their eyes silently, both pairs wide and staring but lacking the ragged irises of a Wretch and shook his head.

Rosie moved aside as two Rangers placed the bodies on stretchers, covering their faces like the others.

The horror continued up the staircase. The Rangers moved slowly and carefully, clearing each room and corridor methodically, lighting the way with electric torches and stepping awkwardly around the dead Wretches.

They reached a corridor and the Ranger teams split in halves, one moving past a closed lift shaft and the other down a long corridor that ended in a heavy closed door. Curiosity drew Rosie and Sinks after them, the dogs' claws clicking on the hard floor.

'WARNING BIOHAZARD'

The words were stencilled on a machine-printed sign, so at odds with the white stone and gilded décor of the Chateau that suspicion was immediate.

Fortis was trying the handle and he raised his eyebrows in surprise as the door moved. Quickly, he pushed it shut.

"We need to check in there." Rosie insisted.

The Lieutenant shook his head "Not without protective gear. We – Oi!"

Rosie shoved him aside and hauled open the door, ramming her own rifle barrel through the opening but another empty corridor loomed, this one walled on three sides by glass ending in a hefty but clear door covered in more warning signs.

"Bloody civilians!" Fortis shoved her back, leading his men down and turning left and right to peer through the transparent walls and ending at the heavy door.

"Is that a laboratory?" Sinks had followed the Rangers and Fortis looked into the room which spanned the width of the building. Rosie could make out several computers and pristine white tables.

"Could be." Fortis tapped the door "That's an airlock. That means no going in without protective gear." He moved between Rosie and the door "I mean it! You go in there, I'll lock you in there else you'll Infect my men."

Rosie did not argue. In any case, they could see the entirety of the room through the clear glass and it was plainly empty with no other exit. She nodded and moved to the two other doors, one set either side of the corridor that led into offices.

"Here…" Sinks had opened one, revealing a small, plain workspace with a computer monitor sat on a desk with a plastic chair behind it. There were no windows on the stone wall and aside from a single framed photo of a small family, no personal accoutrements. The chair was leaning on two legs against the wall as though the occupant had left in a hurry.

Rosie crossed around the desk, trying the two drawers set into the body but they were both empty. The lift shaft they had passed had been silent and she guessed the crashed Puma had knocked out the power to the building but Sinks reached across her, tapping a plastic key on the computer and the screen sprang to life, words plainly typed on the screen in a message.

They both read it in silence. It wasn't long and ended abruptly mid-sentence.

"He was here, then."

"Yes."

"Looks like they took him before he could type where he was going."

Fortis joined them, inhaling sharply as he took in the information. He keyed his radio, signalling Camp Seaside, the excitement making his voice shake.

"This changes everything!"

Sinks nodded "We could take back the entire continent."

"It's not a cure." Rosie pointed out but even she couldn't deny the thrill of Dr Frost's words on the screen before them.

"Why didn't Armstrong release it before?" Fortis wondered.

Sinks grunted "Control. He was always trying to hold on to power..."

Guilt flushed through Rosie as a dog looked at her expectantly and she remembered her real quest. Quickly she stepped away from the world shattering discovery, heading back towards the lift shaft. A small, dark staircase wound its way up to the roof and she followed the Rangers as they made their way up, weapons at the ready.

They emerged into daylight, blinking after the gloom and even the Rangers froze, lowering their weapons in awe.

"Coming out!" Fortis was there with Sinks. Each man, well accustomed to death and war was as frozen as the others. From here, Rosie could see, the pattern of the battle was obvious. The shattered stone where the grenade had exploded, the fire where the Puma had burned and then the fallen Ferals, each lying in the direction they had been surging when they were killed.

Facing towards...

Kyle

The dogs were sniffing the corpses suspiciously, hackles raised as Rosie began stumbling forward, pulling aside grey skin to search for the remnants of living flesh. She ignored the warnings from Sinks and Fortis who frantically directed his men to check the dead, confirming the Ferals were indeed expired.

None were alive.

A dog had stopped moving atop a tangle of bodies, three or four deep. As Rosie watched, the creature began to whine and dig with its paws, futilely attempting to move the Wretch flesh.

"Sinks!" Rosie shouted for him to help as she hauled the first Feral up, flinging the dead monster aside and soon more hands were there, pulling aside the grey skin only to reveal the silent, pale skin of a Warrior who had ridden in glory to Valhalla, his hand still clenched around the hilt of a blade, buried deep in the skull of his final enemy.

The dogs began to howl. The Rangers stood silent, paying homage to this rarest of sights, a true last stand.

Rosie's tears dripped silently onto a face unravaged by the virus that had cursed his fallen enemies. He did not look at peace. He looked like he had died in battle, his mouth still curled into a final grimace of pain and fury.

The devastation around him was monumental. It was unthinkable that one man could stand against so many. Even Sinks in decades of blood and conflict had seen nothing that compared. He shook his head in wonderment at the memory of the boy he had known.

Staring at the face of the man he had become.

The dogs raised their voices in a funeral dirge, the weird tones echoing from the dead as Kyle's body lay motionless with the stillness of death.

Until, with a snarl, it did not.

EPILOGUE – 'A CHOICE'

The tall Ranger moved through the rain soaked camp, heedless of the deluge as it beat its fury upon him. He carried no rifle but a pistol was holstered on his leg, water beading on the black grip. Most soldiers within the camp were under what little shelter they could find but those that risked the weather did so at a run, splashing through the cloying sand.

The Ranger ignored them and those that saw him looked away quickly, hurrying on before they made eye contact.

Everyone knew about Frost.

He turned a corner around a poorly erected canvas tent and ducked under a tarpaulin that was sinking from the weight of the water pooling atop it. A pair of young soldiers were sheltering there and they stared wide eyed at the tall Ranger before they hastily moved, scuttling out to brave the elements rather than shelter with *him*.

A small wooden hut stood on the far side of the makeshift tunnel. It didn't bear the insignia of the Rangers nor did any sign denote it as such but the entire camp knew which unit had claimed the sturdiest structure.

Frost approached the wooden door and did not pause. He twisted the handle and strode into the damp interior, pushing it closed behind him.

Lynch was sat on a rusted metal container facing towards the door. As Frost came to a halt, he affixed the young man with that awful, blue eyed stare.

Lynch looked Frost up and down, judging his demeanour

perhaps. The slightly open mouth and too wide eyes were as ever but there was an almost imperceptible tightening of the small muscles around the blue gaze. A sign of the strain upon Armstrong's Devil.

"Just you and me left, Frosty."

Frost stood perfectly calm, neither by expression nor muscle movement conveying anything but disdain for the monster that sat before him. He did not speak.

Lynch snorted stood slowly, looking Frost in the eye. He had to raise his chin to meet Frost's height.

"We's the same, Frosty." Lynch's eyes did not blink, did not move as he spoke. His swollen red lips moved robotically, the fat tongue visible between syllables "You and me's the same. Ain't about that black dressed slag nor them offi-sah's." the fat tongue darted out to moisten the lips "S'about somefink more."

Frost just looked at him. Waiting.

"S'about killing. S'about slaughter and you fink you're any better 'coz you had a fancy for that gel, you're wrong. I know's wot you are. I seen it way back in Matwood."

Lynch paused as though expecting Frost to respond but the younger man said nothing. A sneer crossed the Sergeant's mouth at the silence.

"You ain't scarin' me, boy so don't waste your time. Fact is, you 'n me got us an opp-or-tu-nity." As ever, Lynch drew the long word out into its component syllables as though enunciation was hard with his swollen tongue and ill-fitting lips "Them In-fec-ted ain't a threat like they was. Still, they gonna need killers, Frosty. There's a whole new world now and men like you 'n me are gonna rule it."

Lynch believed every word, Frost could see that. And there was a part of him that was tempted. Lynch was right, Frost was a killer. More than that, he had gone further than any Warrior into the shadow of death, willingly surrendering himself to the unknown. Now, no fear of the end of his life remained and Frost knew that with this wide eyed devil he could shatter any enemy, crush any threat, living or Infected. The army was racing across the continent, speed borne from the tools left for them by Dr Frost and thoughts of his Father reminded him that secrets remained and the answers were hidden behind that awful stare.

But for a moment, the demonic gaze vanished to be replaced by Amelia Singh's eyes, wide with fear in her final expression as she saw Lynch pause, make his choice, and end her life. Frost realised that the last thing she'd seen was Lynch's stare and that the Sergeant's existence was utterly wrong. In a world torn and ravaged by monsters, this was the true threat.

Look after me, Kyle

But Kyle was gone. Only Frost remained and this Warrior reborn in death could see the world in a different plane to the boy who had left Holden. Two futures spiralled forward from this moment, one filled with strength and victory, the other with pain and struggle.

A choice.

Amelia would have pled with Kyle, begged him to stay his hand but she was dead. Perhaps his Father, Dr Frost would have given cautious advice but he was gone, a mystery to which Lynch might hold the key.

Eric, Sinks, Rosie... all of them would tell him what they thought. That was how Kyle had lived, always seeking advice, and trying desperately to survive the chaos of his life.

Frost did not care for survival. He couldn't have said what he cared about, now. So much was gone.

But one thing remained certain and that was the wide, staring eyes of Sergeant Lynch before him and in a flash, Frost knew that the existence of this creature would spell only more misery and death and it was his task as a Warrior to make the hard choice and to live with the consequences.

Everyone else could go to Hell.

In a motion so smooth that Sinks, had he seen it would have smiled with pride, Frost drew the Glock from the holster and with a tight, two handed grip, aimed it at Lynch's head. The place where Lynch's bullet had ended Amelia's life.

Lynch hesitated, some uncertainty finally creeping onto his face. He looked from the pistol to Frost's eyes and his tongue flicked out to moisten his fat lips. The weight of the moment seemed to hang over the two men as though the universe held its breath, waiting to see which path would be taken.

A slow grin spread over Lynch's face as his too wide eyes bored into Frost's own.

"Your choice, boy."

Frost shot him.

The bullet took Lynch in the centre of his forehead, just above those deceptively child-like blue eyes. It punched a dark hole in his lumpy, pockmarked skin and exited the back of his misshapen head in a spray of dark red gore.

Lynch's face did not react, he did not blink nor did his fat lips close. His awful, wide-eyed glare seemed not to lose its intensity as he held Frost's own gaze. His body stayed upright for an imperceptible amount of time. A second perhaps. An eternity.

Then a metallic tinkling shattered the stillness and the sound of the shot filled the narrow space between the wooden walls as the brass from the round landed on the floor and bounced once. As the noise sounded the final spark of light in Lynch's eyes vanished like the final dregs of water disappearing down a drain and he collapsed. He dropped to his knees first with a crunch of bone and then the heavy body canted sideways, the eyes still locked, impossibly on Frost. His head struck the floor with a thump and the illusion was shattered as the irises rolled upwards revealing nothing but the bloodshot whites.

His mouth still slightly open, revealing the yellow teeth and lolling tongue, Lynch died.

Minutes passed as the rain pounded on the roof of the shack. No-one came to investigate the shot. No storm of vengeful Rangers tore into the small space. Instead, the man who had been Kyle Frost stepped outside, carefully closing the door behind him. He paused on the step, for the first time seeming to notice the rain and wrinkling his nose. Movement caught his eye and he looked down to see a pair of the ridge backed dogs had followed him. They did not bound to greet him with the playful energy they usually flourished but instead, each dog stepped close, sniffed him once and then stood by his side.

Soldiers ready for battle.

The sound of tramping feet filled their ears and the nearest dog turned its head, tracking the movement of a damp squad of troops who marched down a muddy lane between the hastily erected buildings. As they passed, a Private in the rear rank paused, his fellows marching on ahead. There was a moment, a brief tilt on a knife's edge where the threat of violence loomed and the dogs tensed, hair rising on the backs of their necks. But then Frost simply dipped his head and Sinks blinked rapidly several times before he hurried after his squad and out of sight.

When they were gone, Frost bowed his head for a moment, murmuring a single word as though it were a prayer.

"Amelia."

Abruptly, he stepped into the rain, heading towards the camp gates, where black smoke hung on the horizon.

A Warrior heading to war.

THE END

Printed in Great Britain
by Amazon

31078182R00245